Acknowledgments

I wish to extend a special thank you and express my deep gratitude to the following persons for their help and advice. They were both generous and gracious in the sharing of their time, knowledge, and expertise:

The registrar and education staff of the Jewish Museum of Florida, especially Chaim Lieberperson, for providing accurate historical details of Jewish Miami during the 1920's-1950's.

Three Guys from Miami (http://3guysfrommiami.com/) for their advice on all things Cuban in and around Miami for the novel's historical and contemporary chapters.

My wonderful critic partner, Ronelda, for staying with me through the good times and the bad.

And last, but certainly not least, my dear husband, without whose support and advice, my writing would flounder.

MIAMI DAYS, HAVANA NIGHTS

LINDA BENNETT PENNELL

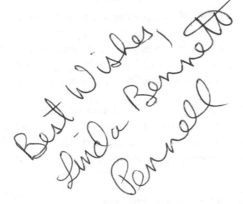

Best Wishes,
Linda Bennett
Pennell

SOUL MATE PUBLISHING

New York

MIAMI DAYS, HAVANA NIGHTS

Published in the United States of America by
Soul Mate Publishing
P.O. Box 24
Macedon, New York, 14502

ISBN: 978-1-68291-759-6

ebook ISBN: 978-1-68291-720-6

www.SoulMatePublishing.com

The publisher does not have any control over and does not assume any responsibility for author or third-party websites or their content.

Chapter 1

May 18, 1926
105 South Street
New York City

Knocking — sharp, loud, rapid — echoed through the empty speakeasy. Sam froze, the notes of a tune stuck in the roof of his mouth. He glanced at the entrance and leaned the handle of his push-broom against his shoulder. Puffs of dust settled on the floorboards around his feet while he remained motionless.

It was late, too late, to be admitting customers, even for the city's illegal watering holes and gambling joints. Although a thick crossbar and several stout locks protected the heavy iron door, an uneasy feeling crawled down Sam's spine. Growing tension over control of the Fulton Fish Market, in fact the entire South Street area, was making a lot of people jumpy, including him.

Several seconds passed without noise from the other side of the door. Sam let out his breath and laughed at himself. Working at the fish market in the afternoon and staying up half the night at the speakeasy didn't leave much time for sleep. It kept him on edge. All the rumors and threats floating around these days weren't helping either. Inclining his ear and hearing nothing, he relaxed and gave his broom a shove.

Bam, bam, bam.

Sam's heart jumped into his throat.

"Open up, Monza. I know you're in there." The shout, colored by an Irish lilt, came from the second-floor landing accompanied by renewed pounding. "I come to talk with ya. We need to settle this business. I got a proposition for ya."

Sam's breathing kicked up a notch as he looked over his shoulder toward the office. The boss didn't like to be disturbed when he was meeting with his guys. The pounding from outside in the hall returned in earnest, but the office door remained fixed.

"You gonna open this damned door or do I break it down?" The doorknob rattled and jerked.

Behind Sam, the office door clicked open an inch. He watched in the mirror over the bar as the muzzle of a .38 Special emerged from the opening, its nickel-plated barrel glittering in the overhead lights. One of the gangsters stepped into the room, met Sam's eye in the mirror, and jerked his head, then the room went dark. Sam dropped his broom and backed into an alcove next to the bar. The office door opened wider. Several shadows scurried across the floor. Metal locks and bolts clanked and the entrance door swung inward.

"Hey, you guys forget to pay the bill? What's with the dark?"

Sam couldn't see the newcomer's face, but given the guy's size, backlit by the stairwell's single bulb, and his accent, it must be William Mack, the labor organizer. Trying to push in on Tops Monza's action at the market was a stupid move. The Irish were losing this war. Heck, they couldn't even win a battle. The big Mick must have had enough. Sam shook his head. *The goy had chutzpah coming here. You had to give him that.*

Shoe soles scuffled on bare floorboards. The door slammed.

"Hey, what're you guys doing? I come here in peace." The Irishman's voice boomed into the room followed by shoes dragging across the floor. "Monza, you chicken shit. Come out here and meet me like a man."

The room filled with light again followed by groans and the sound of body blows coming from the area in front of the bar. Sam squinted against the glare and stepped from his alcove, his heart thumping in rhythm with the punches being administered to Mack. Two guys held the Irishman's arms while he strained and tugged to get free. Another of Tops's men, a former heavyweight boxer, jabbed and pummeled Mack's head and mid-section. When his knees buckled, the boxer stepped back, making room for Tops, who strolled over to the bar from the office doorway.

Tops bent down so that he was eye level with Mack. "So, you gonna insult me and make demands now that we done kicked your sorry Irish asses? Ain't nobody gonna set terms for Joseph Monza. Fulton is mine, and it's gonna stay mine." Tops grabbed Mack's shirtfront. "You got that, you dumb Mick son-of-a-bitch?"

From the slits of his swollen eyelids, Mack looked up sideways at Tops. He spat out a glob of blood. "People know I'm here. You ain't gonna get away with this. You're gonna pay."

"And whose gonna make me? You?" The sound of Tops's laughter rolled around the empty room.

Tops snatched the pistol from his henchman and took aim, firing once into Mack's chest. Sam jumped at the pistol's report. A soft groan floated from Mack as blood bubbled on his lips. Though Sam wanted desperately to look away, he couldn't tear his gaze from the oozing, red stream dribbling down the Irishman's chin. Sam's mouth went dry as though filled with cotton gauze.

Grabbing a fistful of the Irishman's hair, Tops lifted so that Mack had to look him full in the face. Setting the muzzle against Mack's forehead, Tops grinned and counted to five, then squeezed the trigger. Blood and brains splattered over the bar and floor. Tops let go and Mack's lifeless form toppled over.

Sam's stomach heaved. He gagged on the bile rising from his stomach and covered his mouth with a shaky hand.

"Get him out of here, boys." Tops turned, his upper lip curled in a sneer. His gaze lit on Sam. "Let the busboy help. That's about what the Mick was worth. Hey kid. Yeah you, Sammy. Come over here and grab the legs. It'll be good for you. Toughen you up."

Sam's heart dropped to his soles as he shuffled across the floor toward his boss. Handling dead fish was one thing, but the thought of touching a dead person with a gaping hole in his forehead left Sam trembling. He stopped beside the Irishman's body, fighting to keep his churning stomach from emptying at Tops's feet. Although he had worked for the mobster since he was fifteen, nothing had prepared him for what he had seen tonight. Of course he'd heard the stories, but Sam had pushed those stories aside as mere rumors. In addition to Tops paying better than other jobs, Sam admired the boss. Tops was the smartest and strongest man Sam knew, but this was outright murder. The seventh *Aseret ha-Dibrot* in the Torah stated *You shall not murder.*

Tino, the guy closest to the body, bent over and slipped his hands beneath Mack's arms. He grunted and looked up. "Come on, boy. I ain't gonna do this by myself. You heard the boss. Get your ass to work."

Sam bent toward the Irishman's lifeless form. The metallic odor of the blood covering Mack's head and shirt front assaulted Sam as he grabbed the feet. The need to puke made Sam's head swim, but he refused to give in. As stupid as he had been up until now, he couldn't show weakness. No telling what would happen if he didn't follow orders. Straining and grunting, he and Tino lifted Mack while the others made room for them to maneuver. Tops himself opened the speakeasy door.

"Good riddance, you Mick bastard. Your boys come around looking for a fight, we'll send them to meet ya."

Tops leered at the body and lobbed a wad of saliva onto the chest. "Dump him on the union building steps. That'll send a message."

Sam and Tino struggled down the dimly lit stairwell to the ground floor door that exited onto Beekman Street one block east of where the United Seafood Workers Union had their headquarters. The street lamps had been shot out so many times the city finally stopped fixing them. Darkness enveloped the neighborhood. Not even the moon dared shine tonight. Tino stopped in the covered entry and peered back over his shoulder. His head swiveled toward Sam and he nodded. Together, they moved into the street and turned west.

Pain shot down Sam's back and his arms shook. His breath came in short gasps, as much from terror as from exertion. At the corner, they stopped while Tino checked the cross street. He leaned forward while hoisting Mack's body a little higher.

"Shit. Beat cop's up the block. We gotta hurry."

Tino scurried backward over the curb, nearly jerking Sam off his feet. He stumbled once and righted himself but dropped one of Mack's legs. Grabbing a fistful of gabardine, he stumbled after Tino.

"Hey. What are you guys doing? Stop." The sound of the cop's steps picking up speed and his whistle blasting followed Sam and Tino. When they reached the steps of the union building on the opposite corner, Tino swung the upper body once and let it fly. Sam released the legs as the shoulders thudded on the concrete steps. They needed to get back to the speakeasy fast, but Sam turned directly into the beam of the cop's flashlight. He heard Tino running, but he couldn't make his own feet budge.

"Hey, you. Jew boy. Freeze." The cop jumped from the curb on the opposite side of the street.

The dam of Sam's fear broke, sending a shot of adrenaline through him. He crouched and ran.

You're one stupid SOB, Ackerman. You're gonna get yourself killed for sure. What are Mama and the boys going to do with you gone? Starve and lose the apartment most likely.

With shots bouncing off the street's brick pavers, Sam reached the speakeasy entrance and thundered up the stairs. At the top step, Tino grabbed Sam's collar and hauled him through an opening. Hinges creaked, followed by the swoosh of the secret wall panel falling back into place. Sam blinked once. And again. Total blackness enveloped him like a musty, suffocating blanket. Footsteps pounded up the stairs on the other side of the wall setting his heart racing.

"Tin—" A rough hand clamped down on his mouth.

"Shut up." Damp breath smelling of beer floated against Sam's cheek.

Loud knocking accompanied by shouting and a door slamming filled the cramped space. With his free hand, Tino pushed Sam's face against rough brick. Something scraped softly admitting a narrow shaft of light into the closet sized room.

Tino whispered, "Take a look."

Sam placed his eye against the peephole.

Tops stood leaning against the bar surrounded by his men. "Officer, what brings you to my establishment? Beat sergeant forget to give you your cut?"

"Where is he?"

"Who you wanting to see?"

"The kid who ran up here. He's your busboy, ain't he? Where you hiding him?"

"We ain't hiding nobody. Have a look around, Officer . . ." Tops's gaze went to the officer's chest. ". . . O'Malley."

The cop pointed toward the bar. "Where'd all that blood come from?"

Tops's eyebrows rose. His head slowly turned. "That?"

"Yeah. Is that where you killed him?"

"Officer, nobody's been killed here tonight or any other night. The mess was left by a couple of thugs beating each other's brains out. Had 'em tossed out just before you arrived. Surprised you didn't pass 'em on the stairs." Tops shoved his hand into his pants pocket and withdrew his gold money clip. Stripping off a couple of bills, he pushed them into the cop's tunic front. "You run along now and don't worry no more. Nothing here for New York's Finest to worry about."

Two of Monza's men stepped forward. The cop's head swiveled from one to the other. Officer O'Malley took two steps back and turned on his heel heading for the entrance. When the sound of footsteps faded, Tino removed his hand from Sam's mouth. Sam turned and looked into Tino's grinning face.

"The cop saw me. He recognized me." Sam's voice trembled.

Tino chuckled and patted Sam's cheek. "Sammy boy, you're in deep shit now. Tops is gonna be pissed."

Punching Tino would feel really good, but Sam couldn't handle more trouble than he already had. He opened his mouth to ask what would happen next, but something metal clicked behind him. Tino put a finger to his lips.

Another wall, one inside the speakeasy, swung open. Monza watched Sam from the middle of the room. "Looks like we got ourselves a celebrity. Cops are gonna be looking for you, boy. Irishmen take one of their own being killed real personal." The other gangsters laughed. "What do you think we oughta do with Sammy?"

Sam's heart jumped into his throat, then raced like it might explode. "I'm sorry, Mr. Monza. I was so scared I couldn't move. I've never done anything like that before." Sam's knees knocked together and were in danger of buckling altogether.

Tops didn't say anything for several beats while his smile faded. "I guess I shouldn't of sent a boy to do a man's job." He motioned to Sam. "Come over here."

Sam's hands shook, but he didn't try to stop them. When he didn't move, Tino gave him a shove from behind. Sam stumbled from the secret hole and shuffled across the space separating him from the boss.

"Come on. I ain't gonna bite." Tops reached out and wrapped an arm around Sam's neck. Drawing him down against his chest, the boss ran his knuckles over Sam's head and laughed. "Exciting night, huh, kid? You been with me for how long now?"

"Two years, Mr. Monza. Since I was fifteen."

"You like working for me?"

Sam swallowed hard. "Yes, sir. You're a great boss, Mr. Monza."

Tops laughed and let Sam straighten up, then patted his cheek. "You're a good boy, Sammy. I like you. You work hard and don't complain." The gangster put his hands on Sam's shoulders, holding him at arm's length. He turned Sam left and right. "He's a good kid, boys, but I don't think he'll stand up to being grilled by the cops. Sammy, Sammy, Sammy. What am I gonna do with you?"

The room began spinning. Sam shook his head. Words refused to form.

Tops pursed his lips. "I think we gotta get rid of you."

Sam's heart raced so hard that he became dizzy. Images of Mack's blood-covered body danced around his already addled mind. What would happen to Mama and the boys? They wouldn't even know what had become of him. It would be like he never existed. A metallic taste filled Sam's mouth. His knees buckled and everything went black.

Hands shaking Sam's shoulders brought him back. He opened his eyes and squinted in the glare of overhead lights. Dust from the floor swirled up his nose, making him sneeze.

He sat up and rubbed a lump on the back of his head. The guys bending over him laughed and nudged each other.

Tops gripped Sam's hand and yanked. "Get up, kid." Monza turned to Tino and winked. "Take care of him. And do it right."

Tino grabbed Sam's arm. "You got it, Boss."

Chapter 2

Present
Fall Semester
Gainesville, Florida

Crap. Not one blessed thing gained.

Liz bookmarked and closed the archival records web page she had paid a small fortune to access. Frustration knotted the muscles at the base of her skull. She stretched her back against the living room sofa and rolled her head and neck. Months of research and all she had to show for it was a regurgitation of everything everybody already knew. Maybe she was what she most feared— a one hit wonder destined to fade from her fifteen minutes of glory into ignominious mediocrity.

Jeez. How was that for a pretentious mouthful? Liz's lips thinned into a smirk accompanied by a quiet snort. Well, at least she could still laugh at herself. Unfortunately, some people might not find her so amusing.

She glanced across the room at Hugh. Liz drummed her fingers against the edge of her computer. He would probably understand if she didn't meet the deadline. Hugh was a good boss and a good . . . What? She never knew what to call the man she lived and worked with. Boyfriend sounded so lame, childish even. Boss tended to raise eyebrows. Fiancé would work if she had said yes to his most recent proposal.

Liz sucked the corner of her lower lip between her teeth. Of all the things she had ever thought herself to be, a commitment-phobe was not one of them. And now she was on the verge of disappointing him twice in one week. The new course she was designing could still be taught in the spring, but it would be incomplete as it stood now. She had incorporated a plethora of original details about Al Capone, et al., but new, riveting details on Moshe Toblinsky and the Jewish gangsters were proving elusive. As a consequence, *Florida's Underbelly, 1920-Present: the Mob in the Sunshine State* would probably fail to accomplish what the dean expected despite its titillating title. What a depressing thought.

Buzzing against Liz's thigh made her jump. She dug the phone out of her jeans pocket and checked the caller ID. Her heart rate kicked up a notch. She slid her finger over the screen to take the call and listened to the monologue coming through the ether.

Liz tapped the end call icon, slumped a little lower into the sofa cushions, and sighed. Apparently nothing was going to go right today.

Next to the living room window, Hugh lounged in an armchair with the latest historical monograph spread open on his lap, pretending he hadn't listened to her side of the phone conversation. When she didn't speak, he looked up from the book and raised his brows.

"Well?" His voice was kind but direct.

"Well what?"

"What was in that call to make you look so stormy?"

Liz grimaced and crammed her phone into her jeans pocket. "Aunt Mildred says Daddy is going downhill faster than anyone thought possible, something Mom decided to keep from me. Yesterday, he wandered away from the house and was gone for hours. Mom was on the verge of calling the police when a neighbor brought him home. The neighbor stopped Daddy trying to board the ferry to Whidbey Island. He said he had to report for duty at the naval air station." Liz hunched her shoulders and shook her head. "He retired from the Navy in 1995."

"Did Mildred say how your mother is handling this?"

"Oh, according to *Mom*, everything is just fine." Liz inwardly winced at the sarcasm she heard in her voice, but she couldn't stop it. "*She's* adamant that *she* can handle him. This was just an unusual, one off thing. Mom and Dad both refuse to admit there's a problem. Life is rosy and perfect, according to them."

"Has anyone contacted your brother about this? You've said your parents are usually willing to listen to him."

Liz shook her head. "Absolutely not. He's under enough pressure being deployed overseas. He doesn't need to worry about what's going on here. There's nothing he can do about it from halfway around the world anyway."

Hugh came over and sat next to Liz. He put his arm around her shoulders and kissed her temple. "Sweetheart, I'm so sorry. Do you want to go home for a long weekend? With your teaching schedule, it'll be easy enough. Cancel your office hours. Get a flight out Thursday evening. Fly back Monday morning."

Liz nodded. "I would love to, but every time I mention going to Seattle, Mom becomes livid and says she will never forgive me if I come running home over nothing. She ordered me to stay away. Can you believe it? She's so damned stubborn."

Hugh put his finger under Liz's chin and lifted until her eyes met his. A small smile tugged at the corners of his mouth. "Remind you of anyone we know?"

"Yeah, I suppose so."

"At least you admit you come by that tenacious streak honestly. If you want to go home, do it. Your mother will get over it."

"Maybe. Maybe not. With Mom, it's best to get your timing right. She is pretty much a control freak and isn't planning on giving up the reins anytime soon. Everyone in the family gives in to her."

Hugh cut his eyes at her. "Really? I didn't pick up on that when we visited this summer."

"She was on her best behavior. I told her it would be a very long time before I came home again if she didn't keep it in check."

"Oh. So everybody in the family gives in to her, even your dad?"

"Yeah. Everybody. Daddy most of all. It's survival. Mom's a force of nature." Liz tried to laugh but ended up hiccoughing instead. Cocking her head to one side, she thought for a moment before speaking again. "It doesn't make sense. I *know* it's illogical. But I think Mom believes if I come home in the middle of a semester, it means life as they have known it is officially over forever. She's trying so hard to hang on to what they had. It breaks my heart and infuriates me at the same time. She refuses to deal with reality."

Hugh wrapped his other arm around Liz and drew her against his chest, kissing the top of her head. "Do what you need to do when the time comes. Your mom is too close to the situation to be realistic. At some point, she will have to accept the inevitable."

Liz leaned back so that she could see his face as a tear trickled from the corner of her eye. His finger followed the tear's trail down her cheek and wiped it away. His eyes held a softness and sympathy that made her want to bury her head against his shoulder and sob. Life with Mom had never been easy, and it would only get harder from here on.

Hugh kissed the tip of her nose as a rueful smile lifted the corners of his mouth. "Actually, your going to Seattle would be a kindness. Our colleagues could use the break. Since your monograph was published, no one has had any rest. The dean keeps asking when we are all going to discover exciting new information. It's exhausting working with you."

He meant it as a compliment, but Liz's spirit drooped a little more. She hadn't confided to anyone, not even Hugh, the dichotomous feelings that at times threatened to overwhelm her. Success was both a gift and a burden. At an early stage in her career, she had garnered respect and a touch of fame among her peers. On the down side, the expectations bar had risen into the stratosphere. In low moments, fear of failure flooded her mind and soul. What if her success was just a fluke? Visions of one day being exposed as a fraud lurked in the shadows. Why did she do this to herself? Who knew? Liz certainly didn't.

Out of the corner of her eye she saw Hugh's concerned expression. He didn't deserve her dark mood, and she was nowhere near ready to talk about her fears with him. Especially, not with him.

Liz mustered her most impish grin and leaned back so that she could look at him directly. "Don't you have work to do? Isn't your review for that book due next week?"

"It is, but it can wait."

"No it can't, and we both know it. Now, get back to work. Forget about my parents' willfulness." Liz thumped him on the shoulder for emphasis. She'd be damned if her ridiculous family was going to interfere with Hugh's professional life.

He laughed and held up his hands. "Okay, okay. Just trying to be supportive." He kissed her temple and sauntered back to his chair by the window.

Liz gathered her research notes intent upon forcing them into some semblance of order but her attention kept drifting back to Hugh. As her gaze followed the contours of his bookishly handsome face, a twinge formed just under her breastbone. She had come so close to missing out on the love of this truly good man. Pigheaded determination to keep him at arm's length seemed such a foolish notion in hindsight. She was lucky he had waited patiently for her to see him as a lover, not just as her boss. Sometimes she wondered why he had.

Liz drew a long breath and exhaled slowly. Enough already. Wallowing in self-pity wouldn't solve her problems or change anything. It certainly wasn't getting the new history course description and syllabus written.

She stood up from the sofa and grabbed her laptop bag. "Moshe Toblinsky and his company of gangsters aren't just jumping up and revealing themselves. They're needing a good, hard shove. I'm going to the library to look through the sources again."

Hugh glanced up and gave her a swift once over. "Don't go if you don't want to. You've had bad news. If the new course is ready in time, fine. If not, no harm done."

Liz shook her head. "I made you a promise, and I intend to keep. Got it?"

Hugh's mouth lifted at one corner in a lopsided grin. He gave her a three-finger salute. "Yes, ma'am."

Kissing him quickly, she left the apartment and strode to her red Prius, her mouth set in a determined line. *Florida's Underbelly,* 1920-*Present: the Mob in the Sunshine State,* or Gangsters on the Gold Coast as she had nicknamed the project, would be her contribution to keeping the budgetary ax from falling on the department's neck for another year. She had been hired based on her reputation for weaving classroom magic that attracted large numbers of undergraduates. Being a savior created its own special glow, sort of, but sometimes the responsibility left her a little off kilter. Around registration time each semester, a recurring nightmare had her running after students flapping course descriptions at them.

A rueful smile played across Liz's lips as she guided her car through the late Saturday afternoon traffic. There was a time when she thought research and publication a historian's only worthy goals. That changed the first time she saw light click on in a student's eyes. Research might be her professional passion, but teaching became an unexpected joy. History came alive for her students when she revealed its big events and even bigger characters through the experiences of ordinary people. What a rush. It got 'em every time.

Unfortunately, uncovering detailed information on the ordinary citizens sucked up by the mob as it slithered its way onto Miami Beach was proving a serious challenge. So many people she wanted to interview were dead, and those still living refused to talk. The Mafia's reach was long indeed.

Chapter 3

"Wake up, kid. Time to go." Tino's voice cut through the fog of nightmare clouding Sam's mind. He bolted upright from the speakeasy office sofa, rubbed his eyes, and squinted into the pale sunlight streaming through the single window. His heart banged in his chest. It must be early still. He had actually slept. Even more surprising, he was still alive.

Sam scrambled up from the sofa, put on his jacket, and turned to Tino. "Will you tell me where we're going?"

Tino raised an eyebrow. "You'll see. Right now we got to get away from here without nobody seeing. Do as I say, and keep your yap shut."

Sam swallowed hard and followed Tino down the speakeasy stairs to a black sedan idling at the curb, one of Tops's enforcers behind the wheel. Tino yanked the back door open. "Get in." Sam's heart turned over as he hesitated on the sidewalk. Tino shoved him from behind. "Now, and no questions."

Sam tumbled into the car and dropped down onto a well-padded seat. He couldn't stop a sigh of appreciation escaping his lips. Tops had sent his newest, a Chrysler Imperial, reported to do a consistent 80 miles per hour and 0-60 in a flat 20 seconds. Sam ran his hand over the fine wood appointments. Despite its luxurious interior, this car was meant to get a guy away from trouble in a hurry. The kind of trouble he might be heading to set Sam's stomach churning.

They headed north away from the docks and the Bowery toward the heart of Manhattan. At each cross street, Sam expected them to turn away from town and toward the river where a body could be dumped and carried out to sea, never to be found. Mama would never know what happened to him. He hadn't been able to let her know he wasn't coming home after work. It was always long after her bedtime when he got home, so she wouldn't know anything until she got up to make the kids' breakfast. She would be frantic that he wasn't in his bed.

When they turned left on 31st, utter confusion set in. At the Beaux Arts façade of Penn Station, the car slowed to a stop. Sam stared at Tino who laughed so hard he wrapped an arm around his midsection.

When the gangster found his voice again, he asked, "What? You think we should do you in?" Tino snorted and wiped his eyes. "You should see your face. Come on. Get your ass out. The train leaves at nine-thirty."

Sam stumbled after Tino onto the sidewalk and under the columned portico. When they were inside the cavernous reception hall, Sam finally could hold his tongue no longer. "Where are we going? I need to let my mother know. She will be really worried if I don't come home tonight."

Tino turned toward the ticket counters. "Wait here and don't talk to nobody." When he returned, a guy Sam had never seen before came with him.

The stranger's gaze ran over Sam. "This the kid?" the stranger asked. Tino nodded. "Don't look like much. For what Tops should want to do him favors?"

Tino frowned. "Never you mind. That's Mr. Monza's business." Tino turned to Sam and put a ticket in his hand. "Well, kid, this is where I leave you. This here is Joe. Do what he says, and you'll be okay."

Sam looked up at Joe, who had already turned on his heel headed toward the departures tracks. Sam glanced down at the ticket in his hand and froze. West Palm Beach. Florida. Over 1,000 miles from home. Sam watched Joe's retreating back for a second more and went in the opposite direction. He couldn't leave New York like this. He would hide out in his Brooklyn neighborhood. Tops would never think to look for him there.

In the two years Sam worked at the Fulton Fish Market and the speakeasy, Monza never once asked where Sam went after he knocked off work, and Sam never talked about his Jewish family or Brooklyn neighborhood. When he went to work for the gangster, it had felt like a betrayal of his heritage and his faith, but the family needed the money he brought in and Fulton was the best paying job open at the time. Mama didn't know exactly where he worked in Manhattan. He made up a story of working for a Kosher fish monger and she never inquired further. There was no way Sam was going to desert the family now, not with Papa dead these two years and no other male relatives to look out for them.

He'd find work where he wouldn't be seen by the public. Maybe as a dishwasher in a restaurant or an oven attendant in the Kosher bakery down the street from their apartment. Anything that helped pay the bills and kept him out of sight. Mama couldn't make it alone with five kids and only the income from cleaning houses.

Without warning, something heavy bore down on Sam's left shoulder, halting his flight. He glanced toward the source of the vise grip. A hand the size of a boxer's glove increased the pressure on his complaining muscles and turned him around, bodily lifting him off his feet.

"Hey, kid, you going the wrong way. You don't want to miss the train. Tops would be pissed and that ain't never a good thing. Especially after all the trouble he's gone to for you." The expression in the mobster's eyes would have made an ice house in January feel warm. Joe's hand moved from Sam's shoulder to his upper arm. He stumbled toward the tracks under the pressure of Joe's ham-sized fist.

The smell of burning coal and the conductor's call of "All aboard" met them as they entered the departures lanes. Joe picked up speed, dragging Sam along like a willful child. The train's wheels were turning slowly as Joe yanked Sam up onto an iron grate platform, into the corridor, and finally shoved him through a sleeper car door. More jostling, and Sam found himself plopped down on the seat of a private compartment.

Looming in from the passageway, Joe put a hand on each side of the compartment doorjamb, fixing Sam with a cold stare. "Tops must owe you big to put you on this train. My orders are you stay in here and don't come out until we reach West Palm."

Sam gulped. "How long does the trip take?"

"About thirty-five hours."

"What about food?"

"What about it?"

"I've only got a little money. Will the conductor bring me a sandwich?"

"Nope. Conductors don't run errands like that, but I guess you never been on a train like this before, have ya?"

"I've never been on any train except for the subway."

Joe chuckled. "Don't worry. Boss'll probably let me bring you something from the dining car."

"Mr. Monza is on the train?"

"Tops? Naw." Sam must have looked rather confused and frightened, for Joe's eyes softened a little. "Look, kid. The boss and Tops are close." Joe raised a hand with his middle finger stacked on top of the index finger. "Like this, see? Tops wanted a favor. That's the way the world works. If you worked for Tops Monza, you should of figured that out by now."

Sam swallowed hard, dreading the answer to the question he felt compelled to ask. "So who is your boss?"

"Toblinsky. Mr. Moshe Toblinsky."

Chapter 4

Liz eased into a parking spot marked FACULTY ONLY and turned off the engine. She glanced at the laptop on the seat beside her, but her hands stayed glued to the top of the steering wheel. Resting her chin on her hands, she sucked on her lower lip and gazed up at the building in front of her. The library complex's newer brick and glass exterior blended well with the oldest university buildings. The University of Florida was a beautiful campus filled with grassy quads, ancient live oaks draped with Spanish moss, and lovely old red brick buildings. She had come to love the place, but this afternoon, it failed to bring pleasure. Liz eyed the gabled end where the tools of research awaited and did absolutely nothing. Lethargy wrapped its mantle around her. Inertia gripped her, body and soul.

As she continued in her aimless study of the library's exterior, color flashed at the corner of the windshield and a pair of bright, plaid pants came into view. A seventy-something couple strolled by on the sidewalk. Liz's eyes followed them with wistful recognition. From the back they could be Mom and Dad. The late-October Indian Summer sun cast a golden glow over silver heads that inclined toward one another, the couple linked by intertwined fingers. Halfway to the corner, the woman stumbled over a piece of broken concrete. The man's arm went around her, steadying and supportive. Just like Dad would have before he got sick.

A lump rose in Liz's throat. Her grip on the stirring wheel tightened until her knuckles paled. Dad, once so strong, so vital, was disappearing forever and she was three thousand miles away. Liz released the wheel and pounded it with her palm. Unless Aunt Mildred sent up distress signals, Mom's decree that she stay away from Seattle would be honored until Thanksgiving. At that point, it didn't matter how loud the protests. Hugh was right. Mom was too close to the situation to be objective. A firsthand assessment would give a better understanding of whether Mom was being realistic about keeping Dad at home. Taking a deep breath, she flung the car door open. Sitting in a parking lot brooding wasn't doing anyone any good.

As she emerged from the car, a roar rose from the direction of Ben Hill Griffin Stadium. The band's brass section blared the team's signature tune followed by 70,000 fans screaming "Go, Gators" in frenzied unison. She and Hugh would have gone to the game but for his book review's deadline. An ache rose in her chest.

Dad loved football. During her undergrad years at the University of Washington, he came to almost every Husky's home game dressed in his purple hoodie with the big gold W plastered on the chest. He called it the team's lucky shirt. A smile played across her lips, then her spirit fell. Who could tell what he knew or thought about these days? Liz looked wistfully toward the stadium. Dad and Hugh would have enjoyed watching football and going to games together.

Enough. Liz swiped at the tears threatening to stream down her face. Slamming the car door, she turned and marched toward the library.

Passing from the warmth and humidity of the sun-bathed quad into the dimmer, climate-controlled Yong Library foyer fairly took Liz's breath away. She dropped her book bag on the floor and dug. Her own purple and gold sweatshirt emerged from the depths, replete with fraying cuffs and a hole in one elbow. Tying the sleeves over her shoulders, she headed for the bank of elevators.

When Liz stepped out onto the third floor, the odor of aging paper mixed with that of much handled book bindings greeted her. Breathing it in, her shoulders relaxed, and the tension just below the base of her skull eased. The elevator doors swooshed closed behind her. Blessed silence reigned. She headed down the central hall to her own little corner of the rare books enclosure. Being a faculty researcher had its privileges.

With so many resources available online, she didn't really need to spend time in the library to conduct most of her research, but she chose to do so. The smell of old books, the silence, the polished wood, the rows of stacks filled with more tomes than she would ever be able to read in a lifetime— she loved it all. She had spent so many years of her life in libraries that having a personal space in this one felt like coming home, a bird returning to its nest. Her cubbyhole's narrow window looked out over the interior of the campus. Secured behind a locked door, she left her resources spread out, happy in the knowledge that no one would so much as rustle a piece of paper between visits. The library's custodial staff were not allowed in to clean. Haphazard applications of a small electric broom and disposable dusters from Walmart kept the EPA and OSHA at bay.

An old chair left by a previous occupant took up more than its rightful share of space, but placed under the window it created a cozy, well-lit retreat. The sound of creaking leather filled the room as Liz plopped down and tucked her legs tailor fashion in the wide seat, its saggy cushion conforming to her shape. Liz flipped her laptop open and logged into the digital library. She chased down several journal articles, took a few notes, and printed out what she wanted to keep. Running her hand over the spines of several books stacked on the floor beside the chair, Liz selected three. She set to comparing the printouts with the information in the books. A couple of hours later, Liz picked up her phone and checked the time. All that reading and still not a kernel of inspiration presented itself.

Shoving the books onto the floor, she leaned forward and lifted her arms over her head. Twisting from side to side, she worked the kinks out of her back. She wanted to do with this course what she had done in her book on Al Capone, to tell the story of what happens to an ordinary person who gets caught up in larger than life criminal activities.

Liz sighed. Perhaps the task she set herself was too big, the goal impossible. Was it hubris to think she should hit the jackpot with every project? Maybe insecurity drove her to take this road less traveled. A tight smile lifted the corners of her mouth. She had fallen in love with Robert Frost's *The Road Not Taken* as a high school student. As a more mature reader, she now realized the poet had not intended the verses as inspiration, but as gentle mocking of indecision. Indecision certainly plagued her at the moment. Give up, design a course that contained the usual, the expected, the ordinary, or delay and go for gold? But where to find that golden nugget? She shook her head.

Her hands hovered over the keyboard. Where to look next? Liz had just enough energy for something quick. The digitized newspaper files? Maybe. It could do no harm. No need to do more research on Al Capone and the Italians, but the Jewish gangsters needed a lot of work. In that world, one name stood out. She typed in Moshe Toblinsky and clicked the search button. The first few articles that popped up provided only well-known information. Born in Brooklyn, childhood friend of Bugsy Seigal, business partner of Lucky Luciano, Jewish organized crime figure known as the Mob's CFO, instrumental in developing the National Crime Syndicate, bootlegger, one organizer of the Mafia boss murders that propelled Luciano to power, developer of a gambling empire stretching from Las Vegas to Miami to Havana. Nothing that hadn't been hashed and rehashed a hundred times over.

Scrolling through the digital offerings, her cursor paused on a front-page article in the *Tampa Times*. Now here was something new. The name of a moderately well-known investigative reporter appeared in the byline. He published the article in 1989, a few weeks after Toblinsky died, complete with a picture gallery including several photos from an unpublished private collection. Private collections of this sort usually meant Mafia associates. It would be interesting to know how the reporter persuaded the owner to part with the pictures. This might not contain new information, but at least it would be entertaining.

Liz printed out the article and perused the old photographs. *1926, Toblinsky arrives in Miami aboard the Orange Blossom Special. February 13, 1929, Toblinsky hosts a lavish party in his ornate Spanish-style home on Biscayne Bay. That was the night before the Saint Valentine's Day Massacre. 1952, Toblinsky and Cuban President General Fulgencio Batista enjoy a private dinner. Location unknown. 1954, Toblinsky giving directions to staff for a private party at Miami's Fountainebleau, guest list not included. 1957, Toblinsky and Batista having dinner at Cuba's most exclusive hotel, the Habana Real.*

Liz studied the photographs. Expected faces and those she'd never before seen populated the Kodak snaps, as her grandmother called such pictures. The age and low-tech quality of the photographs made facial features hard to make out. Taking a magnifying glass from its home on the windowsill, she studied each face.

Her heart skipped a beat. Once, twice, then a third time. Could it be? Hard to tell for sure, but the same unidentified face seemed to appear in each photograph. She focused on that face in each picture again. Yes, the features were the same. Moreover, it looked like a shadow fell across the man's lower left cheek and jaw in the later pictures. It didn't make sense that the same shadow would show up in photographs taken years apart. Where had it come from? Port wine stain birthmark? Scar? Whatever its origin, the shadow was distinctive. It had to be the same person in each picture. Clearly, Toblinksy must have trusted this guy. But who could have had such a long association with a famous mobster and remain anonymous?

Chapter 5

When Joe, Moshe Toblinsky's guy, had slammed the compartment door shut, Sam locked it as instructed. Turning toward the seats, he got a glimpse of himself in the mirror over the washbasin. The sight caught him off guard and he leaned forward for a closer look, turning his head one way, then the other. The face in the mirror was thin to the point of sharpness, and there were dark smudges under the eyes. He'd been told they were nice eyes. Their amber color stood out in contrast to his dark hair and pale skin. He ran a finger over his upper lip. Not much there yet. He didn't have a razor anyway. Good thing he shaved a couple of days ago. Mama didn't want him taking a razor to his face, but he wanted to fit in with the goyim who surrounded him at work. For a short Jewish boy on the skinny side, sticking out in the rough crowd at the Fulton Fish Market was not a good idea.

Sam glanced over the rest of the tiny compartment. Not much space, but what there was looked shiny new. From the wood-paneled walls to the upholstered seats, this train was designed for the comfort and satisfaction of the wealthy. Sam looked down at his wrinkled, work-stained shirt and grinned. The boys from the neighborhood wouldn't believe where he was even if they could see him. He drew a long breath. Even the air smelled new and clean, kind of like fresh varnish and sweet-smelling soap mingled together. Leaning over the basin, he splashed warm water on his face and neck, then grabbed the little rectangle of hand soap resting on the basin's edge. Lifting his shirt, he did the best he could to eliminate the odor coming from under his arms. As he took one of two linen hand towels hanging on the wall beside the basin, his gaze returned to the soap. Nobody would miss that little, used sliver. Maybe they wouldn't even miss the hand towel. After drying himself, he wrapped the soap in the towel and tucked the package into his pants pocket. There was no telling when these might come in handy.

Couplings clanked and the whole train shuddered in anticipation. Sam rocked on his feet, swaying with the motion of the sleeper car. A little thrill of excitement coursed down his spine as he settled himself in the forward-facing seat. The train started rolling, its wheels crept over the tracks at first, then picked up speed. They moved out of the station, and the city swept past his window.

Sam had never been farther away from home than lower Manhattan. Once on a lark, he walked from the Fulton Fish Market to the Hudson River warehouses and docks on the opposite side of the island, a twenty-minute walk past skyscrapers under construction, St. Paul's Chapel with its peaceful cemetery, and the electronics suppliers on Radio Row. Now he was headed to a place known only from pictures in newspapers and magazines. Sunny Florida. Mama had no idea. His stomach clinched, bursting the bubble of excitement.

Sam let his head drop back against the seat. What a mess. No suitcase, no place to stay, no friends or family, no job. Things could have been so different, if only . . . If only Papa hadn't died. If Sam hadn't taken the job at the Fish Market for a couple of dollars more per week than what old man Rosenberg was willing to pay at the bakery. If he hadn't taken the second job at the speakeasy. The if's rolled on and on until his exhausted mind shut down with the oblivion of sleep.

~ ~ ~

Sam awoke with a start. The train's rhythm had changed. The view outside his window showed they were pulling into a station with signage stating Norfolk. Virginia. How long had he slept? It was hard to tell, but the sun's position in the sky indicated late afternoon. Sam shifted in the seat to get the circulation in his lower body moving again and felt an urgent need for the lavatory. His compartment contained a washbasin, but no toilet. Joe had told him not to leave the compartment, but if he didn't, there was the distinct possibility that his already soiled pants would have a new stain in a very embarrassing place. There had to be a public toilet somewhere in the car. The problem would be finding it without drawing attention to himself.

Sam took two steps and unlocked the door. Seeing no one in the corridor but the conductor, he stepped out.

"Pardon me, sir, can you tell where I can use the lavatory?"

The conductor's gaze traveled over Sam with an expression of distaste. Sam smiled in return. The man probably wondered what a kid like him was doing on their fancy train in a private compartment. Would telling the conductor who paid for his ticket get a faster answer?

"I'm sorry to bother you, sir, but I really can't wait much longer."

The man snapped back into professional mode. "Just along the corridor. Last door on your right, young man. It is clearly marked."

Sam nodded his thanks and rushed to the facility. Business completed, Sam headed back to his compartment. When he swung the door inward, he found he was not alone. Joe glowered at him from the rear facing seat.

"I told you to stay put. Where the hell've you been?"

Sam's heart skipped a beat. "I couldn't help it. I had to use the lavatory." The shaky whine in his voice disgusted Sam, but he couldn't prevent it.

Joe's face split in a broad grin. "Yeah, when you gotta go, you gotta go. I come to let you know the boss says you gotta eat in the dining car. Come in at five, eat fast, and get your ass back here. Understand?"

"Yes, sir." Joe rose to leave. A touch of panic coursed through Sam. "Wait. What time is it now?"

"Ain't you got a watch?" Sam shook his head. Joe glanced at his wrist. "Four-thirty. I'll tell the conductor to knock on your door just before they start serving."

Sam shifted his weight from one foot to the other. "I . . . How . . .? Don't bother with the conductor. I can't pay."

Joe tilted his head to one side as his eyes narrowed. "So how old are you, anyways?"

Sam gulped. His gaze fell to the floor. To make matters worse, when he opened his mouth, his voice cracked, sending flames shooting across his cheeks. "Seventeen."

"You ain't nothing but a kid." Joe ran his gaze over Sam, then put a hand on his shoulder and gave it a small squeeze. "I got a boy a little younger than you. How about I tell the dining car to put your food on the boss's tab? Including dinner tonight, that should be about four meals total. The boss can afford it. You can get the money to him later."

"It may be a long time before I can repay Mr. Toblinsky."

"Don't you worry." Joe chucked Sam under the chin and winked. "The boss always figures out a way to get his money back." Joe grinned and patted Sam's cheek. "Don't look so scared, kid. Just do what you're told ,and you'll be okay."

Sam stared at the door for several beats after Joe closed it behind him. A curl of dread rose at the thought of what form the repayment might take.

Chapter 6

Liz stretched and twisted her torso from side to side. Outside her cubical window on the library's third floor the Saturday afternoon sun was hovering just above the treetops. Gator fans exiting the game would be clogging the roads, so trying to go home now would be a long, slow trudge. Turning back to her laptop, she looked at the reporter's byline again. Finding the source of the news article's photographs would be the critical first step in identifying her boy with the mark on his cheek. And pray God she wasn't following a trail to nowhere. There was no guarantee lightning would strike twice just because she wanted another find like the one she had made by following Capone to a hotel in a small north Florida backwater.

Liz's heart kicked up a notch. Early success didn't glow quite so brightly at the moment. It felt more like a competition, except the person with whom she competed was herself. Liz rubbed the bridge of her nose. This confounded fear of failure should be something she could discuss with the man she loved, except the man in her life was also her boss. As much as she loved Hugh, life with him was sometimes more complicated than any relationship she had experienced. The thought of diminishing his opinion of her professionalism by whining about her fears set her teeth on edge. If Dad didn't need so much of Mom's time and energy, Liz would talk to her, but adding one more worry to already overloaded shoulders was out of the question. Maybe she should join the university's female faculty support group? Naw. Joining wasn't her thing. Liz's mind whirled. She sighed and shook her head.

Oh, just shut up and get on with it! Nothing's gained by negative self-talk and doubt.

She sucked on her lower lip and scanned the newspaper article. It was written in 1989 not long after Toblinsky's death. The reporter's picture portrayed a pleasant looking man with a receding hairline and the beginnings of fleshy jowls. Twenty-eight years ago Richard Whitehead would have probably been between fifty and fifty-five if the photo next to the byline was to be trusted. That would make him around eighty today, if he was still alive. Taking her cell phone from her purse, she did a quick search for the Tampa newspaper's number and pressed call.

After a couple of automated transfers, a male voice announced, "Speak."

"I apologize for calling on a Saturday, but I'm hoping to contact a reporter named Richard Whitehead. He was working at the paper in 1989, but he may be retired by now."

"Never heard of him." The voice on the other end sounded bored.

"Perhaps there is someone who worked for the paper in 1989 who is still working now?"

"Could be. I have no idea."

"Is there someone else I should ask?"

"Maybe HR, but they won't be in until Monday."

Liz drummed her fingers on the chair arm. That was a total waste, but what had she expected on a Saturday afternoon? Liz glanced at the time displayed on her laptop screen. Too early to go home, but too late to start any in-depth research. She opened a browser and typed. Richard Whitehead, Tampa popped up in the search box. Tapping the return key, she watched entries fill the page. According to Whitepages.com, there were two Richard Whiteheads living in the Tampa area, one in a condo on the bay. The other listing showed no address or phone number. On a whim, she called the number listed for the condo.

A youngish male voice announced, "Rich." Was that a statement of his economic situation? Given his address, it certainly might be.

Stifling the urge to giggle, Liz cleared her throat and said, "I'm sorry to disturb your Saturday, but I'm trying to contact a Richard Whitehead who worked as a reporter for the *Tampa Bay Chronicle* in 1989. By any chance have I reached the right Mr. Whitehead?"

"Who wants to know?"

Oops. Liz swallowed hard and tried again. "I'm sorry. I was abrupt. Please excuse my rudeness." Liz went on to give her name, explained her position at the university, and gave a quick overview of her research project. "So without Mr. Whitehead's help, finding my man will be considerably more difficult."

"Yea, I can see that."

"Are you the gentleman I'm looking for?"

"No."

This guy owed her nothing. She had interrupted his day. Still, irritation reared its head. "Oh. Then I'm confused as to why you didn't say so to begin with."

"Because my dad gets all kinds of people looking him up. Some of them aren't exactly the friendly sort." Rich Whitehead's voice sounded firm, aggressive even. "He was an investigative reporter and made some enemies along the way."

"Oh, I didn't think of that. Of course, you must be protective of him. I promise that I only need a few minutes of his time, and I am certainly no threat to him. I didn't even know his name until I came across the article. Is there any way you will let me see him?"

"It's not up to me."

Good grief! How much more irritating was this guy going to get? "So who is it up to?"

Richard the Younger's deep baritone laugh rolled over the ethernet. "Sorry. It's just that you sound so earnest. Do you always take yourself so seriously?"

"Yes. Can I see your father or not?"

"Can you be reached on this number?"

"Yes, it's my cell."

"Okay. Let me make a call. By the way, are you pretty?"

"Exactly why do you need to know that?"

"It might help. My dad likes pretty women."

Liz glanced at her reflection in the mirror on the back of her library cubicle's door. Hair forced against its will into a ponytail, a halo of auburn escapee tendrils curling around her face and the nape of her neck, no makeup, jeans with holes in the knees and ratty U of Washington sweatshirt. A sight that would not exactly drive men wild with passion.

"Miss Reams? You still there?"

"Yes. Sorry. And it's Dr. Reams. I suppose I look okay when I fix up. Will that do?"

"Guess it will have to. Call you back in a few."

Liz studied the Toblinsky photos while she waited. A closer study with the magnifying glass and the dark area on her man's face didn't appear to be a birthmark. Its edges were too uniform. Could be a scar. The cell phone chiming so soon after she said goodbye to Rich Whitehead made her jump.

"Well, you're in luck, *Dr.* Reams. Dad said okay, but only if you can come to the home tomorrow. His social calendar for next week is pretty full."

"The home?"

"The Autumn Leaves Assisted Living Facility in south Tampa. Down on the bay."

"That's great. I can be there by ten."

"Better make it two-thirty. Dad's got a hot lunch date. New woman just moved down from New York to be near her daughter. Dad's got high hopes for the post-lunch hour."

~ ~ ~

At 11:30 the following day, Liz kissed Hugh goodbye and headed toward Tampa. It was interstate all the way, but she gave herself an extra hour to get lost. After several wrong turns, at 2:00 she parked in a slot marked Visitors and surveyed her surroundings.

The day was mild and bright under a lapis sky. Pure Chamber of Commerce weather. A bench set under a cluster of swaying sabal palms seemed like a good place to wait. Liz strolled across the well-manicured lawn and sat down to admire a scene straight out of a landscape design magazine. Oleanders anchored sculptured beds overflowing with a blaze of blooms. Bougainvillea climbed an arbor inviting a stroll down to the water's edge. Sun diamonds sparkled on the azure bay, mesmerizing and calming. When she was old, a place like this would be just about perfect.

A shadow fell across Liz's bench, catching her off guard. "Are you Liz Reams?"

Liz jumped a little and turned toward the slightly accented voice. Shielding her eyes with her hand, she looked up into dark-brown eyes with laugh lines burned around the outer corners. Black hair. Tanned skin. The fine features of the . . . Spanish aristocracy? Ralph Lauren's star model, the Argentinian polo player, came to mind. Her heart rate kicked up a notch. She managed a nod, hoping she didn't look as stupid and stunned as she felt.

Gathering her wits, she held out her hand and nodded. "You must be Rich Whitehead."

He grasped her hand in a confident grip. "I am."

Indecision tinged with irritation floated to the surface. He would be an unnecessary distraction during the interview with his father but being ungracious at this point would not help. Liz mustered her most winning smile. "I hadn't realized you would be joining us today."

"I left my sous chef in charge. He can handle things between the noon crowd and the evening rush."

"So, you're a chef?"

"Right again. I own Fulgencio's. Maybe you've heard of it?"

Liz's brows rose. Outside of Miami, the state didn't have an abundance of Michelin-anointed places. When Fulgencio's received their rating it made the major news outlets, including the *Gainesville Sun's* Lifestyles section.

"Yes, I have. Congratulations on your star."

Maybe it was the sun in her eyes, but Mr. Rich Whitehead seemed to be wearing a rather self-satisfied smile. Fame, fortune, and devastating good looks. A combination almost guaranteed to create a little arrogance, or maybe a lot.

Liz mentally shook herself and glanced at her watch. "It's two-thirty. Do you think we can risk going in now?"

Rich bent slightly at the waist and extended his hand palm up. "After you."

They strode toward a white stucco and red tile roofed building reminiscent of south Florida's early twentieth century Spanish inspired architecture. It looked like an expensive resort. The antiseptic smell that assailed them when they opened the heavy iron front door drove any thoughts of vacations from Liz's mind. They found Richard Whitehead, Sr. sitting in the sunroom holding hands with a youthful looking white-haired beauty. When she noticed their approach, the lady rose from her seat, kissed Rich, Sr. on the cheek, and departed.

"Dad, this is the woman who wants to ask about the Toblinsky photos."

Rich, Sr. squinted up at Liz, and a smile spread across

his face. "Have a seat, young lady. Don't know how much help I'll be, but I'll give it my best."

After a little introductory small-talk, Liz spread the printed copies of the photographs out on the table at the old man's elbow. Pointing to the same face in each picture, she asked, "Do you know who this is?"

The old man bent over the photos for several minutes, then shook his head. "I can see that it must be the same man, but it's no one I've ever identified. Why are you interested in him?"

Liz explained her hope to tell South Florida's mob story via one of the ordinary people affected by it. She started to talk about her Capone book when the old man interrupted her.

"So you're the history professor who discovered Al Capone's connections in North Florida? Damn fine piece of investigative reporting." The old man patted Liz's hand and enfolded it between both of his. "You know, our work, yours and mine, aren't as far removed as you might think. Only real difference is I investigated living people, while you investigate the dead."

Liz withdrew her hand and sat farther back in her chair. Forcing a calm smile onto her face, she continued, "Only with your 1989 article, you were writing about a dead man. Is it possible to tell me how you came by the pictures? Would your source talk to me?"

"She might if she was still alive."

Disappointment engulfed Liz. "Oh. That's too bad. Who was she?"

"Nobody really. She died a few years back. Her claim to fame was being the fourth wife of a mid-level Toblinsky mobster. When the husband died, she found out there was no money left. In fact, they were in debt up to their eyeballs. She sold the pictures to the paper. My editor paid a pretty penny for them, I can tell you, and they were worth every bit. That article earned me a Florida Press Club Award."

"Yes, I was impressed with how comprehensive the article was. It read more like a true biography than a newspaper piece."

"That was no coincidence. It was the first step toward a real biography of Moshe Toblinsky. Up until then, nobody had gotten close enough to write much that could be proven."

"It's too bad you didn't write your book. I'm sure it would have been excellent."

An odd expression came over Richard Sr.'s features. It looked a lot like fear, but maybe it was simply embarrassment or regret. He shook his head. "Writing that book would have been bad for my health."

Rich Jr. cut his eyes at Liz and chuckled. "Now Dad, don't be melodramatic."

An unmistakable look of anger filled the old man's eyes. "You were just a kid. You know nothing. Biggest career sacrifice of my life and I did it to keep you and your mother safe." A red tinge crept across the old man's face.

A little thrill coursed down Liz's spine. Maybe it was time to change the subject. She tapped the pictures. "Do you have any suggestions for how I can identify this man?"

The old man rubbed his chin. "You might have a go at Toblinsky's descendants. Several of them live in the Naples area. Don't know if he still represents them, but you might try contacting them through Sol Bergman. He was their attorney back in '89." The old man frowned and looked searchingly into Liz's eyes. "When he threatened me with a lawsuit and his . . . connections."

Chapter 7

A sharp rap on the compartment door brought Sam near the surface of the waking world. A second burst of tapping sounded and the door inched open. Fuzzyheaded, Sam struggled up from the corner of the seat where he had slumped and blinked several times.

"Please pardon the intrusion, sir." A conductor's dark navy-blue cap leaned through the opening. "I was asked to be very sure that you did not miss the first call for dinner. If you will make your way to the dining car, your table is waiting. Service will begin in ten minutes." When Sam managed a nod, the conductor closed the door.

Serious lack of sleep and the train's soothing rhythm had made for an irresistible combination but left him disoriented with an otherworldly sensation. He stretched his stiff back and tried to roll the crick out of his neck. It took a second to remember why he was on a train then his heart dropped to the soles of his shoes. Mama would be really worried by now. Sam could visualize her leaning through the open front-room window glancing anxiously up and down the street. Next, she would leave the apartment and go into the street, asking neighbors and other boys if they had seen her son who hadn't come home from work last night. She would tell them she hadn't worried too much at first, because what with working two jobs, not coming home at three in the morning was bound to happen sometime. But he was a good boy. He would have let her know. She would already have walked down the street to the bakery several times between cleaning jobs to inquire about a message. Old man Rosenberg had hopes where Mama was concerned and so he agreed to be their message delivery system. The bakery had a telephone. Mama would tell anyone who would listen that Samuel would have called the baker. Except for last night he didn't. It was the first time.

Sam couldn't just drop off the face of the earth. He couldn't do that to his mother and younger brothers. They depended on the money he brought in from his jobs. Mama barely kept food on the table as it was. Sam closed his eyes and ran a hand over his face. How was he going to get out of this jam? It had started out so innocently. All he wanted was to make two extra dollars a week. Taking the part-time job at the speakeasy meant the younger boys could have new shoes for the winter. Their feet grew so fast. Who was he kidding? Everything about them got bigger seemingly overnight. If it wasn't shoes, it was at least two winter coats, one for the oldest of the four younger kids and one for the baby. Hand-me-downs only made it through three boys before they fell apart.

Five boys. Papa had been so proud with each birth. He said the Ackerman line was assured with so many strapping males. The only luck their family ever had was that Mama and all her children were healthy. The kids had never even been inside the neighborhood doctor's office. Too bad Papa's health hadn't matched that of his offspring. Dropped dead at forty-one of a massive heart attack. Now Sam was headed into the unknown and nobody knew where. Geez. Sam slowly shook his head. Could things get any worse?

The first thing he had to do when he got off the train at West Palm Beach would be to find a way to get a message to Mama. When he found a job, he would write letters every week and send money. For now, he needed to do what Joe told him.

Rising to his feet, Sam stretched again and went to the compartment door. Looking right and left, he stepped into the empty passage and made his way through the train cars. The fragrance of warm bread, something fried, chicken maybe, greeted Sam when he opened the door to the dining car. Probably nothing Kosher on the menu, but Sam was beyond caring about dietary laws. His stomach growled so loudly that a waiter halfway down the carriage glanced up from the table setting he inspected.

The waiter left the table immediately and approached Sam as though he was on the lookout for a kid in wrinkled, dirty clothes who really had no business being on this fancy train. Sam ran his fingers through his hair and rubbed his hands down his pants legs. Like that would make him more presentable. Oh, yeah. Sam dropped his hands to his side while a foolish smile spread over his face. The flicker of distaste disappeared from the waiter's ebony features as quickly as it had appeared.

"Good afternoon, sir. Would you be Mr. Toblinsky's guest?" Sam nodded, and the waiter continued, "Mr. Toblinsky's gentleman mentioned that you might be joining us for the first seating. If you will follow me."

The waiter slid out a chair and Sam sat down. Two sparkling glasses, blue and gold-rimmed china with a pattern of red, blue, and yellow flowers in the center, and silver flatware sat on a white linen cloth. He fingered the linen napkin. It was crisp and so snowy, as though he was the first person to ever use it. A small vase of white flowers with shiny dark-green leaves completed the table setting. Sam had never seen anything like it. He bent to the vase. The flowers' fragrance was surprisingly sweet and stronger than expected. Mama would get a kick out of this place. She always loved pretty stuff although she had precious little of it herself.

The waiter put the menu in Sam's hand. He opened the folded-over cardstock imprinted with oranges and white blossoms on a gray ground and his eyes grew wide. How on earth did they keep so much food from spoiling? Heart set on trying the South's most famous meat dish, his spirit fell a little when he read that the chicken used in the frying had been buttermilk dipped before breading. No mixing meat and dairy for a Jewish boy raised by a mother who kept Kosher. The least he could do was try to keep his family's traditions. With further examination, he settled on the sirloin steak. It was the most expensive item on the menu, but it was as close to Kosher as he was probably going to get.

Being the first guest in the dining car, Sam wasn't kept waiting long. His steak arrived within record time, at least he assumed it was fast since he didn't have much experience with restaurants or steaks, for that matter. The meat was crusty brown on the outside and juicy pink and tender on the inside, tasting of no spices other than salt and pepper. The fluffy baked potato didn't need anything but salt and a pat of butter. The fried eggplant was like what Mama made. Sam tried to remember his table manners, but hunger from a day and night without food drove his knife and fork. When he'd eaten about half of his dinner, his voracious stomach allowed him to slow down long enough to look around at the other diners who now filled the car's tables. Elderly couples, white hair illuminated by the early evening sun coming through wide windows, sipped soup and talked quietly, probably about the grandchildren they were leaving behind in northern cities. A girl who couldn't have been much older than Sam sat opposite a young man, her eyes shining as she listened with rapt attention to whatever he said. A corsage of white orchids pinned to the shoulder of her suit jacket announced that she must be a bride on her honeymoon. The way she twisted her wedding ring indicated she wasn't used to wearing it.

A commotion of voices and a door opening at the far end of the car broke into Sam's surveillance of his fellow diners. Joe entered and pointed toward a table in the center on the eastern side of the car. "Here ya go, boss. I made sure that conductor saved your favorite table."

Every diner shifted focus from his or her own private world to stare at the end of the car. Quiet anticipation hung in the air like August humidity at Coney Island. Paused in the doorway stood a slender man of about thirty. His dark eyes swept the length of the car before he proceeded to the indicated table followed by Joe and two other men of equal size and sternness of expression. The man Joe called boss couldn't be more than 5'5" or 5'6", but he seemed to fill up all the space in the car. Once the quartet was seated, Joe waited for a nod from the boss before snapping his fingers in the air. A waiter appeared beside their table with alacrity, poised to receive the order forms required by the Seaboard Line which did not allow its wait staff to take verbal food orders. The quartet took their time perusing the menu despite other diners waiting to be seated or to place orders. No one moved to a table or attempted to draw attention away from the quartet seated at the center table.

Sam couldn't tear his gaze from them either. He had never been so close to a famous person before. Sam watched Mr. Moshe Toblinsky in fascinated awe. He looked like any Jewish man of Eastern European extraction, his features maybe a little sharper than most. He could have been a rabbi, banker, or Kosher butcher. Except he wasn't. Toblinsky wielded extraordinary power among New York's Italian mobsters. The mob's bookkeeper. That's what they called him. But he just looked so ordinary.

Without warning, Toblinsky's gaze shifted like he felt someone staring. The older man's eyes locked onto Sam and lingered there. Flames crossed Sam's cheeks and his appetite suddenly disappeared. He broke eye contact and dropped his gaze to the remnants of his dinner. Taking his knife and fork from the plate's edge, he began to push his food around as though he was still eating. For several uncomfortable beats Sam could feel his benefactor's eyes traveling over him, evaluating his potential, maybe? When he could stand it no longer, Sam's eyes rose to take another look in the gangster's direction. Toblinsky stared unsmiling with one eyebrow rising ever so slightly. Sam's face flushed again. Toblinsky watched him for another second before nodding slowly as though in recognition. Sam felt his food rise from his stomach and hang in the back of his throat. He swallowed hard and nodded in return.

Chapter 8

Liz blinked a couple of times and glanced over the letter. Shaking her head, she moved into the shaft of sunlight pouring through her office window and held out the piece of heavy, white bond covered in words imprinted by an old-fashioned typewriter. Several words and phrases jumped off the page. Cease and desist. Harassment. Civil action. Slander and/or libel. Invasion of privacy. In other words, leave the Toblinsky family alone or else. The legal firm of Rosenberg and Rosenberg had made their position quite clear. Not now or at any time in the future did anyone from the family wish to communicate with one Elizabeth Reams, Ph.D.

The alacrity with which the lawyers responded sent a prickle of alarm coursing down her spine. She had called the firm on Monday. Today was Wednesday. The letter was brusque, pointed, and brutally direct. Aside from all the legalese, it also contained an undercurrent of . . . What? Threat? She read the sentence containing the phrase "recourse to other means" again. Liz shook her head. This was 2017. No attorney would be so bold or risk disbarment by threatening a person with bodily harm, and certainly not in writing. Immersing herself in the history of American crime for so many years must be making her paranoid. Whatever, it looked like the trip on Sunday to visit Mr. Whitehead, the reporter, had been a waste of gas and time. Maybe finding her man with the mark on his face was a nonstarter.

Liz dropped the letter into her briefcase and grabbed her purse. If she hurried, she could get to the grocery store to pick up some things for tomorrow night's dinner and be home before Hugh arrived with tonight's takeout from the Peking Wok. He was scheduled to leave for a conference early Friday morning. Hugh didn't expect her to be the chief cook and bottle washer but making a nice dinner for him gave both of them pleasure, one that they experienced too seldom. They had fallen into a pattern of either meeting for a quick meal at a restaurant or skipping dinner altogether in favor of a salad or a snack as they worked on job related stuff in the evenings.

Their habit was getting old and expensive. They usually set aside Thursday evening for sharing the cooking and spending time with one another. Sort of a date night at home. She was at her office door when her cell rang. Fulgencio's appeared on the screen. Now what could he want?

"Hello, Mr. Whitehead. How are you?"

"Excellent, and it's Rich, please." There it was again. A touch of an accent echoed in his rich baritone. She had noticed it when they first met, thinking it matched his dark good looks. Odd that his father spoke without one.

"Okay, Rich. I really appreciate you letting me see your dad. He's a great guy."

"Yeah. He's a little rough around the edges, but I love him. How did contacting the lawyer go?"

Liz's fingers found her car keys in the depths of her purse. "Not well, I'm afraid."

"I figured as much. Sorry about that."

"That wasn't your dad's fault or yours. It was a long shot really."

"True, but I hoped you would find what you were looking for."

"Thank you. There was no harm in trying, I guess."

"So, where will you look next?"

"I'm not really sure. This may be the end." Liz winced. It was one thing to know a thing intellectually, but quite another to realize it in your heart. Maybe she should just forget the man with the facial scar and move on to something more realistic, something less ambitious. Liz frowned. "Rich, it is nice of you to follow up, but I know you must be busy. So . . ." The keys flipped back and forth over her hand.

"Wait. Don't go. There's another reason for my call."

"Oh? Is there something I can do for you in return for your kindness?"

"No, but there is something I can do, rather did, for you."

The keys stopped mid-flip and clattered against her palm. "Did your dad remember something about the pictures?"

"No. But after you left, I looked them up online and showed them to someone else. I may have a line on your guy."

Liz's heart beat a little faster. "My goodness. That's wonderful." Liz swallowed to control the bubble of excitement welling up in her throat. "I don't know how to thank you. What exactly did you find out?"

Rich chuckled. When he spoke again, his voice took on a husky familiarity. "Have dinner with me tomorrow night and I'll tell you."

His tone caught Liz off guard. This sounded more like a request for a date than a business meeting. Liz scrambled for a reply. "I'm afraid I have plans with my fiancé." Hugh hadn't proposed again since her latest refusal, but Rich needn't know that. "We could drive over on Sunday afternoon. Would that work?"

"Fiancé? No. The invitation is just for you. Dinner. Thursday or nothing. It's our least busy night, and after the weekend, I'm headed out of town. Even chefs need the occasional vacation."

The little bubble of excitement popped. "Of course you do." Liz hoped the disappointment didn't show in her voice. "Going someplace interesting?"

"Miami and the Keys. Staying with cousins to do a little South Beach clubbing and then we're headed for deep sea fishing. We have an old family shack on Key Largo. It's an annual thing."

"Sounds like fun."

"It is. So, how about Thursday? After dinner, I'll take you to meet the person I consulted. Can you be here by five?"

Liz hesitated. "Are you sure this is something that will really help my research?"

"Guaranteed. Is it a date?"

"I don't know." Curiosity and uncertainty dueled for control within Liz. Would Hugh object? Probably not, but still . . . Stop being negative. Hugh will understand. He supported her career, wanted her to succeed. They would have other Thursdays. Liz stuffed down her unease at canceling yet another date night with him. "I'll see what I can do. Can I call you back in the morning?"

"Yeah, but don't make it too late. We do a heavy lunchtime trade with the local businessmen."

Liz tapped the end call button and sighed. Even though she and Hugh worked and lived together, something always cut into their personal time as a couple. It seemed their jobs . . . no, that was incorrect. *Her* job was consuming their life together. Hugh had managed to carve out time for pursuits other than work. Why did she always feel like work had to come first? Just look at the situation with her parents. Wouldn't a loving daughter ignore her mother's assertions that there was no need to fly home to check on them despite her father's growing dementia? Mom could be difficult and overbearing, true. But maybe Liz used that as an excuse?

Liz sucked the soft flesh of her inner cheek between her teeth and rolled it around, a nervous habit that needed breaking. Whatever the answers, putting work first had always been her way. In high school, she broke her date and skipped her senior prom so she could get a last-minute college application packet in the mail, thereby covering her bases many times over. Throughout college and three degrees, she gave up time with friends and boyfriends to work. Gradually, the friends and boyfriends had given up on her. She regretted letting them fall away, but it couldn't be helped. Competition in the field of history was just so intense. At least, that was the excuse she made for herself. By the time graduation with her doctorate drew near, the biggest loss of all punched her in the gut. Walking in on her fiancé in bed with another girl came close to breaking her spirit. Instead of giving in to pain and rejection, she worked even harder and it paid off. She had the job and the man of her dreams. She came by both via an unexpected route, but she had landed on her feet. Following her navy pilot ex-boyfriend, the one who had promised nothing and cheated on her, to Florida turned out exceptionally well, despite her parents' and friends' dire predictions.

Liz's lips thinned into a straight line. By golly, she *would* have it all one day if she just worked hard enough and planned well. One day, her life would come into complete focus. A few new problems weren't going to shake her. Hugh would be fine with her going to Tampa. There would be other date nights. Plenty of them. Mom and Dad would be fine until she could get there at Christmas Break. Mom had declared it, so it would be.

Chapter 9

Thirty-five hours on a train, even a luxury passenger outfit like the Orange Blossom Special, and Sam was ready to jump out of his skin. The muscles in his back and shoulders complained bitterly. Every time he moved electric jolts shot down his spine. Stretching his arms above his head, he twisted his torso from side-to-side. The bunched muscles screamed in reply. He stood up and bent backward until his hair brushed against the curved metal bottom of the closed upper bunk. That was better, but his *tuchis* still tingled like somebody had put a match to it. Placing a hand on either side of the open compartment window, he leaned out and closed his eyes. Wind slapped his cheeks and rushed on. The air was heavier than any he had ever experienced—warm, humid, with a slight tang of . . . what? Salt? Yeah, that was it. The ocean couldn't be far off. He opened his eyes and strained to see, but neither the sound nor sight of the Atlantic pierced the roar of the tracks and gathering gloom of night.

Sam stared at a flat landscape dotted with the outlines of pine trees and some sort of palm tree bushes, at least that's what they looked like. They had fronds like palm trees, but they sat on the ground. Nothing back home in Brooklyn looked like that.

A rush of homesickness wrapped its fingers around Sam's heart and squeezed. He swiped a hand over his eyes as he leaned his head against the window frame. How was he going to let Mama know what had happened? By now she must be thinking he lay dead in a back alley or at least badly hurt. He didn't know where his next meal would come from or where he would sleep, much less how to pay for a call to the Brooklyn bakery where messages could be left for Mama. The Pullman car's rocking suddenly increased, sending Sam stumbling back into his seat. They rounded a curve and the train began slowing. Brakes squealed, and a one-story Spanish-style building came into view. Electric lighting illuminated a black and white metal sign just under the eaves of the red tile roof. West Palm Beach. The end of the line.

Sam rose from his seat and opened the compartment door. No sign of Joe or any of Mr. Toblinsky's other associates. Utterly alone. No home, no family, no money. His spirits fell, but suddenly another thought struck him. If they had brought him this far from home just to leave him to make his own way, maybe that wouldn't be so bad. Working for a gangster, even if he was Jewish, wasn't how Sam had been brought up. Papa would never have tolerated it. Mama didn't know who he worked for in Manhattan. She had accepted his lie about a better job in a delicatessen without question.

Sam stood in the doorway waiting for other passengers to pass. He stared at the electric glow of the small city through the window opposite. Low buildings in a flat land looked nothing like home, but maybe this would be an adventure he could tell his kids about one day. He slid his hand into his pocket, removing its sole contents. He counted his five coins for the umpteenth time. Five pennies, two dimes, and one quarter. Fifty cents. He shook his head and removed his handkerchief from his hip pocket. Dropping the coins in its center, he tied up a tight bundle. They wouldn't buy much, but if he lost them he would have nothing.

A light breeze blew through the window and caressed his cheek. At least the weather was warm. A park bench or even the sand on the beach would make a good enough bed until he figured out what he was going to do. There had to be jobs available to a strong boy willing to work hard and do what he was told. Yeah. That was it. Find a job, earn some money, and go home. Sam's face split into a grin. Heart lighter than at any time during the last two days, he stepped into the corridor and strolled toward the exit.

Passing a conductor, he paused and turned back. "Excuse me, sir. Can you tell me when the train goes back to New York?"

"It doesn't, young man. This is the end of the season. The Orange Blossom Special won't run again until next December."

"Oh." Sam shifted from one foot to the other. "But there are other trains going north, aren't there?"

"Of course, but not as many going either way. Mostly freight going north after the tourist season ends."

"I thought people came here all the time."

"No, folks up north don't usually come down here when the weather gets hot and most who live here full time don't travel much. Times are getting hard for ordinary people in South Florida since the land boom went bust."

Sam's optimism began to crumble. He ran his teeth over his lower lip and asked, "About how much would a ticket cost?"

Sam's eyes followed the conductor's gaze as it traveled over him. Wrinkled shirt and pants. Dirt smudges at the knees, cuffs, and elbows.

The conductor raised one brow. "Probably more than you've got. Now, move along. I have things to attend to."

The depot platform had a couple of porters helping the last of the passengers when Sam stepped down onto its gleaming pine boards. Everything about the place looked shiny and new, but a long walk from the town. He stuck his hands in his pockets, turned toward the area where the lights shone the brightest, and trudged toward the platform steps. At the end of the platform, a hand grabbed his shoulder.

"Hey, kid. Where you going?" Joe grinned down at Sam. "The car's this way." From the other end of the platform, Mr. Toblinsky watched them with a bored expression. Sam's heart skipped a beat.

In the depot parking lot, a lone Cadillac Imperial stood under a street lamp, its black body so shiny you could probably see your face in it. Sam loped along behind Joe and his pals as Toblinsky led the way. Spying the quintet approaching the car, a uniformed chauffeur jumped from behind the wheel and opened the rear passenger door.

Doffing his cap, he smiled broadly. "Good evenin', sir. Did y'all have a good trip down from New York City?"

"Good enough. Get us to Miami and don't spare the gas."

"Where should I take y'all? The Biltmore? Most rich folks stay there."

Toblinsky eyed the man like he wanted to smash his fist into the driver's ebony face and shove his teeth down his throat. "The Biltmore don't have room. They say they're full up for the season. Take me to the Nemo, south of Fifth in Miami Beach."

The chauffeur's eyes widened and his nostrils flared. "Yes, sir. I'm sorry. My boss, he didn't say we was goin' to Miami Beach."

"You got a problem with it?"

"Oh, no, sir. I just didn't know. That's all. I ain't been in that part of town for a long time. Come to think of it, I ain't never been south of Fifth."

Joe stepped forward, fists clinched at his side. "Get in and shut up, why don't you?"

The chauffeur nodded as Toblinsky and his men stepped into the car. Sam was shoved onto the third seat, squeezed between Joe and another guy his same beefy size. Joe leaned forward and pushed the communication window separating the front seat from the two facing seats in the rear. When it clicked shut, he sat back and looked at Toblinsky.

"He didn't mean no harm, boss. He just didn't know."

"Yeah, I guess the expensive suit fooled him."

Joe must have seen the perplexed expression on Sam's face. "Jews can't stay at the Biltmore. Can't own property above Fifth Street on Miami Beach. Can't join country clubs anywhere. Can't stay at fancy hotels." Joe wrapped an arm around Sam's head and pushed him down into a headlock. Running his knuckles over Sam's hair, Joe continued, "Yeah, kid, it's a real picnic being a Jew or Colored down here, but you'll survive if you behave yourself. Welcome to Florida, land of sunshine and opportunity."

~ ~ ~

After a sweaty trip south on the two-lane road leading from West Palm Beach to Miami, the city proper flew passed the car window. Dark expanses broken regularly by the feeble light of street lamps showed little of the scenery. Low, one-story structures with faint light showing through curtained windows gave way to attached two and three-story buildings. A few multi-story structures loomed momentarily as the car slowed for a bridge. Sam leaned forward and peered around the gangster on his left. Lamps atop pillars lining both sides of the concrete expanse cast diamonds on the ripples of the dark water below. The air coming through the window was noticeably cooler and wetter. They must be almost to the beach. As much as he wished he'd never boarded the train south, a little thrill coursed through him. He had only been to the beach once. Papa had taken the whole family to Coney Island after his bar mitzvah the August he turned thirteen. He strained to see between the buildings they passed for a glimpse of the water. Once he thought he heard the sound of waves crashing, but it could have been wishful thinking. They came to the end of the bridge and continued straight for a couple of blocks before turning right for another three. The car slowed and glided to a stop in front of a three-story building where a man in uniform stepped to the curb and opened the door.

"Good evening, Mr. Toblinsky. It's good to see you again." The doorman glanced into the car's interior. "Will all of the gentlemen be staying with us?"

Toblinsky climbed out followed by everyone but Joe. "There will be four staying here."

Sam's heart stopped, then roared back hammering and banging against his breast bone. His head seemed to float up off his neck. He looked at Joe. "Wha-What are you going to do with me?"

Chapter 10

Liz looked across the dinner table at Hugh. "So, are you okay with me going to Tampa tomorrow night? I'm sorry he only invited me, but beggars really can't be choosers." Hugh's expression of relaxed contentment shifted. His eyes widened as his brows rose.

Liz pushed aside a serrano pepper with her chopsticks and picked up a piece of Kung Pao shrimp. It's garlic and ginger laced bite seared her tongue anyway. She must have missed a little bit of pepper still clinging to the morsel. Eyes watering, she chewed until the shrimp was a sticky paste, but still he didn't answer.

Finally, she swallowed and continued, "I didn't mean to hurt your feelings, but this could be seriously important. I thought you'd understand. We'll do something special next Thursday. I promise." She hated the whine that had crept into her voice. For crying out loud! She did *not* have to ask permission to attend a business meeting. And yet, a small finger of guilt pricked her conscience. Rich Whitehead's invitation had held something more than the promised information on her guy in the old newspaper photographs. Reaching across the table, Liz slipped her hand under Hugh's and tickled his palm. He grabbed her wrist and raised it to his lips, kissing the pulse point.

Placing his other hand over hers, he took a long, slow breath. The corners of his lips turned upward ever so slightly. "I'm fine with it and you haven't hurt my feelings. I'm just surprised. That's all. If this guy Whitehead has what he claims, it could get your research off the ground. Go."

"You're sure?"

Hugh paused for only a beat, but it was enough to make Liz wonder if he had only said what he knew she wanted to hear. "I'm sure, unless that tropical depression out in the Gulf decides to come ashore. And as long as you don't let him get any ideas about this being a date or anything. Barring bad weather and interloping swains, I'm fine with it." He grinned and scooped up a forkful of Kung Pao laden rice.

Was his smile forced? Sometimes Liz's memories of other lovers' betrayals crept into her relationship with Hugh. It made her uncertain and overly sensitive. She second guessed herself and him. That was hardly fair to Hugh, but it was a fact of life for her. Liz searched Hugh's face. He tilted his head to one side and smiled, as if silently asking what she was thinking. No signs of subterfuge or his being disingenuous marred his expression. Maybe her imagination needed a good slap down.

~ ~ ~

Late Thursday morning, Liz peered from her office window for the fifth time since her arrival at 7:30. The day had dawned overcast with air so heavy she felt like she was breathing through a wet blanket. Now thunderclouds hung on the western horizon.

Should she go to Tampa or not? Taking her phone out of her pocket, she found Rich Whitehead's number and tapped call. It rang and rang and rang, but no offer of a voicemail box came on the line. Liz had the phone away from her ear ready to end the call when she heard a faint voice coming through the earpiece.

"Professor Lady. Wait. Don't hang up!"

Liz pressed the cell back against her ear. "Hi. I . . ."

Whitehead did not give her a chance to finish her sentence before he charged ahead with, "Glad you're still there. I left my phone in the office and had to run for it.

You're not calling to cancel, are you?" Despite sounding a little out of breath, Rich's tone was flirty, challenging, and a little unsettling.

Liz pursed her lips and tried to keep the irritation out of her voice. "Hello, Mr. Whitehead. I thought I'd better check. How do things look there?"

"I thought we agreed that you would call me Rich. I'm not going to answer to Mr. Whitehead."

How childish could a guy get? "Rich, should I try it or not?"

"Come on down. I've got something special planned for dinner. It would be a shame to let it go to waste. And my contact is rather interested in meeting you."

Liz's heart rate kicked up a notch at the mention of the contact. Go or play it safe? Liz chewed on her lower lip for a moment before asking, "What if the storm changes course?"

"It's not going to. I've lived here all my life. I've got a pretty good handle on Tampa weather."

He wasn't a meteorologist and they both knew it, but that mysterious contact . . . "Well, if you're sure."

"No worries. You'll be fine."

Liz tried to make her voice sound confident. "Okay, I guess that will work. If I arrive early, may I come on to the restaurant?"

"Sure. Text me when you're about thirty minutes out."

Call ended, she checked her desktop to make sure the message canceling her afternoon office hours had been sent successfully and smiled. Having student email addresses on the university central server organized by class registration was a godsend. She gathered up her all-purpose bag that served as purse, laptop carrier, and book bag, and headed down the hall to Hugh's office. She paused by the open door and tapped on the frame. When he looked up, she entered, crossing to the corner of his desk. A smile lit his face as he came to her side.

"What would you say to knocking off early and going for a good lunch and a movie? The one we've been wanting to see just opened."

"Sounds wonderful, but have you forgotten? I've got that meeting in Tampa this afternoon."

The expression in Hugh's eyes darkened. His gaze shifted to a spot on the wall behind Liz then darted back to meet hers. "No, but I thought you might have changed your mind."

A sliver of guilt pierced Liz. She sensed Hugh was trying to be casual, but she heard the hurt and disappointment in his tone. She gazed into his face silently trying to convey how much she needed to meet Rich Whitehead's mysterious source.

"I really think I should go. This is something vitally important. I feel it in my bones."

One corner of Hugh's mouth lifted in a lopsided smile full of doubt. "Your prognosticating bones don't know everything. The weather report doesn't sound good. That tropical depression in the Gulf is on the move. It could come in anywhere between Bradenton and Destin. I'm not sure driving down there is a good idea."

"I've checked the weather service and there's an 85% chance it will make landfall near Panama City. They get a lot more weather in the panhandle than in Tampa. Besides, it hasn't been upgraded to a tropical storm and probably won't be."

Hugh's smile dissolved to a thin line. "So says the girl who hasn't lived through enough Florida weather to know the difference between a tropical depression and a hurricane."

"We get plenty of heavy weather in Seattle." Great. Sounding defensive. Not cool. Liz plastered a self-confident smile on her face. "If I can drive through a blizzard, I think I can handle a little rain."

"And wind? And high water? Tropical events have a way of spreading the joy over an entire region regardless of where they make landfall."

"All right. I'll call and cancel if you really think it will be that bad."

Liz heard the hint of anger in her voice, but she couldn't halt the tide of emotion surging through her. He, of all people, should realize the pressure she felt to continue her early success. He had even teased her about the dean's heightened expectations for the whole department because of the recognition she received for her Capone revelations. Publish or perish was the rule all university researchers lived or died by, including him. A tide of desperation washed through Liz. How could she persuade Hugh that this trip was worth the risk? She didn't want to fight with him over something that seemed to defy common sense. She drew a deep breath and exhaled slowly.

Trying to keep her tone neutral, she continued, "Of course, if I miss this opportunity, it may not come again. Rich Whitehead doesn't owe me anything. He's trying to help me out of kindness and because his dad liked me, I think. And he was very specific about why it had to be tonight. I thought you would surely understand why this trip is so important."

"Look, I just want you safe. I don't know for sure about the driving conditions. No one does where tropical storms are concerned, not even the weatherman. It isn't a crime to worry. And I do understand why you feel compelled to chase after whatever information this Rich guy is dangling, just not in a hurricane." His voice held notes of anger and hurt feelings.

Liz's conscience pricked the bubble of her own anger. "I know. I'm sorry I got cross."

Liz ran her the tip of her tongue over her lips. Why couldn't she just admit to him her secret fear that early success was a fluke, that she was a fraud masquerading as a competent professional? She hadn't expected to make a name for herself so early in her career. Historians rarely achieved the type of recognition she gained through her Capone discovery. She trusted Hugh in all other things, but she kept this one giant issue private. Maybe another, greater possibility compounded her fear of failure. She had always believed that if she worked hard enough, she could have it all: success, love, family, everything she wanted. The burden of that belief weighed heavy at times. One concern, however, overlaid all others. Hugh's respect for her as a colleague meant the world to her.

Liz sighed and gazed into the eyes of the man who was her lover, her friend, and her boss. When your love life intersected with your professional life like hers did, things could get really complicated. How could she make him see it from her perspective without admitting her fears? Certainly not by mentioning that she had already talked to Rich about the weather.

Liz lifted her hand, letting her fingers trail along his jawline. Looking into his eyes, she mustered her calmest tone. "I really want to find out what Rich knows and going to Tampa now is the only way it will happen. He promised that he would introduce me to someone who knows the guy I'm after. This could make all the difference to my research."

Hugh put a hand on each of her shoulders. His eyes searched hers before he spoke. "You think it's that important?" Liz nodded. "All right. Call me when you get there and before you leave Tampa tonight. If things get bad, don't try to come home until the weather gets better. And promise you'll turn back if the rain gets too heavy on the trip down."

"I will. Thank you for understanding."

"I was raised by a Southern mama. She expected me to be a gentleman who takes care of his lady." Hugh shook his head slowly. "Lord, save us from stubborn, self-sufficient, independent career women."

Liz's anger vanished, replaced by gratitude tinged with humor. "Ouch. That makes me sound so difficult, but admit it. You wouldn't want me any other way."

Hugh laughed and kissed the tip of her nose. "You're right. I wouldn't change a single hair on your beautiful head. You're perfect just the way you are." Brushing a stray strand away from her cheek, he looked into her eyes and all playfulness disappeared from his expression.

"Tropical weather can be vicious and unpredictable. Please be careful."

"I will. And to keep my promise, I'm going to leave now to get ahead of the traffic."

~ ~ ~

The first drops of rain made splashes on the windshield, the size of nickels, as Liz neared Tampa's city limits. By the time she reached the restaurant, the wipers barely kept up despite slapping back and forth at full speed. Liz parked in a spot near the front entrance and gazed through glass covered in sheets of water. Only a few cars dotted the parking lot, but of course it was late afternoon in the midst of a howling gale. Most good restaurants weren't open for business at that time of day. When she called him from an interstate rest stop on the trip down, Rich had told her to come on in as soon as she arrived. He said he was glad she was coming and repeated that she needn't worry about the weather. Why had she listened to him? She knew why—her all absorbing research. No one ever said historical research could be dangerous, but it was too late now.

Without warning, the torrent of rain eased up a little. This might be her best chance of getting inside without being completely soaked. Grabbing her umbrella, she pushed the driver's door open. It pushed back.

Chapter 11

Sam's question hung in the air like the scent of a prostitute's perfume floating through a synagogue. What were these men going to do with him? The order to keep his mouth shut had been issued repeatedly since the Mick's murder, but Sam's imagination had gotten the better of his tongue. Nightmarish visions ran through his mind, like a bullet to the head and his body dumped into a swamp where alligators destroyed all evidence he ever existed. To make matters worse, fear had put a whine in his voice. All eyes now glared at him.

Joe grabbed Sam's arm as he bent toward the open car door.

"Sit back, kid. Stop being a *putz*. Mr. Toblinsky don't like whiners."

One of the men on the sidewalk shoved the car door shut. Sam looked up through the open window into Toblinsky's scowling face and slid backward onto the seat. Sam lowered his gaze to avoid the men's contemptuous stares. From beneath his lashes, he searched Joe's face for any sign of what might happen next. All he saw was a relaxed, neutral expression relating nothing more than Joe's pleasure in being near his journey's end. Sam sighed and placed his hands on his knees so that his companion couldn't see them shaking. Showing fear didn't seem like a good idea, even with Joe, who had been kind in his own gruff way. Joe must have felt Sam watching him for he chuckled and punched Sam's shoulder.

"You should see your face, Sammy. Relax. I ain't let nothing bad happen to you so far, have I?"

Sam's tongue refused to dislodge itself from the roof of his mouth, so he simply shook his head. Joe gave the car's roof a couple of whacks and the Caddie sped away from the curb.

"Where should I take y'all, sir?"

"Back into Miami. Bakery over on the river. Scheinberg's. Know it?"

"Oh, yes, sir. It sells the best bagels in the city. Fine man, Mr. Scheinberg."

Retracing their route to the bridge, they passed over dark water again. A brackish odor drifted in through the open car window, reminding Sam of his days spent on the docks and his walks home over the bridge to Brooklyn. A lump rose in his throat. He bit down hard on the inside of his lower lip. Crying in front of Joe would be humiliating and just as dangerous as showing fear. When the car turned left on the other side of the bridge, Sam grabbed the hand strap hanging by the door to keep from tumbling across the seat.

Only a few sparsely spaced vehicles, mostly delivery trucks, traveled along the broad street. Block after block of darkened multi-story buildings flashed by the car window. When the driver made a sharp right, Sam caught a glimpse of water on the left as the car passed an empty lot. Rows of buildings lined both sides of the unidentified waterway. Sam lost count of how many blocks they traveled. The multi-story buildings deceased in number, replaced by one and two-story structures.

The car slowed beside a truck with Wholesale Groceries on its tarp-covered side. The truck stood next to the curb before a two-story building. Lights shone through the storefront's plate-glass windows, the only ones along the street showing signs of life. The fragrance of baking bread, yeasty and slightly sweet, wafted into the car. Sam's stomach growled and his mouth watered, while tears filled his eyes. Bakeries in Miami opened for business in the early morning hours just like they did back home in Brooklyn. Mama had always awakened him long before dawn on bread days to be first in line, so old man Rosenberg could give him the best loaves without offending his other customers. Praying Joe didn't see the tear trickling down his cheek, Sam quickly swiped a couple of fingers over his face as though he swatted at a mosquito.

The driver applied the brakes and guided the car to a spot in front of the truck. He downshifted, looked back over his shoulder, and smiled.

"Here we are, sir. We made good time, if I do say so myself."

"You going to finish the job or what?" Joe asked.

The driver's smile disappeared. He turned off the engine and stepped to the back of the car, removing his cap as he opened the door. Joe looked at Sam and winked, but did not budge. After several beats, Joe leaned forward and removed himself from the backseat at a leisurely pace. Once he stood beside the driver, Joe stuck his head back inside the car.

"Get out, kid. This is the end of the line for you."

The contents of Sam's stomach rose in his throat. His bladder felt like it would explode. All Sam needed right now was to wet himself or puke on the gangster's shoes. Taking a long breath, he crawled from the backseat.

Joe glanced at the chauffeur. "Wait here. I'll be back."

Turning to Sam, Joe jerked his head toward the side of the building where a staircase ran up to a second story landing. At the top of the stairs, Joe raised an iron knocker attached to the door covered in thick plate metal with a Judas gate at eye level. *Tap—tap, tap—tap.*

"Remember that code, kid. You could get yourself hurt without it."

Sam shifted from one foot to the other and swallowed hard. No response came from beyond the door. The only sound was that of water lapping against a bulkhead and something mechanical off in the distance. Beyond the bakery's back wall a wooden dock running the length of the building extended out over the water. Judging by width and flow, Sam guessed he was looking at the river Joe had mentioned. In the darkness beyond the dock, the mechanical noise increased into recognizable form. A motor *putt-putted*, growing louder as it drew nearer and then cutting out completely. A launch containing two figures bumped against the dock. One of the men, at least Sam assumed it was a man, tied a line to the pier.

The boat rocked gently while the two men began shifting wooden crates onto the dock. Sam started to ask what they brought in by river when the Judas gate opened and a face peered at them from behind the door.

"Oh, it's you. Why don't you guys ever show up on time? I ain't been to bed yet waiting for ya." The voice was straight out of Manhattan's Lower East Side. The face had seen hard times. The man had a cauliflower ear and the flattened, enlarged nose of a prizefighter. By the way he bent toward the Judas gate's opening, he must be the size of a heavyweight.

Joe grinned. "So what? Your phone's probably tapped anyways. No need giving the G-men a heads-up."

"Tapped, my ass. I pay good money so that don't happen." The Judas gate slammed shut.

The sound of bolts sliding and lock tumblers rolling came from the other side of the door. It swung inward to reveal a cavernous room much like the one back at 105 South Street. Tables and chairs sat around an open area in the center of the room, a dance floor of sorts by the look of it. On the far side of the room, a dark wood bar with a brass foot rail covered the back wall. Rows of liquor bottles filled the counter space beneath a large mirror. Bare bulbs hanging from the ceiling illuminated the space. The odors of sweat and stale booze permeated the air.

The stranger's gaze ran down over Sam and back up.

"This the kid?"

Joe nodded.

"He don't look like much."

Joe chuckled. "No, he don't."

"Probably too small for the job. What am I supposed to do with him?"

Joe shrugged. "I guess that's up to you. Boss brought him down here as a favor to a friend."

"Yeah? And I'm returning the favor I owe Toblinsky. This makes us even, right?"

"Hell if I know. That you would need to talk over with the boss."

The stranger's eyes bulged and his mouth became a hard line, but he kept quiet.

Joe nudged Sam, pushing him forward. "Look alive, kid. You do what you're told, you hear?"

At the sound of footsteps, Sam looked back over his shoulder. "Joe?"

But Joe was already on the outside stair landing. He didn't stop to look back.

Chapter 12

Liz watched rain blowing in slantwise from Tampa Bay and slid her feet out of her pumps. They were her only pair of Jimmy Choos. She had found them "never worn" in the very exclusive Jacksonville Charity Guild Shop and had fallen in love. The fact that her former romantic interest—the two-timing Navy pilot, the guy she followed across the continent from Seattle to Florida—was with her when she bought them in no way diminished her devotion. She'd be damned if she was going to trot through a howling storm in them. She clutched the shoes to her chest and opened the car door.

The wind's force plastered Liz's raincoat against her body and turned her umbrella inside out. She held the uncooperative contraption in front of her as she bent behind its meager protection. Hopping over puddles, she dashed for the restaurant's door, which swung open just as she ran under the portico's red tile roof. Rich Whitehead grinned at her from the safety of the restaurant foyer.

Liz shrugged out of her dripping coat. Goose bumps rose on her arms and legs as the restaurant's mechanically chilled air settled on her skin. She looked down at her dirty feet and the drenched hem of her dress. Turquoise suede stilettos and a paisley silk shantung sheath had seemed an inspired choice for a business dinner with the chef/owner of a Michelin star rated restaurant. She glanced at her reflection in a large mirror hanging over an antique Spanish credenza. From knees to shoulders, she fit the professional image she had attempted. Below the knees and above the shoulders, she was a sodden mess. Worst of all, her carefully managed mass of auburn curls had exploded in a full-on frizz fest. Sighing, she turned to Rich.

"Has the storm changed course? The radio didn't say anything about it."

Rich took her coat and mangled umbrella. "This is just a sideline performance. The main show is still out in the Gulf."

Liz's face must have betrayed her incredulity, for Rich's expression sobered. For a moment Liz thought she saw anger glint in his eyes, but the emotion, whatever it was, flashed and disappeared.

"The storm's going to Panama City. I promise. I wouldn't have encouraged you to come if I hadn't been sure."

To ease the tension, Liz tilted her head, raised her brows, and attempted a joke. "And I'm thinking you may be brought up on charges of practicing meteorology without a license."

Oops. A decided miscalculation. This time, a crimson flush started at Rich's hairline, filling his forehead, spreading across his cheeks. He looked just like the boy her freshman year of high school who was sure he would be the class valedictorian in four years. She had made a joke at the braggart's expense. He had not been amused either.

Liz summoned a friendly, neutral smile. "Could you point me to the ladies' room."

Rich blinked a couple of times. His face and body visibly relaxed into a professional demeanor.

"Of course. Right through that archway." He pointed toward a short hallway with only two doors.

Paper towels, hand soap, and her ever ready supply of hair serum repaired most of the damage. Thankfully, the paisley pattern helped to hide the watermarks that were sure to remain when the silk fully dried. Liz slipped into her shoes and looked into the full-length mirror next to the restroom exit. Good enough, but not the image she left home with.

When she returned to the foyer, Rich had disappeared. In his place, a waiter stood at the ready.

"Miss Reams?" Liz nodded. "This way, please. Chef Ricardo is already seated."

They passed through a main dining room where tables were set for the evening. Red, leather club-chairs surrounded expansive tables covered with snowy linens, hotel silverware, and china bearing a wide teal-blue rim and gold medallion in the center. Each dining table had an arrangement of fresh tropical flowers. The room exuded a casual elegance underscored by the richness of its material components. Wood paneled walls in the main dining room rose to dramatic heights and contained gilt framed photographs of a city on the water, but it wasn't Tampa. The pictures had a Latin quality to them. A color photo that particularly caught Liz's eye showed a beautiful dark-skinned woman in a red conga outfit: bra-style top with ruffles at the shoulders, bare mid-drift, a fishtailed ruffled skirt that hardly covered her knees in the front and swept the floor in back, fishnet stockings. She danced with a man whose ruffled shirtsleeves ballooned from shoulder to wrist. The couple clung to one another in a seductive pose, alluring and sensual, the woman bent backward over the man's arm. The heat generated between them flowed outward from the picture in a palpable stream, as though the couple danced only for themselves without thought that others might be watching.

On either side of the couple's portrait, posters with titles in Spanish acted as foils to the intimacy of the dance. They advertised bands and musicians Liz had never heard of. The one on the left proclaimed a handsome dark-haired man to be "Mister Babalu." It was not Desi Arnaz, but someone named Miguelito Valdes. On the right, an eleven-piece orchestra of trumpets, clarinets, a flute, conga drums held by men dressed in shirts with huge sleeves, and a woman holding maracas stood poised to play under the baton of one José Curbelo.

Liz stopped and scanned the room's other pictures. Well-dressed men and women stood or sat by bars in Art Deco rooms. Bands and dancers, conga lines, ornate buildings towering over expensive cars lined up by curbs, views of clear water lapping against low seawalls decorated Rich's restaurant walls. Another color photograph, one of a building with a bright neon sign, held place of honor over the fireplace at the far end of the room. *La Floridita, Bar y Restaurante, La Cuna Del Daiquiri*. The room's ambiance transported diners to another time and place, one that had existed and disappeared long before Liz and her host were born.

Liz turned to the waiter who stood patiently by her side. Pointing toward the fireplace, she asked, "Where is the *Floridita*?"

"*Habana*. It's very famous for being the cradle of the frozen daiquiri." The waiter's voice held a slight Spanish flavor, but it wasn't the Hispanic tones she had heard back home in Seattle.

"Are all of these photographs of Havana?"

"They are. Before Castro and his thugs."

"Looks like a good time."

"It was."

"You can't possibly be old enough to remember Cuba before Castro."

"No, but I have heard the stories." A wistful expression filled the young man's eyes. "One day, we will return."

Liz didn't know what to say. The Castros and their minions controlled Cuba as firmly now as they had for over half a century.

The corners of her mouth rose slightly and she nodded. "Perhaps I have kept Chef Ricardo waiting long enough."

The waiter led her to an alcove behind a short wall off the main dining room where Rich sat with his back to the window, leaving only one other vacant chair.

Rich gave her a rueful smile. "The view is not at its best today, but I thought you might prefer it to the looking at the wall."

Liz glanced through the expanse of glass at palm trees bending away from the bay, leaves and small branches tumbling across the lawn, and water spewing up over the bulkhead. The scene was straight out of every TV hurricane news report she had ever seen.

"Well, I wouldn't call it pretty at this point, but it certainly looks . . . exciting."

As she took her seat, Rich nodded at the waiter who hovered at Liz's elbow. "I think we'd better start now. Oh, and tell Sous-chef to prepare three cold plates to go and to pack the usual provisions."

Liz gave the blowing rain one more glance. "Rich, can you suggest a safe hotel away from the bay? I don't think I'd better try to drive home tonight."

"Don't worry about that right now. This will blow over as the storm moves north. Relax and enjoy your dinner, then we'll go see my contact."

Within minutes, two frosted martini glasses arrived, but the contents were not clear like the simple gin and vermouth concoction. Instead, a yellowish opaque slush filled the bowls and a lime slice perched on the sugar-coated rims. Liz took a sip.

"I haven't had one of these in years. It's delicious. A family recipe?"

Rich rolled his glass stem between his palms. "No, this is the original frozen daiquiri recipe perfected by Constantino Ribalaigua at Havana's *La Floridita*. He served it to Hemingway, Graham Greene, Sinatra—all the big names who passed through town."

"Yes, I remember reading that Hemingway favored daiquiris and another drink that I can't remember."

"The *Cuba Libre*." He picked up his drink and tilted the

glass as though offering a toast. "Free Cuba." Rich laughed softly, but there was a touch of bitterness in his voice. "Your basic rum and Coke. The name's something of a joke, don't you think?"

The arrival of dinner saved her from having to think of something appropriate to say in response. With a flourish, the waiter placed a large slope-sided metal pan between them, its contents fragrant with garlic, onions, and peppers. Two lobster tails sat atop a bed of saffron-colored rice and vegetables. Shrimp, oysters, scallops, crab legs, and mussels surrounded the tails and peeked out from the rice, a work of art for eyes and palate.

Liz's stomach growled loudly. Rich's gaze lifted from the dish. He gave her a lopsided grin. Liz's eyes widened as heat flooded her face. "I guess I'm hungrier than I realized. This looks and smells fabulous."

"*Paella Cubana*. Now this one is a family recipe and a secret one at that. Give me your plate. I'll pick out the best pieces for you."

As Liz handed over her plate, her fingers brushed against Rich's. She expected him to take the plate and begin dishing up the food. Instead, he didn't break the connection, but kept their hands poised above the *paella* in an impromptu *pas de deux*. Rich looked into her eyes and let his gaze linger there. Liz's involuntary intake of breath caught her off guard. Trapped by his gaze, an old feeling, one she thought she had banished forever, surfaced from deep within her psyche. His bad-boy vibe communicated itself to her as though it passed over an invisible electric line running from his fingers to hers, an unspoken conversation filled with possibilities. She shook her head and pushed the plate into Rich's hand.

You've learned your lesson about glamor guys. You fell in love with Hugh for good reasons. You are committed to him. He loves you in a way no other man ever has. Hugh. Oh, crap. The call.

Chapter 13

Sam stared at the landing outside the second-floor speakeasy's front door like he expected Joe to materialize any second and motion for Sam to follow. A couple of beats passed before reality set in then a churning sensation began in his midsection. It straightened out and slithered its way into his chest, growing and expanding until Sam's breath jerked in silent gasps. So this is what being set adrift at sea without a life preserver felt like.

"Hey, kid." The stranger before him snapped his fingers in Sam's face. "You stupid or something? I asked if you got a name?"

Sam swallowed the lump in his throat. He managed to project his voice just above a whisper. "Samuel Ackerman, sir. I'm called Sam."

"Well, Sam, move your ass so's I can shut the damned door."

With the door firmly closed and bolted, the stranger turned his attention once again to Sam. The man's gaze flicked over him, then settled on his face. Placing a hand under Sam's chin, the stranger pushed it one way and the other.

"Jew?"

Sam nodded.

The man grunted, a curled lip lifted one corner of his mouth. "It figures I'd be saddled with a runt and a Jew to boot. You know how to drive a boat?"

Of all the questions the man might have asked, this one

would never have occurred to Sam. "No, sir. The closest I've been to a boat is unloading fish on the Fulton docks."

"How about a truck?"

Sam shook his head.

"How much can you lift?"

Once again a question caught Sam off guard. "I guess the boxes of fish at the market must weigh seventy or eighty pounds."

The stranger reached out and grabbed Sam's right arm above the elbow. "Muscle feels firm enough. Show me your biceps."

"Sir?" Sam had no idea what the man asked him to do.

"You know. Like this. Show me what you got." Lifting his own arm, the man bent his elbow and raised a considerable muscle on his upper arm, one like the body builders in the ads of cheap magazines showed. "Now, show me with both arms."

Sam did as directed. A lump the size of a small grapefruit rose on each arm. Hard fingers gripped the biceps and squeezed.

"You must be a lot stronger than you look. I guess you'll do for the job."

"What job would that be, sir?"

"That can wait 'til morning." The stranger turned and motioned for Sam to follow him to the other side of the room. Turning down a narrow hall to the right of the bar, the man went to a door at the end and opened it.

"This is where you'll stay until we decide what to do with you. Toilet's across the hall. The bakery downstairs has been told to give you breakfast. They're your kind, so you'll like the food."

When the man turned to go, Sam could no longer keep silent. "Wait. What's your name?"

The stranger frowned, an impatient glint in his eyes. "Bateman. Now get some sleep. You're going to need it."

Sam placed a hand on the man's arm. "Please, Mr. Bateman. Is there a telephone where I can call and let my family know that I'm all right?"

Bateman shook free of Sam's grip. "No. Long distance calls cost money and can be traced. Write to them. You do know how to read and write, don't you?"

Sam nodded. "But I don't have any paper or pen."

"You can get some tomorrow. Now shut the hell up. I've missed enough frigging sleep on your account."

With that, the door closed and Sam was truly alone. He hadn't cried since the night his father died a little over two years ago. Growing up fast and toughening up hadn't been accomplished by crying over hurts or because life wasn't going his way. Despite all that, Sam's shoulders slumped and his head dropped nearly to his chest. Tears ran unchecked down his cheeks. Would he ever see his mother or brothers again? For the first time in his life he realized how much home meant to him. He'd been too focused on helping his family survive to think about how much he loved them. At times, his family had felt more like a burden than a source of comfort. Now, he would give anything to be able to pick up that burden again, but he was stuck in this hole with no way to even let them know he was alive until he could get a letter to them. Even after he wrote the letter, Mama would be sick with worry for a good while longer because the mail was so slow. Why had he thought two dollars extra a week made working for gangsters worth the risk?

Wiping tears from his face, Sam focused on the space in which he found himself. The room was really rather large. If it weren't for the wooden crates stacked on three walls almost to the center of the room, there would have been sufficient floor space for several pieces of furniture. Sam stepped over to the closest stack of crates and peered into the one on top. Twelve bottles filled with amber liquid rested in the wooden container. Lifting one, he read the label. A little whistle escaped his lips. Canadian Club Whiskey, the best available. This must be an example of what he saw being offloaded from the river.

Returning the bottle to its spot, Sam took in the rest of the room. A single bare bulb hanging from the middle of the ceiling illuminated a folding cot, complete with gray blanket and dingy pillow, set beneath the room's one window. On the cot's leg the words *US Army* had been burned into the wood. Sam walked over to the cot and sat on its edge. Pulling the blanket back, Sam saw the same words woven into the woolen fabric. Must be army surplus from the Great War. He picked up a corner and brought it to his nose—musty as only cloth improperly stored for years could be. In fact, mustiness hung about the entire space. The room had no air moving. The evening was warm and humid even though it was still spring. When they arrived at Palm Beach, the first step onto the platform made Sam think summer had already arrived.

Sweat dripped from his chin and trickled down his back. He leaned over and pushed on the window's lower sash. With some encouragement, it rose until half of the window opening was filled with nothing but rusty wire screening. Next, Sam opened the door and went across the hall to the toilet. Luck was with him. The water closet's smaller window opened as well, its opaque glass rattling in the frame as Sam pushed it upward. With cross ventilation established, a light breeze tinged with salt floated into his bedroom. The air's clean scent and cooler temperature made the room bearable. The breeze's freshness meant it probably came straight off the Atlantic. For reasons he couldn't explain, that was somehow a comforting thought. Maybe it was because that same ocean sent cool breezes into Brooklyn when the winds were just right. Home might be a thousand miles away, but the Gulf Stream waters rolling ashore just a mile or two away at Miami Beach would eventually lap against the sands of Coney Island. Sam couldn't see either beach, but he could follow the ocean's path in his imagination.

Stretching out on the cot, Sam watched the stars through the window, picking out the Big Dipper, the only constellation he remembered from his school science lessons. On summer evenings, he and his brothers had lain on their backs on the apartment building's roof, watching the stars and making up stories about going to the moon or to Mars. The little boys usually begged for him to read H.G. Wells to them at bedtime, the size of their eyes exceeded only by that of their imaginations. A lump caught in Sam's throat, raising a bitter, stinging sensation in his clenched jaws. That part of his life belonged to someone else, someone who lived within a traditional family. The father went to work and the mother took care of the home and the children. The oldest boy in that once happy family was now a stranger, a phantom who might never have existed. Sam choked back a sob, closed his eyes, and tried to shut out memories of what might never be again. He placed an arm over his eyes in an attempt to block out the world. Maybe exhaustion would be his friend tonight. Whatever tomorrow brought, he needed to be rested and ready for it. The breeze picked up, calming his spirit and drying the mingled sweat and tears rolling down his face. Tension melted from him and his mind became quiet. Blessedly, sleep crept in and lay quietly over him within a few minutes.

Chapter 14

Liz's fingers tightened around the shaft of her fork as she fought the urge to kick herself. How could she have forgotten to call Hugh? Hunger and delicious food were no excuse. Hugh was not the demanding, jealous type. He understood her professional need to follow up on the information Rich promised. The one thing Hugh asked . . .

Liz patted her lips with her napkin and slid the chair back.

"Thank you for a wonderful meal. The *paella* was truly amazing. I'm afraid I ate like a starving tiger. What must you be thinking?"

Rich slouched back in his chair and let a small, self-satisfied smile play across his lips. "I think you enjoyed my food. That's the biggest compliment you can pay a chef."

Liz rose from her chair, giving him what she hoped was a playful smile. "That's a relief. I'd hate for you to think me too uncouth to be introduced to your contact."

"Never." He tilted his head to one side and raised one brow. "Going somewhere?"

"Please excuse me for a moment. I need to make a call. I nearly let it slip my mind."

"Fiancé keeps you on a short leash, does he?"

He guessed who she was calling and assumed the worst. Liz mustered a neutral smile, hiding a twinge of irritation. Rich's macho self-confidence and knowing glances contrasted sharply with Hugh's mellow charm.

"Not at all. His only concern is my safety." Her voice sounded sharper than she intended.

Liz walked to the far side of the main dining room. Having jabbed the call key, she was rewarded with a request to leave a message. Of course. Hugh didn't take calls when he was driving, especially not at rush hour. A text would have to do until she could call later that evening. She wanted, no needed, to hear his voice.

When she returned to the table, Rich's gaze flicked up at her as he slipped his phone into his pocket. A languid smile filled his features, but not quickly enough to hide the expression of a moment ago. Guilt, worry, or maybe, stress had darkened his eyes. Whatever was on his mind, he didn't appear inclined to share it with her. She only hoped it wasn't a new weather report with bad news. Liz glanced at the scene beyond the window. The restaurant's garden lights still glowed, but the fixtures bounced and bobbed casting eerie shadows over flowers and shrubs nearly flattened by the pelting rain. Illuminated by bulkhead lighting, the bay churned higher and wilder than before they began dinner. When a palm frond slammed against the window, Liz jumped. The flattened spears dragged over the glass, screeching as though in pain before flying away, driven on by the gale.

"I think the storm has gotten worse. Should we move away from the window?"

Rich looked over his shoulder and back at Liz. "I have a better idea." He snapped his fingers and the waiter appeared.

"We're ready to go. Has Sous-chef prepared the carry out?"

"The bags are waiting on the prep table."

"Good." Rich looked up at Liz. "Give him the keys to your car."

Liz turned to the young man who had served them all evening. "Thank you. I'll meet you at the front door."

"No need. He'll put the car in our covered parking."

"But I'll need it to drive to the hotel after our appointment."

"Solid concrete. Great protection from storms. No need in taking two cars where we're going. Unless you want a limb through your windshield or something."

Liz's fingernails dug into the palms of her hands. It wasn't what he said, so much as how he said it. His words, delivered in a condescending, know-it-all tone, set her teeth on edge. His smart-aleck banter kept her a little off-kilter, a feeling she heartily disliked. If he hadn't sworn his contact's information would be critical to her research, she'd gladly tell him to take what he offered and shove it, go to a hotel to ride out the storm, and go home as soon as possible.

But if she told him off now, she would never know what his contact might tell her. Since she was here, she might as well see it through to the end. She would be a monumental fool if he was lying, but why would he? They hadn't known each other long enough for that kind of game. Liz drew a long breath and exhaled slowly. In the end, she had to admit one thing drove her forward, overriding all doubt. It always did. Every instinct she possessed, every fiber of her being screamed that she was on the verge of discovering a critical clue in her search.

Willing a soft smile onto her lips, she relaxed her clenched fingers. She retrieved her purse from the floor and handed over her car keys. The waiter bowed slightly at the waist and disappeared.

Rich stood and tossed his napkin onto his chair. "We'll go out to the garage through the kitchen."

"Okay. Give me a minute to get my raincoat from the foyer."

"No need. Cover from door to door. You can get the coat when you come back for your car."

Rich turned and headed across the main dining room without seeing if Liz followed.

Liz's smile tightened as she trailed after her host.

"My goodness, covered parking on both ends. How . . . convenient."

If Rich noticed the note of sarcasm in her voice, he didn't respond to it. Instead, he led her through an unexpectedly empty restaurant. It was well past the time that customers should be dining. Perhaps Rich's patrons knew something about this storm that he refused to acknowledge. The thought sent a shiver down Liz's spine, but she didn't voice her dismay as he ushered her down an unadorned hall, through a service door, and into a white subway tile and stainless steel commercial kitchen. Though the mystery he created was wearing thin, she was committed at this point. A loud thump above their heads made Liz jump and set her pulse racing. Seeing the last of Rich Whitehead, Jr. and Tampa would be a relief, great clue or no.

With carryout food bags slung over his arms, Rich led Liz to a rear door. She stepped through it into a concrete enclosure. Wind-driven rain pounded the building's metal roof, creating a soft roar that filled the garage. Liz's nose wrinkled. The odor of motor oil mixed with cooking fumes permeated the space, which looked like the World War II bunkers featured in documentaries she and Hugh enjoyed watching. Gray concrete slab walls enclosed space for six cars. Rich opened the door of the closest vehicle, a red Porsche 911 convertible. Her Prius sat next to the sports car, looking prim and sedate by comparison. Eyeing the Porsche's seat, she turned backwards, sat down, and lifted her legs as demurely as she could. A sheath and pumps did not lend themselves to the graceful entrance of a ground-hugging sports car.

Once seated beside her, Rich pressed the automatic garage door opener and guided the Porsche onto the driveway leading to a side street. Liz glanced his way. Rich drove with one wrist slung casually over the top of the steering wheel as though they were out for a pleasure drive on a sunny afternoon instead of riding in a car being buffeted by a howling tropical storm. Maybe small-talk would calm her twitching nerves.

"I don't think I've ever seen a restaurant with a garage set up like yours. It certainly comes in handy on stormy days. Is it a recent addition?"

Rich grinned. "You didn't have time to notice when you ran for the front door, but my building is actually a restored, converted mansion. The garage was the brainchild of the first owner. Apparently, he had a Rolls he prized more than the mega-bucks it cost to build the thing in 1921."

Liz's phone pinged from the depths of her purse. She peeked at the screen. Hugh's text glowed against her wallet.

Rich cut his eyes at Liz. "Trouble?"

"No. Hugh is telling me to stay in Tampa tonight because the storm is coming in at Tarpon Springs. Maybe as a Cat 1." Liz choked back the accusation of reckless endangerment she really wanted to scream at him and asked as neutrally as she could, "Tarpon Springs isn't too far away, is it?"

"Nope." Rich chuckled as if he enjoyed the storm and her discomfort. "Only about thirty miles as the crow flies. Fifty minutes by car. Tonight is probably going to be a little more exciting than I originally thought."

Liz's lips became a thin line and her eyes narrowed. *What an arrogant ass he has turned out to be.* Taking charge of her anger with a deeply drawn breath, Liz tried to keep her tone conversational.

"That's really close. I think I ought to make a hotel reservation now. Any suggestions?"

"Wait until we get where we're going. My contact may have a better idea."

Liz twisted her grandmother's engagement ring, the one she wore on her right, ring finger. Another nervous habit. Liz bit back the words that she wanted to say. *She better.* Now why did Liz think the contact was a woman? Geez, her imagination worked overtime, no doubt prompted by the storm lashing the windshield.

They traveled a two-lane street lined with storefront businesses, boutiques, and restaurants of various sizes, shapes, and connection. When the headlights flashed on a brick and stucco sign in the median announcing Welcome to Hyde Park, they entered an area with a definite vintage vibe. Buildings of mixed commercial and residential use ranged in design from late Victorian to new construction made to appear old. If it weren't for the storm, Liz would enjoy the passing scenery. The historian in her never let an opportunity to peek into the past go by. Massive live oaks created a canopy over the street and oleanders, hibiscus, and other lush plantings filled in beneath them. The surroundings must be beautiful on sunny days, but in the gathering gloom of this evening, their limbs bent and swayed like dancers in a frenzied modern ballet. The street came to a dead end at another body of angry water fronted by a four-lane avenue following the shore.

Bay? Lake? Gulf? Liz's sense of direction was usually pretty good, but she felt disoriented due to the limited visibility created by the storm. Finally it came to her. Tampa is built on a peninsula. They must be facing the other bay on the city's eastern side. Its name escaped her at the moment. Traffic lights hanging at the intersection blinked red as they bounced and jerked against their tethers. *Please, Lord, don't let us have much farther to go.*

Rich stepped on the brakes and they turned right. They passed between the bay on their left and what looked like large residential estates on their right.

"Even in this storm these houses look wonderful. Is this the historic district?"

"One of them. The homes in Hyde Park were built between the late 1800's to 1920's." The car slowed again. "Here we are. Looks like everything is okay."

Rich guided the Porsche up the driveway of an expansive two-story brick manse. Light poured onto a broad wrap-around porch through large three-over-one-paned double-hung windows. Evenly spaced thick, brick columns supported the porch's roof. The car slowed to a stop under a side-entry porte cochere. Outside lights illuminated four steps leading up to the porch and mahogany French-doors beyond. Behind the lines of the door's leaded glass design, a figure fumbled with the locks and chain.

Rich turned to Liz. "I'll drop you off here and park the car in the garage. Go on in. They're expecting us."

They? He had said nothing about more than one person.

Chapter 15

Sunlight played across Sam's eyelids, calling him back into the waking world. He rubbed his eyes and leaned up on one elbow, peering over the windowsill toward the east. Judging by the position of the rising sun, it must still be early. Noticing the hook and eye holding the window screen closed, he unhooked the frame and pushed it up. Poking his head out the window, he craned his neck for a better view of his surroundings. Only one truck lumbered passed on the street in front of the building. He hadn't realized until that moment that his window overlooked the street. Normally something like that would not have escaped his notice, but the last seventy-two hours had been confusing to the point of confounding his senses. The morning was still, quiet, and peaceful. Sunlight washed the whole area with pale gold. It should prove to be a fine day. The fragrance of baking bread mingled in the sea breeze, making his mouth water and reminding him that it been many hours since he last ate.

A shadow moved on the sidewalk below and then the top of a head appeared, drawing his interest. A slender figure with a bucket in one hand and a cloth in the other emerged from under Scheinberg Bakery's front awning, turned to the plate-glass window, and placed the bucket on the pavement. Water sloshed over its side. The girl shook her head at the bucket, placed the hand holding the cloth on her hip, and looked up at the glass. Shielding her eyes from the reflected glare, she surveyed the job lying before her. The girl caught sight of Sam and frowned. After for a couple of seconds, she waved. A new sensation, one he had not experienced with any of the neighborhood girls in Brooklyn, the only girls he really knew, jolted Sam. As he gazed at this girl, his heart turned over in his chest while his breath caught in his throat. A bronze-haired, green-eyed, rosy-lipped angel had just blessed him with the most beautiful smile he had ever seen. Warmth coursed throughout his body. He lifted his hand in reply and grinned, praying he didn't look as foolish as he felt.

"Hello. They told us you'd arrived. Come on down. Mama has breakfast ready." The girl spoke with an unexpectedly Southern accent.

Sam couldn't help himself. Instead of moving out of the window and toward food, he stood glued in place, watching as the girl bent toward her bucket. His eyes refused to tear themselves from the sight revealed by the cloth of her overalls as it draped across her upturned bottom. The girl dipped her cloth in the water and looked back up at him.

"Are you going to hang in that window all day? If so, I'll let Mama know not to wait for you."

"Uh, uh . . . I'll be down in a minute. I need to, that is, I haven't . . . Please tell your mother I'll be down real quick."

The girl laughed, dropped her cloth into the bucket, and disappeared under the awning. Sam yanked his upper body backward out of the window, whacking his head on the sash in the process. He rubbed the spot where a small lump rose and hurried to the water closet across the hall. Remembering the tiny bar of hand soap he had stolen from the train, he removed it from his pants pocket and unwrapped the towel he had placed it in. Of course, the bar had melted away to almost nothing, but at least the towel could act as washcloth. He did what he could to make himself smell less foul. After rinsing his mouth with warm water and raking his fingers through his dampened hair, he surveyed himself in the cracked mirror over the wash basin. The face that looked back had dark circles under the eyes but was otherwise a fairly pleasant one. His mother, obviously prejudiced, had always told him he was handsome like his father. Sam had to admit that the older he got, the more like Papa he looked. Women had always stolen second glances at his father. Sam had noticed that even as a little boy. He turned his face from side-to-side. Not too bad, all things considered. He paused in his observation and moved in a little closer to the mirror. Was that a shadow of hair on his upper lip? Sure looked like it. He sighed. A razor. One more thing he would need to buy when he got a little money.

After one final glance in the mirror, Sam ambled to the speakeasy's front door. He tried the knob, but it was locked tight with no key in sight. Bateman surely did not expect Sam to wait to get something to eat until the bar opened. Of course he didn't. He had said the baker would provide breakfast and the girl seemed to expect him to come downstairs. There must be another staircase. Sam returned to the hall where his bed-storeroom was located and looked around. At the end of the hall beyond the water closet was a door he had not noticed before. He edged it back to reveal narrow, dark stairs. The fragrance of baking bread, accompanied by the sounds of laughter and the clacker of pots and pans, greeted him as he descended.

He paused on the bottom step and took in the sight of the bakery's busy kitchen. Five younger versions of the window washer, at least in coloring, sat on benches on either side of a long rectangular wooden table. Four boys ranging in age from about seven to twelve scooped bites of latkes and applesauce into their mouths between poking each other in the ribs and arguing over who would get the last crisp pancake. The youngest, a girl of about three, watched her brothers with duplicates of her sister's big, green eyes. When the boys weren't looking, the little girl slipped her dimpled hand onto the platter and grabbed the last latke. Jumping down from the bench, she skipped to the open back door and paused, apparently waiting to be noticed. The oldest boy, winking at his brothers, yelled for her to bring it back to which the child responded by sticking out her tongue and pushing through the screen door onto the dock over the river. At that point, a middle-aged version of the window washer turned away from her stove.

"Ruben, stop teasing that child and go get her before she falls into the river. You boys finish and go help in the shop. Give me some peace on the busiest day of the week." The mother glanced at Sam and frowned. "Well, why are you standing there? Sit. Your breakfast will be ready in a minute, not that I don't already have enough people to feed without Bateman sending me his bootleggers."

Sam swallowed hard. He wasn't a bootlegger. He just worked for one, at least that is what he had always told himself, but now he really had no idea what would be required of him in this new life, a life he had not chosen. He nodded toward the lady and dropped a leg over the long bench.

"Thank you for the food. It's been a while since I ate last. Everything smells wonderful."

The woman stopped dropping lakes into her skillet and ran her gaze over Sam. Her frown lifted, replaced by a softer, kinder expression. "*Oy vey*! You're nothing but a boy. No beard? How old are you?"

"Seventeen, ma'am. Eighteen the end of August."

"Old enough, I suppose. So who are you and what are you doing with the likes of Bateman?"

Unsure what to say about why he had been placed with Bateman, Sam introduced himself and stuck with the simplest truth he could manage. "I'm Sam Ackerman. The man I worked for in New York needed someone he knew down here, so he sent me. Are you Mrs. Scheinberg?"

"And who else would I be?" The woman raised one eyebrow. Her lips pursed in an expression stating loudly and clearly that she had believed very little of what Sam said. "Samuel, you are welcome to your secrets, but understand this. We know who Bateman owes and why, who he works for, and what he does."

Sam smiled weakly. "Then you know more than I do." He paused for a second, casting about for a change of subject. "I've been wondering. I was told Jews can't live—"

". . . Wherever they want? That's true of Miami Beach, but Miami proper is different. Sort of. We set up a bakery here, instead of below fifth in Miami Beach because Jews aren't the only people who like baked goods. Bateman and *your* kind make sure we aren't bothered by the goyim."

Sam wasn't sure exactly what she meant by "his kind," but from her tone it couldn't be good. Mrs. Scheinberg probably wouldn't appreciate his asking why a man like Bateman acted as her protector either. Perhaps she would be more understanding if she knew his story. Sam told her about his family and going to work on the Fulton docks, ending with, "The truth is I saw something that meant I had to get out of New York fast. At first, I thought they might get rid of me another way, but the boss liked me, so here I am. My mother doesn't even know what's happened to me."

Mrs. Scheinberg's brow wrinkled with concern. "She must be out of her mind with worry."

"I was told not to call. I'm going to write when I have money for a stamp."

Mrs. Scheinberg leaned toward the door into the shop and yelled, "Ruben, go to your father's desk. Get paper, an envelope, a pen, and a stamp." She cast a maternal gaze over Sam. "You will reimburse me for the stamp out of your first pay, ill-gotten or no. The paper is a gift. Write to your mother before you eat. She deserves to know what has become of you."

Sam sat at the table with his mouth watering and his stomach growling. Between the yeasty smell of baking bagels and raging hunger, it took all of his determination to do as Mrs. Scheinberg directed. Taking the fountain pen, he scratched across the paper.

Dearest Mother,

I can't tell you where I am or why I left without saying goodbye, but I want you to know that I am safe and with good people. You will know by the postmark that I am in Miami, but I cannot tell you the address. This is for your safety and mine. Please tell the boys that I miss them and to be good. I will send money when I can. Please don't worry.

With love,

Your son, Samuel

Sam felt a presence at his shoulder. He glanced up at Mrs. Scheinberg, who stood with a hand on her hip reading over his shoulder.

"Is that the best you can do? Your mother deserves an explanation."

"I appreciate your concern, but you really don't understand. It would be dangerous for her and my brothers to know anymore."

"Dangerous for them or for you?"

"Both. Like I said in the letter."

"Letter? More like a note that might be sent to the butcher, but it will help your mother to know you are alive and unharmed." Mrs. Scheinberg stepped over to the stove and grabbed a plate of food. "Eat. Your mother wouldn't want you to go hungry."

Sam gave Mrs. Scheinberg a grateful smile before cramming food into his mouth with the appetite of the starving. The latkes and applesauce tasted so much like what his mother made that tears lurked in the corners of his eyes. He swiped at them when no one was looking and kept on eating. When no more grated potatoes remained, Mrs.

Scheinberg saw him eying the bagels she took from the ovens. The fragrance meant home, family, and love. Sam couldn't stop a tear from rolling down his cheek. He ducked his head and swiped his hand across his face. Without comment, Mrs. Scheinberg placed cream cheese and a couple of bagels on the table. He laid waste to the last crumb.

A small head appeared at the opposite end of the table. Big eyes watched Sam with interest. A tiny finger pointed. "Mama, that boy is eating up everything, and he wiped his mouth on his sleeve. Aren't you going to make him stop?"

Sam looked from the little boy to the mother. Both of them shook their heads at him. Heat crawled up Sam's face. "I'm sorry. I guess I was so hungry I forgot my manners."

The child cast another appraising glance over Sam. "Why are his clothes so dirty and wrinkled?"

Mrs. Scheinberg stopped transferring bagels from the baking pan onto a large parchment paper covered tray and turned to her son. "Jacob, which is worse? Wearing wrinkled clothes or being rude to a guest?"

"But he's not a guest. You and Papa said so last night. You didn't want him here, and Papa said we had no choice."

"And what does the *Aseret ha-Dibrot* say about boys who argue with their mothers?"

"To honor your mother and father." The little boy mumbled his words like he had been asked the question several times before.

"That's right, so you will speak no more about it. Is that clear?"

The little boy rolled his eyes, pushed his lips into a pout, but nodded in agreement. Mrs. Scheinberg watched her youngest son wander into the shop and then turned to Sam.

"So, tell me. Why are you wearing such?"

Sam looked down at his shirt and pants. Dark patches colored the knees and elbows. A blotch of some unknown origin stained the left side of his shirt and everywhere the cloth was puckered and creased. "I left New York with what you see. They wouldn't let me go home for my stuff."

Mrs. Scheinberg shook her head. "My, my, Samuel. You're in a mess, aren't you?"

"Yes, ma'am."

"What kind of mess?" The window washer stood at the screen door peering into the kitchen from the dock. Drops of water spotted the denim overalls she wore over a man's blue, work shirt that was too big for her small frame. She couldn't have been more than five feet tall and maybe ninety pounds. Her side parted bronze hair dipped in waves to her chin and rose up in the back in the latest Flapper fashion. The girls at Tops's speakeasy had worn the style. They called it a Marcel wave bob or something like that. Sam couldn't keep his eyes off her. She was modern, tiny, and perfect with a sparkle in her eyes that spoke of impishness and a becoming self-confidence. Adorable popped into his head. That was it. The word described her completely. He had never met a Jewish girl like her.

She cut her eyes at Sam and wrinkled up her nose with a grin. Sam felt the heat rising in his face again, but this time it was like the sun had suddenly come out after a storm. The warmth of her smile washed over him bringing the first calm he had felt in days. Sam opened his mouth to say something, anything no matter how stupid, just to hear the music of her voice again in reply, but her mother beat him to it.

"Never you mind the mess, Miss Nosy Pants. Are the front windows clean?"

When her mother turned back to her bagels, the girl raised her eyebrows and grinned again. "Yes, Ma'am. Those windows'll blind anyone driving by."

"Very good. Now get the clothes your aunt and uncle sent, the things your cousins have outgrown. None of the boys are big enough to wear them yet, but they'll be just about right for Samuel. They're in the storage closet under the stairs. Next, go to the pharmacy and get a toothbrush. Tell them to put it on our account."

The girl shrugged and made a comical face at Sam. After dumping a box into his lap, she shot another grin at Sam and disappeared into the shop. A bell, like the ones merchants placed above their front entrances, tinkled followed by the slam of a door. Sam felt eyes boring into him. Mrs. Scheinberg's smile had been replaced by a thunderous glare. Probably because his gaze had followed the girl, staring even after the girl had passed through the shop's front door.

Mrs. Scheinberg put a hand on each hip. "Our Rebecca may look like a modern *shiksa*, but she is very chaste despite the unfortunate hair. Hear me now. She is not for the likes of you. I will be kind to you for your poor mother's sake and as part of my *Tzedakah* obligation, but our daughter is destined to marry a good, observant Jewish boy, maybe a rabbi even, not a gangster. Understand?"

As much as Sam wanted to shout that he was not a gangster, he realized how he must look to this kind, conservative woman.

"Yes, I understand." Looking for something less painful to talk about, he asked, "Are the schools already out for summer here in Florida? It seems kind of early."

Mrs. Scheinberg appeared puzzled. After a moment, comprehension dawned in her eyes. "This is Sunday. The children will return to school tomorrow as usual. What will you be doing?"

"I don't know."

"Humph. A likely story. You'll probably be—"

". . . doing exactly what he's told. Get your ass up and come out here. We got work to do." Bateman had come to the back door without making a sound.

Heart in his throat, Sam looked at Mrs. Scheinberg, whose mouth hardened into a thin line. "Yes, Samuel, go with your master. I'm sure he'll have a lot of work for you from now on."

Chapter 16

As Liz dashed up the porte cochere's steps, the French door opened to reveal an older woman dressed in casual slacks and top. She looked to be in the neighborhood of sixty, but a rather well-preserved sixty. Only a scattering of sunspots on her hands and the beginning of sagging at her jawline gave away her true age.

"Come in out of this storm, honey. We've been expecting you all evening. We're so glad you're finally here. Quite a night, isn't it?"

Liz returned the smile and held out her hand. "I'm Liz R—"

"Oh, we know who you are. Rich, Jr.'s told us all about you." The woman chuckled as though there was some sort of unspoken conspiracy between them. "I'm Mrs. Gray, Mrs. Hernandez's companion and nurse. She's anxious to meet you because she likes talking about the old days. Of course, she doesn't get out much these days, you know."

No, Liz didn't know. Should she ask about this Mrs. Hernandez? Clearing up misunderstandings now might be the best way to get off on a good footing here. "I'm afraid Rich has told me virtually nothing, not even the name of the person he's brought me to interview."

"And you came anyway?"

A flush crawled from Liz's throat up onto her cheeks, prompting a nervous laugh. "He was adamant that meeting his contact would be critical to my research. He was quite persuasive."

"Clearly." Mrs. Gray's right eyebrow rose as her head tilted to the left. She must have been a mother, teacher, or head nurse at some point. The look said more than mere words ever could have. Liz's cheeks burned with the heat of a blast furnace. Mrs. Gray pursed her lips and continued, "His contact, huh? Well, I guess you could call her that. Come on in and meet Mrs. Hernandez. You can decide for yourself how helpful this visit turns out to be."

Mrs. Gray led Liz through an updated kitchen replete with commercial stainless-steel appliances, furniture-grade wood cabinets, and granite countertops. The glow from the overhead recessed lights completed a scene straight out of an expensive home décor magazine. Liz couldn't resist running her fingers over the cool, glossy surface of the granite as they passed the enormous island in the center of the room. Her heels tapped on richly hued travertine covering the floor. The same stone created the backsplash above the counters. Serious money had been spent to create this chef's dream. One day, if they worked really hard, she and Hugh would have such a kitchen in a house like this. On pretty Saturdays, they sometimes drove around Gainesville admiring the old homes and dreaming out loud about what the interiors must look like. They had even picked out one they would like to own and refurbish one day.

Mrs. Gray pushed on a swinging door and they entered a long hall at the end of which stood a pair of French doors surrounded by divided sidelights. Liz blinked as her eyes adjusted to the lower light. Beveled wood panels formed the lower third of the front doors, while divided light glass filled the upper two thirds. Formal living and dining rooms opened on either side of the hall just beyond the staircase. Liz took a quick glance at the formal rooms. What she saw made her want to spend time in those rooms. The furniture was clearly antique and expensive.

She didn't want Mrs. Gray to catch her gawking, so Liz dragged her gaze upward. Crown molding ran around each of the fourteen-or-so-foot ceilings and medallions anchored each of three hanging fixtures, none of which was illuminated. Instead, light from sconces set in the cream-colored plaster walls and a table lamp set on a carved antique console glowed softly, creating a scene of both luxury and peace. Hugh would love this place!

Near the front doors, a tall, case clock chimed seven o'clock. A sinking feeling settled over Liz. She hadn't realized it had gotten so late.

"Mrs. Gray, is there somewhere that I may make a quick call? I promised my fiancé I would let him know when I reached Tampa, and I haven't been able to get through to him."

"Fiancé?" A surprised frown creased Mrs. Gray's forehead. "Well sure, honey, just step back into the kitchen. I'll wait for you here, but make it quick. Mrs. Hernandez doesn't like being kept waiting. She's a dear but a bit of an autocrat, if you know what I mean."

Liz nodded and retraced their route. A little knot twisted in her stomach. What had she gotten herself into? If this meeting turned out to be a dud, she would feel like a gigantic fool, and Hugh would probably ask her to drop the whole project, something she was unwilling to do even for him. She loved Hugh deeply, but living with her boss complicated life beyond measure. She dug the phone from the depths of her purse and tapped Hugh's number. This time, there was no voice mail request. The number didn't even ring. It seemed that service had been disrupted due to the storm. Maybe he would see that she had tried to call. She glanced at her missed calls. He had tried to reach her, but she hadn't heard her phone ring. She sighed as her heart sank at the thought of Hugh worrying about her. Sometimes a text could get through when a call couldn't. She tapped out *Am fine Will stay Tampa tonight & return Gainesville tomorrow a.m.* That would have to do for now. The muscles in her neck bunched up into a brick at the base of her skull. She shoved her phone back into her purse, rolled her head from side-to-side to ease the tension, and went to rejoin Mrs. Gray.

A thick, hall runner in a red, cream, and black Persian pattern softened their tread as they continued down the hall. With each step, her insecurity over this little adventure grew. Mrs. Gray led her beside a wainscoted wall leading to the staircase. When they reached the first step, Mrs. Gray placed her hand on the carved, mahogany newel post and turned toward the stairs.

She paused on the first tread and shook her head. "I asked her to stay downstairs in the back parlor, but she would have none of it. Said a little storm wasn't going to run her out of her sitting room. Stubborn as a mule, that one. Thank goodness this house was built when they knew how to make them strong and secure."

Great. Even this experienced Floridian believed the storm would turn dangerous. Rich Whitehead, Jr.'s promises had better pan out or she would . . . Oh, hell, she wouldn't do anything except tuck her tail and run back to Gainesville empty-handed. Liz swallowed hard. *Let's hope his assessment had been accurate regarding the usefulness of his contact's information.*

At the top of the stairs, they walked toward double-pocket doors of the type found in grand turn-of-the-century mansions—thick, richly dark, paneled, polished brass handles. If the old lady hoped to intimidate her guests by receiving them in all her state, her goal was on its way to being achieved. Mrs. Gray slid one door open and stood back, gesturing for Liz to pass through. She stepped not into a sitting room in the traditional sense, but rather a library. Floor to ceiling bookcases covered three walls. A fireplace centered the fourth. A chintz-covered sofa faced the fireplace across a polished dark wood coffee table.

In a wing chair beside the mantle sat a woman with a book resting on a rolling reading table against her waist. She was dressed in expensive looking loose, black slacks and a rose-colored silk shirt. The gold beads of a necklace showed at the shirt's open throat and simple half-dome gold studs adorned her earlobes. Her appearance declared understated elegance in a language spoken only by the truly wealthy.

Liz felt Mrs. Gray move in beside her, but she didn't move toward the figure in the chair. Instead, Liz held back, observing, trying to get a sense of who the woman might be. Aristocrat came to mind. Mrs. Hernandez's hair, drawn up in a chignon, glowed black and silver in light from the table lamp beside her. The lamp also highlighted fine lines in her otherwise flawless complexion. Gold-framed glasses perched on her nose as she bent toward her reading. She did not seem to hear them enter nor feel their presence in the room. Mrs. Gray cleared her throat and took Liz's elbow, pressing her forward. Liz drew a deep breath and mustered her most confident smile.

"Consuelo, dear, Rich, Jr. and Dr. Reams, the young lady he told us about, have arrived."

Mrs. Hernandez barely lifted her eyes from her book, but she waved in the direction of the other wing chair opposite hers. Liz walked to the chair, but remained standing, breathing in the room's familiar odors. The scents of old paper, leather, lemon oil, and the remains of log fires told Liz this library wasn't just for show. A crystal bowl of old-fashioned roses on the occasional table at the elderly woman's elbow added their delicate fragrance to the scene. This was a beloved space. It was easy to understand why its occupant preferred it above other rooms in the house. That they shared a passion for reading comforted Liz and eased the tension that had built since she entered the house.

After a few seconds without any form of acknowledgment, Liz stepped toward the old lady and extended her hand. "It's very nice of you to allow Rich to bring me here. I hope this isn't an inconvenience."

At last Mrs. Hernandez looked up. Removing her glasses, her gaze ran over Liz from frizzy hair to rumpled hem to rain dampened Jimmy Choos. "At my age, young lady, most things are an inconvenience, but one learns to endure them. Please stop hovering and be seated." A trace of Spanish accented the old lady's words. "Now, where is that confounded boy?"

"Right here, Aunt Connie." Rich spoke from the door. "And stop being rude to my guest."

"She's my guest, as are you." Consuelo's eyes softened with what could only be described as deep affection. "Come in, you rascal, and tell me why you insisted this young woman come to Tampa during a hurricane."

Liz glanced at Rich, who had the good grace to look sheepish, like a kid caught sneaking a peek at his Christmas presents hidden in a closet. He grinned at Liz, shrugged, and turned back to his aunt. "Dr. Reams is not a woman to let a little rain interfere with something she wants. And it's still a tropical storm, according to the radio weather station, so stop trying to instill guilt and offer us a drink instead."

"Gray will bring up refreshments presently." The old lady's lips thinned in exasperation. "Oh, do sit down. Why do young people feel compelled to hover?"

Rich settled himself on the sofa, crossing one knee over the other and flinging his arms atop the seat back. Liz glanced his way. He appeared completely relaxed and at home. It made her wonder. Consuelo looked to be anywhere between eighty-five and ninety-five, really too old to be Rich's aunt unless his mother had been a seriously much younger child in her family. Liz waited for him to offer a conversation starter, but he just smiled and waggled his eyebrows at her. After enticing her with promises of critical information, he seemed disinclined to help the process along. Liz drew a shallow breath and donned her most professional demeanor, but a sudden loud thump made her jump.

Swallowing hard, she asked, "Goodness, was that a tree limb hitting the roof?"

Rich leaned forward and patted Liz's hand. "Probably, but it's nothing to worry about. This house has made it through storms much worse than this. We had a metal roof put on a few years back to make sure it lasts for many more to come."

Liz laughed and eased her hand away from Rich. "I'm glad to hear it." She returned her attention to Mrs. Hernandez. "I really appreciate you're agreeing to see me, Mrs. Hernandez."

"Yes. You've said. Go on. Ask your questions before we're all blown away."

Liz's gaze darted to Rich, who grinned like he enjoyed watching his aunt toy with her guests. "Rich tells me he showed you the pictures I found on the internet, the ones from Mr. Whitehead's 1989 article. I found them fascinating as they have not been published before or since. What did you think of them, Mrs. Hernandez?"

Consuelo lifted her book from its perch on the rolling table and withdrew a folder from a tote bag on the floor beside her chair. She opened it and spread the copied Whitehead article photographs on the coffee table. The man with the mark on his face had been circled in each picture. Consuelo picked up the one labeled *1952, Toblinsky and Cuban President General Fulgencio Batista enjoy a private dinner.* She tapped it with her index finger and handed it to Liz.

"I've always liked that photograph of my uncle. He was a handsome man, don't you think?"

Liz's eyes opened wide as she glanced at Rich with a quizzical expression. "You didn't tell me you were related to General Batista."

Rich's mouth spread in a self-satisfied grin. "I thought it would be a nice surprise. Aunt Connie is actually my great-aunt. She and my grandmother were Juan Batista's daughters."

"Juan?"

"Fulgencio's younger brother."

"And that explains your restaurant's name. I wondered why you chose it." Liz turned back to Consuelo. "Mrs. Hernandez, your uncle was indeed a handsome man. How much has Rich told you about my research project?"

"Enough to know that your interest in my uncle and my family is merely peripheral to your work. Otherwise, you would not be here. Understand this, young lady. I will countenance no disrespect toward or defamation of my uncle. There has been enough of that over the years. Castro and his hooligans saw to that."

"I assure you that I only want to trace the man whose face is circled in the photographs. As you can see, he appears in all of these photos. He clearly was a trusted associate of the gangster Moshe Toblinsky. It is American crime in which I am interested."

"So I understand. You know, of course, that my uncle and Mr. Toblinsky were business partners of sorts."

"I do. Did you ever meet him?"

"Yes, once. My uncle invited him to a family gathering. Mr. Toblinsky was in Cuba for a business meeting and his flight back to Miami was canceled due to weather, I believe. He was a quiet, nice man. I liked him."

Liz's fingers tightened on the arm of her chair as she bit down on her lower lip. It took all of her effort not to laugh aloud with released tension. Rich's great-aunt had actually met Moshe Toblinsky. What a find she might turn out to be.

"And the man I'm interested in?"

A sudden boom sent the house into darkness. Liz felt,

rather than saw, Rich rise and move to the mantle. A match scraped over a striking surface and candles flamed to life.

Shadows danced across Rich's handsome face. "There. That's better. Aunt Connie's always prepared."

Mrs. Gray, flashlight in hand, appeared in the sitting room doorway. "I'm afraid that loud noise was the transformer in front of the house blowing up. I think a limb fell on it. The whole street is dark."

"And likely to stay that way until this storm passes. Well, it's close enough to my bedtime. I'm rather tired. Gray, make up the guest room for Dr. Reams."

Liz felt her head snap back in surprise. "I really couldn't impose on you like that. I'm sure I can find a hotel room."

"Perhaps, but it would be the height of foolishness to go out again in this weather. We'll talk again in the morning. I have a few things to tell you."

Liz looked up at Rich, who nodded. She turned back to Consuelo. "Thank you so much. I look forward to your revelations."

Rich rose to his feet when his aunt raised herself from her chair. "Yes, thank you, Aunt Connie. You're the best."

Consuelo paused beside the sofa and shot him an appraising glance. "You, my boy, will occupy the room you used as a child. It seems somehow fitting considering that you finagled getting your way in having this young lady stay overnight during such terrible weather. Of course there is nothing unusual in that."

As Liz watched her hostess make her way to the library door, disappointment at the interview's ending so soon mingled with other emotions. Liz's hackles rose at having been so manipulated by a near stranger, but without Rich's intervention on her behalf she would never have met Consuelo Batista Hernandez, niece to Cuba's former dictator and one-time acquaintance of Moshe Toblinsky. Liz's instincts about the importance of Rich's information had been vindicated, but from the very beginning this trip had not worked out as she planned. Every time she thought she had things under control, some new surprise cropped up, like foolishly leaving her car at the restaurant. What had she been thinking in allowing Rich to talk her into being without her own transportation? She drew a quiet breath and exhaled slowly. Hugh had certainly been right about the weather. Would he understand all of this? Especially her staying on in Tampa later than she planned?

Of course he would. He of all people understood the importance of following up on research leads. But another unwelcome thought surfaced. Hugh loved her, of that she was certain, but he was also a man who had been deeply hurt by love in the past. A quiver of apprehension slithered through Liz.

Chapter 17

So, the only hope Sam had for normal friends, the Scheinburg family, died before it could draw its first breath. Mrs. Scheinberg had made that very clear just a moment ago. She had practically ordered Sam to keep away from her daughter, Rebecca. Now, Bateman waited for him on the back porch and there was no turning back. Rising to his feet, Sam leaned against the table and looked toward the bakery kitchen's screen door. Bateman had one hand shoved into his pants pocket jingling his change. The coins clanked against a larger piece of metal that created a small bugle in the pocket's fabric.

Sam took a couple of steps away from the table. The distance across the concrete floor to the door could be covered in about seven or eight strides. It was such an ordinary, commonplace thing, this walking across a kitchen. He had made such a journey nearly every day of his life, but the end of this short trip would seal his fate and would make him exactly what Rebecca's mother believed him to be, a gangster without conscience or regard for the things that were lawful and wholesome.

As he passed near the ovens, Sam fought the urge to drop on his knees at Mrs. Scheinburg's feet and beg for help, anything that would keep him from being beholden to and under the control of men like Bateman, Tops Monza, and Moshe Toblinsky. For the thousandth time, he cursed himself for ever thinking he could work for gangsters and not become like them. The extra two dollars per week he got for working at the Fulton Market had cost him everything he loved. Sam glanced her way, but she had already turned her back, busying herself with the next pans of pastries ready for baking. If he hadn't been so afraid of showing weakness, he would have given in to the tears threatening to pour down his cheeks. Every instinct screamed at him to run, no matter the consequences. If he managed to get away, to hide, to disappear even, hunger and sleeping under bridges would be small prices to avoid being sucked farther into the gangsters' world.

The entrance to the shop was to his left. Freedom felt so close, mere steps, a run for the shop door, and no more Bateman, no more Tops, no more Joe or Tino. He might even find a way to get back home to Mama and Brooklyn. Could he make it to the front sidewalk before Bateman caught him?

A shout came from the other side of the screen door. "You dumb kid. Don't even think about it. You got a debt to work off. It'd be ashamed to get a hole blown in ya before the boss gets what's owed him."

Either Bateman could read minds or something in Sam had given him away. He approached the screen door but couldn't bring himself to touch it without one last backward glance. Mrs. Scheinburg had turned toward the pair, her attention no doubt drawn by Bateman's tone and volume. She searched Sam's face and something in her demeanor, in her attitude shifted. The angle of her body relaxed. Her head tilted slightly to one side. The haze of anger and condemnation that had hung about her only moments ago evaporated. The expression in her eyes softened as they met Sam's gaze. Her mouth lifted a little at the corners, but the movement didn't qualify as a real smile. Ever so slightly, she nodded.

When she spoke, her voice had lost its gruffness. "Do what Mr. Bateman says, Samuel. It will be best for everyone." She paused and fixed Bateman with a look that only a mother protecting her young can give. "Please see that he drinks plenty of water. It is going to be a hot day."

A guttural sound somewhere between a growl and a laugh was the only reply she got from Bateman, but her words meant a lot to Sam. Maybe Mrs. Scheinberg understood after all. Sam smiled, nodded, and moved toward Bateman, but he couldn't keep his hand from trembling as he reached out to push the screen door open.

Standing on the dock beside Bateman took Sam's breath away, but for the worst reasons possible. His calf muscles and knees shook like they had minds of their own. Sam willed his tongue to be still. It betrayed him instantly. Words tumbled out of his mouth like a river rushing over a cliff.

"What am I going to do? Will it be for just now? Can I go home soon?"

"Shut the hell up. I get enough diarrhea of the mouth at home. Get in and sit down. Don't open your mouth again until I tell ya."

Sam lowered himself into a shiny wooden boat with Chris Craft on the stern. He settled himself on the forward seat, running his hand over the tan leather, his lips forming a silent whistle. He had only seen such boats as they passed the Fulton docks making their way from the East River toward Long Island Sound, usually steered by guys in white shirts and pants with captain's caps perched on their heads. Boats like this weren't cheap. Millionaires owned them. Bateman pressed the starter and the motor roared to life.

At the last moment before they floated away from the dock, Sam felt eyes upon him. He looked up to the kitchen window where Rebecca stood watching. Her face held a troubled expression until their eyes met then a broad smile lifted her features. She raised her hand and gave him a small wave. He nodded in response. A feeling of surprised contentment mingled with an edge of excitement washed over him. It was unlike anything he had ever felt before.

Was this what they meant by love at first sight? But this wasn't really first, because he had a similar feeling earlier this morning when he first glimpsed her preparing to wash the shop's front windows. She had taken his breath away just like she did now. She was definitely a girl a man could fall in love with. He could have stayed right there in the glow of her gaze all day, but the boat's engine signaled their private moment's end. He lifted his hand in reply and smiled. With a jerk, the boat leapt into action, pushing his body back against the seat and they were off.

Sam knew nothing about boat motors, but at the sound this one made, he felt sure it had more power than anyone needed for a casual outing. This rig was built for speed. Sam craned his neck so that he could see farther down the river. If he tilted his head just right, he could see where the river widened and the water turned from muddy brown to shades of aqua and blue. Biscayne Bay extended to the horizon. Instead of heading toward the bay, Bateman made a sharp half-circle bringing them about face with the bow pointed inland. He shoved the throttle forward and the boat leapt into action, picking up speed as it seemed to hover over the water. It cut not just through water, but through the air as well, creating a wind force that stung Sam's face.

Soon, the buildings of downtown Miami faded behind them. The scenery evolved to low banks covered with scrubby trees, mostly pines and palms, broken only by the occasional higher white-sand cliffs topped with spiky grass. The river narrowed, forcing Bateman to pull back on the throttle. Relief from the sun's mid-morning blaze disappeared as the wind created by the boat's former speed ceased. Buildings and other signs of human habitation grew farther apart. Just the occasional farmhouse appeared in the distance. They passed a dilapidated shack with a short dock slumping into the river. Not far beyond the shack, they entered an area that couldn't really be called "river" anymore. Water spread out in all directions as did trees with Spanish moss hanging from their branches, wide swaths of grasses, and low palms that looked like their fronds grew straight out of the water. Humidity and mosquitoes clogged the air. Sam's skin burned. Worse yet, he could smell himself. He desperately needed a real bath.

The boat wove in and out between trees and little tussocks of grass where long-legged birds with blue-gray feathers and long, pointed beaks jabbed at the water, occasionally spearing a fish. They passed a log where a line of turtles lazed in the sunshine. Next to the turtles' perch, another log floated much lower in the water. Its bark had a pattern that didn't match any tree Sam had ever seen. He blinked and lifted his hand to shade his eyes. On second glance, he wasn't sure it was a log. As they drew closer, eyes snapped open and blinked at the glare coming off the water. Alligator. It had to be. What else would be lurking in the water like that? A shiver ran down Sam's spine despite the day's growing heat. The alligator's eyes followed the boat's progress, perhaps judging the possibility of its next meal. A spasm ran over Sam and he averted his gaze. The reptile's stare felt as though it might mesmerize him, drawing him into the water to certain death. An unwelcome vision arose of being held between jaws clamped down with the strength of a steel trap. Sam drew a long breath, shaking his head. Foolishness. Pure and simple. His imagination had taken a wild turn. He clearly needed more sleep than he had gotten recently.

They passed through stands of what Sam guessed might be cypress. Cone shaped things stuck up out of the water at the bases of the trees. Sunlight filtered through a sparse canopy, providing little shade from the growing fierceness of the sun. Sweat trickled down his back and forehead. It couldn't be May. The temperature was way too hot, but then, he was over a thousand miles from any climate he understood.

Bateman steered the boat ever deeper into the watery terrain until the swamp closed around them like some ancient world not yet disturbed by man's intrusion. Sam had no idea where they were or how far they had traveled. He was completely dependent upon a rough talking gangster who only an hour or so ago had threatened to shoot him if he didn't do as he was told. If Bateman had been ordered to get rid of him, this would certainly be the place to do it. Sam's heart rate kicked up a notch as Bateman slowed the boat even more. The boat pushed on through much denser growth. Instead of a constant roar, the engine putt-putted and coughed, apparently struggling with the unaccustomed drifting pace. After about fifteen minutes, the vegetation suddenly fell away and an island lay before them backed by thick forest appearing to grow straight out of the water. At the island's center sat a large two-story building covered in unpainted, weathered, gray boards. Bateman guided the boat to a dock that looked much newer than the building. After tying off ropes, he looked at Sam and jerked his head. Sam scrambled onto the dock with his heart in his throat.

Bateman led the way over a well-trodden path leading to tall barn like double doors with a man-sized entrance on one side. A brass padlock held together the ends of a heavy chain, preventing any casual passersby from entering the building. Taking a wad of keys from his pocket, Bateman unclasped the lock, drew the chain out of its holes, and gave the door a shove.

"After you, kid."

Sam stepped inside, temporarily blinded by the difference between bright daylight and the interior gloom. Except for light filtering through a single, filthy window beside the door, the structure was in complete darkness. When his eyes adjusted, Sam looked upon row after shadowy row of boxes and crates. The stacks filled the space as far as he could see. There must be hundreds of them. He turned toward Bateman who held the cork of a bottle between his teeth. Yanking the cork free, he took a long swig from the bottle before dragging a flask from his hip pocket. After pouring amber liquid into the flask, he held the bottle out to Sam. Canadian Mist in large script covered the upper half of the label.

Sam shook his head, but Bateman shoved the bottle into Sam's hand. "Better get used to whiskey. It's one of the benefits of working for the boss. He don't get upset if a little of his hooch disappears down his employees' gullets."

Afraid of offending the gangster, Sam raised the bottle. The smell of liquor had always made him queasy, but he brought the bottle to his lips anyway. Tilting it up, he took as little into his mouth as possible. His stomach lurched, threatening to empty itself of its contents. Sam gagged, choked, and coughed. Bateman's laughter echoed in the cavernous space and bounced off the wooden rafters.

Slapping Sam on the back, Bateman spluttered between fits of mirth. "You should see your face. You're as red as a boiled lobster. Boy, you better toughen up if you're gonna survive."

Sam smiled weakly and handed the bottle back to Bateman. He eyed Sam for several beats. Bateman's eyes narrowed. "You don't say much, do you?"

Confusion mixed with fear turned Sam's tongue to lead. Bateman had told him not to talk, yet now he expected conversation. Which was it? Instinct told Sam to humor the guy. Arguing or pointing out the contradiction might prove a harmful mistake.

"No, sir. I guess not." Sam's voice came out in a croak.

"Probably just as good. Might as well get on with it."

"What am I to do, Mr. Bateman?"

"See that first stack of crates?" Sam turned in the direction Bateman pointed. The crates were stacked three across and head high. Sam nodded. "Start taking them to the boat. The hold hatches are between the seats and in the bow. Fill 'em both." Bateman pushed a breaker on the first support-post and the space filled with electric light. With that, he sauntered over to a single crate next to the doors, plopped down, and threw a pudgy calf across the opposing leg's knee. He leaned his head against the wall. Soon after, raucous snores came in rhythm with the rise and fall of his chest.

Sweat poured in rivers from Sam's head and body. The crates weren't so heavy, but the rough wood poked into his skin leaving splinters that became more painful with each load. By the time crates filled the holds, blisters and red blotches covered his hands. Sam's head spun and his throat ached with thirst. Looking around for a source of clean water, he found nothing. His only choice appeared to be the swamp. Unable to go another step without drinking, he bent over the edge of the dock until his face grazed the water. It was surprisingly sweet for being black as ink. He slowly lowered himself for his next gulp, this time really noticing the water. It possessed a peculiar quality. Although it was indeed black, it didn't look dirty. In fact, it was clear, not cloudy at all. He took a second longer swig, and thirst quenched, he dunked his head and upper body. A hand grabbed his pants waist and haul him bodily to his feet.

"You trying to get snake bit or dragged off by a gator? Stupid Yankee kike. Get in." Bateman's mood had not improved with a nap. If anything, it was fouler. He shoved Sam, sending him stumbling into the boat.

The engine revved, the boat moved away from the dock, and within seconds Sam's head slumped onto his chest. The thump of wood on wood woke him. He squinted at the sunlight, still strong despite what must be fairly late afternoon. The sun drooped over the western rooftops. They were back at the bakery's dock. Time had disappeared in a haze of exhaustion.

Once out of the boat, Bateman again slung himself onto the closest chair on the covered porch and shouted orders. "Get the crates out of the holds and up to the storeroom. Make sure you stack 'em with the others just like 'em."

By the time Sam had lugged all of the crates up the stairs and rearranged the storeroom's contents by label, Bateman was long gone. Dusk bathed the city, the bay, and the river with a burnished bronze that covered all blemishes, leaving Miami floating on a rose-gold sea. Sam stood on the dock and stretched his aching back and shoulders. A growl deep in his midsection reminded him he hadn't eaten since breakfast. Putting one foot in front of the other seemed an impossible task but going back into the building was his greatest desire. On his last trip down the stairs from the storeroom, Rebecca came in and sat down at the scrubbed wooden table. Hearing his tread, she turned and smiled up at him. Instead of the controlled bob of earlier in the day, her hair looked damp. Gone were the tight finger waves replaced by a halo of soft curls. The sun slanting through the open door and windows set her golden crown afire and intensified the creaminess of her skin. Her simple, clean, fresh washed beauty had taken his breath away, but something else had stopped him stone cold in his tracks. A different kind of light shone from within her, a glow that would brighten the darkest corners or raise the lowest spirits. An entirely new, unexpected feeling washed through Sam. A quiver of sensation shot to his very core, settling in the area of his heart. A guy could bask in her smile forever.

With that vision burned into his memory, Sam turned and shuffled quietly to the back door. He didn't want to disturb her, just wanted another glimpse. She bent in concentration as she pushed needle and thread up and down darning socks. Even in her overalls and work shirt, she had to be the loveliest thing he had ever seen. Just standing there looking at her gave him renewed energy. His exhaustion melted and any thought of hunger floated away. A random thought popped into his head, one he had never before experienced. Could a girl like Rebecca ever fall for a boy like him? Probably not, but at least he could admire her from afar.

Across the room, a throat cleared loudly, breaking the spell. Sam looked up to the shop entrance. A middle-aged man stood in the doorway frowning at him with an expression that contained anger, fear, and distrust. He could only be Mr. Scheinburg, Rebecca's father.

Chapter 18

It was the silence that woke Liz. No wind, no rain lashing the windows, no stuff bouncing off the roof. Just calm, peaceful silence. After having her sleep interrupted on and off all night by the sounds of the hurricane, Liz's eyes opened to a room filled with sunlight and glowing lamps. With only a flashlight to guide them last night, it had been difficult to see the room Mrs. Gray conducted her to or to get a feel for exactly where it was located on the second floor, but Liz hadn't really cared about the details. She had struggled into the loaned nightgown, crawled between the high thread-count sheets, and fallen asleep surprisingly quickly despite the raging storm.

Liz sat up in the middle of the four-poster double bed and looked at her surroundings. Marble topped mahogany antiques and a Persian carpet that looked like the real deal. Wallpaper in a variegated cranberry, navy, and hunter-green stripe topped by thick, dark crown molding. Faceted glass knobs on the doors. The room was lovely in an Old-World sort of way, like the rooms she had seen downstairs. What she would give for a house like this. She could imagine herself sitting by the room's fireplace with its carved mantle and decorative tiles on a winter evening enjoying a good book and a cup of tea. She and Hugh had promised each other such a house. If she weren't feeling so guilty about not reaching him yesterday, she would have loved to snuggle down for a few more minutes and just soak in the atmosphere. The tangy odor of lemon oil drifted from the wood grain of the furniture and the bed linens and nightgown were scented with rose water. The room felt like sitting on her grandmother's lap with arms wrapped around her—secure, safe, and comforted. Thoughts of returning to the hectic pace of her real life and other people's expectations made her wish for a little respite, but that was not meant to be. Grabbing her phone from the bedside table, she tried to look at the time.

Crap. Lifeless as last Thanksgiving's turkey and her only charger cord was in the car back at the restaurant garage. Liz stepped out of bed and padded over to the dresser where an old-fashioned Big Ben Timex alarm clock ticked softly. Her heart thumped. 9:00 a.m. She had hoped to be on the road by now. What must Hugh be thinking?

A soft tap sounded on the bedroom door followed by Mrs. Gray's well coifed head appearing around the edge. "Oh, good. You're up. Breakfast, or brunch really, will be ready at ten." Holding out her hand, she gave Liz a toothbrush and paste. "I thought you might want these. There should be plenty of everything else in the bathroom just through that door by the fireplace. Use whatever you need. I took the liberty of leaving a couple of my own things there. I hope you will feel free to wear them. Rich is most concerned that you are comfortable." Mrs. Gray took a step to go, but turned back, no doubt arrested by the look of confusion on Liz's face. "The bathroom has a connecting door to the next bedroom, but no one is using that room. I used the connecting door so I wouldn't disturb you. You will have complete privacy."

Liz thanked the older woman and turned to the pile her clothes made on the chair by the fireplace. Whether Mrs. Gray's clothes were comfortable or not, they would certainly be better than her winkled sheath and Jimmy Choo stilettos. Hopefully Mrs. Gray had thought about panties, as well.

Taking the clock with her, Liz padded across the bedroom to the en suite bath. A glass-front cabinet contained an array of shampoos, conditioners, and deodorants. Thank goodness. Gathering a selection for her bath, Liz turned on the taps of the claw-foot tub that had pride of place under a shuttered window. Within minutes, steam filled the space and Liz slipped into chest-deep water scented with citrus bath oil. Sighing with pleasure, she soaked for a few moments, then began cleaning herself in earnest. It would have been heaven to remain in the bath until the water cooled, but the clock showed nine-twenty. After wrapping a plush towel around her body and one around her hair, she finished the cleaning process at the pedestal sink, wondering how she was going to bring some control to her mane of auburn frizz. It took the right products to make it presentable. She combed through the cabinet's offerings. Glory be. Hair oil. Exactly what she needed. Consuelo, or perhaps Mrs. Gray, certainly knew how to stock a guest room.

The clothes Mrs. Gray had left surprised Liz. The old girl definitely had another side to her. Stylish slim jeans, a sailor stripe boat-neck T-shirt, a sailboat themed scarf, and navy boat shoes lay on a chair beside the door. On top of these, a pair on granny panties completed the ensemble, but who cared about their less than feminine appearance? They were clean and smelled like lavender. The shoes were a little large, but everything else fit well enough. Liz rolled the jeans' hem up a turn and glanced at herself in the cheval mirror next to the chair. A girl with clear, creamy skin, bright green eyes, and auburn spirals held back by the scarf looked back. Without makeup, Liz realized she looked much younger than her thirty years. She hadn't looked this relaxed or felt this calm in some time. Was this what life in this house would be like? Pampered, cared for, spoiled? Would Rich one day live here?

Liz's next breath came in a gasp. She had no interest in Rich Whitehead's future or what he wanted. Why would she even think such a thing? Hugh was her future. Giving her head a shake, Liz left the room and followed the fragrance of frying bacon. She found everyone already gathered in the kitchen. Consuelo sat at the head of a long refectory style table. Mrs. Gray stood at the range dishing up eggs. Rich poured himself a cup of coffee. At the sound of her step, they all glanced toward Liz.

"I hope I haven't kept you all waiting. Your guest room is so comfortable I'm afraid I overslept."

Consuelo smiled and glanced at Rich. "We want our guests to feel at home. Hospitality demands it, and I wish nothing less. Ricardo, get this young woman a cup of coffee. Come, Dr. Reams, sit by me so we may talk."

Liz felt momentarily confused. As Rich set coffee before her, she asked, "I thought you were Richard, Jr. Are you really Ricardo?"

Rich slumped into the chair on the other side of Consuelo and grinned. "I'm only Ricardo when Aunt Connie wants to remind me of some fault or breach of manners. She never quite forgave my mother for naming me Richard instead of Ricardo."

Consuelo turned a raised brow to him. "I do no such thing. I've always spoiled you, to my great discredit, and you know it. Your father never lets us forget how poorly behaved you always were after a visit here when you were a boy." A fleeting sadness entered her eyes. "I suppose he may have had reason to criticize, but surely he understood why we doted on you."

Rich reached out and took his great-aunt's hand. "Of course he understood." Bringing the hand to his lips, Rich kissed it and then continued, "Dad loved Mama. He wanted whatever she wanted, and she wanted to share her child with you and Uncle Raul."

Consuelo glanced at Liz. "I apologize for this maudlin display. You must be wondering what on earth we are talking about."

Unsure how to respond, Liz smiled and tilted her head to one side. "I think you are reminding each other of how much love there is in this family."

Consuelo's eyes became bright with unshed tears. Mrs. Gray stepped in with platters of food and bustling efficiency. "Let's eat before this gets cold. Thank goodness they restored the power early this morning. Luckily for this street, the transformer was the only problem."

"Thank you, Gray. You are a treasure." Consuelo smiled up at her companion-nurse. To Liz she said, "After we eat, you will learn all. I promise."

~ ~ ~

While Gray cleared the table, Consuelo put the folder of pictures on the table. Tapping them, she said, "Before we get to these, I think Rich and I owe you an explanation for our little scene."

"You owe me nothing that you don't want to tell me. I'm just delighted you are willing to talk to me about the pictures."

"No, I feel you should know. It will help you understand other things." Consuelo looked at Rich, who nodded. A wistful expression played across her features as she raised her gaze to a spot on the wall above his head. Drawing a slow breath, she exhaled and began. "Castro killed my child."

Liz blinked as her head snapped back. She certainly had not expected that. "My goodness. How awful."

"Yes, it was." A faraway expression came over Consuelo's face. "Our little Ricardo was a miracle. It took several years of trying for us to have a child. When our baby was born, I nearly died and the doctors advised against having more children, so Raul wouldn't hear of trying for another. Little Ricardo was all we had. He was such a beautiful little boy." Consuelo's voice cracked with emotion. Her gaze shifted to the ceiling.

After a silence longer than was comfortable, Rich picked up the story. "When it became clear that Castro was going to take over, Uncle Fulgencio departed for Spain, and the rest of the family made arrangements to leave. Aunt Connie refused to go on the last plane out because two-year-old Ricardo was very sick with a chest cold. The doctor told her flying might be harmful, so they delayed. But when Castro entered Havana, Uncle Raul felt they had no choice. They boarded a friend's sailboat and left for Miami in a storm. Between the rough weather and an unexpected cold snap, Ricardo had pneumonia by the time they arrived in Miami. The doctors did all they could, but he had never been a strong child. Aunt Connie had him moved to Tampa when they settled here. His father is buried beside him."

A lump rose in Liz's throat. Surprised by the level of emotion Consuelo's story elicited, Liz swallowed hard before speaking. "What a tragic story. You must still feel his loss deeply."

The older woman sighed. A thoughtful expression entered her eyes. "One never gets over losing a child. One simply survives and endures." Consuelo reached out and patted Rich's hand. "And one finds ways to fill the void." The look that passed between them revealed deep affection.

This side of Rich surprised Liz. She had known plenty of glamor boys like him over the years, but none of them had exhibited this level of family devotion. In this way, he reminded her a lot of Hugh. In fact, they actually shared several commonalities. Both men were very successful in their chosen fields. Both were handsome in their own way. And both of them loved their extended families. Who would have thought such a comparison possible?

Liz mentally kicked herself. Musings like this were a complication she neither needed nor wanted. In the most important way, Hugh and Rich were nothing alike. Hugh was steady. Rich was . . . well, what exactly? Liz let out her breath slowly. Rich was exactly the kind of guy she would have gone for before Hugh, but not anymore. Enough said.

Liz glanced from Rich to his great-aunt, trying to decide how best to resume the conversation. "I suppose we all handle loss with some form of filling the void. While I've not experienced your level of grief, I've certainly tried to fill unexpected empty spaces in my life, usually with my work."

"And work is why you are here, so we'll delay no longer." Consuelo opened the folder and spread all of the pictures out on the table between them. Picking up one in which the man with the mark on his cheek showed fairly clearly, she studied the photo for a moment before passing it to Liz. "I've thought about this man since Rich gave me these photographs. I do have some vague memories of him. Things that I had forgotten until now. I'm afraid I've spent many years trying to put my life in Cuba behind me."

"That's certainly understandable. Is it too painful to talk about this?"

"No. This man was nothing to me. He was nothing to my family. He was, however, someone to Mr. Toblinsky. He performed services such as catering, even in Havana. Can you imagine bringing your own caterer to a foreign country? Apparently, Mr. Toblinsky had issues of trust, even with his close business associates."

Liz couldn't hold back a chuckle. "Perhaps his experiences with business associates dictated his caution."

"Of course. It would, wouldn't it?" A thin smile lifted the corners of Consuelo's mouth. "At any rate, this man served Toblinsky. I remember hearing he was involved somehow when Havana fell."

Liz's heart stopped for a tick, then bumped back to life. Consuelo surely couldn't mean what she had just implied. "Do you mean Toblinsky's caterer supported Castro?" Her voice came out louder and higher pitched than intended.

Consuelo's brows rose in surprise. "Oh, I doubt it. Mr. Toblinsky and Uncle Fulgencio were friends. They wouldn't have tolerated a revolutionary in their midst, but it is possible your man could have gotten tired of being a lackey. Or he may have had secret communist leanings. Who can say? All I really know is that he was in Havana when the Castro brothers entered the city and that there was some mystery or subterfuge where he was concerned."

"I suppose it is too much to hope that you remember his name."

"If I ever heard it, I forgot it long ago. We would not have been officially introduced. There would have been no need. I remember he was from Miami. Odd, the things that surface from the past."

"Was there something particular that made you think of Miami?"

Consuelo slipped her hand into the pocket of her robe and withdrew a square of paper. She passed it across the table. When Liz turned it over, her breath caught in her throat. Looking up at her was the man they had been discussing. The mark on his face showed clearly as a scar, like one caused by a cut that had not healed smoothly. Rather than detracting, the scar gave his rather attractive face a rakish appearance. A modern-day pirate stared into the camera over the heads of a man Liz recognized as a Toblinsky henchman and that of Fulgencio Batista. Her man bent toward the gangster as though he was about to communicate something. Toblinsky's guy looked up expectantly. The background held what looked like a party in full swing. She could make out couples whirling on a dance floor, streamers hanging from the ceiling, and balloons tied to various surfaces.

"This is wonderful. You can clearly see his face, but I still don't get the Miami connection. "

Consuelo smiled and pointed to a patch embroidered on the man's shirt above the chest pocket. The letters M, I, A, and M were clearly visible. The rest of the logo was lost in the folds created by his posture. "He owned a business with Miami in its name."

"Ah, so he did. I should have noticed that." Liz studied the picture a little while longer then turned it over. Her eyes grew wide. Giddy to the point of lightheadedness, Liz stifled laughter threatening to burst out as a loud whoop. Not once since she began this quest had she expected something this incredible. She had been satisfied to look for a low level Toblinsky associate to make the new Florida crime course come alive for students, but instead, she had stumbled onto something rather incredible. Maybe her fears of being a professional fraud were unfounded after all. Maybe Liz's rising star would shoot a little higher instead of falling back to earth. A tingle of anticipation rushed through her. This could mean another important discovery similar to her Capone find.

Inscribed on the back of the photo was a date and location: *December 31, 1958, Hotel Nacional*, mere hours before General Fulgencio Batista flew away from Havana never to return. Consuelo might not know the guy's name, but she had provided pure gold — proof Liz's man was in Havana as Cuba fell to Castro. Now if she could find him in Miami, her world would be perfect. Or at least her professional world would be. Hugh's face flashed before her mind's eye. Somehow he didn't look pleased, but her imagination must be working overtime, because Hugh would be as thrilled as she was with this new information.

Chapter 19

Smiling at the bakery kitchen's occupants through the back porch's screen door, Sam shifted his weight from one foot to the other. All he had wanted was a glimpse of Rebecca. He hadn't intended to interrupt her work, but the way Mr. Scheinberg looked at him, the older man probably thought Sam was a weirdo or maybe even a stalker. Sam sighed, lifted his hand in greeting, and hoped he didn't look too much like a fool.

Mr. Scheinberg's frown deepened. He looked like he wanted to order Sam to jump into the river and swim out to sea or into the Everglades. Whether Sam drowned in the Gulf Stream or was eaten by alligators would probably make no difference. Either way, the baker would be rid of his unwelcome lodger.

A wooden floor slat squeaked as Sam's weight shifted more heavily than he intended. Rebecca looked up from her darning, smiled briefly, and ducked her head back to her work. Warmth spread through Sam, traveling downward and settling a few inches below his belt. Rebecca's effect on him was like none he'd experienced. He watched her silently, mesmerized by the very being of her. He never knew oversized denim work clothes could look so good, so lovely, so . . . sexy. Love at first sight was a crock, at least he had always thought so until now. All that poetry shit about dying of unrequited love had always made Sam laugh. Until now. He wanted so badly to tell Rebecca's father not to worry, that he knew Rebecca was beyond his reach, that all he wanted was to admire her from afar, but saying it aloud would make the girl and her father think he was nuts.

Feeling like a fool, but unable to think of anything else, Sam said, "Good evening, sir. I'm Sam Ackerman. You must be Mr. Scheinberg."

The man's gaze ran over Sam like a Hoover carpet sweeper, sucking up details and information as it went. Mr. Scheinberg pursed his lips as though deep in thought before he asked, "How long will you be here?" A strong German accent colored the question.

Sam gulped and stammered, "I don't know. Nobody's said. I'll try real hard not to be a bother." Sam searched for something that might cast himself in a better light. He finally settled on, "I'd be happy to help you with any work you want done when Mr. Bateman doesn't need me."

"Humph. Unlikely. Bateman will work you until you drop dead or run off. That is his way. He is not a nice man." Mr. Scheinberg's voice held an angry edge. "Stop lurking and come inside. You look like a specter standing there behind the screen."

Mr. Scheinberg turned back toward the shop. Over his shoulder he said, "Some of us have work to finish before we can leave. Do not be long, Rebecca. You have school tomorrow." Within moments, the clacking of a ten-key adding machine sounded throughout the bakery.

Sam grabbed the door handle and grimaced. From the corner of his eye, he watched a concerned expression cross Rebecca's face. "What's wrong with your hand? Come over here, and let me have a look." Her wish was his command.

Sam went to the table. Rebecca grabbed his wrists and turned his hands palm up. "Good grief, you must have a hundred splinters. Sit here while I get the rubbing alcohol. These have to come out."

Rebecca came back from the restroom carrying a bottle, a bowl, and a pair of tweezers. Pouring some of the clear, pungent liquid into the bowl, she dipped her instrument in the alcohol long enough to sterilize them to her satisfaction, wiped his injuries with the stinging liquid, and went to work. The painful probing of a needle had never been so welcome.

"Why didn't you wear gloves? If these become infected, you could be in for a bad time."

Sam laughed softly. "I'm afraid I don't own any."

"I'll see if there's an extra pair of oven gloves. They won't be as good as leather, but better than nothing."

"If your father doesn't mind, I'd be very grateful."

Rebecca glanced up from her digging and grinned. "Leave Papa to me. He may seem like a grizzly, but he's really a teddy bear."

Sam wanted to argue the point, but looking into Rebecca's face stopped him. Her eyes shone with affection for her father. He quickly changed the subject. "So, how did your father become a baker? Was his dad in the business?"

Rebecca shook her head without taking her eyes off her work. The needle continued to pick and the tweezers to pluck. "My mother's father was."

When she didn't elaborate, Sam leaned in a little. "And so?"

She frowned in concentration over a particularly recalcitrant splinter. "And . . ." Pick. "So . . ." Pick, dig. "What?" Pick, gouge, pick.

A shout of pain hovered in the back of Sam's throat. He closed his eyes and gritted his teeth. Showing fear or weakness was the last characteristic he wanted to display in Rebecca's presence.

Click.

Holding the tweezers up in triumph, she waved them at Sam. "There! It's finally out, the little stinker. I think that's the last one. Now, for the alcohol." Dipping cotton wadding into the bowl, she began swabbing his palms.

A howl would have felt so good, or at least so right, given the multiple points that screamed at him from his palms. He drew a deep breath and let it out slowly. "So, how did your dad, who doesn't sound like he was born in this country, come to be a bakery owner in Miami?"

Rebecca looked up from massaging alcohol into his open wounds. "Oh, that. Well, he came over to New York from Germany and went to work for my grandfather. I don't think becoming a Kosher baker was his life's ambition, but it was the only job he could find. He learned the business, married my mother, and they came south for the weather after my grandparents died."

At long last, she placed his hands on table and cast an evaluative gaze over her work. "I think that'll do, but you better keep your hands clean. They could still get infected if you're not careful." Rebecca stood and began gathering her medical supplies.

"I'll do my best." Grabbing her by the shoulders and forcing her to sit down again probably wouldn't go over too well, so Sam settled on being nosy. "Why did your dad leave Germany?"

It worked. She looked thoughtful and lowered herself onto her chair. "Oh, the same reason anybody does, I guess. He never really said. He doesn't like talking about the old country."

"Have you ever asked him directly?"

"Once. When I was about twelve. He said that people like us had a better chance of a good life in America than in Europe."

What else to ask? Anything to keep her sitting across from him. "Do you remember your grandparents?"

"Not really. I was a baby when we moved here."

"Do you ever think about going back to New York?"

"No. This is home." A wistful expression played across her face. "I never want to move away from Miami. I don't care that Jews have to live south of 5th on Miami Beach or that we can't go to the Biltmore and fancy places like that. I wouldn't want to leave. Not ever."

"Do you live in the Jewish section at the beach? I sort of thought your family might live somewhere near the bakery."

"Nope. We've always lived at the beach. Mama doesn't want to live near here." Rebecca's gaze lifted toward the ceiling. "She says the neighbors are a bad lot."

Mrs. Scheinberg had hinted at some agreement between Bateman and Mr. Scheinberg. He had been afraid to ask her mother, but Rebecca's comments piqued his curiosity. "So how did your dad's business wind up in this part of town?"

"Papa used to have a job south of 5th on Miami Beach with a Kosher baker there. One day he walked in and told Mama he had quit his job because he got a great offer to start his own business."

"I'm guessing this is the place?"

"Yeah."

"And the speakeasy on the second floor?"

"Papa neglected to mention that little detail. The offer came with one minor string attached. We provide a veil of legitimacy for the whole building. For all the police know, the second floor is our storeroom."

"So Bateman set your dad up in business and makes you all act as cover for his other activities."

"It wasn't Ole Fishbait."

"Who?"

"Bateman. Ole Fishbait. That's what my brothers and I call him. He looks like a fish and smells like one, too. It was his boss who set Papa up. Some man Mama has never met. She suspects he works for Moshe Toblinsky or maybe even Al Capone."

Sam's heart skipped a beat. Of course. It would come around to that. "Why does she think that?"

"It was something Bateman let slip once when he and Papa got into an argument. Something about people who owed the mob's favorite Jew big time needed to shut up and stop complaining."

"Sounds like good advice." Sam didn't pursue the topic. It reality hit too close to home. "Your dad mentioned school. What grade are you in?"

"Eleventh. I'll graduate in June."

"So that makes you sixteen or seventeen?"

"Sixteen. I'll be seventeen in August."

"My birthday's in August. I'll be eighteen. What date?"

"August 1st."

"Hey, that's my birthday too. That makes us twins." At the sight of Rebecca's lifted brow, Sam quickly amended, "Well, sort of."

"I suppose, if twins can be born a year apart with different parents."

Sam laughed at his own foolishness. With nothing else to say, he watched Rebecca rise again and push her chair back from the table. As much as he would have loved to keep her there talking into the night, exhaustion crept over him, keeping his tongue still.

Her hands filled with her medical supplies, she smiled down at him. "Well, I've got school tomorrow and you have whatever it is you do, so I guess it's time for me to go home. Goodnight. Remember to keep those hands clean."

The sudden quiet caught Sam off guard. He had been so focused on Rebecca he had been blind and deaf to everything else. Mr. Scheinberg's adding machine no longer clacked. No light came from the bakery office. The shop lay in complete darkness. Footsteps echoed. Rebecca's father appeared in the kitchen's entrance. He fixed Rebecca with meaningfully raised brows.

"You'll have to stop playing nurse. The children and your mother are in the car." His voice was sharp with irritation. "You've kept us waiting long enough working on this gangster's errand boy. Everyone wants their supper."

Rebecca's eyes grew enormous. She blushed and mouthed "I'm sorry" to Sam. He shook his head ever so slightly and smiled reassuringly. He wanted to argue with the older man, but his conscience poked and pricked him into remaining silent. If Rebecca were his sister, he wouldn't approve of her associating with someone like himself. A father would be all the more protective.

Rebecca put the medical supplies on the table and hurried after her father without so much as a glance back over her shoulder. Sam watched her until she disappeared through the shop door. The click of the big Yale lock's tumblers shifting into place drifted softly through the bakery, then all was quiet. The only illumination came from the single bulb hanging above the kitchen table. The only sound in the place was the kitchen tap's slow drip onto the cast iron sink's enamel-covered surface.

Plonk. Plonk. Plonk.

A place had never felt so empty. Only one other time had he ever felt so alone, so utterly lonely. If it would have helped, Sam would have thrown himself across the table and bawled like he did when Papa died, but the last three years had taught him that crying didn't help. Only action improved circumstances.

His stomach growled loudly. Would Mrs. Scheinberg be angry if he ate whatever leftovers from the family's lunch he could find? Probably, but finding him dead from hunger in her kitchen wouldn't do her much good either. He went to the icebox and rummaged around. Balancing the remnants of a roast chicken and a tomato in one hand, he grabbed a hunk of bread from the breadbox on the counter. The pilfered chicken tasted of garlic and herbs, just like Mama's. The simple meal was both nourishing and poignant.

Glancing at the kitchen clock, Sam cleaned up the evidence of his theft so he could get into bed for an hour or so before the noise started on the second floor. He figured he needed to get to sleep before the speakeasy opened or the laughter, music, and general din would keep him awake. After tromping up the steps, Sam went to his bed, striped down to his skivvies, and stuffed cotton into his ears. Sleep came quickly.

~ ~ ~

A hand shaking his shoulder woke Sam. "Get up, kid. Time to clean up."

He rolled over and looked up into the bleary eyes of the burly man who leaned over him. The man's breath smelled of beer and limited oral hygiene.

Sam blinked several times and stammered, "Who are you?"

"Barkeep. The brooms and mops are in the closet at the end of the bar. Make sure you wipe down my bar real good." The barkeeper yawned and wandered out of the room. He had clearly finished work for the night.

Nobody had said anything to Sam about being the cleanup crew, but it apparently ran true to form for these guys to think nothing of working him night and day. Mr. Scheinberg had said as much.

No rosy glow hovered on the eastern horizon, but it must be in the morning hours because car headlights shining and engines roaring on the street below told him the speakeasy had just closed. Whatever the present time, Mr. and Mrs. Scheinberg would arrive sometime before first light to start the day's baking. Sam hoped he would be finished with the cleaning quickly so he could crawl back under the sheet for another hour or so of sleep. Breakfast and Bateman's orders would come all too soon.

Sam dressed and stumbled sleepily to the main second floor room. Trash lay strewn over the floor and empty glasses sat on tables and the bar. Someone had broken a bottle and the shattered remains had been kicked into a corner. The whole place reeked of liquor. He began by turning chairs seat down onto the tables. By the time he was finished and returned to his bedroom, the sun was peeking over the rooftops.

Mrs. Scheinberg shouted up the staircase, "Samuel, you'd better come down here before all the breakfast is gone. The wolves are already here."

There would be no time for rest. Sam shuffled down the stairs and settled himself between Scheinberg numbers three and four. He hadn't learned their names yet because he'd only seen them once, the previous morning at breakfast. Rebecca and the baby sister were nowhere to be seen. Sam wanted to ask, but dared not. He and the boys fell on stacks of pancakes covered in melting butter and with streams of dark cane syrup running down the sides. Heaven on a plate. Sam ate his stack and was about to get up from the table when a hand came from behind him and flipped more cakes onto his plate. He looked over his shoulder into Rebecca's smiling eyes. How she had managed to slip up on him was a mystery. Maybe his brain was more befuddled with exhaustion than he realized.

She bent close to his ear while serving the brother on his left, the side away from her mother's penetrating gaze. "You need your strength." Her voice was so soft that he wondered if he had imagined it until she spoke again. "Eat up. Fishbait will be here soon enough."

But he didn't come, and Sam was left on his own.

~ ~ ~

A hand shook his shoulder, but this time it belonged to Mrs. Scheinberg. "Sit up, boy. I've got to clear the table. My husband wants his dinner."

Dinner? Sam jumped up like he had been kicked in the butt. How could it have gotten so late? He must have dozed all afternoon. "I'm so sorry. I meant to work for you this afternoon. Anything you wanted me to do to repay you for the chicken I stole last night."

The woman looked at Sam like he had two heads. "There's still plenty of time for you to do some chores for me. As to the chicken, you were welcome to it. It was left for you." She tilted her head to one side. Her eyes narrowed. "Did you really think we would let you starve?"

Sam opened his mouth, but closed it without comment. He shook his head in answer. Complete confusion filled his mind. He wasn't sure what he had thought, given all that he had experienced in the last week, but Mrs. Scheinberg was a kind woman and a good mother, that much he had already learned. He should have known more than to think any less. It dawned on him that she had said there was plenty of time to work. He glanced up to the wall clock. 12:00. Noon.

"I thought you said it was dinnertime."

She chuckled at his confusion. "We've fallen into Florida ways. Down here, dinner is the noon meal. Supper is served in the evening. You'll get used to it." She gave him a little push on his shoulder. "Get up now. Go take a shower. You need one. Bathroom is at the back of the storeroom. I've put your towel and washcloth out. Dinner will be on the table when you return."

Hot water and lots of soap made him a new man. Mrs. Scheinberg had even washed and ironed the clothes he had worn on the train. Maybe things weren't going to be so bad after all. Bateman might be a hard boss, but Rebecca's family would surely make up for it.

As Sam entered the kitchen, Mrs. Scheinberg gave him the once over. "Better. Much better. Take your place at the table so that Mr. Scheinberg can say the *brachah rishonah*."

Mrs. Scheinberg placed lamb chops, garden peas, and potatoes on the table and turned toward the shop.

The thought of being left alone with Rebecca's father sent a chill down Sam's spine. "You aren't going to eat with us?"

Mrs. Scheinberg stopped long enough to reply, "Someone's got to mind the store. I'll eat when you two have finished."

The meal was taken in complete, frustratingly awkward silence. It was as though Rebecca's father was unaware of Sam's presence. When Sam could bear it no more, he asked, "Mr. Bateman hasn't come around today, has he?"

The older man looked up from his plate, fork half way to his mouth. "No."

"Is that normal?"

The older man shrugged. "What is normal?"

"I mean for him not to show up."

"Sometimes."

"How often does it happen?"

"Now and again."

Sam held on to his temper. "Look, could you please help me out here. I don't want to get on that man's bad side."

"He has another side?"

Sam shrugged. "I certainly hope he does."

Mr. Scheinberg put his knife and fork on his plate while he eyed Sam. After a moment, the older man drew a long breath and let it out slowly. He made a tent of his fingers and rested them against his lips for a moment. "My boy, I fear it is a vain hope."

A sense of desperation coursed through Sam. He fought to keep his voice steady as he asked, "Please tell me as much as you can about him."

"He comes and he goes. Sometimes we see him every day and then not for two or three weeks. Everything else you already know."

"If he doesn't show up today, please let me help out around the bakery." Sam heard the hint of desperation in his own voice. Shame washed over him. All he needed was for Rebecca's father to think him a weakling.

Mr. Scheinberg's expression softened. "Have you slept recently?"

"You mean other than between breakfast and lunch, er, dinner? Not much."

"Sleep today. We will talk after the shop closes this evening. There are some tasks that you can perform."

~ ~ ~

Bateman didn't show up for weeks, allowing Sam to fall into a pattern that provided some semblance of normalcy in his life. He went to bed right after eating the leftovers from the noon meal that Mrs. Scheinberg always seemed to have. He awoke around 3:30 a.m. to work in the speakeasy after it closed before helping in the bakery. He learned to mix and roll out the bagels and how to operate the ovens. He rode around Miami on a bicycle with a special box on the back making deliveries. He washed the front windows so Rebecca could concentrate on her impending graduation. He even entertained the younger boys with fishing from the dock and walks around the neighborhood so Mrs. Scheinberg could have Sunday afternoons to herself where she read or did some mending in the bakery's little sitting room behind the office. The parents never invited him to their home, but they allowed him to accompany them to the beach or to take the children to the soda shop. Sam began to feel a little like he was part of their family, someone they trusted and cared for. He began to feel like he belonged somewhere and to someone again. The fact that Rebecca was usually nearby made his borrowed life all the happier. Her place in his heart grew larger each week, but he kept this to himself. She was a goddess on a pedestal, one to be admired, but not touched. The fact that he sometimes caught her looking at him with an odd expression didn't make it any easier. If he didn't know better, he would say it was affection shining in her eyes during those brief moments, but that couldn't be. She was too far above him.

The week of Rebecca's graduation, Sam watched her trying on her cap and gown while begging her mother to let her go to the after-graduation party in the school's gym. Jealousy of the boys lucky enough to dance with her haunted Sam's thoughts and absorbed his attention.

A shadow fell across the table. The little boys became uncharacteristically quiet.

Sam turned. "Hey, you guys. What . . .?" The question stuck in his throat. Bateman stood at the end of the table.

"Miss me, kid? Come on. We got work to do."

With his heart in his throat, Sam hustled after Bateman, but drew up short once on they were out on the dock. Whatever the gangster had in mind, it must be important. "Where did that come from?"

"Nowhere you need to worry about."

"It looks like a speed boat. Is it very fast?"

Bateman placed his foot on the hull of the long wooden vessel and grinned. "You bet. Of course, it takes a fast boat where we're going."

Sam dreaded the answer, but he couldn't stop himself asking, "Where would that be?"

"Untie the bow line and get aboard." Bateman swung himself down behind the boat's wheel. "We're leaving the country."

Chapter 20

Consuelo's final revelation took Liz's breath away. She turned the photograph from front-to-back twice more, then looked at her companions. Three pairs of eyes studied her in amusement. Maybe Rich and Mrs. Gray had known all along what Consuelo planned for her grand finale. Liz drew in a deep breath and let it out slowly. Consuelo would probably find someone jumping, whooping, and clapping wildly more than a little unseemly.

Gaining control of her excitement, Liz held the photograph out to Consuelo. "This is more than I ever expected to find out about my man. Evidence that he was in Havana at a New Year's Eve party attended by your Uncle Batista and a Toblinsky associate is . . . is unbelievable luck. Thank you seems rather feeble in light of this incredible gift. Unpublished information of this nature is so rare. You have no idea what it means to my research." Continuing to gush and stumble over her words might be more than a little off-putting to her hostess, so Liz fell silent while warmth crept over her cheeks.

The older woman smiled, but did not accept the picture. "Oh, I think I have an inkling of its importance. The photograph is nothing to me or my family, but it is obviously of great value to you. Keep it and I hope it brings you much success."

Liz tucked the photograph into the pocket of her borrowed shirt. The smile that split her face must have made her look like the Cheshire Cat, but she didn't care. She was giddy with excitement and a desire to tell Hugh what

Consuelo had revealed. It took Liz less than twenty minutes to eat, retrieve her belongings, and issue a promise to get Mrs. Gray's clothes back to her clean and within the week. She checked the bedroom one more time for anything she might have forgotten, gave the lovely space a final glance, and went into the hall. At the top of the stairs, she paused and looked down to the first floor. Rich stood waiting for her at the foot.

She lifted the grocery sack containing her dress and shoes. "Got my bag packed and ready to go."

Rich smiled and held out his hand when Liz reached the bottom step. She tilted her head, giving him a quizzical look.

He grinned, moved closer, and murmured, "A southern gentleman never lets a lady carry her own luggage." He leaned in.

Whether it was to kiss her or to take the sack by force, Liz would never know. She flinched and inched back. Her heel became tangled in the unrolling hem of her jeans, nearly sending her into Rich's arms in the process. She saved herself by grabbing the banister railing. What a graceless klutz. Jeez, why did she react like that?

Rich raised his brows. "Did I say something wrong? I sure didn't mean it as an insult."

Embarrassed, Liz fumbled for a reply. "Of course not. It just reminded me of something Hugh, my fiancé, says sometimes. And I'm way overdue getting back to Gainesville."

Rich chuckled as his mouth lifted in a sneer. "Oh, I get it. The fiancé. I forgot he keeps you on a short leash."

Liz's eyes widened and her nostrils flared. "He does no such thing. He just worries. That's all." Her voice was sharper than she intended.

Rich reached out and took the sack from Liz. "Look, I was teasing. I didn't mean to make you mad." His hand lingered against hers a little longer than necessary.

Liz stiffened unconsciously and swallowed hard. "I really need to be on the road. Will you please take me to my car?"

The smile faded from Rich's eyes, replaced by an expression that might be offense or even hurt feelings. "Of course. I'm sorry. Sometimes I let my warped sense of humor get out of control. If you were my girl and stayed away with another guy, even because of a hurricane, I guess I'd be pretty pissed."

He turned on his heel and led the way to the porte cochere where his car waited. Throwing her sack behind the driver's seat, he got behind the wheel without a word.

The trip back to the restaurant was silent to the point of being uncomfortable. Considering the events of last night and the amount of storm debris covering the streets this morning, lack of conversation felt abnormal, but Liz could think of nothing to say that didn't make her feel foolish. Instead, the scene at the bottom of the staircase replayed itself in her mind. Why had she reacted so strongly to him leaning toward her? All he had wanted was to take the bag from her. But, she hadn't known that at the time.

A truth she didn't want to acknowledge presented itself. Rich was handsome, successful, glamorous, in a word, a player—just the type she had always been drawn to. To be completely honest, the term "drawn to" didn't really do justice to her previous romantic relationships. Obsession came closer to reality. A damned lifelong obsession with the wrong kind of men. Surely she had learned her lesson. Rich's attention was flattering, but that's all it was. That's all it could ever be. She loved Hugh. Rich could never take his place. The two men could not be more different.

Guilt washed through her, but honestly, she had no reason to feel guilty. She had done nothing wrong, unless feelings of attraction served as an indictment. But, she had no intention of encouraging Rich's pursuit of her, if he was pursuing her. Was he? He hadn't really said or done anything concrete. Confusion replaced the guilt. She stretched her neck and rolled her head trying to clear away the conflicting emotions. Maybe it was a good thing she had offended him. When they reached the restaurant garage, she would express her sincere gratitude and that would be the last they would ever see of each other. Quick, harsh, dismissive maybe, but necessary.

When Rich parked beside her Prius, Liz turned to him. "Thank you for everything you've done. You, your father, and your great-aunt have given me more than I could ever have hoped. I'm not sure why you helped a perfect stranger, but I am very grateful you did."

With a condescending nod, he lifted one corner of his mouth. "Let's not play games, Liz. I think you know why I went to so much trouble, but you've made your wishes clear." His eyes narrowed while his mouth settled into a thin line. He regarded her for a moment before he continued, "So. For you, it's home to the fiancé. For me, it's back to running the best restaurant on Florida's west coast. Simple. No worries. No complications."

Liz blinked at his unexpected directness. "Rich, I'm sorry if I in any way gave you the wrong idea or somehow led you on. It was not my intension. I'm not like that. And I'm quite certain I mentioned Hugh during our first or second conversation."

Rich slouched against his seat and grinned, but the humor did not reach his eyes. "Yeah, you probably did. If you get this stuff published, give me and Fulgencio's a little free PR." He leaned across her and shoved the passenger door open. "See you around sometime."

Liz's cheeks stung like she had been smacked. She didn't know if she was angry or her feelings were hurt. Maybe both. "Of course. I always acknowledge people who have helped me in my research. Well, thank you again for all you've done."

Rich Whitehead's abrupt dismissal affected her more than it should have. It was stupid to care what he thought or felt. They didn't really know each other that well. Even if she were unattached, he wouldn't be good for her nor she for him. But she was attached and Liz wouldn't hurt Hugh for anything or anybody, so why did this little episode with Rich cut her? There were just too many inappropriate, unanswered questions. Liz didn't like herself very much in that moment.

She fairly leapt from his car. As she fumbled in the dim space with the automatic key fob, the smell of something dead mixed with the odor of gasoline made her gag. It was definitely time to get away from Tampa.

The drive back to Gainesville became a blur of interstate and exits. At one point, the speedometer needle hovered at 90. Easing up on the accelerator, she pondered the last two days. They had left her in a state for certain, but of what she couldn't be sure. Gratitude, anger, hurt feelings, maybe hurt pride to be more accurate, tumbled around inside her like fruit in a blender. The resulting concoction tasted bitter, like confusion of the worst sort. Getting home to Hugh couldn't come fast enough. Kind, loving, patient Hugh. He was one in a million.

The Prius slid into the apartment building parking lot just after 2:00. She was surprised to see Hugh's car parked outside their apartment. Since no one wanted to teach classes on Friday afternoon, he always assigned the slot to himself and his historiography/research methodology block that all senior history majors were required to take. He gave himself the worst schedule to cut down on complaints and to improve departmental morale. The liberal arts were under virtual siege from the bean counters when it came to undergraduate course enrollment. Leading by example helped keep his colleagues sane despite the constant worry about tenure and job security. No wonder they loved him.

Liz dragged her laptop and purse from behind the driver's seat and trotted to the apartment door. It flew open as she stepped onto the front stoop.

"Why the hell haven't you answered your phone?" Hugh's voice rang across the courtyard.

Too late, Liz realized she had failed to call him when she left Tampa. How stupid! "Oh crap. I was so intent on getting home I forgot to put it on the charger in the car. I'm sorry. My text didn't get through, did it?" One more thing about which to feel guilty.

"No. It didn't." Hugh's voice held a sharpness Liz had not heard before. "Not only have I been worried sick, but your Aunt Mildred has called every hour on the hour since five this morning." He handed her his cell phone. "Call her now before you take another step."

Liz's heart lurched. All thoughts of explanations and apologies flew from her mind. Tapping the number, she listened to endless rings while the bubble of apprehension inside her chest threatened to explode. In the end, she could only leave a message.

Turning to Hugh, Liz's voice wavered as she whispered the question to which she already feared she knew the answer. "Did she say what she wanted?"

"Our flight leaves Jacksonville at ten tonight. Get your bag packed. We're going to Seattle." His voice held both determination and anger.

"We? You're going too?"

A fierceness Liz had never seen before shone from Hugh's eyes. "I don't let people I love fight battles alone."

Chapter 21

Sam scrambled over the side of the long, sleek boat and dropped onto the seat behind Bateman. He craned his neck outward over the side to try to catch a little air as they moved slowly away from the dock. A light breeze traced the lines of Sam's face, bringing with it the tangy, slightly fishy fragrance of salt water and a dampness that clung to his skin. Early June, but it already felt like high summer. The air was positively liquid. Although the sun hung low over the rooftops, its heat raised a line of sweat on Sam's upper lip, or maybe, it was simply nerves. Bateman said they were leaving the country, but not where they were going. Sam knew better than to ask too many direct questions.

They moved south toward Biscayne Bay past the Gautier Funeral Home and the other businesses that lined the river. As they passed the Granada Grill and Apartments, Sam looked up at its Spanish façade and wondered what it would be like to have the money to live there or to eat in the restaurant. He had observed the activity around the building when he had taken the younger Scheinbergs joyriding down river in their father's old Jon boat. The Grill's veranda, overlooking the river, usually held lots of people eating and drinking no matter what time of day or night. The tables on the veranda were covered with white cloths and the diners where dressed in elegant cloths. At night, the apartment windows glowed invitingly. It must be pretty nice in there. Of course, he would never know. Even if he had the money, as a Jew, he probably wouldn't be allowed inside the place.

They continued on, passing in and out of the shadows of multistory downtown buildings and into the bay proper. Islands dotted either side of their watery path, then without warning, they cut through incoming ocean waves and on into the open Atlantic. Here, Bateman pushed the throttle forward, the engine roared, and the bow rose up in response. The boat cut through the wind and water as though it had wings instead of a mere propeller. Sam glanced back over his shoulder. The beach and its buildings were just a dark line on the horizon. Once land was completely out of sight, Bateman eased back on the throttle so that they were going at what seemed more like a normal cruising speed. All around them lay nothing but emerald water. Even the seagulls had disappeared. The sun grew more intense with every mile. Sam had no idea where they were or where they headed. Perhaps his boss would be open to a little conversation. With luck, Sam might even be able to ask about their destination.

Sam cut his eyes at Bateman, whose expression seemed relaxed enough, if not exactly pleasant, at least as much as Sam had ever seen him in that attitude. Nothing ventured . . . "So, Boss, this is a great boat. Never knew this kind could go that fast. What kind of motor does it have?"

Bateman glanced at Sam and gave him a smug look. "It don't have a motor. It's got a engine, a airplane engine to be exact."

Sam let out a low whistle. "That's impressive. Why did you slow us down?"

"We're outside the three-mile limit, so we can save a little on the gas. Coast Guard can't touch us out here."

"How far out into the ocean can this boat go?" Sam could hear the tension in his words.

Bateman turned to get a good look at Sam and laughed. "You think maybe we're headed to Europe or Africa? Don't get your panties all in a twist. We'll get where we're going in under three hours."

Sam racked his brain for memories of his geography lessons from his school days. Two to three hours east from Miami would take them across the Gulf Stream. But what was out there? It must be the Bahamas. British territory. No Volstead Act. No Prohibition. They had to be on a liquor run and in broad daylight, no less. That took chutzpah.

As promised, in a little under three hours, the boat bumped against a wooden dock that stretched out into the Atlantic from a beach dotted with thatched cabanas. Beyond the sand lay manicured lawns with graceful palm trees swaying in the breeze coming off the water. Crushed oyster shells created a path leading away from the beach, through the grass, and up to a large four-story building. By the look of the place, it could be a first-class hotel.

Bateman hopped up on the dock. "Welcome to the Bimini Bay Rod and Gun Club, kid. And you don't need to worry about a passport. We're always welcome here. Let's go up to the bar. I'm thirsty."

Sam climbed onto the dock but followed Bateman as slowly as he thought he could get away with. Dread built in him at the thought of spending time in a bar with his boss, even if it was located in a palace like the one that lay before them. Sam paused by crates marked with the names of various Canadian and British distilleries that crowded one side of the dock. Bending down, he pretended to tie a shoelace and sighed deeply. The scene beneath his feet, visible between the dock's treads, looked so peaceful, like it belonged to another world. It did, of course. The creatures below the surface of the crystal-clear water probably had their own enemies and times of terror, but at the moment, they looked so peaceful. No cares. No worries.

A starfish lay motionless against the white sand bottom, perhaps simply basking in the combined luxury of clean water and warm sunshine. A school of tiny fish darted under the dock and back out on the other side. Were they playing a game of chase? Did starfish and minnows have enough brain capacity to luxuriate or play? Who knew? Sam certainly didn't. At the moment, all he knew was that he wished he'd never left Brooklyn. Homesickness washed over him in a suffocating wave, drowning him in a misery that he knew was mostly his own fault. Why here and why now, he could not say. This place neither looked, smelled, nor felt like home, but missing his family and their shabby apartment suddenly grew into a physical ache. To his shame, a tear actually rolled down his cheek and dropped onto the gray, weathered boards of the dock.

Out of the corner of his eye, Sam saw Bateman stop and look back. Damn. All he needed was for Bateman to see he'd been crying. Sam swiped his hand over his forehead and down over his cheeks as though he was wiping away sweat.

"Hurry up, kid. I'm thirsty and I ain't looking to die of heatstroke out here."

Sam nodded and trotted after his boss. Apparently Bateman thought he had to keep an eye on Sam. Where the hell did the guy think Sam could run off to? The island wasn't so big that he could hope to hide out indefinitely. Even if he did run away, he had no friends and no way to survive. He was stuck.

Shuffling along behind Bateman, Sam blinked at the sudden change from searing sunlight to the dim interior of the Rod and Gun Club's lobby. When his vision adjusted, he realized the place wasn't as lavish as he had thought it would be. In fact, it was pretty ordinary for a resort that hoped to attract tourists from the mainland US. Dark wainscoting, white plaster, dark wood floors, ordinary iron fixtures, a mahogany desk of no great design pretty well summed it up. The bar, just off the lobby, was even drabber. Instead of the fancy stained glass, beveled mirrors, brass railings, and good quality polished wood of the speakeasies he'd seen in the States, this one looked more like something out of the Old West. Rough sawn planks and shelves, bottles, and plain glassware created a rustic retreat that served the Club's patrons after a day of fishing or swimming or whatever guests did here besides guzzle booze. They had passed crate after crate upon crate of the stuff stacked about the lawns ready for loading onto boats. This place was a bootleggers' paradise.

Bateman marched over to the bar and ordered a bottle and two glasses. He glanced at Sam and back at the barkeeper. Jerking his head toward Sam, he told the barman, "Give the kid a Coke and a sandwich." He slapped a bill onto the bar. "Here's a fiver to see I'm not disturbed."

Bateman gathered up the bottle and glasses and wandered toward the main staircase, stopping by the newel post as though waiting. Within minutes, an ebony-skinned woman in a light summer dress that had seen better days wandered through the lobby's front door and strolled over to Bateman. At her approach, the gangster's face split in a broad grin — more like a leer, really. The woman stepped in close and wrapped her arms around Bateman's neck. After gazing into his eyes in the most explicit way possible, she gave him a long, slow, simmering kiss. The gangster finally broke her embrace and slapped her on the bottom.

"It's good to see you too, Maria."

The woman ran her fingertips along his jawline. "I have waited so long for your return. My heart breaks for lack of you." Her simpering reply held the accent of the islands.

"Yeah, I bet it does." He draped an arm across her shoulders and turned to Sam. "I'm going to be busy for the rest of the afternoon. Stay outta trouble. If you wander off, don't get lost. Be here ready to go to work at five."

Sam watched the pair sashay up the stairs and disappear from view. Girlfriend or lady of the evening? It was hard for Sam to know from his limited experience with women, but his close acquaintance with Bateman told him the woman was more likely a prostitute. He couldn't imagine any decent woman having anything to do with his vulgar, smelly boss. Sam had often wondered if the man knew what water and soap were for.

The room had become over warm. Sam ran the back of his hand over his forehead where beads had formed and were threatening to run down into his eyes. He wandered back to the bar and took the meal that awaited him. On their way into the building, they had passed tables and benches placed under swaying palms. Taking his sandwich and warm Coca-Cola outside, he sought out a bench as far from Bateman as he could find and settled down to eat.

The sandwich tasted surprisingly good. The thick slices of bread had a sweet flavor that complemented the crispy fried fish. The sandwich contained no condiments. It didn't need any. Even the Coke without ice seemed right. The breeze off the ocean picked up, setting the palm fronds rattling. Brightly, flowered shrubs dotted the lawn between the crates stacked about. Even with the liquor taking up so much space, the place still looked and felt like a vacation spot. Did they allow Jews to stay there?

Without warning, Rebecca's face drifted before his mind's eye. Had she ever been to a real vacation location? Visions of the two of them strolling along the beach with their arms around one another's waists popped into his head. They stopped, lay down, and began to undress one another, not even minding the crunch of the sand against their bare skin.

Sam jumped to his feet and shook his head. Thoughts like that could get him into trouble. Mr. Scheinberg didn't seem like a violent man, but he would probably be capable of murder if he knew what Sam daydreamed about. The ache in his groin told Sam he had to do something or go crazy. He walked to the end of the property and stepped behind a chest high bush. Glancing left and right and seeing no one, he stripped down to his underwear. The water lay a few feet away rolling in to shore in gentle waves with only the smallest head of foam. He ran in and waded out quickly until the water washed over his shoulders. He lifted his legs until he lay on his back, floating, rocked in the arms of the sea. The sun warmed his front and the water cooled his back. The relaxing motion and the water's saltiness began easing his pains, both the aches of strained muscles and scratched flesh and the despair of knowing he was in love with a girl he could never have.

Drifting out to sea to never be seen again held some appeal, but that meant Sam would never see Rebecca again. Of the two options, the latter held the far greater terror. He rolled over and waded back to the beach. Once dressed, he decided to walk off his doldrums. If simply thinking about her could drive his spirits so low, maybe throwing himself into hard physical activity would block her from his mind, at least for a little while. At first, he walked, then he trotted, finally in an effort not to think, he broke into an all-out gallop. The deep sand road leading away from the Rod and Gun Club sucked at his feet, making running a heart-hammering, lung-bursting chore. He ran anyway. When he finally slowed because he could run no more, he found himself on a village street lined with one story houses topped by corrugated tin roofs. The street ended at a town square where old men sat on benches fanning themselves in the afternoon heat.

Sam stopped at the corner before entering the square. Shading his eyes with his hand, he looked up to try and gage the time. Mid-afternoon probably. Crossing to the first group of men, he asked, "Do you have the time?"

An old man laughed. "We got all the time. Which particular time you be wanting?"

Despite his low spirits, he smiled. "The time of day, please."

"Oh, dat one be easy, mon." The man looked at his wrist. "It be exactly four-thirty."

Sam's heart rate kicked up a notch. He had no idea how long or how far he had run. "Can you tell how far is it to the Rod and Gun Club?"

"That all depend on how fast you want to arrive."

"The quickest way."

"That would be drive back down the road you came. Twenty minutes."

"And by foot?"

"Depends on how fast you run."

As pleasant as continuing to trade banter with the old man would be, Sam had no time to waste. He lifted two fingers to his forehead in a parting salute and started running back down the sand road. He arrived at the Rod and Gun property to find Bateman sitting on a stack of crates.

"Where you been? We're late getting loaded." Pointing at the crates closest to Sam, Bateman growled, "Start with those and work fast. You get us caught 'cause you been wandering around and you won't need to worry about the G-Men shooting you 'cause I'll do it for 'em."

It took three hours to get everything stowed away. The sun hovered on the horizon as they moved away from the dock. By the time they reached the mouth of the Miami River, only the lights from the apartment buildings, clubs, and restaurants along the river broke the darkness. Bateman had said they would be returning under the cover of fishermen returning from a day of deep-sea sport, but now they were late enough to attract the wrong kind of attention.

They were about even with the Granada Grill and Apartments when the glare of a spotlight hit their boat. Sam put a hand up to shield his eyes. The light came from a rapidly advancing craft from which sirens screamed and a voice projected by a loudspeaker demanded that they halt immediately and prepare to be boarded. A cruiser. They were being chased by a fucking law enforcement cruiser. G-men or Miami Police, it made no difference. The cops would put Sam and his boss in the darkest hole they could find, if they caught them.

Bateman shoved the throttle forward, throwing Sam back against his seat. Popping sounds reached them as they raced forward. Bullets whizzed close by their heads. Sam dropped and flattened himself against the boat's floorboards. Pure terror descended. Sam's pulse roared against his eardrums while his heart tried to pound its way through his rib cage. Bateman returned fire while steering to keep the boat on a path straight toward the low-lying bridge about a quarter mile ahead of them. If they could just make it under that bridge, the pursuing cruiser couldn't follow. It was too tall.

Visions from the night Mack the Irishman had been killed rose in Sam's mind, evolving into a specter. The unearthly spirit's bony finger pointed toward a future of misery and despair. Someone other than Sam controlled his life, his future, his very existence. If only there was some way to get out of this damned boat and away from Bateman. Sam could disappear. The gangsters he worked for would think he had been killed in the gun battle.

Pop. Pop-pop.

The shots were getting closer. If ever he was to act, it had to be now.

Sam rose up just enough to peer over the side of the boat. Reflections of lights floated and flashed on the water. How hard would he fall if he slipped overboard from the speeding craft? Would he be shot going over the side or would the force of impact when his head hit the water break his neck? The boat entered the shadow of the bridge. It was now or never.

Chapter 22

The plane bumped once as its wheels touched down on the wet tarmac, but it was enough to rouse Liz from dozing. She lifted her head from Hugh's shoulder and looked into his eyes. He smiled back at her with a mixture of affection and sympathy. His arm slid arm around her shoulders as he kissed her forehead.

"It will be all right. Your mom will be glad to have your help." Hugh's arm tightened around her shoulders in an encouraging hug. "No matter what decision y'all make, I'm sure it will be for the best."

"I wish I had your confidence. Mom is a first-class control freak. You have no idea."

"That may be, but she isn't a stupid woman. She can be brought to see reason."

"Yeah. Maybe after a ten-round match in which she will use every trick to get her way, including, but not limited to, hysterics and heart palpitations, if all else fails." Liz mentally shuddered. Hugh had not seen Mom in full cry. Images from the day Liz announced she was following her former boyfriend across the continent without a ring on her finger flashed through her mind.

"Maybe there won't be a fight. Perhaps she already realizes things must change."

"I doubt it."

"How do you know?" Liz heard an edge of irritation in his voice. "You haven't even talked to her. Don't you think you should at least call her once we are in the terminal?"

Liz's fist hit the side of the armrest. "Absolutely not. That would give her time to plot her response and create a cover-up. I want to see how things really are firsthand."

"Okay, but at least call your aunt and let her know we've landed. Sounds like it might be well to have backup."

Fellow passengers began stirring as the plane rolled up to the gate. A visual image of Mom and Aunt Mildred in full on sister drama brought a rueful smile to her lips. Hugh had no idea. He and his sister had such a wonderful relationship he assumed all families functioned like his did.

Liz brushed her fingers against Hugh's cheek and let them run lightly along his jaw until her hand cupped his chin. "I'll call Aunt Mildred in the morning, but I have the best backup anyone could want right here beside me. There is no way I can ever repay you for making these reservations and coming with me."

An expression she did not expect crept into Hugh's eyes. "Why would you think I need repayment? I do things for the people I love because I want to, not out of charity or obligation. Why would you think otherwise?"

"I'm sorry. That came out wrong." Confused at her misstep, Liz kissed his cheek quickly and bent down to get her carryon from under the seat in front of her.

The jet-way's accordion entrance thudded against the side of the plane followed by the click of the hatch opening. A whiff of jet fuel made its way through the plane. The buckle seatbelt light went off. Within minutes, they were shuffling down the jet-way along with two hundred or so other bleary-eyed folks.

The sound of their carryon wheels rolling on the terrazzo floor echoed through the near-empty terminal. The kiosks and the food counters were shuttered. Even the newsstands had their gates down and padlocked. It would be very late by the time they arrived at her parents' home.

On the way to baggage claim, she let Hugh walk ahead while she mulled over what he had said to her on the plane. His reaction to the way she thanked him nagged at her. Why, indeed, would she think he wanted or expected repayment? Good question. Maybe she needed to go into analysis because she hadn't a clue. Liz sucked the edge of her lower lip between her teeth. Perhaps she had no idea who she really was on the most fundamental level. In retrospect, the majority of her pre-Hugh life seemed like a dance between warring personalities. On the one hand, her professional life had always been in complete, tightfisted control, but her personal life had been another matter entirely.

In truth, she had never really expected much of the guys in her life. She had been satisfied to let them call the shots for the most part. She had been happy to be the giver to their taker. She had no idea why she had been such a milksop in her romantic life. Another question probably best explored on a shrink's couch. The only place she held firm was her academic pursuits, and those she protected like a grizzly with a freshly caught salmon.

Hugh was the best relationship she had ever known, and here she was doing her damnedest to screw it up. Thank goodness he possessed the patience of those two guys who sat forever on a park bench waiting for somebody named Godot.

Outside baggage claim, Hugh hailed a cab. Liz gave the driver her parents' address and sent Aunt Mildred a text just in case she was still awake. Liz's cell phone rang in an instant.

"You've arrived?" Aunt Mildred's head-nurse voice barked through the earpiece.

"Yes, we're in Seattle and headed to Mom and Dad's."

"I'll be on my way as soon as I get dressed."

"No, really, I don't think you need to come over tonight."

"It's late. Your parents are in bed." No doubt, Aunt Mildred was in bed, too. "Do you have a key?"

"Yes, I still have my key." Liz sighed at Aunt Mildred's rapid-fire questions. She and Mom were clearly sisters in more ways than blood.

"Have you let your mother know you're coming?"

"I'll call them when we are a few blocks away. I wouldn't want Dad to mistake us for intruders and shoot us."

Mildred harrumphed. Liz could visualize her aunt's face—one eyebrow raised, her mouth set in a rueful expression, her laser gaze boring through the object of her derision. The Look ran in the family. "Honey, he doesn't know where he is most of the time, much less that he owns a shotgun."

"Oh, I guess I hadn't thought about it that way." Liz wanted to get off the phone before she dissolved in tears. "Well, I'll let you get to sleep. See you in the morning and thank you for all that you are doing to help Mom."

She tapped the end call button and shoved her phone back into her purse.

Hugh took her hand and asked, "What did you not think about?"

Liz's lower lip trembled slightly when she started to speak. She ran her teeth over it before replying, "Dad doesn't remember he has a gun or much else, apparently. Anyway, I forgot Mom locked it up a good while ago. She didn't want to get shot either." For some reason, that last statement sent Liz into hysterics. She laughed until her sides hurt, then burst into tears.

Liz wiped her eyes and face, while she spoke. "Sorry about that. I'm not crazy. Or at least I wasn't the last time I checked." Liz mustered a half smile.

"I know." He raised her hand and kissed it. "I think what you need is a bath and bed. You've had way too much excitement and worry lately."

"I had a long soak this morning, but bed is a definite go." Had it only been this morning that she bathed in the lovely claw-foot tub at Consuelo's home in Tampa?

The cab turned onto the street where she had grown up. Hugh looked at her and raised his brows. She shook her head in response to his unspoken question. Her phone stayed in her purse.

The cab stopped in front of the shingle covered Cape Cod where Liz spent her childhood and youth. Liz cast a glance up the short flight of front steps leading from the sidewalk to the front walk. Her heart sank. The house blazed. Lights shone from every window. Something wasn't right.

Seeing the same scene, Hugh leaned across Liz and opened the cab door. "Go on up to the house. I'll see to the cab and luggage."

Looking at him, she noticed the dark circles under his eyes for the first time and her heart swelled. He must have lost sleep over her being in Tampa during the hurricane and Aunt Mildred calling so often from early morning. It was now 1:00 a.m. their time. "Thank you. You're the best."

He smiled and kissed her lightly. "This is easy." A serious expression filled his eyes. "I'd do anything to make you happy. You know that, don't you?"

Liz flung a reply over her shoulder as she leapt from the cab. "I love you too."

She dashed up the brick steps leading to the yard and up the walk to the front porch steps. Muffled cries and shouts filtered through the door. Without thinking, she grabbed the knob and turned. It was unlocked. She pushed the door open and drew up short at the scene laid out before her.

Daddy stood in the hall leading out of the living room, Mom's best lamp held aloft while she pleaded with him.

"James! I'm Lillian, your wife. Please put the lamp down."

Daddy's eyes held a wild, confused expression. "No . . . you . . . I don't know you!" His howl rang down the hall and out into the night, then he swung his weapon. Mom jumped back and let out a yelp.

Placing a fist on each hip, she shouted, "Put the damned lamp down, you son-of-a-bitch!"

Mom never swore, had a real revulsion from it, yet there she was screaming profanity at Daddy. Remarkably, he lowered his arm and shuffled toward the living room table where the lamp resided when not being used as a truncheon.

He turned to Mom. "You don't have to shout or swear at me, Doris." Catching sight of Liz, he rocked on his heels and stared. "Who the hell are you, and why are you breaking into my house?"

Liz heard Hugh drop the bags on the porch and then he was beside her. Dad took one look at Hugh and grabbed the lamp again. This time he threw it directly at Hugh's head. Hugh ducked and the lamp flew through the front door. It landed on the front walk in a great crash of glass and metal.

"Daddy, it's me, Elizabeth, your daughter." Liz's voice sounded high pitched and screechy. Perhaps she had screamed. Her pulse thumped against her eardrums with such force that she became lightheaded for a second. "Daddy, don't be afraid. I'm your Lizzie." She took Hugh's hand and pulled him forward. "This is Hugh, my . . . my boyfriend." She had nearly said fiancé. "You two talked about football when we were here last summer."

Mom turned around, her eyes big, her expression hard. Liz couldn't decide if her mother was angry or afraid.

"What are you doing here?" Mom's voice held a sharp edge. Angry. Clearly. "You're supposed to be in Florida chasing around after another one of your precious gangsters. Why you couldn't have specialized in constitutional law and become an attorney is beyond me."

"Hi, Mom. I'm glad to see you too." Liz clenched her jaw. Mom could be hurtful and manipulative when she didn't get her way. She refused to go along with this little head game Mom was trying to play.

Liz adjusted her features to their most casual expression and kept her voice light. "What's up with the profanity and who is Doris?"

"Doris is nobody." Mom's gaze shifted toward Daddy. "Can you believe it? Cursing seems to be the only thing that gets through to your dad when he's in one of his moods. All those years working for the Navy stick with him like barnacles on a ship's hull, but he can't even remember his own family."

"That's very frustrating." Doris was nobody? Really? Dad had moods? Surely Mom wasn't so far into denial. Liz went to her mother, put her arms around her, and hugged her close. Mom stiffened at Liz's touch. Liz kissed her mother's cheek and looked down into her eyes. "This must be so very, very hard. I can only imagine. I love you, and I want to help."

Uncharacteristically, Mom's eyes brimmed with tears and slipped into an unfocused stare. She put her hand to her temple before slumping against Liz. Hugh caught her elbow to keep both women from tumbling to the floor.

Liz held her mother at arm's length and searched her face. "Are you dizzy? What's the matter? Are you sick?"

Mom shook her head. "No, just tired. I'll be okay after I get some sleep."

Hugh's intake of breath swooshed close by Liz's ear. "Lillian, do you have these dizzy spells often?"

Mom shot him a surprised look. "Only when I've been running around too much."

"Do you own a blood pressure cuff?"

"We have one for James. He's on medicine for his blood pressure."

"Would you let us check your blood pressure?"

"I don't have that problem. I'm just tired." Irritation tinged Mom's voice.

Hugh smiled and patted her shoulder. "Would you humor me? Please? I won't rest until we've checked it, and I really need a good night's sleep."

Mom studied Hugh for a moment. Giving him a sheepish smile, she said, "Well, if you insist. You do look tired, and I don't want to be the source of unnecessary concern or lost sleep."

Mom pushed out of Liz's embrace. "It's on the bedside table in our bedroom. Liz, you do remember the way, don't you?"

Zing! That was a shot over the bow of Liz's having moved to the other side of the continent. Never mind that mom had ordered her to stay away from Seattle until the semester break.

Liz's lips twisted in a sardonic smile. Some things didn't change. They probably never would. Mom reacted to Hugh the way she always had to Jake, Liz's brother. Almost from birth, Mom pushed Liz hard to become an early success in everything from potty training to school. With Jake, she had equally high expectations, but Mom was also putty in his hands. Liz could ask that something be done and Mom would refuse outright without discussion. Let Jake ask and Mom acquiesced before he finished speaking. It must be nice to be the favorite.

When Liz passed the single bathroom, she glanced at the green and black 1950's ceramic tile that covered the floor and went half-way up the walls. Sometimes, things that didn't change provided a sense of security and comfort. This house was one of them. Not so much as the kitchen linoleum had been changed since Mom and Dad bought it when they were first married. This would probably always feel like home.

When she reached the bedroom door, her progress halted at the doorway. The sight of a hospital bed with wrist restraints attached to the rails made her stomach turn over. Her hand flew to her mouth as she choked back rising bile.

Things must be much worse than even Aunt Mildred knew. Liz grabbed the blood pressure cuff from the nightstand and marched back toward the living room, anger bubbling up hot and ready to flow. Mom should not have kept the truth from her. But when Liz entered the living room, she sensed a shift in the climate.

Mom looked at Liz through narrowed eyes filled with challenge. "So, tell me, exactly why have you come rushing home when I told you not to?"

Chapter 23

Sam leaned over the side of the speeding boat. Bateman, in the forward seat, only turned every so often to fire over his shoulder at the pursuing police cruiser. If Sam timed it perfectly, he could slip over the side with his boss none the wiser. Injury, arrest, or worse would be worth the risk if that's what it took to get away from Bateman. The water's surface looked so close. Just a moment more and he would be in the river. He wasn't a great swimmer, but he would swim underwater for as long as it took to keep Bateman from seeing where he had gone. If he was picked up by the police cruiser, well, he would deal with that when it happened. Surely the information he had on Bateman and Tops would buy him a reduced sentence or maybe get him off completely. Selling them out carried its own peril, but that, too, was a concern for another time.

The low bridge raced toward them. If he didn't jump now, he would be stuck as Bateman's lackey until another chance to get away presented itself, if it ever did. The police cruiser was too tall to follow them under the bridge. If they made it under without getting killed, Bateman would win. Sam raised himself higher over the side, but his timing stank. The police cruiser spotlight swept over him and arced back, stopping directly on him. The gunfire increased. With Sam struggling to push himself back into the safety of the backseat, Bateman returned fire, but only got off a couple of rounds before the boat swerved dangerously out of control. He righted the vessel with Sam still tittering on the side. *Pop-*

pop. A sharp stinging spread across his temple and lower jaw. Sam's hand flew to his face, then the world disappeared in a miasma of spray from the river and fuel fumes.

~ ~ ~

A voice that seemed to be coming through a long tunnel tapped on the door of Sam's consciousness, bringing with it a pounding in his head that made opening his eyes painful. He rolled over and vomited into a basin that miraculously appeared, then flopped back onto the pillow. His headache eased enough for him to attempt concentration. Someone wiped a cool, wet cloth over his forehead, face, and around his mouth. Sam's eyelids lifted as though they had lead fishing weights attached to them. He squinted through his lashes at the form seated by his bed.

"He's awake." Rebecca spoke to someone beyond Sam's line of sight. "I'll come to the shop as soon as I'm sure he'll be all right left by himself."

"This one's a survivor. He'll be fine. We need you in the shop." Impatience filled Mrs. Scheinberg's voice.

"Not until I'm sure he's okay. He's been shot in the head. Have a little compassion. How about it?"

"Do not get a smart mouth with me, young lady. The bullets only grazed him. And really, he is no one to us. Our family's needs come first." Gone was the caring mother figure of the weeks before Bateman had reinserted himself into Sam's life. In her place stood a tigress watching over her young.

"I will not leave him until I know he will be okay." Rebecca's voice held a defiant edge that Sam never expected to hear when she spoke to her parents. "He is hurt, and he has no one but me." Rebecca's breath hissed with rapid intake. "I mean us. He has no one but us. Please, Mama. He needs us." Rebecca looked away from her mother and down at Sam, her eyes filled with an emotion he dared not hope for. "He needs *me*." Her voice lost its edge, replaced by a quiet strength. She slipped her hand into his under the sheet. "Ordering me away won't do any good. I will not leave him."

"Hmmm. Well, we'll see what your father has to say about that." Mrs. Scheinberg turned on her heel and left the room, the force of her steps in the hallway communicating her displeasure.

Sam tried to speak, but his voice refused to cooperate. Swallowing hard, he finally managed to croak, "Don't get yourself in trouble on my account."

Rebecca raised her brows and turned her head a little. She gave him the "look", the kind mothers give naughty children. "*I* will do as I please. *You* will do as you're told until you are able to take care of yourself. Now go back to sleep. When you feel like you can keep something down, I'll bring you some clear chicken broth." She rose from the chair beside his bed and grinned at him. "It cures everything, you know."

Sam watched Rebecca walk from the room. Even with his head pounding and his stomach threatening rebellion once again, he couldn't take his eyes off that lovely bottom swaying its way through the door. Sam groaned and rolled away from the sight. Who did he think he was to hope that Rebecca would ever find him acceptable?

He must have slept because when Sam opened his eyes this time, the room in which he lay had long fingers of bronze sunlight slanting across the floor through its single window. He looked around and realized he must be in the bakery's backroom where Mrs. Scheinberg had her retreat. Having never been in the space, he had no idea it was outfitted as a bed-sitting room. There was even a fireplace for cool winter evenings, though it didn't look as though it got much use. Maybe Rebecca's mother wasn't completely unsympathetic after all.

Sam slept much of the next couple of days, waking to eat and take care of personal needs, but always finding Rebecca at his bedside. Despite his injury and doctor's orders that he not get excited or stressed, Sam couldn't help but hope Rebecca kept vigil because of affection. Each time he caught sight of her, his heart lurched a little, and he said a silent prayer that she wasn't simply being kind to someone she felt sorry for.

One afternoon, Sam awoke to find the white-haired doctor sitting in Rebecca's chair. He held Sam's wrist between his fingers, nodded, and placed his stethoscope on Sam's chest. Another nod and the old man shoved a thermometer under Sam's tongue. While they waited for the mercury to crawl up the glass vial, the doctor examined Sam's wounds and checked his eyes.

"Well, the boy is definitely on the mend. Other than some unfortunate scars, I believe he will recover completely and be no worse for wear."

Scars? Sam hadn't looked at himself in the bathroom mirror since the shooting because it took all of his energy to keep himself upright getting to and from the toilet. Sam ran his fingers along the stitches in the hairline at his temple and over his jaw. His heart tumbled to the soles of his feet. Rebecca wouldn't want a guy scarred up like a thug. She deserved a guy who wouldn't cause questions about his background, someone she would want to wake up to every morning, someone she would find as alluring as he found her.

The doctor put his instruments back in his bag and rose from the edge of the bed. "Stay in bed at least another week, young man. Take it easy. Be slow going about. Another blow to your head could have very serious consequences." He turned to Mrs. Scheinberg. "It's odd that a simple fall could have caused those injuries. You're sure that's all there was to it?"

"Well, I didn't actually see him fall, but it's the only possible explanation. Why else would we have found him unconscious at the foot of a ladder? He must have been getting the Jon boat paddles down from the porch rafters and lost his balance. The paddles were scattered on the porch."

"And the deep cuts to his face? What caused those?"

"There are nails sticking out of the porch posts. I told Mr. Scheinberg they must be fixed before someone got hurt on them and someone has been. Maybe now he will listen and remove them."

"Yes, I guess it could have happened that way. Of course, if those were gunshot injuries, I would have to report them to law enforcement."

"I assure you he was injured by an unsteady ladder and nails where they should not be."

The doctor looked down at Sam. "Is that how you remember it, son?"

Even in his confused state, Sam knew better than to tell the truth. "I don't remember. I remember going out on the porch, but everything after that is gone."

"Well, that makes sense. Head injuries can certainly cause short-term memory loss. Like I said. Take it easy. No heavy lifting, bending over, or rushing around. When you do go back to work, make it half days at first." With that, the doctor headed for the door.

"Rebecca, remember your manners and see the doctor out. I'll clean up in here. Samuel won't dash off while you're gone."

Mrs. Scheinberg waited until Rebecca's and the doctor's steps faded. She came to the bedside. A deep frown darkened her features. "That doctor costs money, and I expect you to repay us for our trouble."

"As soon as I get back on my feet."

She placed her fists on her hips. "Another thing, I don't want you to get any ideas about my daughter. She may sit by your bed and take care of you, but that is the limit of the relationship. Do you understand?"

Her vehemence shook Sam to the core. He studied her for a moment. The woman actually expected him to swear off her daughter. If he weren't so dependent on her kindness, he would tell her to go to hell. On the other hand, he owed her more than he could ever repay. He sighed and said, "Yes, ma'am. I understand."

"Promise me that you will not let it go any farther than that."

"I promise." Wait. Promise that *he* would not let it go farther? Could that mean she had lost control of Rebecca? That happy thought fell shattered as soon as it popped into his head, broken on the rock of his own pride. A promise had already tumbled from his lips. He had lost a lot of himself in working for Bateman, but he still wanted to believe he would keep his word once given. "Thank you for your kindness. I don't know what would have happened to me if I'd landed somewhere else."

Mrs. Scheinberg's features softened. The nurturing mother, her true nature, made a brief appearance before being shoved aside by the mother protecting her child. "We didn't really have a choice, but you are welcome. Remember your promise to me."

Sam nodded. The pain of what he had just willingly given up took his breath away.

Over the following week, Sam found his strength returning, and along with it, his ability to think clearly. He had given away his hope at happiness. If he had been in better condition at the time, he would have found a way around Mrs. Scheinberg's demands, but as it was, his pride would not let him go back on his promise now. And anyway, he couldn't offer Rebecca the type of life she needed and deserved, not being indentured to Bateman like he was.

Bored beyond sanity with being in bed, Sam sat up and leaned against the wall. He gazed out the window at the only vista he had, the brick wall of the building next door. He would carry Rebecca in his heart forever. Of that he was quite confident, but he had to find a way to live without her. Footsteps sounded in the hall outside his door.

Rebecca came into the room with his lunch tray and placed it across his lap. When she had it adjusted to her liking, she sat in her chair and smiled at him. Flustered, Sam did not return her smile. Instead, he kept his eyes of his food and ate in silence. Without warning, she reached out and grabbed his hand that held the spoon, sloshing soup onto the bedclothes in the process.

"What's the matter with you?" Anger colored her words and filled her eyes. "I bring you food. I wash your clothes. I dress your wounds. And you act like I am some kind of servant beneath your notice."

Sam's head jerked back in surprise. He never considered that his caution might have such an effect. "I'm sorry. I guess the hit on the head knocked the manners out of me."

"Oh, really? You weren't like this when you first woke up from the accident. You weren't like this until after the doctor's last visit. What did he say to you?"

"Nothing. He was great."

"So what's changed?"

Her eyes held a challenge he could not meet, so he mustered his own anger instead. "I told you. Nothing." He hated his tone, but he could not let her see how much heartache this was causing him. "I'm sorry I was rude to you, but you can be a pest sometimes."

"Is that so?" The edge in her voice matched the flash of anger in her eyes. "You've been more than rude. You've been down right cold. You used to like me. I know you did, so don't you dare deny it."

"So what? I said I'm sorry." Great. He sounded just like a little kid who was being scolded.

"That's not good enough. When you were unconscious, you kept calling my name. I know that you care for me, so why are you pretending like you don't?"

"Good grief, just leave it alone." Sam couldn't keep the misery from his voice. "It's best for everyone."

"Really?" The edge in her voice became a razor. "How do you know what's best for me?"

"That's not what I meant."

"Then tell me what you did mean," she hissed.

"I don't know. I'm still kind of confused."

"*Bubba maisa*! Your head is just fine." She grabbed his shirtfront and shook it. "Tell me what's wrong."

Because he could think of nothing better, Sam laughed, but it sounded forced even to him. Still, he pushed on. "I didn't know you spoke Yiddish."

Rebecca blinked as tears rolled down her cheeks. She let go of his shirt and pushed him back against the headboard. Rising from the chair, she turned to leave, but Sam grabbed her wrist. He couldn't stand to see her cry knowing it was his fault.

"Look, I'm sorry. I'm just all mixed up. You shouldn't want me to like you. I'm not for you. You deserve better."

"Who says?" Her eyes, still bright with tears, bore down on him. "Tell me why you've changed when I haven't."

Sam's heart split apart. He fought back his own tears. Crying in front of Rebecca was the last thing he wanted to do. He gave the inside of his cheek a vicious bite to redirect the pain.

Breathing hard, he mustered as much anger within himself as he could. "You don't know me. You have no idea what I do for Bateman. For all you know, I've killed a dozen men, robbed banks, or kidnapped somebody's kid for ransom."

Instead of being put off and leaving the room, Rebecca sat back down on the chair, looked at him through narrowed eyes, and started giggling. She laughed. She chortled. She guffawed until she bent double holding her sides. When she regained enough control to look up, she pointed a shaking finger at him. "You look like you sucked on a lemon. If you're going to tell lies, you'd better improve your *schtick*. Nobody in the world would believe that line you just tried to spin."

Sam turned his face away from her and he groaned. "Oh, god, Rebecca. Why do you have to make this so damned hard?"

"So, you're admitting you care for me. Now, tell me why that's so hard?"

Sam shook his head. "You simply do not understand."

"Well explain it to me. That's what I asked at the get go."

There was no way he could tell Rebecca about his promise to her mother. It would hurt Rebecca and damage their relationship. In the end, Rebecca would probably wind up resenting him for causing a rift between them. Situations like this usually turned out like that. Maybe if he gave her part of what she wanted, she would give up on the rest.

"Ok. I admit it. I'm in love you. I have been since the first time I saw you on the sidewalk getting ready to wash the front windows. This in no way changes the fact that you have a wonderful life ahead of you, a life that I will not be part of. I'm no good for you."

An emotional cloud passed over her features. Her brows twitched as the light of comprehension dawned in her eyes.

"It's my mother, isn't it? I remember she stayed here with you when I walked the doctor to the door. Exactly what did she say to you?"

When Sam refused to answer, Rebecca continued, "Let's get something straight. I love my parents dearly, but they are not going to live my life for me. This is 1926, not 1896. I've bobbed my hair. I wear flapper dresses when I go out. I can vote when I turn twenty-one. No one but me will determine who I love or who I marry."

Love. She said love. And marriage. Sam swallowed hard. How was he going to get out of this? Better yet, could he even force himself to try?

Chapter 24

Liz's nostrils flared and her breath came in little gasps. Mom's question and accusatory tone made the palms of Liz's hands itch. Even at her angst-filled teenaged worst, Liz had never, ever dreamed of striking either of her parents, not even when they forced her to break up with her grunge-band boyfriend. Not until that exact moment had she considered herself capable of physical violence against someone she loved so deeply.

She dug her fingernails into her palms in an effort to keep her hands at her sides. Drawing in a long breath and exhaling slowly, she tried to keep her voice level. Screaming would not solve anything. "I think the answer is obvious as to why I've come home without your express permission." Liz heard the hard edge of sarcasm in her own voice, however rage drove her on. "But in the interest of complete clarity, I'll explain. You've let the situation here get completely out of control. You have to tie Daddy to his bed because he wanders away from the house and has no idea what day or year it is. He doesn't know who you are, and he has forgotten he has a daughter. He thinks you're somebody named *Doris*, for God's sake. Cursing at him seems to be the only way you can get him under control. Is that explanation enough?"

"You don't know the first thing about what it's like living with your father. I tie him down so that I can sleep at night. He's turned into a two-hundred-pound toddler. Next, I'll be changing diapers again."

"He can't help what's happening to him." On some level, Liz regretted her tone and volume as soon as the words left her mouth, but there was no way to change them now, even if she had wanted to do so.

Mom's face turned ashen. Her hands began to shake. "Don't you think I know that? Don't you dare criticize me for the way I deal with a situation you turned your back on."

A tingling sensation took hold in Liz's temples. Her heart thumped as though it wanted to jump out of her chest. "I absolutely did no such thing. You have been dishonest for months now. I would have come home back in September, but oh no. *You* decided unilaterally that there was no need. You ordered me to stay away. Said you'd never speak to me again if I disrupted my career over one little episode. From what I've seen tonight, you can hardly handle yourself, much less a man twice your size in the late stages of dementia." Her words echoed throughout the house, then the room settled into a profound silence. Liz took a couple of steps back from Mom, whose silences often preceded explosions of monumental proportions.

Mom's lips thinned and a hard expression filled her eyes. "Alzheimer's." Her voice was quiet and her tone calm.

Liz's head jerked back. "What?"

"If you're going to lecture me, *Dr.* Reams, at least get your terms correct. Your father has Alzheimer's and it's mid-stage, not late-stage."

Words failed Liz. Her head tilted slightly as she tried to decide what she might say to get Mom to see that Dad was beyond her ability to care for him. Nothing productive came to mind. Liz felt Hugh move to her side. He took her hand and gave it a little squeeze.

Hugh cleared his throat. A quick smile lifted the corners of his mouth. "Ladies, this situation has got to be very painful for both of you. It's late. Perhaps we should all go to bed and try to get some sleep. In the morning, you two can continue your . . . discussion. I'll take James for a walk or entertain him in some other way so y'all can have some privacy."

Shame and gratitude filled Liz in equal measure. "Look, Mom. I'm sorry I yelled at you. Hugh's right. It's late and fighting isn't going to solve anything. Can we help you get Dad to bed?"

All eyes shifted to the spot where Dad had been standing. Since they would have seen him pass them had he left by the front door, Liz and Mom rushed toward the back of the house where a door led from the kitchen to the backyard. It was not until she heard Hugh's voice, that Liz realized he had not followed them.

"He's in here." A chuckle drifted from the bedroom. At the sound of their approach, Hugh turned toward them and grinned. "James has apparently put himself to bed."

From the other side of the room, Dad's voice rang as true as what Liz remembered from her childhood. "Damned right I went to bed. Nobody wants to be around Elizabeth and Lillian when they go at it." Dad gave Hugh a conspiratorial look. "You know what teenaged girls and their mothers are like. All drama, all the time." With that, Dad rolled toward the wall and pulled the covers up to his chin.

Mom cut her eyes to Liz. She smiled, then she giggled. The laughter was contagious. Within moments, she, Hugh, and Mom held their sides while trying to control snorts and chortles. They turned as a body and fled to the living room. Wiping her eyes, Liz leaned against the fireplace mantle and looked down at her mother's equally tear-soaked cheeks. They fell into each other's arms and laughed until the sound became choked, and they were near hysterics. When she finally caught her breath, Liz leaned back and held her mother at arm's length.

"Mom, you look tired, and I know I'm exhausted. Let's go to bed."

Mom cast her gaze over Hugh. "I suppose he's going to sleep in your room. We only have beds in two rooms now."

Liz glanced at Hugh. The apples of his cheeks flamed and deepened to the color of ripe pomegranates. "Lillian, I'll get a hotel room. I don't want to intrude or violate your sense of propriety. I'll call a cab right now."

Mom grabbed Hugh's arm as he started to tap on his cell phone. "You'll do no such thing." Mom stopped speaking and her expression became earnest. "Just make an honest woman of my daughter. That's all I ask. And sooner rather than later. We want her to be happy, and we think you're the man for the job. We love her more than anything, you know."

The flames reached the tops of Hugh's ears. His mouth became a thin line as he glanced at Liz. "I've tried. So far, she's refused to give me an answer."

Mom's gaze ran over Hugh. "I didn't take you for someone who would give up easily. Keep at it. She'll cave eventually. She always does."

Just when Liz thought Mom had softened, had become more like other mothers, the demonstrative, supportive, doting kind, she ups and shoots yet again another zinger. *Thanks, Mom. Love you too.* It hurt all the more because both of them knew exactly what Mom referred to. Too tired to keep the skirmish going, Liz shot her mother what she hoped was a withering look and moved toward the hallway stairs to the second story, dragging Hugh along in her wake.

Hugh paused on the top step and glanced into the room opposite Liz's childhood bedroom. "Why did they get rid of the bed in here? Do they really think you and your brother will never again be home at the same time?"

"Jake's bed was shot by the time he joined the Marines, so they got rid of it. They haven't replaced it yet. Mom says she'll get around to it some time." Liz waved toward a stack of boxes at the room's center. "For now, she uses it for storage. In fairness, she doesn't have time for shopping now."

Liz paused at the door to her old room and glanced around. Nothing had changed here since she and Mom redecorated when she turned thirteen. The same sweet pink-ribbon-striped and daisy-sprinkled wallpaper covered the walls. The same pink cushions sat on the window seat where she had spent hours reading and dreaming about the future. The same white and gold French Provencal furniture bore evidence of years of sleepovers and friends hanging out—not badly marred, just enough to show that the room had been lived in and loved by a teenaged girl. Frilly organza pink bedspreads that she wouldn't be caught dead using as an adult had filled her younger heart with joy. She went to the twin beds and lifted a corner of each bedspread. Sure enough, the white and yellow daisy print sheets were in place. They emitted the fragrance of the floral scented fabric softener Mom always used. They smelled like home.

Liz knew her mother loved her. This room proved it. Mom saved little bits of her housekeeping money for years to give Liz this room. The bubble of irritation Liz had carried up the stairs with her after their confrontation burst in a rush of affection, but it was tinged with a touch of guilt and an old sense of burden created by expectations. Liz could never interact with her mother without conflicting emotions surging at some point. Mom gave so much. She loved so much. But in return, she expected so much. Did all family relationships have a price attached or was it simply Liz's reaction to a mother who pushed her to achieve what the mother never had a chance to do? Liz pushed her hair behind her ears and sighed.

Hugh moved up behind her and whispered in her ear, a hint of humor coloring his words, "A less confident man might feel threatened sleeping in this room." He slipped his arms around her waist and kissed the nape of her neck. Liz relaxed against his chest. Her stress melted away in the safety of his arms. "A less-confident man certainly wouldn't make any moves on his lady in this room, but I grew up with a sister who was pure girly-girl. I understand pink. I hold it no ill will neither do I fear it."

Liz laughed and turned to face him. She slipped her arms around his neck as he bent to kiss her. How this man managed to stir her senses no matter the circumstances always amazed her. As the kiss lingered, their bodies pressed together. The pink room in no way dampened his ardor despite the distance they had traveled and lateness of the hour.

The sun slanting through the bedroom window inched over Liz's face until it reached her closed lids. The sounds of breakfast preparations and fragrance of frying bacon floating up from the kitchen brought her fully awake. She yawned, rolled over, and peeked at the other bed. No Hugh. After sitting up and sliding her feet into her slippers, she wandered down to the kitchen in search of him. She found him dressed in jeans and a t-shirt with one of her mother's frilly aprons tied around his waist standing at the stove pushing a spatula around a pan of eggs. She stopped in the doorway, her steps halted by the wave of love that swept through her. Hugh never ceased to amaze her. She had never known someone so comfortable in his own skin, so full of quiet confidence. He possessed the kind confidence that produced consideration and kindness, the kind that made other people feel better about themselves rather than that they were less than he.

The emotion swelling beneath her breastbone lifted the corners of her mouth, but the fountain of coffee bubbling up in Mom's old percolator brought joy to her soul. Mom and Dad refused to give up that old pot. Liz loved it too. The fresh-roasted fragrance drew her to the kitchen counter. In some ways, her relationship with Hugh had been helped along by their mutual love of good coffee. Hugh kept the departmental coffee room supplied with the kind she liked once he knew her preference. When she went for a cup, he would accidentally need a refill too. His little game of the past now made both of them laugh when they talked about it.

Filling a mug, she added sugar and milk until the liquid turned the color of Mom's homemade caramel sauce. Maybe that was why she liked her coffee like that, because it looked like home. Mom always said Liz had the metabolism of a hummingbird. She never gained weight from all that sugar in her coffee. Liz took a long sip. The tawny liquid rolled down her throat, smooth and soothing. Aw, coffee—her life's blood since the study marathons of college. It was just possible that coffee had become her addiction, and Hugh made the best she had ever tasted, rich and strong enough to stand up to her heavy-handed additions. Reaching for his mug, she filled it, but added nothing else. He liked his black.

He turned to put the skillet on a trivet and bent to kiss her a quick good morning. "Feeling better after some rest?"

"Um-hum. Did you sleep okay in all that pink?"

Hugh chuckled and nodded. "Like I said last night, I have no problem with pink."

Liz pursed her lips and waggled her brows at him. "I thought you might have said that simply as a ruse for what you hoped would come next."

"Yeah? Well, it worked, didn't it?"

Liz play punched him on the shoulder and kissed him on the cheek. "You don't have to play games for that, you know."

"But it makes it more fun, don't you think?"

"I suppose." Liz caught sight of her father's favorite coffee mug in pride of place on an open shelf above the counter and her mood shifted. She couldn't stay upbeat for long considering the purpose of their trip. She rolled her lower lip between her teeth in concentration. "Tell me the truth. What do you think about Daddy's condition?"

Hugh stopped putting bread in the toaster and searched Liz's face. He didn't answer for several beats. When he finally spoke, his voice was quiet, almost hesitant. "I think he is beyond what a woman your mother's age can or should be caring for 24/7. But it's not my call or my decision. My opinion really doesn't count. It's what you think that matters."

Liz sighed. "You're right on all counts, of course. I keep hoping some way will present itself to not have to tangle with Mom over this. So far, nothing brilliant or even remotely sensible has come along."

"Maybe you should wait for your aunt before you tackle the subject. She said she'd be here whenever you called. Your mom and dad aren't up yet. Let it rest until later today."

After breakfast, Liz and Hugh settled in the living room and opened their laptops to clear their emails. With that job finished, Liz worked on organizing her notes from her conversations with Consuelo and Rich's father. She read them and reread them. The longer they waited for Mom and Dad to appear, the tighter the muscles at the base of Liz's skull wound. At 10:30, she could bear it no longer. She tiptoed to their door and eased it open just a crack. "Mom?"

Opening the door a bit wider, she slipped into the room. The beds were empty. "Mom?" Again no answer. The room was too small for anyone to hide in. She went to the closest and opened the door. Nothing.

Running back to the living room, she managed to shout over the pounding of her heart. "Help me search the rest of the house. They aren't in their room."

Chapter 25

Sam watched in consternation as Rebecca leaned across the bed and grabbed both of his wrists. She leaned in until their noses were only inches apart. "Say it again."

"Say what?"

"Say you love me." She squeezed hard enough to make him wince. Who knew there was so much strength in those little hands? "I'm not letting go until you say it."

Any intention he had of keeping his promise to her mother dissolved under the pressure of her fingers, replaced by fire traveling up his arms and into his heart. Despite her being a half foot shorter than he and at least sixty pounds lighter, Sam was lost. He could no more fulfill his promise to discourage their relationship than fly to Mars. In fact, the latter might be easier. He glanced toward the window trying to break the spell cast by her touch.

She jerked his arms. "Look at me, and say it."

He opened his mouth intending to tell her to let go, to leave the room, that they could never be. Her gaze, regal and demanding, clouded his brain, turning him into her willing subject. "I'm not right for you, but I doubt I'll ever love anyone else."

The sun rose in her face. "Good. That's very reassuring. So here's how it is." She released his wrists and raised her left hand with fingers spread. With her right index finger, she ticked off her list. "One. We love each other. Two. My parents don't want you for a son-in-law. Three. I love my parents and don't want to hurt them unless I have to." She tilted her head to one side and waggled her eyebrows. "Ergo, we have a job ahead of us. We've got to find a way to change their minds."

Sam's head spun from the onslaught of her words and the emotions they engendered. "Aren't you moving a little fast? Love is one thing. Marriage is in a whole other country. Besides, you're too young to get married."

"Sheesh. And just when I thought we'd made a breakthrough." Her lips formed a thin line. Her eyes narrowed. "Ok. Let's review. You love me. I love you. You will never love anyone else, which means your life is pretty much going to be a garbage dump without me. I can see you in thirty years. Old, too wrinkled for a woman to want to look at, and a complete grump because you missed out on the love of your life."

Her head tilted to one side, her index finger tapped the side of her chin, and her gaze drifted toward the ceiling. "Yeah, I can see how that might work out really well for you." She dropped her gaze to look directly at him. Laughter danced in her eyes. "Or, we get married, have a bunch of kids, and live happily ever after. Yep, I can see how not marrying me is the thing to do." She stopped short and became very still. The humor slipped from her expression. Anger took its place. "Or, maybe you think you'll be getting a certain something from me without putting a ring on my finger." She leaned in and poked his chest in rhythm with her words. "Hell will freeze over first, buster. I may look like a flapper, but I'm also a good girl. Chaste, like Mama says. My knickers stay firmly where they belong until my wedding night."

Heat rose from Sam's cheeks to the tops of his ears. His hands flew up in a gesture of self-defense, palms out, fingers spread. "Hold on. I'm not like that. But about marriage, the guy is supposed to ask, and you didn't even give me a chance."

"Oh, really? Like you were going to get off the pot anytime this century?" Sarcasm colored her words, but the humor had returned to her eyes.

"I guess that's fair." Sam sucked on his lower lip. Apparently, it was up to him to think logically in a situation so driven by pure emotion. Rebecca wasn't being realistic about a future together, so he had to be mature and farsighted for both of them.

He drew a long breath and let it out slowly. "Okay. Say we get married. Are you prepared to live with Bateman breathing down your neck and ruling your life?" An edge sounded in his voice. "Because that's how it would be. Are you prepared to live in a storeroom behind a speakeasy because your husband is in debt to a big-time gangster? Are you prepared to be scared all the time?" His final words came out raw, filled with fear and hatred.

Rebecca's face fell. Her confidence slipped away. The joy that lit her face shifted. Doubt and unhappiness clouded her features as tears welled up in her eyes. And he had done this to her. In that moment, Sam's hatred of Bateman turned inward on himself. He had hurt this precious girl. He hadn't meant for his voice to be so cutting, so filled with sarcasm, so filled with rage. Despite his promise and his belief that he would ruin her life, Sam couldn't stand it. He reached out and drew her to himself, his arms forming a barrier against the world to shield her from the reality of his life. Her arms slipped around his torso. They clung to one another as though the world would end in the next moment.

He nestled his lips against her ear. "I'm sorry. That was brutal, but you have to see it now. You've got to understand that I'm the last person you should love."

She laid her face against his chest. "Too late. The deed is done. So what are you going to do to make this right?"

He had no idea, but any resolve he had about living without her melted in the tears that fell from her cheeks onto his chest. His arms released her. He cupped each side of her face with his hands and lifted so that she looked up into his eyes. Using his thumbs, he wiped away her tears and bent down until their lips met.

~ ~ ~

The weeks following Sam's recovery passed peacefully. He and Rebecca kept the secret of their growing love without anyone suspecting. Her parents never seemed to notice the glances that passed between them or the accidental touches of their hands as they worked together in the bakery kitchen. The quiet family life of the period during Bateman's previous absence returned, and Sam began to wonder if maybe it would last this time. A small storm in July blew the awning off the front window, giving Sam an opportunity to ingratiate himself to Mr. Scheinberg as he worked on the cleanup and replacement. Mrs. Scheinberg baked a cake for their mutual August 1 birthday, though she had no idea that Rebecca tapped Sam's foot under the table in time to the singing of "Happy Birthday" or that he turned eighteen on the exact day her daughter celebrated her seventeenth. Life felt close to normal, almost like when Sam was a boy and his father was alive.

In September, Rebecca began a course at the local business school so that she would be able to become the bakery's bookkeeper/secretary. Sam spent his time making deliveries by bicycle during the day and cleaning the speakeasy after it closed at night.

On a sultry afternoon in early September, Sam leaned the delivery bike against end of the bakery's back porch and glanced toward the door, which stood open to allow heat from the ovens to escape onto the river, for all the good that did. The day had started with a watery sunrise, the clouds strange in their patterns and unusual in how they just hung over the city neither moving lower nor moving west along their normal path. Sam had seen plenty of rainclouds, but these were different in a way he couldn't quite figure out. He glanced toward the sky, tugged his handkerchief from his back pocket, and ran it across his face. To the east, a line too dark even for midday ran along the horizon. Not a whisper of a breeze stirred the palms along the street. The atmosphere sat like murky puddles in the lungs and raised rivers of sweat on the brow. The air smelled of rain, but none fell.

Instead of going into the kitchen, Sam went to the faucet at the base of the porch steps and soaked his face and head. The inferno inside could wait another minute or two.

"That you, boy?"

Sam's stomach turned over. He looked up toward the location from which the voice had come. Bile rose. Sam swallowed hard to keep it from spewing onto the ground at his feet. Bateman stood behind the screen door, his face obscured by the shadows.

"Haul your ass out to the dock. We got work to do."

The screen slammed and the gangster stomped down to the dock where a sport fisherman squatted against the pilings. The speedboat was nowhere in sight.

"See to that bow line and hustle. We gotta go." Sam had never seen the man show fear, but it colored his words and flared in his eyes. "We may've already left it too late."

Sam climbed down to the deck and settled on the seat beside the wheel under the canopy. Bateman pushed the throttle full forward, and the boat jerked into action. Within seconds, they were bouncing over the water headed toward the river's mouth and the Atlantic.

The wind became higher, the waves grew fiercer, and the horizon grew darker the farther east they went. Apprehension filled Sam with each nautical mile the boat covered. In the few months spent in Miami, he had learned that summer rain was a frequent occurrence in south Florida. In fact, you could set your watch by the daily four o'clock showers, but this looked and felt different. If a weather formation could be said to possess emotion, billowing rage described what they were speeding toward. Sam leaned forward and tapped Bateman on the shoulder.

The older man sneered as he looked behind him. "What the hell do you want?"

"Don't you think we should turn back? That sky looks dangerous."

"How the fuck would you know? You're just a sniveling New York Kike. Sit down, and shut your yap."

After another few miles fighting an ever-growing headwind, a boat Sam did not recognize raced toward them with someone on board frantically waving a white flag. Bateman pulled back on the throttle, coming to a stop as the other boat came alongside.

A silver-haired gentleman in a sweat-stained white linen shirt leaned over the railing of a cabin cruiser. "Turn back now. Get to shelter as fast as you can. There's a tremendous blow coming. Word came up from the southern islands to Bimini. So long and good luck." With that, the cabin cruiser's bow lifted, and the vessel flew away toward Miami.

Bateman took his lower lip between his teeth while giving the eastern horizon a long, searching stare. He obviously struggled with whether to go forward or do as the stranger advised. His mouth became a thin line. Finally, he slapped the boat's side.

"Shit. A whole load of prime hooch is gonna be blown the hell and gone into the goddamn ocean."

He gave the wheel a vicious jerk and the boat leaned onto its side doing a 180 degree turn. Bateman shoved the throttle forward, and they raced off in the direction from which they had come. Sam said a quick prayer of thanks for the Good Samaritan who had flagged them down. That man clearly had more sense than Bateman, but of course most people did. Sam laid his head against the padded seat back and closed his eyes. Relief to be headed away from danger instead of rushing toward it allowed him to relax a little. Sleep crept in.

A sudden deluge slapped Sam in the face, soaking him to the skin within seconds. He sat up and squinted toward the horizon. Miami made a dark line across the edge of the earth. By the time they reached the river's mouth, the wind blew hard, making it feel like the boat traveled sideways. The rain came at them on a slant so sharp it seemed it might actually pierce the skin. By the time they were alongside the Granada Grill and Apartments, tree tops and pieces of roofing flew above their heads. Sam leaned over and placed his lips as close to his boss's ear as he dared.

"Where are we going?"

"Warehouse."

Sam's pulse raced. "Pull in at the bakery. Please. The Scheinburgs should be taken to safety. That old building won't stand if this gets much worse."

Bateman shoved Sam hard. He landed on the slick seat and slid to the floor. Scrambling to his feet, Sam leaned toward his boss once more.

"Stop and get them. You've got to. You can't leave a whole family to die."

"I ain't stopping for nobody. Stay back, or I'll dump your ass in the river."

Rebecca and her family would die if Sam didn't force Bateman to stop for them. He was sure of it. The wind howled around the buildings along the river bringing debris with it. Bateman struggled to keep the boat aimed upriver as they pushed on. Day became demi-night with rain so intense it cut visibility to a few feet. The bakery had to be nearby at this point. Sam had traveled the river enough to know where the landmarks were even in this storm. In a few moments, it would be too late to make the turn toward the bakery. The wind was becoming too strong.

Sam had no weapon, no way of forcing the gangster to do his bidding. One thing for sure, though, this boat was Rebecca's only chance. Bateman was taller and heavier by a good bit. Sam feared his boss more than anyone he had ever known. Sam closed his eyes and saw Rebecca's face filled with fear. He heard her voice pleading for help. Desperation won out over fear.

He grabbed the wheel and yanked it hard. The boat jerked in response. Bateman, his face a study in pure rage and hatred, turned on Sam and slammed a fist into his temple. The blow left Sam dizzy, but not out. The frenzied rain blowing in through the bridge roof's open sides became an ally in his fight to remain conscious. From his position lying across the seat next to the wheel, Sam looked up at his enemy. His heart pounded, but it wasn't fear that drove him. Rage burned in him with an intensity he never knew possible. This terrible man, this gangster, this damned goy bastard refused to help innocent people, people Sam loved. There had to be a way to make the son-of-a-bitch stop for them. Then it came to him. By knocking Sam flat, Bateman just might have put him in an unexpected position of power. There would only be one chance to get it right. He would have to make it count the first time or he was dead. The gangster would have no qualms about killing him. It had to be now.

Lifting his feet, Sam used his heavy work-boots like a battering ram against the man's head. The blow broke Bateman's grip on the wheel. A second blow to the head and Bateman slumped against the boat's edge. Sam jumped up and grabbed the gangster by the belt. Using strength driven by rage and fear, he lifted the much heavier man until his torso balanced on the boat's side. One more heft and Bateman tumbled overboard. The only sound he made was that of his shoes banging against the side as he tumbled into the river.

The boat careened out of control, nearly sending Sam to join his boss overboard. He grabbed the wheel and peered through the driving rain. The boat rushed straight toward a dark form sticking up out of the water. Sam jerked the wheel hard left as he sped past the pilings of an old pier. He wondered momentarily if the SOB had come to and was flailing around, but he didn't stop, and he didn't look back. Rebecca would die if he didn't get to her fast.

Chapter 26

Searching the small house and backyard took very little time. Still no sign of Mom and Dad and the car was still in the garage. Liz went to the front porch and rushed down the steps. She looked up and down the street, straining for a glimpse of them without result. Where on earth could they be, and how had they gotten out of the house without her hearing or seeing them? Taking her phone from her jeans pocket, she pressed the call button. Aunt Mildred answered on the first ring.

"They've disappeared." Liz heard the high and screechy quality of her voice but didn't try to control it. "Do you have any idea where they could have gone?"

"No. I'm coming over right now. Stay where you are." Mildred ended the call before Liz could say anything else.

She took one more hard look in either direction on the street before she turned back to the front steps. Hugh waited for her on the porch.

"Have you tried your mom's cell?"

"Mom refuses to join the modern world. Bedouins traveling the Sahara have cell phones. Mongols living in yurts have them. Sherpas climbing the Himalayas have them, but not Mom. She insists they're a waste of money because she doesn't go out much and never travels. It's been inconvenient in the past, but now it's downright dangerous."

"Looks like it's time for some changes here."

"You bet there are going to be changes. Mom and Dad have clearly gone beyond any shred of common sense."

Liz's mouth narrowed to a thin line as she placed her fists on her hips. "The way they are living is simply insane."

Hugh took Liz's hand and led her to the old, metal porch-glider where they sat waiting as instructed. Within fifteen minutes, a car whipped up against the curb. A sharp application of the brakes sent tires sliding along the gravel in the gutter. The driver door flew open and a head of white, tightly curled hair popped up just above the doorframe. Aunt Mildred shoved the car door closed and paused to wave before bustling up the front steps to join them on the porch. Hugh's southern training took over as he jumped to his feet. Mildred came to rest at Hugh's elbow, her head just reaching the lower part of his shoulder. Liz stood with arms outstretched. Keeping her ample bosom tucked in the curve created by hunched forward shoulders, Mildred leaned out and stretched up to peck Liz on the cheek. After giving Hugh the same, she turned glittering eyes on her niece. Perpetual motion and dynamo always came to mind when Mildred, Mom's much-older sister, whirled into Liz's life. It was a good thing she was tiny. The world probably wasn't ready for a larger version.

"Still no word on your parents?" Liz shook her head. "Have you called the police?"

"Not yet."

"No time like the present. Give me your phone."

"Aunt Mildred, the police usually won't take a missing person's report until twenty-four hours have passed."

"Just pass me the phone, please."

Instead of pressing 911 as Liz expected, Mildred tapped in an entire number. A couple of rings and they heard a male voice answer.

"Hi, Virgil. Yes, it's me. Borrowed phone." After an exchange of pleasantries, Mildred took charge of the conversation. "Listen, Virg, I need a favor. Uh-huh, you guessed it. Nope. No idea. Last time he tried to get on the

Whidbey Ferry. My sister's gone too. Probably trying to find him before anyone notices they're gone. Yes, it's silly, I know, but she's lost perspective lately. The car?" Mildred looked at Liz who shook her head and pointed to the garage. "Still here. That would be great. Thanks ever so much. Give my love to Roberta."

Liz cocked her head to one side. "So who is Virgil, and what can he do?"

Mildred smiled sweetly and patted Liz's arm. "Seattle PD Chief. His wife, Roberta, and I play bridge every week. We are all also members of the same small, group supper-club at church. Nice people. Good friends. Great guy to know in a crisis."

Mildred never ceased to amaze. Liz chuckled. "Is there anyone you don't know?"

Mildred pursed her lips in thought. "The governor. He was elected during Harold's last illness." Mildred's smile weakened a little at the mention of her deceased husband. "So, I didn't meet the governor, but he's going to speak to the Seattle League of Women Voters in a few weeks. He's up for re-election, you know."

No, Liz didn't know. Washington state politics were the furthest thing from her mind and completely beside the point, but Mildred's wide-ranging connections might prove to be a godsend. "It's fabulous that Virgil is willing to help."

"He'll see that they're found. He said for at least one of us to stay at the house, so Hugh, why don't you come with me? I've got a couple of ideas where to look, but I'll need help if we find them. Liz, call us if they come home while we're out."

Mildred took Hugh's arm and tugged him toward her vehicle. He shot an enquiring look at Liz, who hunched her shoulders, grinned, and shook her head. Hugh got the message that resistance was hopeless. He followed meekly and did as instructed. Mildred was a force of nature, just like Mom.

With nothing else to do but wait, Liz returned to the living room and plopped down on the sofa. She opened her laptop and tried to focus on her Moshe Toblinsky project, but with every sound of an approaching car, her gaze darted to the front window. In about an hour, her vigilance was rewarded. A police cruiser pulled up to the curb with two white-haired heads huddled together in the back seat. A burly giant of a patrolman stepped from the driver's seat and went around to open the door for Mom and Dad. Instinct told Liz to stay at the window and observe them when they didn't know she was watching. Greater truth was often revealed in this way.

Mom and Dad exited the back seat looking disheveled, their nightclothes rumpled and stained by God only knew what. Mom appeared at her wit's end. The expression on her face communicated she was as confused as Dad. When the officer bent down to speak to her, she didn't seem to understand at first, then a look of extreme relief spread over her exhausted features, and she allowed the young man to take her elbow in one hand and Dad's in the other. Dad resisted at first, but Mom peered around the officer's chest and said something. Dad settled into a docile shuffle and together, the trio made their slow progress up toward the house.

A growing anger at herself and Mom mingled with relief coursed through Liz. Mom had bullied her into staying away, and she had told obvious lies under the guise of supporting Liz's career. Those acts were perhaps understandable given Mom's nature and history. Maybe. Mom never lost sight of what she had given up when she got married right after college graduation. She had put her deep love of historical research on the shelf in favor of teaching high school and having children. By all accounts, she had been a wonderful teacher who inspired her students to go out into the world and make something of themselves, but she never let her family forget that she could have accomplished so much more if she had the time and opportunities.

The fact that she tried to relive her life through her daughter's career sometimes galled Liz and goaded her into keeping things to herself. Mom wanted a constitutional lawyer in the family. She had nominated her daughter for that honor, so Liz's choice of history of American crime appalled Mom, but she still devoted herself to supporting Liz's career to the detriment of the truth and common sense. Well, Mom had made her choices. Just when it seemed like Liz might explode in frustration, a jolt of realization seared her mind and heart.

Perhaps she subconsciously wanted to believe Mom could handle Dad by herself. Liz's own complicity in the deception and acquiesce to bullying had to be acknowledged. After all, going to Seattle earlier in the semester would have been very disruptive to her teaching and her research. She would probably not have met Rich Whitehead, his father, or his Aunt Consuelo. At the thought of missing out on their momentous revelations, Liz's heart beat a little faster.

Dear lord, what kind of person had she become? Had she really put her career before her parents' wellbeing? Mom raised Liz to believe she could have it all, but what did that really mean? Was it even possible? At this point, Liz couldn't be sure. So far, she seemed to be striking out in every aspect of life except her career.

Wait a minute. That was completely unfair. Hugh had asked her to marry him, but she kept putting him off for reasons that weren't clear even to her. Liz drew a deep, quivering breath and let it out slowly. Hugh deserved better than her flippant responses to his proposals. Mom and Daddy deserved more from her than the weekly obligatory call where they only got a portion of her attention at best. But how could she give Hugh an answer when she didn't know the answer herself? What held her back? She had no idea. And how could she stay on top of Mom and Dad's situation from 3,000 miles away? Had she followed the navy pilot to escape responsibilities she didn't want to deal with? Geez, that made her a real self-absorbed bitch.

The door opened and Mom and Dad shuffled inside. The officer smiled inquiringly at Liz while he led the pair to the sofa.

"Thank you so much for finding my parents and bringing them home. We've been so worried."

The officer nodded. "I was happy to help, ma'am."

"Where did you find them?"

"Sitting on the curb near the Whidbey Ferry."

Shock blazed through Liz. "My lord, that's nearly five miles from here."

"Yes, ma'am." The officer hesitated before speaking again. "I'm afraid I had a hard time getting your dad in the cruiser."

"I can only imagine. I'm sorry for any trouble they may have caused."

A tight smile lifted the corners of the officer's mouth. "It's all part of the job. I just didn't want them to say something later that you might not understand."

"Believe me. I would understand completely. I know how difficult they can be. Well, if that's all, I don't think we should take any more of your time. I'm sure you have other things to do besides chasing down wandering parents."

Liz thought the officer would turn to go, but he stayed in place, shifting from one foot to the other. When the silence drew on, a serious expression replaced the one of professional affability on his pleasant features.

"I hope you won't think me out of line, ma'am, but my conscience won't let me leave without speaking." Here it came. Condemnation and accusation, both of which she deserved. "I couldn't help noticing that your dad has serious memory issues. Is your mother his sole caregiver?"

"I'm afraid she is, but that's going to change."

Out of the corner of her eye, Liz saw Mom bow up. "Nothing is going to change, and you're going back to Florida tomorrow."

"We will discuss that later, Mom." Liz turned back to the officer. "Clearly things have gotten out of hand here, but I will be making some corrections before I return to my job."

The officer smiled and extended his hand. "I'm glad to hear that. I'd hate to have to call Senior Services."

The implied threat was not lost on Liz. She took his hand in a firm grip and shook it. "I assure you this is the last you will be seeing of us."

"Well, you take care now."

Liz accompanied the officer to the door where he paused and reached into his pocket. "Call me if you need help again." With that, he gave Liz his card and left.

When she turned away from the door, a red-faced fury advanced upon her. Mom shook with rage. "How dare you speak about me as though I'm not present or mentally incompetent. I've taken care of your father for years now without your help, Dr. Reams, and I don't intend to stop just because you came running home at the first sign of trouble."

"Mom, please. Let's not do this now. Let me make a call, and I'll help both of you get to bed. You need rest."

"Don't tell me what I need. I goddamned well know what I need. It's for you to go back to Florida and make something of yourself. I didn't work so hard all this years to see you give up."

"That's not going to happen. Now, it's time for bed for you two."

Liz reached out to take her mother's hand. Mom snatched it away. "I'm perfectly capable of putting myself and your father to bed. When we awake, please be so good as to have eggs and bacon ready. You do remember how to cook, don't you?"

Liz turned away before she lost it somewhere between

anger and misery. Tears rose as she reached for her phone to let Mildred and Hugh know one drama was over. She didn't have the heart to mention that another one was about to start.

Chapter 27

Sam fought to keep the boat in the channel. It was almost impossible to figure out his exact location. Driving rain kept visibility low, but the bakery dock had to be close by. He ran a hand across his eyes. The force of the storm was so strong that if he missed the dock, he might not be able to turn back. The engine roared in the struggle against the storm's westward drive. With the bakery on the eastern bank, the going was becoming a serious struggle. Sam's muscles ached and trembled with the strain of staying on course. He sensed the boat drew near the bakery and Rebecca, but the storm's rage turned everything on the riverbank into hazy, unrecognizable shadows. Sam's heart rate increased with each lashing of rain or howl from the wind. He strained for a glimpse of the familiar rectangle anchored to the wooden bulkhead.

Unexpectedly, the storm began to ease. It was like some giant hand slowly turned off a faucet. The rain slacked off and the river current didn't fight him so much. In a few moments more, weak sunshine broke between the heavy clouds highlighting the bakery only a few feet ahead. If this could be called good luck, Sam would take it. Maybe the storm had moved on. Realistically, that was probably too much to hope for. During the small hurricane back in June, this let up had happened only for the storm to come back full force.

Sam studied the height of the river against the bulkheads lining the bank. Water lapped over the tops. Normally, the river lay a good three feet or so below the bank's edge. The respite from wind and rain also revealed that the bakery porch listed to the left and the speakeasy's staircase was missing. That couldn't be good. Sam's heart thumped harder in his chest. Rebecca was somewhere inside a building that had suffered the storm's pummeling, but neighboring structures had fared worse. Everywhere entire buildings had been pushed off their foundations, flattened, or shoved into the river. The whole area looked like photographs of villages destroyed by mortars during the Great War. When the calm passed, there was no telling if the bakery would continue to be habitable. How much time did they have to load the family into the boat and head inland before the deluge started again? It was anyone's guess.

Sam guided the boat to the bakery dock, tied off the bow line, and ran to the back porch. He pounded on the locked door. Maybe the family had already left for higher, safer ground. He jiggled the knob again, then pressed his face against the door's window. The kitchen and shop beyond lay in darkness. No kerosene lamps lit any interior space. Sam stepped out onto the bank and surveyed the secondary story. No signs of life came through the windows. He went back to the door for one more try. As he raised his fist to knock, the sound of feet pounding down the stairs echoed from within and Rebecca's face appeared in the glass. The door flew open, and she threw her arms around him.

"I thought you had drowned in the ocean. How did you get here?" Rebecca sobbed against his shoulder.

He wrapped his arms around her, his voice gruff with emotion when he spoke. He told her about the stranger's warning and how he had fought Bateman to get to her.

"You left him in the river?" Her voice contained surprise and something else. God, she seemed to think he had done the wrong thing.

"You want I should go back for him?" He had done the right thing, the only thing he could do to save Rebecca. Still, her question gut punched him.

She hiccoughed and looked up at him with a watery smile. "No. Not really. I just . . . oh, I don't know what I think."

"I think it is best for everyone that Mr. Bateman will not be joining us." Mr. Scheinberg's voice came from the staircase, his tone soft and low. Sam's gaze shot toward him. The rest of the family peered at him from behind Rebecca's father.

"Sir, we've got to get all of you out of here. The river's rising and the building looks like it's been damaged pretty bad. This calm may not last much longer."

"Where would we go and how?"

Sam pointed toward the dock. "I've got a boat. There's a place I know back in the Glades. It looks like a huge shack from the outside, but inside, it's built like a fortress. It will hold during the storm."

Mrs. Scheinberg peered around her husband. "We can't take the children out in this." Her shrill voice rolled around the quiet kitchen. "We can't leave the bakery. It will be looted."

"Ma'am, you don't have a choice. If you stay here, all of you will most likely be washed away. This storm will pick up again and the river is already over the bulkhead. You haven't seen what it looks like out there. There's a lot of damage, and it will only get worse."

Mr. Scheinberg placed his hand on his wife's arm when she drew a loud breath. "I think we must do as Samuel suggests, Mama. We've already felt the building shift. He is right. It may not withstand another assault from the storm."

Mrs. Scheinberg's eyes glittered with desperation. "But our home in Miami Beach. We can't leave it to the thieves."

"My dear, in all likelihood the house is no longer standing. It is time to seek shelter elsewhere." Rebecca's father looked back at Sam. "Can you help me gather the account books, the cash register, and empty the safe? There is no reason to leave those things for the looters. We should fill jugs with water and empty the larder."

"Of course, sir, but we shouldn't stay here much longer." Sam held Rebecca at arm's length. "Can you help get the children to the boat? There's a cabin that is dry and big enough for all of you. I will need your father's help at the wheel."

"Can't I help you and Daddy once we are under way? Surely more sets of eyes would be better."

"No, I need for you to stay below and keep everyone calm. Look at the kids. They're scared to death. Your mother is going to need your help taking care of them."

While Sam filled jugs with water from the kitchen tap, Mr. Scheinberg gathered account books and the cash box. Sam scanned the kitchen. Satisfied that nothing useful had been left unpacked, he and Rebecca's father headed for the boat. They followed one another down the narrow dock. At the sounds of frightened voices, Sam stopped and looked back toward the bakery. Rebecca herded the children down the steps onto to the dock, the older two boys lugging baskets of food, but there was no sign of her mother.

"Mr. Scheinberg, stay and help the kids. I've got more water jugs to get. I'll go look for Mrs. Scheinberg."

Sam raced to the kitchen and stopped at the larder door. Mrs. Scheinberg turned from one item to the next, filling baskets to overflowing.

"We've got to go. Please." Sam picked up one basket.

"No. Wait. Just a few more things." Her voice quivered. She held up a bunch of dark-skinned bananas in a trembling hand. "We may need these." She took a closer look, shook her head, and put them back on the shelf. "No, they're too ripe. We need something fresher."

Her dithering chewed up precious minutes. Sam picked up the other basket. "We'll take these to the boat now." Trying to reason with her seemed fruitless at this point. Maybe she would just follow if he led the way. The sound of her shoes tapping on the linoleum behind him gave him the answer.

Once they were all aboard, Sam placed a hand on Rebecca's arm and leaned in close to whisper. "There are life preservers down there. I don't know how many, so start with the kids."

She looked at him with frightened eyes. "But you and Daddy will need them too."

"We don't have time to argue." Sam gave her a little push. "Get down there now. If there are any life jackets left, pass them up after you've seen to the kids, yourself, and your mother." Sam's rough whisper came through gritted teeth. He hated himself for speaking harshly, but time was running out.

Sam heard the sounds of storage area doors opening and closing. The kids' frightened voices came up through the open hatch door as they asked how to put the vests on. No life preservers came up to the wheel deck.

Sam closed the hatch door and looked east. The sun still hovered listlessly in the watery sky, but dark, swirling clouds were moving inland like ocean waves. It wouldn't be long before the hurricane was on them again. He pushed the throttle forward. His fingers itched to shove it full open, but speed had to be balanced with avoiding the debris that float all around them, and more dangerously, lay submerged out of sight. Mr. Scheinberg stood beside him scanning the river. The second pair of eyes helped Sam steer the boat around mangled pieces of buildings and ruined trees now littering the water.

Their luck held better than Sam expected. The storm didn't hit in earnest until they were well into the Glades channels, but it returned with the full force of its furry. The tops of cypress trees, live oaks, and pines whirled, spun, and tore free, flying over their heads like demented birds of prey ready to devour all in their path. A branch crashed onto the boat's long, wooden bow, bringing screams from the cabin below, but the sturdy cypress hull held.

As the storm roared, Sam eased the throttle back to a crawl. Water poured in solid sheets reducing visibility to no more than a few feet. Sam's heart moved up into his throat as he peered through the storm. The channel no longer looked familiar. When it divided a while back, he took the fork to the left. It was the right direction. It had to be the correct one, but everything looked so different.

A sudden jerk rocked him against the wheel. Mr. Scheinberg grabbed a railing to keep himself upright. The sound of the hull scraping sent a chill down Sam's spine. The motor churned and growled uselessly. The boat refused to move forward. Sam switched off the power and looked down through the hatch.

"Everybody okay?"

Rebecca's frightened eyes looked up at him. She nodded and opened her mouth like she would speak, but the baby threw her arms around Rebecca's legs and howled. She picked up her sister and moved away from the hatch and the rain pouring in through its open door.

Mr. Scheinberg raised a trembling finger, pointing toward the bow. "What are we lodged on?"

"By the sound of it, I'd guess a sandbar. I'm going to need plenty of help to push this tub free. Call the two oldest boys to help while I get in the water to see how we stand."

"But they are just children. I can't risk their lives doing men's work."

"You'll be risking all of our lives if they don't. We may not be able to move this boat even with their help." Sam sat with one leg over the side of the boat. Rain and wind lashed him like whips in frenzied hands. "We don't have time to argue. Get them up here."

Sam dropped down into the water, clinging to the side's wooden edge, and hand-over-hand eased his way toward the bow. Half-way there, the water became shallow. His feet hit bottom and sank into grass and muck up to his ankles. The goo sucked at his boots, but Sam slogged on, gripping the boat's side with fingers that slipped in the pounding rain. If they survived this, he would marry Rebecca no matter what her parents said. As it was, they would most likely drown without seeing the warehouse.

Sand rolled beneath Sam's feet. It was indeed a sandbar on which they sat. He pushed against the hull to see if it would respond. The boat squatted on the sand like a gator protecting its territory. It didn't budge, not even a fraction of an inch. A tap on his shoulder drew his gaze upward. Mr. Scheinberg and his two eldest sons, both in life jackets, clung to the bow deck railing, their eyes wide with terror. The wind and rain lashed them without mercy.

Sam let go of the bow and cupped his hands around his mouth. "Leave one boy with me. You and the other one get into the water on the other side. We've got to rock the boat until she moves off the sandbar."

Sam positioned himself ahead of Ruben, the eldest boy, grabbing the bow line and nodded to the others. He and Ruben pushed. Nothing. Mr. Scheinberg and the other boy pushed. Still no movement. By some unspoken directive, they all pushed and shoved. Sometimes strength comes through desperation. Slowly the bow leaned to one side, then the other. Inch by painful inch it rocked until the sound of cypress scraping on sand whispered up through the water. The bow lurched and slipped backward, nearly jerking Sam off his feet when the boat's full weight dropped into the water. His grasp hardened on the line as it dragged itself along his palms, and he dug his boots into the river bottom's gunk. The vessel slowed enough for the Scheinbergs to scramble aboard the bow's deck. Ruben caught the line as Sam threw it up. Mr. Scheinberg lay on his belly and leaned a hand out to Sam. He bent his knees to push off the bottom. Together the quartet slipped and slid their way back to the wheel well.

A thunderous crack followed by a thud that rocked the boat sent four heads swiveling. The boys' eyes grew wide at the sight of a huge limb standing where the bow had been just moments before. Its broken end must have buried deep in the sand for it to hold upright so firmly. A shudder passed through Sam. If the boat had not moved when it did, they would have been stranded. If the limb had hit one of them . . . he shook his head. It would have been the end.

Back at the helm, Sam guided the boat on through lashing rain and screaming wind. The thick trees lining the channel did little to break the storm's force. If he didn't find the warehouse soon, he might never get the Scheinbergs to safety, not Rebecca, not her family. Sam's gut clenched. Instead of moving on across the peninsula to the Gulf, the hurricane seemed to have stalled. A crash behind them made Sam jump. As screams sounded in the cabin below, he peered over his shoulder. A huge cypress lay across the channel where they had just passed.

Mr. Scheinberg put a hand on Sam's arm and leaned close to be heard over the tumult. "How much farther? The children can't take much more of this."

"Not so much. We'll be there soon." A spasm of guilt gripped Sam, but the need for the others to remain calm superseded the need for honesty. He had no idea how much longer before the warehouse came into view. He had lost all concept of where they were. He said a silent prayer they were even in the right channel. They chugged on.

After fifteen or so minutes, Sam guided the boat around a treetop covering half of the channel and they moved toward the mouth of a wider waterway. Across the expanse a large shape rose up. It looked like it was floating, but it had to be the warehouse. It had to be. Sam pulled the throttle back to a standstill. As the boat rocked from side-to-side on the wind whipped channel, he peered at the open area between them and the safety of the warehouse on its island of raised earth. The trees along the channel had been more protection than he realized. Rain coming in on a slant meant the wind was at its worst. Would the boat's engine be equal to the directional force of the hurricane? Sam had no idea, but they couldn't stay where they were.

He turned to Rebecca's father. "I think you need to bring your family up here. If we capsize or start to sink, they would be trapped below." He pointed to the dark, hulking shape on the other side of the expanse of water. "That's where we're headed. If we have to go into the water, don't lose sight of that."

When the family stood crowded beside Mr. Scheinberg in the wheelhouse, Sam took inventory. Only the children wore life vests. Damn whoever owned this boat for leaving it so unprepared for disaster, but then, it probably wasn't meant to carry seven people through the Everglades during the height of a hurricane. Sam gripped the wheel firmly with one hand and eased the throttle forward again.

They pushed out onto the open water. Wind and rain slammed the vessel, pushing it sideways. Sam held the wheel steady with all of his strength, arm and shoulder muscles twitching and trembling under the strain. The bow remained pointed at the warehouse despite the stern being pushed toward the south. Moving at an angle, the boat edged its way across the open water.

A gust stronger than previous ones lifted the boat and tilted it, but not enough to swamp them. The children's screams floated above the wind's shrieking as they slid toward the lower side. Mrs. Scheinberg moved behind the children and braced them with her body. Mr. Scheinberg snatched her dress front while Sam grabbed Rebecca and jerked her to him. He placed her hands on the wheel.

"Do what you can to keep us moving forward." She nodded and gripped the wheel with white knuckled hands.

Hanging on to a metal railing that ran on the decking behind the wheel, Sam edged toward the kids. One-by-one, he lifted them up and away from the lower side. With the last one clinging to Rebecca, he grabbed Mrs. Scheinberg's arm and hauled her upward until she, too, came to rest beside her daughter. Mr. Scheinberg moved to the center, and the boat settled back into a normal balance.

Sam reclaimed the wheel and pushed the throttle forward again. Either they got out of the middle of this open area or the next blow would swamp them for sure. The risk of hitting submerged debris seemed less than being washed away to certain death. Sam guided the boat close enough that the warehouse took on its true form. A few more feet and the vessel drew alongside the dock that still protruded into the water.

Sam turned to Mr. Scheinberg. "Take the wheel and try to keep us steady. I don't trust the dock with the banks flooded like they are. I'll test it first."

Sam stepped out onto the dock, which swayed and buckled under him. He jumped back onto the boat's bow as the dock broke apart and bashed against the hull. Within moments, fragments of the now demolished dock floated away, driven by wind and a frantic current.

Sam cupped his hands around his mouth. "Mr. Scheinberg. Give the wheel to Rebecca and bring the boys out here. We're going to have to drag the boat onto the bank and up far enough that it won't float away."

Sam signaled for Rebecca to guide the boat as close to the bank as they dared. It bumped against something below water level, slid sideways for a foot or so and edged forward again. The bank had to be just inches away, maybe no more than three or four feet. So close, yet was it close enough?

Sam eyed the distance between him and what he hoped was firm ground under the water. Had he judged the bank's location correctly? There was only one way to find out. If he made it, maybe he could pull the boat a little closer, if not, well, he couldn't get any wetter than he already was. Of course, if he landed on something sharp hidden beneath the water, he could break a leg or be impaled. That was a risk he had to take. They couldn't stay as they were. Sam crouched until his calf and thigh muscles bunched, ready to spring, his heart in his throat.

He launched himself at what he prayed was the bank. His feet hit water-soaked earth. Muddy, jarring, blessed, solid ground lay beneath about five inches of water. All those months of lifting and lugging loaded crates of booze had finally brought about something good. He nodded to Mr. Scheinberg, who threw him the bow line. After Mr. Scheinberg and the boys joined him on shore, they hauled on the line until the bow scraped on the bank.

Sam wiped rain from his eyes and looked around. "We'll need to tie this off secure, or we'll be stuck here until someone decides to check on this place after the hurricane passes. Mr. Scheinberg, get the women and kids into the warehouse. You may have to break the window and crawl through it." Sam jiggled the line. "I'll figure this out."

Sam watched until all of the Scheinbergs walked on firm ground, then turned back to the boat. Tugging with every ounce of strength he had left, it still took about half an hour of struggle to haul the boat closer to a stand of trees at the edge of the warehouse clearing. After tying the rope to a cypress that hung out over the bank, Sam slogged toward the hulking building. Despite the raging elements, it stood steadfast and firm. Relief washed through him. Rebecca and her family were safe. He had made that happen. Surely now her parents wouldn't object to their marrying. Leaning into the wind driven rain, he stumbled and slid his way to the warehouse. As he figured, the door still bore its chain and padlock, but the window was no longer in place. Shimmying through the opening, Sam strained to see through the gloom.

"We're over here sitting on crates." Rebecca's voice held a slight tremor. "It's dry. Not a drop of water anywhere."

Sam raced toward the sound. When he found Rebecca, he enfolded her in his arms and hugged her to his chest. She leaned back, put her arms around his neck, and looked up at him with glittering eyes.

"I was afraid we had lost you."

Light coming through the wall opening cast a ghostly illumination over everything in the forefront of the building. Even in the semidarkness, he could see tears shining on her cheeks. Holding her in one arm, he lifted his other hand and wiped her cheeks with his fingers, then tucked a curl behind each ear. Without speaking, without thinking, he bent to her upturned face and pressed his lips against hers. The kiss blocked out the sounds of the storm, the terror of the day, even the glaring gazes of her family sitting only inches away. The world disappeared in the strength of their love.

Sam lifted his head so that he could look into her eyes, thereby breaking the spell. He sensed her parents' displeasure without looking at them, but he would have his say. "I love you. I would do anything to be with you, to marry you, if you'll have me."

"Yes. A thousand times yes."

Mr. Scheinberg cleared his throat. "You are underage, Rebecca. Your mother and I will never give our consent. Marriage to this . . . this gangster, even considering how much we owe him, will never be."

Chapter 28

Liz stared into the empty fireplace, her open laptop resting untouched on her knees. Moshe Toblinsky's dramatic life couldn't hold her attention, his appeal defeated by a different type of drama that had no chance of a happy ending for the main characters.

Mom and Dad were still asleep after their nocturnal adventure. If they didn't awaken soon, she would get them up. Daddy getting his nights and days mixed up would be a disaster. He had a hard enough time keeping track of reality without Mom being so sleep deprived she couldn't function.

Liz shifted her weight, trying to get comfortable on the lumpy sofa that had rested beneath the living room windows for as long as she could remember. Mom and Dad could afford better, but they insisted on getting the very last nanosecond of good out of everything they owned. The sofa could remain where it was until it fell to rags and splinters, but the living arrangements in this house were going to change no matter the cost to her relationship with Mom. Some things were worth fighting for.

Hugh strolled in from the kitchen with two cups of coffee. He gave one to Liz and plopped down beside her on the sofa.

He tapped the computer. "Why don't you put this away and come sit with me on the porch? It's a beautiful day. Breathing fresh air might help make things clearer."

Liz glanced at the brochures Aunt Mildred had given her and gathered them up before following Hugh. Once they were ensconced on the old aqua and white aluminum glider, she focused on the distant speck of blue she knew to be the bay. She tilted her head and squinted so she could make out the ferries as they chugged toward the Clinton terminal on Whidbey Island. A flurry of gold, red, and bronze leaves floated across the yard, driven by a chilly breeze. Liz shivered and huddled closer to Hugh.

He put his arm around her and rested the back of his hand against her cheek. "You're really cold. I'll get your sweater from our room."

Before he moved away from the glider, she grabbed his hand. "You're a truly good guy. You know that, don't you?"

He grinned and nodded before moving through the front door. The need to reassure him came over her from time-to-time. Why now at this exact moment? Liz's cheeks puffed out with a held breath then deflated as she pushed the air out in one swift swoosh. Perhaps his being the first romantic partner who put her needs before his own meant more than she cared to admit. His kindness and compassion had been made particularly clear by his actions since they had become a couple, even more so during the last forty-eight hours. Hugh was about as perfect as a guy could get—handsome, smart, kind, successful, good lover. So why did she still dodge his marriage proposals? She loved him. Of that, she was sure, so why did the idea of a lifelong commitment to him scare her so? Discovering herself to be so complicated, so conflicted, so unsure was a novel experience, one that definitely sucked big time. Maybe his perfection scared her. Maybe his being her boss held her back. Maybe deep down she thought she didn't deserve him. She rolled her head and hunched her shoulders to release the knot building up at the base of her skull. Whatever the reason, if she messed up this relationship, she would certainly be the world's biggest fool.

Geez. She needed distraction from this depressing train of thought.

Sorting through the brochures, she picked out the one touting the place Aunt Mildred had politicked for before cruising off to her bridge game. The price list made her heart lurch. Grabbing the other two brochures, she quickly scanned them. Some difference in the prices. The two less-expensive facilities looked sterile and institutional even in their own ads. Mildred's choice at least appeared homey, cozy even. It promised the best in memory loss care for patients in all stages of dementia and Alzheimer's. The grounds were lovely, and according to the brochure, were secured by a sturdy wall accessed only from one facility door. The photographs of the patients' rooms and common areas showed a subtle decorating hand adept at creating an atmosphere both welcoming and neutral, a difficult task to carry out. Families were encouraged to decorate patients' rooms with furniture and other personal items to ease the transition, to make it familiar, to make it more like home. Clearly the irony was lost on the brochure's author. How long did people in their condition remember home? A shudder ran through Liz. She drew a shaky breath and wiped a tear from the corner of her eye.

"So, what do you think?" Liz jumped at the sound of Hugh's voice. "Will any of those work for your dad?"

Liz wrapped the sweater he offered around her shoulders and handed him the brochures. "I hate the idea of all of them, but Mildred's recommendation seems to be the only choice based on what I've seen so far."

"Yea, I see what you mean. I guess we'll know more after y'all's visit this afternoon."

"I dread Mom's reaction, but I don't see that she has any choice. Since the appointment is for four, the coward in me is going to wait until after lunch to tell Mom what's up."

"No, not cowardice. Wisdom, if you ask me."

Liz took his hand, drew it to her cheek, and kissed it.

"You are my rock, my knight in shining armor. You know that, don't you?"

Hugh dropped down beside her and took her in his arms. "Glad to be of service."

The day crawled by. Corralling Mom and Dad turned into a full morning job. They didn't eat lunch until 2:00, after which, they put Dad back to bed for his afternoon nap.

When Mom returned to the living room, Liz could wait no longer. She stood as Mom reached the sofa. "There's something we've got to do this afternoon with Aunt Mildred."

"Well, you and Hugh can run along. We'll be fine right here."

Liz inhaled deeply, held the breath for a moment, and exhaled. That little trick usually calmed jangling nerves, but it didn't help much this time. "Mom, it's an appointment for you, Mildred, and me. Hugh is going to stay here with Daddy."

Mom's eyes narrowed. "And just where do you think we will be going?"

"I'm going about this all the wrong way. I love you and Daddy with all my heart, which is why this is so difficult."

"Well, spit it out."

"We, I mean, I don't think you should be trying to care for Daddy here at home anymore. His condition has become too severe."

"I haven't been *trying* to care for him. I take care of him just fine, thank you very much."

Grief settled over Liz like a wooly blanket, nearly smothering her, but giving in to Mom as she usually did was not an option. "Oh, Mom, how can you say that? He was threatening to assault you with a lamp when we arrived. Last night he led you on a chase until the early morning hours. You had to be brought home in a police car. He is clearly beyond your control."

Fury flashed in Mom's eyes. "I didn't sacrifice my life and my dreams for all those years to have you speak to me like this." Mom paused and glared at Liz. Here it came. The recitation intended to induce guilt and to maintain control of their relationship. It had ever been thus. "I fought your father when he thought sending a girl to a premier college was a waste of money. I stood up for you when you decided to major in history when everyone said you would never find a job after college. I sent money to help cover your living expenses during all those years of graduate school. I wanted you to have what I didn't. I wanted you to have it all, and this is how you choose to repay me for my sacrifices?"

There was nothing Mom loved more than a good fight. Her strong-willed approach to life had served her well. She'd had years of practice in getting her way. Liz's gaze swept over her mother. She looked old and tired. Perhaps giving her the fight she wanted might not be the best idea. This situation called for a cool head and calm disposition. Instead of speaking, Liz smiled gently and took her mother's hand. Mom's arm stiffened, but she didn't snatch her hand away. That was a good beginning.

Liz chose her words carefully, determined to keep a soothing, even tone. "Yes, you gave up a lot. I wouldn't be where I am today without the unfailing support you have always given me. I know that. I'll never be able to repay the debt I owe you." Some of the tension eased from Mom's arm and hand. "But now it's time for you to let me do something for you."

Mom sucked in air and moved a step away from Liz. "How dare you plan this without talking to me first? A nursing home is out of the question." So, Mom's ESP was working overtime as it usually did when a member of the family was in trouble. "How could you do this to me? To your father? It's unthinkable. Those places are horrible, for old people about to die. I won't have it. Do you hear me?" Mom raised her index finger and poked Liz in the chest "I. Will. Not. Have it."

One more poke and Mom would do permanent damage to the thin skin over Liz's breastbone. She caught the offending hand by the wrist and drew it to rest on the spot Mom had been in the act of assaulting. "I love both of you, and I want you around for a very long time, but that won't happen if you work yourself into an early grave or Daddy escapes and gets himself run over. Mildred says this place is the best. She has a friend there. She says it doesn't smell, has good food, and is clean. She says the staff is kind and patient with the residents."

"Residents? Is that what they call the poor people incarcerated there? And that's what you want for your father whom you claim to love so much? A place whose best recommendation is that it doesn't smell, for God's sake?"

"Mom, please. Give this a chance. I don't see how—"

"Exactly. You don't see a damned thing. Otherwise, you wouldn't have run off to Florida when that jerk of a navy pilot wiggled his little finger. You wouldn't be chasing around after criminals instead of working on something useful. You wouldn't be getting your information secondhand from my busybody sister. You would be here at home where you belong. You would have a right to give me advice."

Hugh moved to Liz's side. He placed a hand lightly on Mom's shoulder. "Lillian, it wouldn't hurt to keep the appointment. You don't have to make a decision right away. Think about it when you are well rested. Important decisions shouldn't be made when you're sleep deprived. Last night couldn't have been very restful."

Hugh had the magic touch with older women. Mom's shoulders relaxed and the fear-fueled rage faded a little from her features. She slumped down onto the sofa and looked up at Hugh.

"As usual, you're the voice of reason." Mom, her eyes narrowed and her mouth a thin line, glanced at Liz for a split second, then looked back at Hugh. "I suppose I should take a look for future reference. For when the time comes. I do know it will come to that someday. I'm not completely delusional."

~ ~ ~

Mildred's car pulled up to the curb at precisely the moment she had told them to be ready. Never one to waste time or energy, she honked the horn twice. When they didn't appear immediately, she waited two minutes and honked again.

Liz took Mom's elbow. "Next, she's going to sit on that horn until she sees us. You know how the neighbors feel about noise."

"Let go of me. You don't have to push me. I'm not a child."

"Well stop acting like one." Dear God, where had that come from? "I'm sorry. Please. Come on."

Mom ignored Liz and turned to Hugh. "You are sure you can handle him?"

"You won't be gone that long. We'll be fine, won't we James?"

Daddy looked up at Hugh from the card table and nodded, but there was no sign that he recognized his keeper. His arthritic fingers shuffled a deck of cards with the precision and attention of an automaton. A sense of desolation tinged with dark humor settled over Liz. Of all the things Daddy had forgotten, Gin Rummy was not one of them. Amazing. He didn't know what day it was and didn't always recognize the important people in his life, but he could remember what constituted a Gin hand. The brain's mechanisms truly were the last frontier in medical science.

The trip to the facility took about ten minutes. Mildred pulled into a parking spot, but did not open her door. Instead, she took Mom's hand.

"I have a dear friend who's here for skilled nursing care. She and I have a plan. Her name is Carrie."

With that mysterious pronouncement, they all got out of the car and proceeded to the main entrance of a building designed to give the impression that it was much older than it really was. They walked up stone steps that led onto a wood-floored, front porch. Fussy Victorian corbels topped the porch posts and supported the hand railings. They passed through mahogany French doors with ovals of frosted glass centering each side. The lobby would have been right at home in an Edith Wharton novel, though the furniture and colors of the walls were somewhat lighter and brighter than true Gilded Age style. The receptionist greeted Mildred by name. Obviously, she spent a lot of time there visiting friends and relations of friends.

The facility director gave them the official tour and answered their questions. At least, she answered Liz and Mildred's questions. Mom's stony silence created an awkwardness.

As the interview wound down, the director stopped speaking and looked meaningfully at Mildred. "Do you or Mrs. Reams have any other questions?"

"I think we've got a pretty good idea of what you offer."

"Well, don't hesitate to call if you think of something more. My secretary will be happy to see you out."

"That won't be necessary. We're also here to visit a resident."

Once they were away from the administrative offices, Mildred led them into a yellow sunroom, indicating a grouping of white wicker chairs.

"Well, now you've heard the pitch. The official party line is all well and good, but seeing things like they really are is the only way to get a true feel for a place. Carrie is going to give us her personal guided tour."

Mildred took her cell phone from her purse and started typing out a text message. In a few moments, the tap of a walker sounded in the hallway. Liz looked toward the sunroom's entrance where a white-haired woman in a floral housecoat shuffled toward them with a gleam in her eyes. The old lady stopped by the first chair, held up a cell phone, and waggled her eyebrows.

"Got your text, Mildred. I see you have your spies with you. Let's be off."

The walker skidded in a 180-degree turn, leaning at a slight angle. Carrie righted the object and gave it a pop with her hand. "Darn thing is going to learn to do what I want or it's headed for the trash bin."

Alarm kept Liz from following Carrie's lead. "Are you sure you should be walking around with us? We don't want to tire you out."

"Physical therapist wants me making 5,000 steps a day as part of my rehab." Carrie held up her wrist. "Fitbit keeps up with how many I've done. Great thing, technology. Wouldn't be without it."

Carrie and Mildred took off with surprising speed requiring long strides for Liz and Mom to catch up. They stopped at the corner, looked both ways, and sped down the corridor to closed double doors with a sign proclaiming authorized personnel only. Carrie took an ID card out of her pocket and swiped it against the reader on the wall next to the doors. They swung inward, revealing another wing of the facility. A pretty brunette seated at the nurses' station looked up and smiled.

"Are you going to see Mrs. Cochran, Miss Carrie?"

"I am. Some days she knows me. Some days she doesn't. Either way, she seems to like the company."

"I'm sure she does. Thank you for thinking of her. I see you've brought guests."

"Yes, this is another of Mrs. Cochran's bridge friends and her daughter visiting from Florida."

As they headed off down the corridor, Carrie tucked the card back in her pocket. "They got tired of opening the door for me, so they gave me the card. I pretty much have the run of the place."

Liz listened for the crying, shouting, and moaning one expected to hear in a ward for people who had lost their minds. Anxiety crept over her. Maybe Mom was right. "It's so quiet here. Do they keep everyone sedated?"

"Well, I'm sure when they need it. It's hard to tell with some of them. It's their condition, you know." The sound Carrie's walker made as she pushed it down the hall made the empty space all the more eerie. She stopped by divided light French doors. "This is the unit the director will probably recommend for your husband, Lillian. Right now, they are in the sunroom. It's exercise hour."

Mom hadn't said a word since they left the director's office. Suddenly, she grabbed Carrie's arm. "Are the patients happy?"

Carrie took Mom's hand. "Follow me and see for yourself."

Chapter 29

Sitting all night with his back against crates had left Sam stiff in places that didn't have names. Rebecca moved against his side, probably adjusting herself to a more comfortable position, an impossible goal. The arm he had kept around Rebecca all night tingled from being trapped between the crate and her shoulders, but he hadn't dared move her. Her parents hadn't been able to see them in the absolute darkness, and he didn't want to attract their attention. Mr. and Mrs. Scheinberg would have been less than pleased had they realized their older daughter had her body pressed against the guy they considered a gangster.

He opened one eye. The soft light of dawn brightened the space where the window had once been. It must have been the quiet that woke him. He had tried to stay awake to guard over the others, but exhaustion had won out, and he had drifted off somewhere during the night with the storm still shrieking.

While the wind howled, the warehouse had heaved, sighed, and groaned. Sam peered into its cavernous depths, checking the deepest corners and tallest rafters. Other than a few pieces of roofing tin way down at the far end, the old building had held on to its outer skin—no boards gone, no door torn off its hinges, no water splashing through the roof where Sam and the Scheinberg family huddled together.

Sam placed his lips against the hair covering Rebecca's ear. "I need to get up and check on things."

She jerked a little and looked up at him with dazed eyes that closed again almost at once. He settled her weight against the crate and kissed her on the top of her head. After slowly lifting himself off the floor, Sam moved toward the opening in the wall, his heart thumping a little harder with each step. The warehouse had protected them from the wind and rain, but not the roaring of the storm. If the cacophony that pummeled them through the night was any indicator, the hurricane had been intense. Sam peered from the building at the spot where he had tied the boat and his heart lurched. The boat was gone. The tree it was tied to was snapped in half with the upper part laying on its side, its canopy stripped of foliage. He raced through the opening, his head swinging from side-to-side. Everywhere he looked, trees lay broken, their trunks and branches tossed about like children's Tinkertoys.

That boat was the life line that would get them back to civilization. If it was damaged, or worse, had disappeared for good, it could be weeks before anybody wandered by this uninhabited island in this isolated part of the Glades. Bateman had chosen it precisely because it was so out of the way.

Sam's step slowed. He blinked and swallowed hard. Bateman. Sam hadn't given the man a single thought since pushing the SOB into the Miami River. So why did the image of Bateman flailing around in the water crop up now? A darkness snaked its way through Sam. Goddamned Bateman. Sam had left him to drown without a backward glance. Why should he care about that bastard's fate? It made no sense, but this felt an awful lot like guilt pricking his conscience. He had never once thought himself capable of ending the life of another human being. Visions of another death crept into his mind. As though it happened in the moment, Sam saw Tops Monza gripping William Mack by the hair. In slow motion, he heard the pistol's firing pin crash into the bullet's primer and the explosion that followed. Blood and brains flew through the air in a macabre dance.

Maybe Sam was no better than Tops. Perhaps he was worse. Big Mack had died quickly, but Bateman may have struggled for some time before sinking below the surface. On the other hand, he may have managed to swim to the bank and hoist himself out of the river. Sam sucked on his lower lip. The chance of Bateman saving himself seemed unlikely. Did doing nothing to help a drowning man qualify as murder? Sam clenched his teeth. He refused to consider the answer. There was much more important work to do.

He reached the spot where the boat once sat. The stripped tree trunk still bore the loop of rope used to secure the boat. Sam picked up the frazzled end and tossed it in his hand while he scanned his surroundings. The position of the debris pointed to the storm's westerly path. At some point during the night, water had been high enough to flow over the island. The warehouse sat on a raised pier and beam foundation. The rising water must have flowed under the building. Weighted down as it was with 100's of crates of booze and being constructed of heavy timbers, it had withstood the force of the wind and water. A new confidence eased through Sam and he relaxed a little. At least he had done something right for a change. Bringing Rebecca and her family here had saved their lives.

He dropped the rope and followed the water's course. If the boat still existed, it would be west of where he stood. The shattered trees and debris were all that was left of undergrowth once so thick that a man would have needed a machete to hack his way through it. Sam slogged through water covering his ankles, praying that he didn't inadvertently step into a bog. He had never explored the island so had no idea of its size. One thing for sure, the islands creatures were awake. Clouds of mosquitoes swarmed, biting, stinging. Not too far ahead, gators grunted. Frogs croaked a cacophony of tones. Perhaps the island wasn't that wide after all or maybe it had a lake in its center. Whatever, Sam veered away from the direction of the sounds.

Just up ahead, the trees appeared to thin out. A flash of movement on the ground caught Sam off guard. He froze mid-step. Just in front of his foot, a cottonmouth slithered away. Bateman said they were vicious and aggressive, but this one didn't seem to want to do anything except hide. Maybe it had gotten its fill of fighting for its life during the storm. As its tail disappeared into a stand of palmettos, Sam put a hand over his eyes to shield them from the fully risen sun. He searched the horizon for any sign of the boat. Sweat tickled down every part of him, stinging his eyes and soaking his clothing. He would give a lot for a bucket of cool, clean water to ease his thirst and clear away the dizziness that washed through him in waves. It dawned on Sam that he hadn't eaten or had anything to drink in many hours. How could he have been so stupid? People died from heat stroke and dehydration.

He stopped and leaned against a tree to rest and clear his head. After wiping the sweat out of his eyes, he searched the horizon once more. His heart rate kicked up a notch. Maybe it was the heat and exhaustion, but he could swear there was a splotch of white up ahead. His energy renewed by hope, he started toward the image, praying it wasn't his addled brain playing tricks on him. Another ten minutes or so pushing through scrub brush and struggling with sucking mud brought him to a sliver of sand bordering a wide body of water broken only by green spikes protruding from its glassy surface. Their boat sat stern toward Sam on the edge of this inland sea in about two feet of water, its hull resting on the grasses that gave the Glades its name. A fit of hysterical laughter gripped Sam. He had not noticed the vessel's name until now. How fitting. *Miami or Bust*. Sam howled until his sides ached.

When he finally got control of himself, he shook his head to try and focus on his next task. He really needed something to drink. The name of the boat wasn't really all that funny. Dehydration must be messing with his mind. Did he dare drink from the Glades? Did he really have a choice? Even if he managed to push the heavy boat into water deep enough to float it, there was no telling how far he had to go until he would be able to reach the side of the island where the warehouse stood. The island wasn't wide, but it might be long.

Sam waded in and dropped to his knees. Sunlight shining through the clear water illuminated everything, including minnows scurrying along the bottom. Sam eased himself down until water washed over him completely. He turned onto his back and looked skyward. It was like looking through wavy, old-fashioned glass. He sucked in and swallowed. Sweet. The water was sweet. Sitting up, he gulped from his cupped hands and shook the water from his hair.

Sam returned to the strip of sand and trotted over to the vessel. He ran his hands over its wooden surface. From what he could see and feel, it seemed seaworthy, but there was no telling what kind of damage the hull might have sustained. There was only one way to know if it would float. Sam waded around to the bow and grabbed the tattered end of the rope hanging from the bow. Using what remained of his energy, he tugged on the line, his heels sinking into the silt covered bottom. He rocked the bow from side-to-side until he felt it loosen and slip forward a little. Sam stepped backward hauling on the line until his muscles screamed. Sand scraped the hull. Sam now stood in chest deep water. The boat swooshed as it dropped into deeper water nearly yanking him off his feet. It sank to the bottom, setting Sam's heart thumping, before it bounced up and floated. If there was damage to the hull, it must not be too bad. Sam bent at the waist, resting his hands on his knees while he panted.

The rope jerked from his hands and the boat floated south, paralleling the island. The momentum created by its weight and a current Sam had failed to notice promised to carry the vessel out of reach. He lunged, but the line wiggled free from his fingertip grasp. As the boat picked up speed, he dove after it, managing to reach the stern and grab the ladder attached to the right of the prop. Hauling himself aboard, he checked for leaks. Finding none, he went toward the wheelhouse and prayed that the engine would start. Five tries and the thing finally turned over and spluttered to life. It seemed that God was on his side after all. Maybe Rebecca's parents could be persuaded too.

Within about fifteen minutes, Sam rounded the south end of the island and turned toward the warehouse. Rebecca, her oldest brother, and her parents sat on the bank, while the little kids threw sticks at one another and pretended to sword fight. The younger boys caught sight of him and began shouting his name, waving, and jumping up and down.

Sam guided the boat to a safe spot on the bank. He went to the bow, grabbed the line and jumped into the water. The two older boys ran to help. Together, they hauled the boat onto the bank far enough that it would not float away. Wiping sweat from his eyes, Sam looked at Rebecca's parents as they made their way toward him.

When they reached the boat, Mrs. Scheinberg let out a cry. "Praise God. We thought you had deserted us."

Sam felt the heat rise in his face. "What makes you think I would do that after I fought Bateman and probably killed him trying save you?" His tone was harsh, filled with anger, but he didn't care.

Rebecca's mother looked like she had been slapped. "Of course. We should have known better. Rebecca tried to tell us you had gone to find the boat. We were just so afraid."

"Why can't you understand? I love Rebecca. I'm grateful for the kindness you've shown me. I will never do anything to harm any of you." Sam's words ended on a shout.

Mr. Scheinberg's intake of breath was audible. "Except try to marry our daughter."

Chapter 30

Liz held her breath while Mom stared into the exercise room. Patients stood in two rows reproducing the movements of a leotard-clad young woman as best they could. Some of them were near perfect in their performance. Others moved like confused automatons. No surprises there, but as she surveyed the room, Liz blinked and her gaze snapped back to the middle of the group. A man who couldn't have been more than forty-five shuffled in time to the exercise music. Tears rose in Liz's eyes, and she stepped behind Mom to wipe her cheeks. Mom would dig in her heels for certain if she thought Liz weakened. But still, seeing someone so young in such a place shocked Liz. Her brow furrowed. Enough rumination. Getting maudlin wouldn't help Mom and Daddy.

Liz lowered her lashes in an attempt to sneak a covert glance at her mother. Mom's eyes glittered with uncharacteristic tears. She wouldn't appreciate someone drawing attention to her distress, so Liz remained still and quiet. Mom must be allowed to draw her own conclusions. If she failed to reach a sensible decision, only then would Liz assert herself and take charge of the situation. Such a role reversal would be a first for Liz, as long as you didn't count moving across the continent to follow a man who had ultimately proven himself to be a cheating, lying bastard just as her friends and family had predicted. A serious lack of understanding of what made a good relationship had driven her decision to throw away her life in Seattle and move to

Florida. She thought she couldn't live without the man. Jeez. She had been stupid.

A small sob escaped Mom's firmly clamped lips. She dodged the arm Liz extended, turned away from the exercise room doorway, and fled. Liz pursued Mom through the facility, but lost her at the junction of two main corridors. Liz's head swiveled.

The sound of a throat clearing behind her made Liz jump.

A male nurse with kind eyes asked, "Are you looking for a lady in a red sweater?" Liz nodded. "She headed toward the lobby. She's probably in the parking lot by now." A sympathetic smile lifted the corners of his mouth. "This happens a lot on first visits. It's hard, but they usually come around. This is a great facility. They adjust pretty quickly because the level of care is so good."

Liz gave him a weak smile in return. The man seemed to think Mom would be the newest resident. The irony made the tears return. She did not have the courage or energy to correct him. "Thank you. That's good to hear," Liz replied, her voice barely above a whisper.

She headed for the front entrance and did not look back to see if Mildred followed. Pushing through the double doors, Liz searched for a glimpse of her mother. She wasn't on the front porch nor was she at the car. A flash of red between the trees of the forest bordering the facility's property signaled that Mom sought solace in nature, a habit of long-standing. Liz ran across the parking lot in pursuit, heart filled with the knowledge of the confrontation that lay ahead.

The red blotch stopped moving through the trees and sank toward the ground. Presumably, Mom had run out of steam and had stopped to rest. Liz went several yards farther into the forest. A bird perched on a low hanging branch startled at her approach, in turn making Liz jump as it shrilled and flapped away. The fragrance of rich, moist, compost-laden earth reminded her of the many happy childhood hikes she, her parents, and siblings had taken in the parks around Seattle. Mom sat on a fallen log, her shoulders heaving with silent sobs. She looked so forlorn, a very unusual state for her. This might be the best opportunity to get her to see things Liz's way, while she was vulnerable. A shock of guilt seared Liz's mind and heart.

Dear Lord, it wasn't as though she was going into battle, but Liz slowed her pace and studied Mom. Memories of past arguments played out in her mind like shaky VHS home movies. Some of them got pretty hot. A couple were downright nasty. Maybe battle was exactly what she faced.

Although Liz often laughed when she described her mother as a force of nature, truth underpinned every word. Mom could muster unnerving stores of will power when other people would fold and toss in their cards. Mom's courage and strength showed brightly when her own parents, brother, sister-in-law, and niece were killed in a car crash and again when Jessica, Liz's older sister, died of leukemia at age fifteen. Those terrible events would have been enough to sink a lot of people, but not Mom. She had grieved and come out on the other side seemingly stronger. Now, she looked so frail sitting on that moss-covered log. Daddy seemed to be the one loss Mom could not bear. Liz would never believe that Mom loved him more than other family members, but he was clearly her heart, her center. Odd that Liz had not noticed that until now. A rueful smile played across her lips. Children, even as adults, were so often ignorant of their parents' inner lives.

She approached with care, not wanting to startle Mom. When she was about ten feet away, Liz called softly, "Are you okay?"

Mom looked up as though she didn't understand why Liz was there. "You have to ask?" Anger flashed in her eyes. "No. I'm not."

Thoughtless move there. Mom never reacted well to condescending solicitousness. On to Plan B. "Look, I know this is really, really hard, but we've got to talk about the future."

"Future? What makes you think there will be a future? Every day he slips farther away from me. There is no future."

So, Mom did have a clear understanding of what lay ahead for Daddy. Liz hesitated, searching for the right approach. Keeping her tone soft and gentle, she said, "Daddy will never get better. We all know that. Eventually the Alzheimer's will kill him. We know that too. You, on the other hand, have many years of life ahead of you. You owe it to me and my brother to be here for us and our eventual children."

"Children? Your brother, maybe, if that scatterbrained little girl he's engaged to waits out his deployment. You, on the other hand, refuse to marry a wonderful, kind, successful man. Hugh's the best boyfriend you've ever had. I don't know why he puts up with you."

Liz felt gut punched, but she kept a firm grip on her temper. Mom was spoiling for a fight. Liz refused to give her one. It would accomplish nothing. "You're being mean. That's not like you. Too much stress and too little sleep does that to people."

A deep crease formed between Mom's eyes, which glittered with emotion. "As long as I'm on a roll, I need for you to tell me something." Liz dreaded what Mom would say next, but kept her mouth shut. Mom needed to get it out. "I've given up nearly everything I ever wanted to accomplish merely so that you could have the life I never had. I wanted so much for you to live more, to accomplish more, to be more than I am. Somehow I failed you. Look at you. What you've become. Sure, you're a success professionally, but your love life has always been a disaster." Mom searched

Liz's face, pain visible in her eyes. "Could I have done more? Do I somehow owe you more?"

Mom's words made razor cuts on Liz's heart. Instead of lashing out as she would have in the past, she held her own emotions in check. She had to if Mom was to be convinced to do the right thing for herself and Daddy. "No, you don't. What I said was badly put. No one could have done more for her daughter. If anybody owes a debt, it is me. I am so grateful to you, and I know I can never fully repay you for the life you've made possible."

Mom's shoulders heaved. She wrapped her arms around her body and stared off into the distance for several moments. She turned to Liz, tears trickling down her face. She tilted her head to one side, raised her hand to Liz, and ran the tips of her fingers over Liz's cheek until they came to rest at her chin. Looking deeply into Liz's eyes, Mom said, "I don't need repayment. What I need is to know that I did right by you." Mom drew a long breath and let it out slowly. "Did I push you too hard to have a career, to be a star? Is that why you're so afraid to have a committed relationship with a man?"

Surprise made Liz's brows rise. "I'm not sure what to say. I've never really thought about it."

But that wasn't quite true. After her previous relationship ended in disaster, there had been a shift in Liz. A spark of personal reflection had flared. Before Hugh, Liz only wanted the bad boys, the ones with a fatal combination of glamor and danger who were as emotionally unavailable and unreliable as they were beautiful and exciting. Unaccountably, she had always been willing to carry most of the emotional load with those guys. She was still working on why it never occurred to her to expect as much from her romantic partners as she expected from herself. From the secure vantage she now enjoyed, she saw just how incredibly, and in some respects, undeservedly lucky she had been. She landed on her feet with both Hugh and her job, but that was not something she was going to tell Mom now. And why she couldn't manage a simple yes to Hugh's proposals was a worry for another day. Instead of answering the questions, Liz smiled softly and slipped her arm around Mom's shoulders.

Mom tensed at first, but finally relaxed and slipped her arm around Liz's waist. "You know, I may have tried to live my life through you to make up for my own dissatisfaction. Your poor dad understood, bless him, and put up with my bad moods. That's what makes it so hard. I always thought there would be time for us once you kids were adults." Mom shook her head. "I've left it too late. Time has run out for your dad and me."

Liz's heart split in two, but she couldn't give up now. Here was a breakthrough at last. Mom seemed finally ready to talk realistically about the future. Liz tightened the embrace in which she held her mother and brought her closer. Mom drew a shaky breath and placed her head on Liz's shoulder.

Liz ran her tongue over her lips. Her words needed to be just right. "What's happening to Daddy is terrible. It breaks my heart for him, but I am much more frightened for you."

Mom jerked away and straightened up. Consternation filled her eyes as she rose from their log perch. "I can't imagine what you mean by that."

Liz grabbed Mom's hand before she could bolt. "I mean that you will not do anyone any good by destroying your health trying to care for someone who needs watching 24/7. I love you and Daddy, but he is leaving us. You still have a lot of living ahead of you. I want you to have the energy to experience some joy in the time you have remaining."

"And your suggestion is to put your dad here, I suppose." Mom spat her words like they were globs of rotten food.

"Would it be so bad?"

A wail of pain came from Mom, showing just how raw her emotions had become. "It would mean that we had given up. I can't desert your father. I'm not a quitter. I'm not a coward either."

"Of course you aren't. I don't know anyone who has more strength and courage than you. You are a very loving, caring wife. You are also a wise and intelligent woman. Let's look at this another way. If Mildred had been in this situation with Harold, what would you have wanted for her? I know how much you love your sister. What would you have advised her to do?"

A faraway expression entered Mom's eyes. She sat back down on the log, shoulders slumped, her gaze on the forest floor. After a full minute of silence, she turned tear filled eyes to Liz. "I would have told her to put him in a memory care place like this one."

Chapter 31

Sam lifted Rebecca's younger siblings into the boat while struggling to keep his temper in check. He didn't respond to Mr. Scheinberg's accusation because what the man said was true. Sam intended to marry Rebecca with or without her family's approval. He would do what he could to change her parents' minds about him, but in the end, they would either accept him as a son-in-law or risk losing their daughter. Rebecca had pledged herself to him. She would take his side no matter what her parents tried, at least Sam prayed she would. He held out his hand to Mrs. Scheinberg and helped her into the boat. Getting all of them out of the swamp and back to Miami took top billing for now.

Navigating around fallen trees and dealing with changes to the landscape and waterways prolonged the return trip. As they entered the river's main channel into town, Sam adjusted the throttle, making the boat idle in place. A sensation akin to grief rose in him. Fear for the future, for what might come, and for the strength he needed to survive along with this family washed over him. A scene of complete devastation played out before them. Not a single building stood in its original condition. Some had simply disappeared altogether. Trees lay on their sides or floated in the river. The sickly-sweet odor of decaying flesh drifted on the hot, muggy air. A dead cow bumped against the boat, its body bloated and discolored. Sam's stomach clinched. He pushed the throttle and the boat edged forward again.

Rebecca moved up beside Sam and slipped her hand

onto his arm. "What will have happened to the bakery? Do you think it's still standing?"

"That's anybody's guess. It may have survived. We'll just have to wait and see."

Sam took Rebecca's hand in his and lifted it to his lips. Giving it a quick kiss for reassurance, he scanned the horizon for any sign of hope. He saw none.

The journey toward town took far longer than it would have prior to the hurricane. Sam steered around wreckage from destroyed buildings and partially submerged watercraft torn from their moorings. The sun hung low in the western sky by the time they came alongside what remained of the bakery dock. Sam placed his hand over his eyes to shield them from the glare coming off the building's white stucco. Amazingly, it still stood square on its foundation. Bare concrete showed where chunks of stucco had been ripped off, no glass remained in any window, and sheets of roofing tin lay crumpled on the ground, but the outer walls remained intact.

A sharp intake of breath sounded near Sam's left shoulder. Glancing behind him, he took in Mrs. Scheinberg's pale, stricken face and the trembling hand that pointed at the bakery. "We are ruined. How will we ever recover?"

Tempted to speak soothing platitudes, Sam stopped himself before they fell from his lips. He wouldn't insult her with empty words that any fool could see through. "That's a possibility, but standing here guessing about the future isn't helping. Let's see what can be salvaged."

Sam assisted the Scheinbergs out of the boat and then they all scrambled over the rubble to the bakery's backdoor. The back porch lay in a heap against the neighboring building's bulkhead, so Sam gathered boards and a couple of wooden crates that had floated onto the bank. With these, he created makeshift steps up to the door.

Once everyone was inside the kitchen, they stood in the center of the room and took in the damage in the growing gloom. The odor of rotting garbage and mildew filled the once pristine space. Muddy water covered the tile floor. Mrs. Scheinberg went to cupboards miraculously still standing in place and yanked on a drawer. It didn't budge.

She turned to Sam. "Can you get this open? I have clean dishtowels in it that we can tie over our faces to lessen the stench."

As darkness enveloped Miami, Sam and the Scheinbergs continued their survey by the light of kerosene lamps that had survived the storm The door that separated the store from the kitchen had somehow remained in place. Sam opened it cautiously. A tinkling clump of debris fell at his feet. He held his lamp aloft. Gaping holes where the big plate-glass front windows once stood let in the evening breeze. A bulky object of indeterminate description had crushed the bakery display cases, their wood and glass joining that of the front panes scattered over the floor. Puddles of water and vegetation occupied territory over, under, and around the shards of glass. The scene looked like the photographs of French and Belgium villages that were mortared and bombed into oblivion during the Great War.

Backing away from the opening, Sam closed the door and lifted his gaze to the kitchen's ceiling. The speakeasy was right above it. Only minimal water marks showed in the plaster. Maybe the roof was still intact over the back of the building.

Rebecca was on her knees inspecting the foodstuffs on the lower shelves of the pantry. He leaned down, put his hand on her shoulder, and whispered, "I'm going to check the second story."

She looked up at him, a concerned frown wrinkling her brow. "Please be careful and don't take too long. I have an awful feeling this whole place will come crashing down on us any second." Sam heard the catch in her voice.

"I'll be quick, but we've got to figure out where we're going to sleep tonight."

Sam grabbed the newel post and gave it a shake. The banister stayed firmly in place. He started up the stairs, testing each step as he went. The staircase held without shifting and only a little groaning. At the second-floor landing, Sam halted. The prevailing ocean breezes that blew in the evenings were stronger up here. The door to the speakeasy stood open. Sam peered into the space. Since it had no windows, no broken glass appeared on the floor nor did any stars peek down into the room from above. Water marks showed in places on the ceiling, but the floor remained relatively dry. Only a couple of small puddles indicated that the room had been through a storm.

Satisfied that the back of the building would provide shelter until better could be found, Sam moved toward the room where he slept. The door dangled at an angle, held to the jamb by only half of one hinge. The odor of liquor hung heavily in the air, making Sam's stomach churn. Moonlight illuminated the entire space. His cot and the top two layers of liquor crates were simply gone. The remaining crates lay in shambles across the floor, covered in debris from outside the building, splintered wood, and broken glass. Another step forward and the floorboards buckled and groaned beneath his feet. Time to get back downstairs.

Over subsequent days, they discovered there was no better shelter to be found than what the bakery provided. They were, in fact, luckier than the many who didn't have even a leaky roof over their heads. Rumors spread throughout the city saying that 25,000 people were homeless, some said 45,000. It was hard to know what to believe, but one thing was certain. The storm had devastated Miami and Miami

Beach. The storm surge covered Collins Street in sand and piled it into expensive hotel lobbies. The death toll varied with the messenger. The worst thing they knew for fact was that a family of six had been discovered crushed beneath the collapsed walls of a nearby apartment building.

Sam and the older male Scheinbergs worked daily to clear the bakery of debris. They made repairs as best they could with the scraps of construction materials they foraged from the debris piles mounding on the sidewalks and in the gutters as the city tried to shake off the ravages of the storm. Eventually, they dried-in the roof over the back of the building and made the speakeasy into a dormitory for Sam and Rebecca's brothers. Her parents, baby sister, and Rebecca all slept in Mrs. Scheinberg's sitting room. They ate whatever Rebecca and her mother could prepare from their nearly exhausted supplies. Sam boiled water in Mrs. Scheinberg's best stewpot over a fire out by what remained of the river bulkhead.

After an afternoon of dragging boards and roofing tin from four streets east of the river, Sam plopped down on a bench at the kitchen table hoping for a bite to eat before continuing construction to restore the back porch. A shadow fell across the salvaged screen door. Sam's head jerked and he blinked several times. For a moment, it seemed like Bateman had returned to take revenge for being pushed into the river during the hurricane.

The figure at the door placed his hand over his eyes, pressed his face against the repaired screen, and peered into the kitchen. "Hey, you at the table. This the Scheinberg place?"

Sam breathed a sigh of relief. He didn't recognize the voice. "It was. Can I help you?"

"I'm looking for Bateman. He ran the business upstairs. You seen him around?"

Sam's heart lurched into his throat. He swallowed hard before answering. "Not since the hurricane." The less said, the better. He had no idea what this guy might know.

"Yeah, that's what our guys said. How about the kid that worked for him?"

To tell the truth or lie? How likely was it this man knew that Bateman had tried to go to Bimini the day the storm hit? Maybe as close to the truth as possible might be best. Sam ran his tongue over his lips. "That would be me."

"Good. I come to get what's left of the liquor. Take me to the storeroom."

Sam's head jerked back in surprise. "I suppose a few crates might have survived. We haven't had time to clear that part of the building yet. We had a pretty big storm here, in case you haven't noticed."

"Don't be a smart ass. Show me where they're at. The boss has plans for them."

Sam really didn't want to go into that part of the building. It wasn't safe. The floor creaked and shuddered when you walked on it. Delay with questions sometimes proved a good strategy. "Boss? Which boss?"

"The only boss. Mr. Moshe Toblinsky."

Surprise thrilled through Sam. "He's here in Miami?"

"Yeah, came in by train last night." Sam had no idea train service had been restored.

"Why on earth would anyone be in Miami who didn't have to be here?"

The stranger shrugged. "That ain't nobody's business but his. It certainly don't concern you."

An idea formed. It was a long shot, but this was as good a chance as he'd likely get.

"Sorry. I don't mean to offend. I'll help you move the liquor, if you want. Did you bring a truck?"

"Yeah. I borrowed one from a citizen." The stranger's tone implied the loan might not have been voluntary.

"Can I catch a ride?"

The stranger shrugged. "Suit yourself, but you'll have to get back here on your own. I ain't running a taxi service."

Chapter 32

It took Sam and the gangster, who didn't see fit to share his name, a couple of hours to pick through the broken glass and splintered wood. They salvaged twenty crates that by some miracle remained intact. Since the best of the liquor had been stored in the room's back corner, their haul represented a tidy sum in future ill-gotten gains. Once the stuff was loaded on the truck, Sam climbed into the cab beside the driver. As they bumped and swerved their way toward the train depot, Sam formulated what he would say if he got the chance. Act smooth or go for full on pleading? It would be nice to know what kind of reception to anticipate.

After several detours and backtracks caused by roads blocked by debris and police barriers, they arrived at the depot and parked beside a boxcar. A couple of muscular gents peered at them from the car's open doors. Sam jumped down from the truck's cab and wiped his damp palms on his pants legs. His nerves jangled at the thought of his actual mission.

Loading the crates of liquor into the boxcar made for the work of only a few minutes. When the last crate was stowed, Sam ran the back of his hand across his forehead to keep sweat from running into his eyes. The state of his nerves reached a new low. His pulse kicked up a notch at the thought of his next task. The gangster turned to get into the truck cab, but Sam placed a hand on the man's arm.

"Is Mr. Toblinsky here at the depot?"

The man brushed Sam's hand away and gave him a quizzical look. "Yeah. What's it to you?"

"I need to talk to him. Can you tell me where to find him?"

The man crooked his thumb toward a lone passenger car coupled into the line of boxcars. "Try in there, but don't expect he'll see you. The boss is a very busy guy."

"Thanks. I owe you one."

The gangster chuckled knowingly. "From what I hear kid, you owe just about everybody who counts."

Sam's head jerked back, and he blinked a couple of times. That this stranger knew who he was or anything about him came as a shock. His plan might not be such a great idea after all, but it was his only hope at this point.

"Well, thanks anyway. I'll be going now."

The gangster's laughter followed Sam as he turned and went to the passenger car. Another goombah greeted him when he hopped up on the car's platform. The man blocked the entry to the carriage. He looked Sam over with a suspicious glare.

"Whatcha want?"

"I would like to see Mr. Toblinsky."

"He ain't receiving at the moment, but give me your name just in case."

Sam did as instructed and the man entered the car, returning shortly. "Go to number seven. Boss says he'll give you a few minutes."

Pulse thumping against his eardrums, Sam made his way through the car. All the windows and compartment doors stood wide open, but not a breath of breeze stirred the heavy air. He arrived at compartment seven where electric fans whirred at full speed. They did nothing to mitigate the stifling heat. Toblinsky sat at the drop-down table with a couple of his men, their white shirts soaked with sweat. Toblinsky wiped his forehead and face with an equally damp handkerchief. Sam cleared his throat and tapped on the door frame.

Toblinsky looked up with a less than welcoming expression. "You've got two minutes."

Sam shifted from one foot to the other and swallowed. "Mr. Toblinsky, I've met a girl, and we want to get married, but her parents won't allow it unless I leave bootlegging. I've come to ask your . . . your permission."

Toblinsky frowned and his eyes narrowed. His gaze traveled over Sam as though he couldn't quite place him. Finally, recognition flickered in his eyes. "Oh, yeah. Sammy. The kid Tops asked me to get out of New York on the sly." Had the gangster really forgotten Sam or was this pretense simply for effect? He couldn't say. "I see you survived the storm."

"Yes, sir, but it was a close call."

Toblinsky's expression became neutral. "So tell me. Seen or heard anything from our guy Bateman?"

Sam stopped breathing. Of all the questions that might have been asked, this was not what Sam expected. He had thought Bateman a low-level flunky beneath the boss's notice, but maybe he was something more. What did Toblinsky already know? How much should Sam say? He made his decision.

"No sir. I haven't seen him. I don't know what happened to him."

Toblinsky's head tilted to one side and his eyebrows rose. "I thought you guys were going to try to save the hooch on Bimini."

Panic coursed through Sam, setting his heart racing.

"Well, we did try, but we couldn't make it. The storm was coming too fast. We had to turn back. I haven't seen him since we got back to the bakery just before the storm reached Miami."

"And what? Bateman just wandered off?"

"He left the building to go get supplies. He never returned."

"So how is it you survived?"

"When Mr. Bateman didn't come back, I knew I couldn't wait for him any longer. I took the boat to the warehouse to ride out the storm."

"And you just left the Scheinbergs to their fate?"

"No, sir. I took them with me."

"I see. So this girl of yours. Would she be the Scheinberg kid?"

"Yes, sir."

Toblinsky glared until Sam broke eye contact. Doom settled over him like a musty shroud while the gangster pursed his lips in contemplation. After a few seconds, Toblinsky hit the table. "Okay. Looks like we've seen the last of Bateman, but that leaves us a dilemma. Who's going to get the booze from Bimini to Miami?" All three men in the compartment looked directly at Sam. "I'm thinking it's going to have to be you, Sammy. What with you not knowing where Bateman is and all." Sarcasm bled from Toblinsky's words. He frowned, drummed his fingers on the table top, and carved a crater through Sam with his eyes. "You know the route and the Bimini people. You've got my boat. Consider yourself promoted. Is the bakery building sound enough to keep the speakeasy there?"

With a sinking feeling, Sam conjured an answer. "I'm not an engineer, but I'd say it still needs a lot of work. We've done what we can to make repairs. The roof doesn't leak anymore, but I'm not sure how long the repair will last. The outside staircase is gone and so are all of the front windows."

Toblinsky spoke to the men at the table with him. "Give the kid here some cash to get the stairs rebuilt and make permanent repairs." To Sam, he said, "Get the place up and running by the end of the month. One of my guys will notify the barkeep we're back in business. Get what's left of the liquor from Bimini. Turning a profit by the end of October will ensure the health of everyone at the bakery." Toblinsky's attention shifted to the papers spread before him on the table.

To his horror, tears welled in Sam's eyes. "But, Mr. Toblinsky . . ."

The gangster closest to the door rose to his feet. "Your two minutes are up. Get out."

Sam trudged back to the car platform and hopped down. Cinders and gravel crunched beneath his feet. The odors of burning coal, decaying debris, and his own sweat combined with the realization of what his future held made his mid-section clench. He turned toward the nearest boxcar and heaved the contents of his stomach onto the track. He could have disappeared like Bateman. Why hadn't he? The corners of his mouth lifted in a wry smile. The question didn't even require an answer.

Chapter 33

Transitioning Dad to the memory care facility was ultimately easier than Liz ever thought possible. Ms. Carrie, Aunt Mildred's friend who had taken an apartment in the assisted living section after rehab, helped ease Mom's mind and convince her that Dad would get the best of care and that visitation was not limited in any way for family. They would even put a bed in Dad's room for Mom when she wanted to stay the night with him. Between the excellent meals and the wonderful staff, Mom became at peace with the inevitable.

In her room at Mom's house, Liz bent over the bed where her suitcase stood open. She studied the stack of clean laundry ready for packing and tried to make herself feel better. In a few hours, she and Hugh would be on their way back to Florida, leaving Mom alone in the house, Daddy confined to the facility, and Mildred to watch over both of them. Guilt, pressing yet subtle, like an old ache to which one had become accustomed, washed through Liz. It seemed to be the chief emotion she felt these days, other than the heavier one of grief. Being around Mom for any extended period tended to do that to her. As much as she loved Mom and Daddy and as deeply appreciative of their sacrifices for her as she was, there were times when the pressure of their expectations, especially Mom's, seemed as though it would sink the leaky ship of her emotional peace.

She had never been quite sure whether Mom's high expectations or her own expectations of perfection had come first. Perhaps they sprang up simultaneously from deep within the mystical bond between mother and child, which developed into a symbiotic relationship with each participant nurturing the other until it was difficult to know where the one left off and the other began. Mom had been hard on Liz while she was growing up, but no harder than Liz had been on herself. A wise teacher had once told a stressed-out teenaged Liz that all families were complicated, but that each family was complicated in its own way. Mom's drive for her daughter's academic achievement and professional success had been their family's complication.

From the perspective of independence and adulthood, Liz now realized that the pressure had been relentless. Mom really believed that Liz could have it all if she worked hard enough. Compromise had been a dirty word. Liz had never failed or disappointed her mother, not even as an angst-ridden adolescent, except in one way. Mom had never approved of any of Liz's boyfriends before Hugh, and he was admittedly very different from his predecessors. Liz had never considered herself a rebel, but maybe the history of her love life proved otherwise. It was worth thinking about when she wasn't so damned tired and emotional.

A step on the bare floorboards behind her broke the spell of her musings. She turned to find Hugh standing in the doorway holding out her cell phone.

"That guy in Tampa has called three times in the last hour. Maybe you'd better call him back." Hugh's face had lost some of its usual good humor.

Liz took the phone and pressed the return call icon. Rich Whitehead's voice came through the ear hole before the first ring finished. An unexpected thrill passed through Liz.

"Rich, I'm surprised to hear from you. To what do I owe the pleasure?" Liz glanced at Hugh whose slight frown had morphed into full on scowl. Liz shook her head, hunched her shoulders, and pointed to the phone with her free hand.

"I have something that belongs to you." Rich's mellow baritone floated to her warm and flirtatious, like he was talking to a sweetheart. His tone imbued his words with several layers of meaning, catching Liz off guard and making her laugh.

"And whatever could that be?" The effort to keep her own voice businesslike failed if the expression on Hugh's face was any indicator.

Rich laughed softly. "A silk dress and a pair of matching heels. I had them cleaned. They look good. You'd never suspect they'd been through a tropical storm."

"Oh my goodness. Thank you. I'd completely forgotten about them."

"But not about me, I hope."

"Of course not. I'll always be grateful to you for introducing me to your father and your great-aunt."

"And would another introduction increase that gratitude?"

"I suppose that would depend on who I'm being introduced to."

"One of my cousins in Miami has found someone who thinks he might know the man you're chasing. Interested?"

Liz was beyond stunned. She had almost given up hope of finding out more about the man in the pictures. She hadn't worked on her research since arriving in Seattle. Hadn't even thought much about it, in truth. Worry for her parents' situation had driven all else from her mind.

Her words came in a stutter. "I . . . I . . . Absolutely. How did your cousin find him? Can he give us a name?"

"Whoa. Slow down. First, my cousin knows a lot of the old folks who were born in Cuba. Second, I asked him to check with some of them. It seemed the best way of seeing you again."

"My goodness, that was . . . kind of you." Stuttering

and verbal stumbling did nothing to bolster Liz's confidence. Rich popping up out of nowhere was having an unexpected effect, one she had not noticed being so strong when she last saw him. In fact, their parting had been rather abrupt and dismissive on each side.

"Kindness born of self-interest, if I'm honest. Of course, if I had found your clothes in my car first, I might not have called my cousin."

"Well, I'm glad you didn't. Find the clothes first, that is. We're in Seattle, but we're catching the red-eye back to Florida tonight. Do you think the person your cousin found might see me soon?"

"Oh, it might just be possible. In fact, you've got an appointment at eleven-thirty this coming Saturday, so you'd better get yourself on that plane. And who are we?"

Liz cut her eyes to see if Hugh was still nearby. He stood in the doorway looking stiff and unhappy. "Hugh is with me." Liz couldn't remember if she had ever actually mentioned Hugh by name to Rich. She couldn't refer to Hugh as her fiancé like she had when she was in Tampa since it was her fault that it would be a lie. "We've been seeing about my parents' situation. Daddy is going downhill fast."

"I'm sorry to hear that. Will you be able to make the appointment?"

"I'm looking forward to it. Should I come to Tampa or meet you in Miami?"

"Meet me at the Fontainebleau's bar at eleven."

"Fabulous. See you then." If it would not have been so unseemly, Liz would have jumped up and down while clapping her hands and whooping with joy.

Hugh took a step into the room. "Why're you meeting this guy? I thought your business with him was finished." Exasperation colored his words bursting the bubble of her excitement.

Liz explained what Rich offered. "Do you mind that I'm going away so soon after we get home?"

"Yes, I mind. I mind a lot. On the other hand, this could be a big break for your research. That's why I'm going with you." The expression on his face made it clear that she would not be going to Miami alone.

Chapter 34

8:30 P.M.
October 29, 1929

The music coming from the radio stopped abruptly, followed by the crackling of a microphone being shifted into place.

"We interrupt this program to bring you breaking news. The greatest volume of trading in the history of the New York Stock Exchange occurred today. In a slide that began last Thursday, the Dow Jones Industrial Averages lost an additional thirty points today, reaching an all-time low of 230.07. Trading was so intense that tickers did not stop running until seven-forty-five this evening. Losses are so great tabulations will not be complete for some time to come. One source estimated they could run into the millions, perhaps even the billions."

The radio news announcer's voice shook while he read the report. Sam, sitting at the bakery's kitchen table, looked at Mr. Scheinberg over the remains of their supper. "Do you think this will affect your business?"

The older man glanced at him without any of his usual antipathy. "Who can say? People have to eat and bread keeps body and soul together when all else fails. What about the speakeasy?"

A rueful smile tightened Sam's mouth. "Like you said. People have to eat and sometimes they have to drink. If this thing doesn't get better, they may be drinking a lot more."

"A lot more of what?" Rebecca asked as she wandered into the kitchen from the storefront. Sam died a little each time he saw her. Despite her being of age and making her own money as a secretary, she refused to defy her parents and marry him. It was because he would not free himself from Toblinsky and the speakeasy. She refused to see the impossibility of his situation despite having declared her love for him long ago. As far as he could tell, she wasn't going out with any other guys, but Sam couldn't be near her without wanting to shake her and demand that she commit herself to him completely. She said she would gladly do so when he left the world of gangsters behind. They existed in stalemate, so he had started keeping his distance.

Sam rose from the table and dropped his napkin on his chair. "Sir, excuse me. I've got work to do."

As Sam reached the second-floor landing, the sound of running steps ascending behind him echoed in the stairwell. Sam knew those footsteps simply by their sound. He refused to turn around, went to the speakeasy door, and slipped his key into the lock.

Rebecca grasped his arm. "Please wait. I need to talk to you."

"Are you ready to be your own woman? Ready to live your own life?" The words tumbled from him rough, harsh, but he didn't care.

"Sam, don't be like this. I can't hurt my parents like that. I just can't. Can't you leave bootlegging?"

"I guess I could, but would you really be happy living life on the run? I'll never be free as long as Moshe Toblinsky wants me working for him. I owe him my life."

"But you used to say you'd leave him so that we could marry. You promised."

"I know what I said, but that was before I got stuck with this, when I still thought I could be rid of him."

She leaned into his chest, her shoulders shaking with silent sobs. He did not push her away. He didn't have that much strength. She worked a magic on him that he was powerless to resist. He had learned a lot about life since coming to Miami. He had grown up a lot, too. Observing speakeasy customers over the last three years had taught him that women could work all kinds of magic, some of it good, most of it bad. If good and bad witches existed, Rebecca was as good as they got. Her magic, while personally painful to him, represented nothing but the purest forms of kindness, caring, and love. That made being around her hurt all the more. If she were a conniving bitch like so many women he met, he could easily turn her away. As it stood, all she had to do was look at him with those big, beautiful, soulful eyes to melt his resolve.

When she started sniffling, he slipped his arms around her. Her tears split his heart in two and shattered his determination to keep her at a distance.

She tilted her head so that she looked into his eyes. "Oh, Sam. What are we going to do?"

He smothered her question with a kiss filled with longing. He didn't have the courage to tell her he didn't know the answer to her question. Without that answer, they would struggle on in the limbo they had endured for these three years. He couldn't have her, but he couldn't let her go and move on either. They were stuck. They had no way forward and no place to turn for help.

~ ~ ~

10:35 P.M.
December 5, 1933

Sam looked up from his table next to the speakeasy's bar. A commotion near the back door drew his attention. To his horror, Rebecca bounced toward him through the crowd of drunks and lowlifes. She wore an unaccountably sunny smile as she ignored the catcalls and slapped away hands reaching out to grab at her. When she reached him, she dragged out a chair, plopped down in it, and placed her elbows on the table.

Resting her chin on her upturned palms, she looked at him with sparkling eyes. "Have you heard?"

"What are you doing in here?" Sam purposefully kept his tone gruff. Encouraging a display of intimacy between them in full view of this crowd would not end well for anyone. In fact, keeping Rebecca at a distance was the only way to preserve his sanity.

"Prohibition is over! Utah ratified the amendment today. I just heard it on the radio."

"So why are you so excited? You don't drink. You don't like the stuff, and I doubt you ever will. And before you ask, no, seder wine doesn't count."

"Don't you see? Bootlegging is finished. No more Prohibition, no more need for bootleggers or speakeasies. You're free."

"People will always drink. Who knows what my bosses will do? They may turn legit and expect me to continue to run the business for them."

"Or maybe not. You'll never know unless you ask. Call him."

"Call who?"

"You know. Call the main man."

"No, now get out of here."

But after Rebecca left, the idea of calling Toblinsky ate at Sam like wildfire through drought parched timber. A small spark grew rapidly into a raging inferno.

Sam waited a month before picking up the phone and calling the number he was instructed to use only for emergencies. After the second ring, a male voice came across the wires.

"Speak."

"I need to talk to Mr. Toblinsky."

"Who are you, and what do you want?"

Sam drew a slow breath. "My business is with Mr. Toblinsky only."

"No name, no Boss."

Sam stated his name but remained silent about his purpose. The receiver clicked against what must have been a wooden table. While he waited, his anxiety increased as the second hand on his watch swept around and around. At least ten minutes passed before the familiar tenor voice came on the line.

"Sammy. I'm surprised to hear from you. What's the emergency?"

Now that the moment had arrived, Sam was unsure of how to begin. He ran his tongue over his lips and blurted out, "It's not an emergency, but I need a big favor."

"And that would be?"

"Now that booze is legal again, the speakeasy and the Bimini runs seem sort of unnecessary. Business has dropped off a lot because our customers can go wherever they want and it ain't our place. They're hanging out at the beach hotel bars, which are up and running at full steam again. Seems like a new bar opens every other day. Our place can't compete."

"This is not news. We are working on organizing other areas of . . . interest. But this can't be the reason for your call, so spit it out."

"I want to get married, and I need to be done with bootlegging and speakeasies so her parents will agree it."

"But, Sammy, you are more to my business than a bootlegger and speakeasy operator. No one can organize a dinner meeting like you do. Are you saying you want to disengage from my organization?"

Sam's heart lurched, but he plunged on. "Mr. Toblinsky, I'll always be grateful to you and Mr. Monza for getting me out of New York. If it hadn't been for you, I might be in prison or worse. The thing is, I've waited for this girl for seven years. Please. I'll do whatever it'll take to make things right with you."

"I see. You and Issac."

"Sir?"

"Issac. From the Torah. Tricked into marrying the wrong girl. Had to work for his SOB of a father-in-law for another seven years before he got the girl he wanted."

"I hadn't thought of it like that, but I guess it's sort of the same."

"So, you're saying I'm an SOB?"

"No." Sam hadn't meant to shout, but a sense of desperation had taken control. He struggled for a more reasonable tone before continuing, "Of course not. You've always been great to me. I'm not saying things right."

A soft laugh sounded on the other end of the wire. "Calm down. I'm having a little fun at your expense. So, you want out of the booze business?"

"Yes, sir."

"Okay." Sam couldn't believe he had heard correctly, that it had been so easy. "Monza was right. You've been a hard worker, and you don't complain. I tell you what. Close down the speak. Do it tonight. The business is finished anyway. You go ahead and marry that girl. Scheinberg will be lucky to have you as a son-in-law."

"Thank you, Mr. Toblinsky. I'm really grateful to you."

"That's good. I'm glad to hear it. And I'm gonna do something else for you. Young men need money starting a family. I'm sending you $500 as a wedding gift. Something to tide you over until you find a job now that you ain't working for me."

"I don't know what to say. Thank you seems so inadequate."

"There's no need to apologize. I'm giving you the money in the spirit of friendship. Friends help each other out. Think of this as a debt of friendship against the future. One day I may need a friend in Miami and you'll be the guy. Agreed?"

"Of course."

"Well, I think that concludes our business. For now." The way Toblinsky placed extra emphasis on the last two words sent a chill through Sam.

"What if you don't know where I am when you need the friend?" Geez, what a stupid thing to say.

"Don't worry. I always know where to find my friends." The receiver clicked down and the line went dead.

Sam sat in silence for a good half-hour before he jumped to his feet and started shouting, "Get out. We're closing for good. Finish your drinks and leave. Boss is closing us down as of tonight."

After he hustled the last drunk through the door, he went to the kitchen in search of Rebecca's father. He found him sitting in his small office behind the store working on his bookkeeping for the business.

"Sir, can I talk to you?"

Mr. Scheinberg looked at Sam over the top of his bifocals. "You are talking to me now."

"I've got something important to tell you."

The older man sighed, took off his glasses, and rubbed the crease between his eyes. He looked up at Sam with an expression of resignation. "When is it ever not important when you come to speak to me?"

Sam swallowed the lump in his throat. "I don't have to run booze ever again." Mr. Scheinberg just stared at Sam. "It's what you said would have to happen before Rebecca and I could get married. Don't you see? I'm free."

"I don't recall ever giving you permission to marry my daughter under any circumstances."

A light step behind Sam revealed that Rebecca must have been eavesdropping. How had he not seen her? "Yes you did, Papa. You said I couldn't marry Sam while he was a bootlegger."

"That is hardly the same thing. This is not the man for you, my daughter."

"I'm of age, Papa. I can marry who I want, and I want Sam. He's not a bootlegger anymore. You'll never have to work for that Toblinsky ever again, will you, Sam?"

"No. I won't have to work for him." Sam didn't see the need to tell them about his agreed upon debt to the gangster. He doubted Toblinsky would ever need his friendship or help despite what they had said. What could he ever do for a man like that?

Chapter 35

Miami, 1946

Sam hoisted the last tray of baked goods onto the shelf in the hotel pantry. Those damned trays seemed to get heavier every week. He bent over and placed his hands on his knees while he panted to catch his breath. Geez, he was only 37, but some days he felt 101. The army doctor who declared him 4F during the war had called it right about his heart being dicey. He hadn't noticed it when he was younger, but now he felt it a little more every year.

When his breathing returned to normal, he wandered toward the restaurant manager's office to leave his invoice. Becoming the main supplier of bread and bagels for two of Miami Beach's big hotels had been a godsend during the lean years of the Depression. From time-to-time, he still wondered why Scheinberg's had been chosen from among all of the struggling bakeries in Miami, but it didn't do to question prosperity too closely.

As he approached the office, an angry voice boomed through the open door. "What the fuck do you mean you can't get the linens here by this afternoon?"

Sam stopped in the hall. All was silent in the office for a moment, followed by, "I don't give a shit your machines all broke down at once. We've got a contract. If you want to keep it, you're going to get those goddamned linens here in time for us to set up for this banquet. The clients are paying for clean, starched, linen tablecloths and napkins. Trust me when I tell you these are not the kind of people you want to disappoint. You disappoint me and I'll make sure they know who to blame."

The manager slammed the receiver down and glared up at Sam. "What the fuck do you want, Ackerman?"

"I've just finished a delivery. Here's the invoice."

"At least you're dependable. Same order for the rest of the week. After that, we may want to change things up a little."

Sam hesitated at the door, trying to judge whether the time was right. Being in and out of the hotel restaurants everyday had shown him there were holes in Miami's restaurant supply chain and he had an idea of how to fill it. Maybe now was as good a time as he would get.

"I couldn't help overhearing. Looks like your linens guy dropped the ball again."

"Second fucking time this month."

"Maybe you need another supplier."

"That's the goddamned problem. He's the only one in town. What I'd give for that son-of-a-bitch to have some competition."

"What would it take to give it to him?"

"What are you asking?"

"Like how many tables per week? How many deliveries per week?"

The manager showed Sam the most recent invoices from the linen service. Sam made a quick note of the figures. "You think you can beat this? Work up a proposal. I'd love to stick it to that guy."

"And I'd love to expand our business, but my father-in-law hates change."

"Then go out on your own. You're a young man. Old Man Scheinberg has sons to pass his business down to. You aren't going to get anything from him when he's gone."

That was the truth. Rebecca's father believed in the patriarchal tradition of inheritance going from father to sons. He would no more think of leaving Rebecca, and by extension Sam, a part interest in the business than he would eat pork or skip the observance of Shabbat. Sam's spirit sank at the thought.

Times like these made Sam miss his mother and brothers all the more. Watching his brothers-in-law grow into the family business reminded him of how much he had lost. He had felt secure enough to reestablish contact with Mama and the boys after he and Rebecca married, but it was the Depression. When Mama died in '39, he hadn't had the money to go back for her funeral. He had thought there would be time to get to know his brothers again when money wasn't so tight, but then the war came. The three older boys joined the army. At fifteen, the youngest had been placed in an orphanage. No one had even thought to give Sam a chance to offer the boy a home. Sam had become a stranger to his brothers, someone they vaguely remembered who had disappeared from their lives when they were children, someone who became a shameful family secret. The final blow to any sense of family came when two of the boys were killed in the Pacific and the other one on D-Day. His youngest brother had not responded to his letters. Sam lost all contact with the boy and had no idea where he was.

~ ~ ~

For weeks, Sam mulled over the figures and did research on the costs of rental space, bulk linens, and commercial laundry equipment. Organizing the occasional dinner for Mr. Toblinsky back in the early 30's had taught Sam a lot about the service industry, but this idea of his would require investment capital. He used a cost analysis system of his own design. Having only finished eighth grade before he dropped out to go to work, he established a first name acquaintanceship with the circulation ladies of the public library. He read every book they had in the business section. When there were no more books on their shelves, he struck up conversations with business owners and inconspicuously picked their brains. He didn't share his dream with anyone, not even Rebecca. There was no need talking with her until he knew it was even a possibility. If they used the kids' college funds, they would have enough for a down payment on the equipment, but not enough to pay for it outright. They would need a loan to make up the difference, provided Rebecca went along with his idea.

Sam yawned and dropped his pencil. Stretching his arms over his head, he rolled his shoulders to relieve the tension that always built up when he worked on his plan. Rebecca and the children went to bed hours ago, but Sam couldn't sleep. The plan would work. There was no doubt about it, but the damned banks refused to make him a loan to get started. He didn't have any collateral to put up, and he wouldn't ask Rebecca's father to co-sign the loan. After all these years, the Scheinbergs finally considered him family, but their familial feelings did not extend to finances. Sam was Papa Scheinberg's employee and Rebecca's husband, pretty much in that order.

There might be a way to get the financial backing, but did he dare? An unexpected conversation of a few weeks back replayed through Sam's mind.

~ ~ ~

He had been minding the store in the predawn hours when the shop bell jingled. Sam glanced at his watch, rose to greet this unusually early customer, and dropped his newspaper on the chair behind him. When he turned toward the arrival, a shock of recognition jolted him. A face from the past grinned at him over the display case.

"Hello, Sammy. Scheinbergs still make the best bagels in the city?"

Sam struggled to keep from gasping. "Of course. How have you been, Tino? It's been a long time."

Tino looked older than he should have. Gray hair covered his head and lines creased his face. Life in the mob must be taking a toll.

The gangster considered the array of offerings and ordered two dozen mixed variety. After Sam gave Tino the boxes laden with warm goods, Tino remained in place, watching Sam with a speculative expression. "Ain't you interested in why I showed up here after all these years?"

"Yeah, but asking would have been rude." Sam grinned, hoping Tino saw the humor too. "Offending customers is against the rules. You still with Mr. Toblinsky?"

"Who else? He moved down here a couple of years ago. Didn't you know?"

"No, I wasn't aware of that. What business is he in now?"

"You mean with Prohibition over a long time ago?" Tino chuckled. "He invests in real estate, hotels, stuff like that. You could say he's an entrepreneur. The boss always lands on his feet."

"So why the sudden yearning for bagels?"

"We had some for breakfast at the hotel yesterday. The chef told us about you and the bakery. Mr. Toblinsky remembered you guys right off. Wanted to know how you were doing."

"That's nice." Fear trickled through Sam. Why should Toblinsky be interested in him after all this time? He worked to keep his voice even. "We're doing fine. Tell him thank you."

"Yeah, but that's not all. Mr. Toblinsky is looking to— Whatcha call it?" Tino snapped his fingers. "Diversify, yeah, that's it. He's looking to diversify. He's wondering if old man Scheinberg might want a partner."

"My father-in-law has all of the partners he wants or needs. The boys each have part of the business."

"Well, if you think he might change his mind or if you come up with an idea of your own, come see the boss. He always liked you, Sammy."

Tino left as the sun peeked over the tops of the buildings across the street from the bakery. Sam was glad to see his black Caddie pull away of the curb. Tino's sudden reappearance had awakened bad memories.

~ ~ ~

Sam rubbed the creases between his eyes and went over his figures again. Nothing on the page had changed. Perhaps it was time to do as Tino suggested. And Rebecca? So maybe one of the banks had a change of heart. Maybe a silent partner offered financing. Maybe a long-lost relative sent money. If he made the lie believable enough, maybe Rebecca would never guess where the money came from.

Chapter 36

The Fontainebleau's bellman opened the car door for Liz at precisely 11:00 p.m. on Friday. The four-and-one-half-hour drive had been tiring after a long week of catching up on everything left undone while they were in Seattle. Liz unfolded herself from the passenger seat and rubbed the small of her back. A warm, humid breeze caressed her despite it being early November—so different from Seattle, even from Gainesville.

Hugh had made a reservation for them, but he wouldn't tell her what type of room they would have or what it cost, which was probably astronomical. She had suggested they stay at a cheaper place off the beach, but he would have none of it. Extravagance was so unlike him. In fact, he was being rather mysterious, as though he was trying to put on some kind of show.

Liz looked through the lobby's curved glass front into the mid-century modernism of a space created before she was born and as storied as any place on Miami Beach. This was where the Rat Pack had hung out. Sinatra and company had made the Fontainebleau their own. At a glance, you could tell their brand of 1950's cocktail lounge cool still permeated the place. From the back and white photographs on the walls to the clean lines of the retro style furniture, cool still held sway. The hotel had lost none of the glamor of that post-war period when the world had reawakened to new life after the long nightmares of World War II and Korea. Liz loved the ambiance instantly.

Once checked in, Hugh led her to a room on the seventh floor. Liz dropped down onto the king-sized bed and sighed.

"This is really comfortable. I could stay in bed all weekend. Thank you for insisting we stay here. This room is so luxurious."

"That's not the best part." Hugh took Liz's hand. "Come to the window."

He yanked on cords and opened the curtains to reveal a balcony overlooking the famous bowtie pool with a full view of the Atlantic beyond. The glass door slid back at his touch. The sound of soft waves and the scent of fresh salt-laden air filled the room. Liz stepped onto the balcony, placed her hands on the railing, and breathed deeply. The stress of the last weeks ebbed in rhythm with the water as it kissed the sand and ran away. The night, like the Atlantic, rested peacefully under a starry sky.

Hugh stepped behind Liz, slipped his arms around her, and leaned in. "We can sleep with the door open, if you want to. Nobody can see into the room after the lights are off."

Liz settled into his embrace. "Lovely thought. I've always wanted to see the sun rise over the ocean."

He kissed the back of her neck, awakening senses as only he could do. With that simple gesture everything — piled up work, research worries, registration numbers, needy parents — all of it disappeared under the warmth of his lips and the gentle pressure of his body.

~ ~ ~

Sunlight slanting into the room turned the backs of Liz's eyelids red, waking her from the first full night's sleep she had experienced in weeks. She opened one eye and squinted into the dawn. Although not exactly cold, the air had turned somewhat cooler overnight. She reached down, drew the duvet around her shoulders, and rolled over. Hugh lay on his back with one arm stretched up against the headboard.

Gentle snoring escaped his slightly parted lips. Devotion to weekly workouts in the athletic department's weight room kept him in good shape for an academic, nothing outlandish, but firm where it mattered. His bare chest rose and fell in deep slumber. She let her index finger hover lightly above his lower lip and traced its beautiful outline. For a man, he had the reddest cupid bow mouth she had ever seen. His dark wavy hair stood mussed on the top of his head and the stubble on his chin and jaw gave him the appearance of a model on the cover of a romance novel.

The fact that she knew he was naked beneath the covers made the comparison all the more apt. Liz stretched her arm across his belly and closed her eyes. There was time for another couple hours' sleep and maybe something more before they had to get ready to meet Rich.

Liz and Hugh strolled into the hotel bar at 10:50 expecting to be early for their appointment. Liz's gaze swept the space looking for the best table for conversation. To her surprise, she found Rich already seated in a corner booth. He stood as they drew near and extended his hand.

"You must be the fiancé. I'm afraid I don't recall your name." Rich's tone sounded somewhat dismissive, but his expression seemed to hold a challenge.

Liz bit down on the tip of her tongue. She wanted to slap Rich for his attitude and kick herself for lying about being engaged. Beside her, Hugh visibly stiffened and cut his eyes at her before a confident smile took charge of his features.

He stepped forward and gripped Rich's hand. "Hugh Raymond and you must be the acclaimed chef, Richard Whitehead."

Although Hugh's words were perfectly cordial, Liz recognized a particular inflection that usually portended the building of a cold wall of professionalism. Hugh was the consummate diplomat, so Rich may not have noticed, but something hard flickered in his eyes. Wanting to distract them from their little drama, Liz made a display of looking at her watch.

"Isn't our appointment at eleven-thirty? Shouldn't we be going?"

Rich blinked a couple of times as though snapping out of a trance. "Yeah. The guy we're going to see is a tough, old bird. He can be difficult if he thinks he isn't being given sufficient respect."

"Sounds like he's a bit touchy. Any idea why?"

"Could be because he's something of a fake. Has a 24K gold signet ring with a family crest on his pinkie. Wears expensive suits and rides around in a chauffeur driven Bentley. Claims he's from an old aristocratic family, but by his accent when he speaks Spanish, I'd say it's more likely he stole the ring and invented the family. Nobody seems to know where his money came from. Rumor has it he's connected."

"He sounds interesting in his own right. He may find a place in an article, if he agrees."

"Yeah. He's a colorful character." Rich cut his eyes at Hugh. "If I'd known there were two of you, I'd have brought Connie's Mercedes."

Liz's mouth thinned. She was pretty sure she had told Rich that Hugh would be with her. She opened her mouth to comment, but Hugh cut her off. "No problem. We'll take my car. Plenty of room for three."

With Rich navigating from the backseat, Hugh guided the car away from the beach and over a bridge into Miami proper, turning left onto Bayshore Drive.

After a few blocks, Rich leaned forward and pointed toward limestone block walls. "Turn in at this gate."

The car's tires made a soft slapping sound as they passed over the brick paved driveway beneath a tunnel of foliage. Liz gasped at first sight of the home. Lush gardens surrounded the two-story structure giving it a feeling of seclusion and privacy in the midst of the busy city. Red-barrel roof-tiles and deep, overhanging eaves established it as an example of Miami's early 1900's mission style. The stucco exterior, heavily framed casement windows, and arched entrance demonstrated that care had been taken in maintaining the home's original aesthetic. One day, she and Hugh would have a home like this.

At the chiming of the doorbell, a uniformed butler opened the door. Not even Rich's great-aunt Consuelo had a butler. This was a world unlike any Liz had entered. She glanced down at her plain navy business suit and tried to smooth away the travel wrinkles.

The butler conducted them down a central hall that ran straight through to the back of the house. Liz peeked into the rooms lining either side of the hall. Each room looked like it had been staged by a decorator whose tastes ran to high quality antiques. She did a quick calculation. Nope. She and Hugh would never have a place like this unless they won the lottery.

At the door to the patio, Liz shielded her eyes from the glare coming off the bay. In a corner next to the balustrade under the shade of mature ficus trees an elderly gentleman rose from a table set for three. A maid hastily laid a fourth place.

"Thank you, Sonya. I think that will do. You may bring the wine now." After brief introductions, their host waved toward the vacant seats. "Please join me. I thought we might enjoy sitting out here. The day is so beautiful." He waited until Rich pulled out a chair for Liz and for his guests to sit before he resumed his seat facing the water. He turned to Liz. A twinkle lit his eyes when they met hers. "Winter in South Florida is beyond compare. Don't you agree, my dear?" A handsome charmer shone through the veil of age. He must have been serious eye candy in his youth.

"It is indeed, Mr. Cruz. You are so kind to meet with us. I'll try to be brief so that we won't intrude on your lunch."

"Intrude?"

"There are four places set for what I assume is lunch with family or guests. We'll be on our way quickly."

"But my dear, the table is set for you." The subtle gesture of his hand included them all. "Richard promised me a vision of loveliness to brighten my day, and he did not disappoint. Please allow an old man the pleasure of your company at a meal. My health doesn't allow me to get out as much as I would like. Your visit is a gift."

Liz glanced at Hugh and Rich. They nodded in unison. "Your invitation is as gracious as it is charming. We are delighted to accept."

While gracious and subtle, Mr. Cruz made it apparent that prolonged conversation over a saffron-laced seafood paella and a good pinot grigio was the price of his cooperation in Liz's project. After a maid cleared away the meal, he finally looked expectantly at Liz.

"I believe you have some photographs you wish for me to see?"

Liz's heart beat a little faster while she laid her cache out before their host. "I'm hoping you will recognize this man." She tapped the face with the scars.

The old man took a magnifying glass from his breast pocket and squinted at the pictures, stopping over the clearest ones, nodding. He swiveled several times between the two from the 1950's.

"Yes. I recognize him." He picked up the 1952 picture of Toblinsky and Batista, location unknown according to Rich, Sr.'s article, and held it close to his face. He seemed to breathe in the very essence of the image. A rueful smile settled over his features as he returned it to the table. "I was there that night. In fact, I am in the background of the picture." A broad smile lit the old man's face. "I see I have surprised you. You are perhaps wondering how a much, much younger version of myself could be in such a place? I reinvented myself once I arrived in Miami." He cut his eyes at Rich and raised an eyebrow. "People are more receptive when they believe a man has breeding. Wouldn't you agree, young man?"

Rich did not answer immediately. He seemed to search for the right response. "I believe that a man is whatever he makes of himself. Breeding is an old-fashioned idea."

"Perhaps for your generation. If so, the better for it." Mr. Cruz returned his attention to the picture and pointed at a figure in the background. "That's me. I was a bellboy. I was twelve. I've come a long way, haven't I?"

Compassion for the boy the old man had been filled Liz. He must have been about nineteen when he arrived in the US. "You have certainly done very well. It must have been difficult to be so young and leave home with no hope of returning."

Emotion clouded his eyes for a moment. "It was, but we had no choice if we were to live as we wished."

"Your courage and perseverance are an inspiration." Liz smiled and gathered up all of the pictures save the one bearing the clearest image of her man. "By any chance do you remember this man's name?"

Mr. Cruz traced the scared face with his finger. "His name, if I ever knew it, left me long ago, but I do know this. He was a caterer or party planner of some kind and his business was located here in Miami. All of us hotel employees wondered why an American outsider was brought in when we had the best trained staff and the best kitchen on the island."

"So this photo was taken in Cuba?" Liz stopped breathing.

"It was. In the restaurant of the Riviera, Moshe Toblinsky's Havana hotel built with generous cooperation from General Batista."

Liz breathed in and out slowly. "Do you remember the name of the man's business?"

"No." The old man glanced up at Liz, the desire not to disappoint clearly evident in his eyes. "However, I know someone who might have information or who could at least point you in the right direction."

Liz feared she was grinning like a jackass as she placed her business card on the table. "My goodness, how wonderful. I would call or meet with him whenever he wants. I am so very grateful for your help. This means so much to my research. If there is any way that I can return your kindness, please allow me to do so."

A twinkle lit the old man's eyes. "I will give your request some thought. For now, I will see what my contact says about supplying information. If he agrees, I will have Richard call him."

"He wouldn't speak to me directly?"

"Do you speak Spanish?"

"I'm afraid not."

"So having Richard translate is the best plan, I believe, provided my acquaintance is willing to help." Mr. Cruz smiled coyly. "And I have thought of something you can do for me."

Liz grinned in return. "And what would that be?"

"Bring yourself and these two young men here for New Year's Eve. I am hosting a small gathering of friends. You would be an ornament to the evening, and I suspect observing the competition for your hand could be entertaining."

A chuckle colored by surprise escaped Rich's crookedly, grinning lips. Angry heat pouring off Hugh was palpable, matching the fire crawling from Liz's throat onto her cheeks. She hadn't the courage to meet either guy's gaze.

Chapter 37

"Liz, your phone has gone off at least a hundred times. Do you want me to bring it to you?" Hugh's niece yelled from the bedroom wing of the ancestral Raymond farmhouse in Cross Creek. "It's somebody named Rich."

Leave it to an inquisitive adolescent to breach the peace of everyone's Thanksgiving afternoon stupor. Apparently she also felt the need to check the caller ID while assisting Liz with her phone. The reason for such an invasion would be a topic for later discussion when the whole Raymond clan — Hugh, his sister, her husband, and the girl's three older siblings — weren't gawking at her.

Liz smiled at everyone and replied, "Yes, please. I probably need to call him back."

"Got some competition, Uncle Hugh?" The girl actually giggled as Liz took the phone.

She glanced at Hugh. He appeared anything but amused. His smile barely lifted the corners of his mouth and the crease between his eyes had deepened. Tilting her head, she returned his gaze, raised her shoulders, and arched her brows. He broke eye contact and sighed. After a couple of beats of silence, he gave her a curt nod. He seemed to see a threat in Rich. This was so unlike Hugh's normal confident, professional demeanor when it came to business, but apparently he thought there was more to Rich than business. Liz ran her tongue over her teeth and swallowed. Hugh's ex-wife had taught him a lot about violated trust, just as a former fiancé and a feckless boyfriend had taught her. If nothing else, their previous romantic attachments proved that gender equality existed in terms of pain and rejection.

Maybe Hugh needed to feel included in the call. Taking his hand, she pulled him to his feet. "Let's take this down by the lake. It's so pretty there, and I need to walk off dinner."

The path to the lake led beneath bald cypress trees draped with Spanish moss, knees poking up around their bases like creatures rising from a primordial swamp. Liz had laughed when she first saw the trees. The moss looked so much like curly gray beards. She had grown to love those bearded trees with their pointy knees. They dotted Hugh's farm like gentle sentinels protecting all beneath their outstretched arms. This was a lovely little corner of old Florida. The Cracker style farmhouse and attendant acres inherited from his grandparents held Hugh's heart. He once told her that no matter where he spent the majority of his time, the farm at Cross Creek would always be his true center. Having visited many times, she now understood his devotion. There was something completely comforting in the frumpy old furniture, the stands of planted pines covering fields where crops once grew, and the marginally manicured lawn. Simply put, the place just felt like home.

As they strolled, Liz glanced at Hugh from beneath her lashes. He looked troubled, which sent a twinge of guilt and regret twisting through her. He loved her enough to reveal his vulnerabilities, a novel experience in her romantic life. She had always been the one to work harder and love more. The responsibility that came with holding another person's heart in the palms of one's hands weighed heavily at times like this. Liz felt nothing for Richard Whitehead, Jr. despite his glamorous lifestyle, his dark good looks, and the fact that his type had traditionally been her type, usually with devastating consequences for her. Equally handsome and certainly her equal in education, perhaps her superior in intelligence, Hugh was the safe, the sensible, the far better choice. She leaned closer and grabbed his hand, giving it a squeeze. He smiled and raised her hand to his lips.

The wooden bench, silvered with age and weather, where he had proposed to her the first time faced the lake on its eastern side. Sun diamonds danced on water rippled by a cool breeze. Liz wrapped her sweater a little closer around her body, sat down, and pressed the return call icon.

"Hey, pretty lady. I was afraid I wasn't going to hear from you. That would be a shame considering the trouble I've been to for you." Rich's voice came through the ether flirtatious and slightly slurred. In the background, Liz could hear laughter and the clatter of dishes and cutlery.

"You're entertaining. Should I call later?"

"No, now is fine. I'm at Dad's place. We're having late dessert with his friends. It's a wild bunch here on Tampa Bay."

Why hadn't he taken his father to Consuelo's for the holiday? Perhaps Richard, Sr. did not want to leave his new lady friend even for the short time it would take to share Thanksgiving dinner with his former aunt-in-law. The thought made Liz smile.

She glanced at Hugh, who asked questions with his eyes. She hunched her shoulders and shook her head. "I can only imagine what you and your dad are getting up to. You said you have some news for me?"

"Indeed I have. How much time do you get between semesters?"

"Not as much as you might think. Why?"

"Interested in a little trip in the name of research?"

"Where did you have in mind?"

"Havana. Mr. Cruz's friend gave me the name of someone you will want to talk to. If the man is still alive, there's about a 90% probability he knew your guy."

"Is this for real?" Liz tingled with anticipation.

"Would I be suggesting the trip if it weren't? Aunt Connie is furious that I want to go with you."

"A member of her family going to Cuba brings back terrible memories, I'm sure."

"It's more than that. She thinks the current regime still has its sights set on everyone in the family. She thinks I'll be gunned down the minute I set foot in Havana."

"Oh, my. Do you think she could be right?"

"Of course not. It's a ridiculous notion. How would they even know who Richard Whitehead is, for Christ's sake?"

Liz could feel Hugh's eyes boring into her and hear his fingers drumming on the bench's arm. His agitation was distracting, so she turned away. A sharp intake of breath behind her did nothing to dampen her excitement, but it sent her guilt meter's needle edging into the red.

"When do you think we should go? I need to go back to Seattle sometime during the holidays to check on my parents."

"How about at the beginning of the break? That way you can be home for Christmas."

"Sounds great. I can't wait." Liz tapped the end call icon and turned back to Hugh.

"So what's got you all hot and bothered?" Hugh's voice held no pretense of casual enquiry. Anger lit his normally kind eyes, and his mouth had hardened to a thin line.

Liz explained what Rich had discovered and what they planned. Hugh's mood deepened. "Havana, huh? With Rich. Great." Hugh drew a deep breath and exhaled slowly. "I don't think it's particularly safe for you to go gallivanting around Cuba with a member of the deposed dictator's family. I'm going with you."

The urge to lash out at him filled Liz. He was acting like a controlling husband. She prepared a worthy retort, but the expression in his eyes stopped her. Behind his anger lurked a deeper emotion. It wasn't jealousy. It looked more like fear.

Hugh seemed to be afraid for her to be alone for an extended time with Rich. He must fear she would betray him, too. Ex-wives could leave their marks on men long after the marriage ended.

Liz choked back her own harsh words and anger, replaced by empathy for this fear she so well understood. "Of course. I want you to come. It will be a working vacation."

~ ~ ~

The trip from Miami to Aeropuerto Internacional Josè Martì—La Habana had only taken an hour and fifteen minutes, but Liz felt like she stepped into another era as they waited for a taxi outside the terminal. Cars produced in 1950's Detroit lined the curbs and dotted the street. Many of them were in oddly good shape with polished paint jobs and clean interiors. The drivers looked James Dean cool with their bare forearms resting in the open windows.

Rich flagged down a taxi and spoke to the driver in Spanish. Liz caught the name of their hotel. The driver nodded and began loading their luggage into the trunk. Rich slid onto the front seat, leaving the back for Liz and Hugh.

While they traveled toward the city center, Rich talked nonstop with the driver, apparently asking questions about life in Cuba from what little Liz understood. The driver occasionally cast a speculative gaze over his front seat companion, who seemed not to notice or maybe he simply didn't care. Rich's expression and his voice showed how pumped he was to be in the country of his heritage, but which he had never been allowed to visit. Did he feel like he was coming home? It wouldn't be a surprise if he did, given the emersion in Cuban expat culture he had received from his mother's family.

They edged into the old central city, greeted by a warm December breeze flowing through the taxi window, caressing Liz's cheeks and tightening the frizz around her face. Humidity wreaked havoc on her hair no matter how much time she spent forcing it into compliance. Maybe she would just go natural while they were in Cuba. After all, the glamor the city had known before Castro must surely be as faded as the paint on the buildings they passed. At one time, these places would have been considered mansions, but evidence of decades of neglect showed in soot and mold running in wide rivers down the crumbling formerly white stucco. Iron gates allowed the occasional peek into interior courtyards where barefoot children played or adults lounged in the shade of trees planted before the revolution.

All at once, Rich gasped and pointed to an ornate Spanish colonial style building. He looked over the seat at Liz, his eyes wide with excitement. "See that house? I think that's where my grandmother and Consuelo grew up. At least, it looks like the pictures. I'd love to see inside."

The taxi driver's gaze snapped toward Rich, then turned back just as quickly. Although the man pretended to not speak English, it seemed he had understood what Rich said. An uneasy feeling crawled through Liz. Consuelo had warned Rich not to come on this trip. Liz prayed the old woman's fears did not materialize. Clearly Consuelo's final experiences in the land of her birth colored her perceptions and imaginings, but what if she was right? After all, what did ordinary Americans really know about Cuba's political climate or her citizens' feelings toward their once politically prominent former neighbors?

Chapter 38

Miami, Florida
January 5, 1959

Damnit, the schmuck was at it again.

Tearing his gaze from the one-way mirror looking out into the showroom, Sam pushed back from his desk, went to the office door, and yanked it open. "Get back to work. I'm not paying you to stand around yakking."

Grumbling loud enough to be heard throughout the store, he gave the door a vicious shove, filling the small, windowless office with the sound of rattling glass. Over the years, several panes in the door's upper half had fallen victim to displays of temper, but only Rebecca knew it was all for show. A guy had to control his emotions, not let them control him. It had kept him alive back when things were different.

Sam glanced toward the mirror. Message received? A tight smile lifted the corners of his mouth. The back of a silvery sharkskin suit passed through the store's front entrance and disappeared behind the wheel of a black Caddie parked at the curb. Making nice with that goombah got harder every Monday. As slick a guy as you'd ever likely meet.

To make matters even more of a pain, next he'd have to deal with the blowback from his little display of temper. Sam glanced at his wrist and followed his watch's second hand. Five, four, three, two, one. A face appeared in the door's window followed by a hesitant knock.

Sam's lips pursed as he jerked his chin toward the office interior. "It isn't locked."

Sam's college-boy salesman, Jimmy, stepped into the office, a little furrow creasing his forehead. "I'm sorry about that, Mr. Ackerman, but he stopped me and wanted to talk. I didn't want to be rude."

"It's okay this time, but I don't want you to talk to that guy again." Sam jabbed his index finger at Jimmy. "He wants to talk, you send him to me. Got it?"

"Yes, sir." Jimmy shifted from one foot to the other. His mouth opened, closed, and opened again. "Mr. A, he was asking me about school and stuff. Like what I'm majoring in." The boy shrugged. "I thought he was just being nice. I didn't want to offend one of your friends."

Sam rolled his lower lip between his teeth. The kid really didn't know any better. "He's no friend of mine. He just works for somebody I know." Jimmy's eyes filled with confusion. How much to tell? Not much, for sure. Sam placed his hand on the boy's arm. "Look, stay away from guys like him. Your wife gets sick, your mother needs an operation and you ain't got the money to pay for it? You come to me. That guy's bosses are always on the lookout for smart, educated young guys. They promise you'll get rich working for them, but it would be the biggest mistake you'd ever make. Once they get their hooks in you, you'll never get free."

Jimmy's eyes grew with each sentence Sam uttered. "Is . . . Is that guy in the mob or something?"

Sam suppressed a bitter laugh. "Yeah. The mob or something." Holy crap. Each word grew harder and louder. Some things he didn't seem to be able to control so much anymore. *Get a grip. Be a mensch.*

The boy tilted his head to one side. "So what does he do?"

"What you've seen him do every Monday you've been working for me."

"But all he does is carry a briefcase back into the office with you for a few minutes and leaves. He doesn't stay long enough to do much of anything. Do you think he's ever killed anybody?"

"Maybe. Probably not. He's just an errand boy."

"So how come you know somebody like that?" Jimmy's words came in a rush.

Sam's frown deepened. "Never you mind how I know him. That isn't any of your concern." The boy broke eye contact, his face turning crimson from chin to hairline.

Sam walked to his desk and sat down, but Jimmy remained rooted in place, his face a study in fascinated curiosity. He wasn't a stupid boy, but he hadn't seen much of the world outside that little swamp near Jacksonville where he grew up. Sam sighed. The kid probably needed to be told enough to keep him from blundering into trouble.

Sam waved at the visitor's chair on the opposite side of the desk. "Sit."

Jimmy moved from the door and dropped onto the chair in one smooth motion.

"You remember me telling you I was a kid in Brooklyn?" Jimmy nodded. "You wouldn't have recognized me back then. My parents were good, observant Jews. We went to synagogue every Saturday. I went to Hebrew school in the afternoon after regular school. My mother wanted me to be a rabbi. Maybe I would of been, but my father died and I had to quit school to go to work. Got a job on the loading docks at the Fulton Fish Market. Know anything about the Fulton Market?" The boy shook his head. "I was fifteen when I started there. Tops Monza ran the whole operation. Ever heard of Lucky Luciano?"

Jimmy half grinned as though he thought Sam might be having him on. "You mean the Mafia guy?"

"That would be him. Lucky Luciano was Tops's boss and Tops was mine."

"But . . . I thought you had to be Italian to be in the Mafia."

"You do. I'm not Mafioso. I just worked for them." A trickle of pride tinged by anger ran through Sam. "I was a good worker. Monza liked me and took care of me when I needed help."

The boy's intake of breath made a little whooshing sound. "What kind of help?"

Sam eyed his employee, irritation bubbling just beneath the surface. Such a persistent kid, but he'd probably do well after college. "Mind your own business. And no more answering questions for the errand boy. Now get back to counting those returns before I fire your redneck ass."

The boy jumped to his feet as though he'd been slapped. "Sorry, Mr. Ackerman. I'll have everything counted and restocked before quitting time."

"You better," Sam barked. "Just because you stayed up late watching the Friday Night Fights doesn't mean you can make up for lost sleep on my dime." Employees shouldn't get to thinking you were soft. Tops Monza had taught him that.

When the door closed, Sam returned to his ledger, but the figures danced and wiggled across the page. Taking off his glasses, he massaged the frown lines between his brows, and blinked several times. Returning the glasses to their perch, he squinted at the ledger, but the edges of the handwritten debits and credits still blurred. Straightening his back and rolling his shoulders, he glanced toward the one-way mirror. Jimmy's curiosity had stirred up events that wouldn't leave him alone.

His gaze drifted up to the fan oscillating on the top of the bookcase, but his eyes didn't focus on anything in particular. Memories. So many memories. Things that ought to stay locked away pushed themselves forward, uninvited, unwelcome. Stupid waste of time. Dwelling on the past didn't do anybody any good.

Sam shifted in his chair as a twinge built in his chest, sending a warning shot down his left arm. His old enemy was at it again. Just beneath Sam's ribs, an invisible pump inflated an inner tube of pressure wrapping itself around his heart. With each up and down of the pump, the tube expanded, stretched, thinned. Sam rubbed his arm and opened the desk's top drawer. Withdrawing a vile of nitroglycerin tablets, he placed one under his tongue, clenching his teeth as the medicine washed through his mouth in a metallic wave, bitter, stinging. Sam massaged the area over his heart with his knuckles, waiting for the pain to ease and the headache to begin.

He leaned back in his chair, resting his head against the wall behind him. As much as he tried to keep the past buried, it sometimes came sneaking up on him, snaking its way into his consciousness when he wasn't looking, preying on his mind, stealing his peace. The past crept in now and turned on a projector in his head. Scenes rolled like 8 mm Kodachrome home movies, a little jerky at first, but sharp and clear where he dreaded them most. The grand finale— Bateman floundering in the river during the hurricane, the years of bootlegging, the lies to Rebecca about where he'd gotten financing to start the business, the favors done for and received from Toblinsky—played in full technicolor.

The telephone's jangling broke his reverie. He snatched up the receiver. "Ackerman."

"Hello, Sammy. Do you know who this is?"

Sam swallowed the lump in his throat. "Yes, sir."

"That's good. It's unkind to forget old friends. Friends help each other, just as I once helped you." A brief pause electrified the air around Sam. "Sammy, the time has come for you to return the friendship I have always shown you."

Fear wrapped its icy fingers around his heart, chilling his very core. He had always known this day would come, but he still wasn't prepared to learn what form the repayment would take.

Chapter 39

"Sammy, you still there? Ain't you going to say something?"

"Mr. T-Tolbinsky." Sam had never stuttered in his life, but that voice filled with pretense of friendship and kindness set his heart thudding and tied his tongue. "It's been a long time."

"But not so long that you've forgotten a debt of friendship." It was a statement, not a question.

Sam drew a long breath before he answered. "Of course not, sir. I'll always be grateful for the start you gave me."

"Good, good. Gratitude is an important quality in a person." Toblinsky paused. Sam could hear him breathing on the other end of the line. When he spoke again, his voice came in soft, almost thoughtful tones. "I doubt you've ever been told, but it was a debt of friendship to Tops that persuaded me to bring you to Miami all those years ago. He hated to bump off a good kid, but he didn't have a choice unless I took you. He figured you'd cave under police questioning."

Sam had always suspected there was more to the story than Toblinsky doing a favor for Tops and now here was confirmation. How do you respond to a thing like that? A twinge built in his chest as he cast about for a sensible response and settled on, "Then I am doubly grateful to both of you. It must have been a powerful debt for you to take on a kid like me."

A soft chuckle came over the wire. "Not exactly. To tell the truth, I said no at first, but when Tops said you was a good Jewish kid fallen on hard times, how could I say no? Us Jews gotta stick together, don't we?"

"Absolutely."

An uncomfortable silence settled between them. Finally, Toblinsky asked, "Ain't you gonna ask how you can repay me for saving your life and setting you up in business?"

Sam's voice stuck in the roof of his mouth. He cleared his throat and asked, "What do you need for me to do?"

"I need for you to take a little trip to Havana to see about some people and pick up a few documents for me."

Sam choked back a gasp. "But the country is overrun with Castro's Revolutionaries. Everything is in chaos down there."

"Which makes the job even more important. Nobody there really knows you, so you can move around Havana without people getting suspicious." Toblinsky became quiet while Sam's thumping pulse grew loud against his eardrums. An intake of breath and the gangster continued, "How's that pretty wife of yours and the kids, Rachel and Jacob is it? I watched them leaving your house earlier today. Real nice family you got there. Nice house, good business, nice life. You're a lucky guy, Sammy."

Toblinsky didn't threaten Rebecca and the kids directly. He didn't need to. Sam swallowed hard. "Tell me what to do."

~ ~ ~

January 6, 1959

Sam pulled back on the throttle of the big sport fisherman and gazed up into a moonless sky of the predawn hours. The stars somehow looked bigger and brighter down here. Rebecca had always wanted to come with him to Cuba, but he had put her off by saying that he would be working the whole time. He had never once mentioned that those business trips were in service to Toblinsky. Nor had he ever told her how he managed to get his own business started when the banks refused to make him a loan. If she suspected, she didn't say anything. But why would she suspect? He didn't cheat on her. He told her everything that was going on in the business and in his mind and heart, with that one exception, the biggest lie of all, the lie that he was indebted to a gangster. To top it all off, he had lied to her about where he was going this time. He told her he was flying to New York to meet with a potential client, a guy who was building a hotel in Naples. Sam was considering expanding to the Gulf Coast and offering Jimmy a partnership after he graduated college. Lies. All of it. Regret, guilt, and deep sadness settled over him like a sodden fishing net. At least this job would be finished quickly, if all went as planned. Of course, that was a pretty big if considering the state of things in Cuba at the moment.

Sam found the river mouth he had been told to enter and guided the boat through the mangroves until his destination came in sight, a small, secluded loading dock beside acres of sugarcane fields. The odor of spawning fish and rotting vegetation greeted Sam once the smell of the boat's exhaust dissipated. He climbed onto the dock as the boat bumped against its wooden piers. After tying off the bow line, he strained toward where he thought the city should be. It was hard to tell whether he had it right. Only a grayish blotch hovered on the horizon where the glowing lights of a vibrant nightlife should have been. Standing there staring into the gloom wasn't accomplishing anything. Best get on with it.

He strode toward what had been described as a sugar warehouse and stepped through the unlocked door. Clicking on his flashlight, he went to a tarp covered mound in the center of the building. A couple of hard tugs revealed a farm truck large enough to shelter a small number of livestock or several human beings beneath its canvas top and sides. After opening the warehouse doors, Sam scooted behind the wheel, pressed his foot against the floor starter, then depressed the clutch and shifted the stick into first gear. The truck rolled forward into the balmy night.

Once beyond the bounds of the sugar plantation, it bounced over a rutted farm to market road for about an hour before the outskirts of the city began surrounding it. Havana by starlight would have been alluring, even romantic under other circumstances. As it was, Sam dreaded entering the city and the tasks that lay ahead of him.

Chapter 40

The taxi bearing Liz, Hugh, and Rich twisted and turned through Havana past ancient buildings in need of significant refurbishment and shiny, late-vintage glass towers. Liz craned to catch every possible glimpse of the city most Americans thought of as a mysterious den of communism and decay. The scenery had a surreal quality. Antiquated structures squatted in the shadows of modern high rises making Havana look like it had a bi-polar disorder, the manically new and the depressively old contained within one dichotomous whole. The city felt simultaneously sinister and alluring.

A thrill crawled through Liz, equal parts excitement, curiosity, and trepidation. They had come into a closely guarded society against the advice of friends and to the horror of her mother and Aunt Mildred. She traveled in the company of a man who might well have a price on his head due to his family connections. Liz had never thought of herself as particularly brave, but perhaps she had underestimated her attraction to outright danger.

From the cab's front seat, Rich gave a running commentary on various points of interest, turning frequently to make sure Liz missed nothing. For someone who had never been to Cuba, he sure knew a lot about the place. When the aqua water of the Florida Straits appeared ahead, the cab turned right onto the famous Malecòn, the broad esplanade, roadway, and seawall that stretched from the mouth of Havana Harbor in the old town to the Vedado neighborhood.

As the cab whizzed along, glittering boutiques, bistros, and bars popped up among less fortunate neighbors.

Prosperity seemed to be returning to what had once been the most glamorous eight miles south of Miami Beach. A sharp right onto a palm-lined divided drive sent Liz sliding into Hugh, who put his arm around her shoulders and kissed her temple. Rich's smile froze for a moment, then he grinned and recovered his usual bravado.

"Well, here we are. The Hotel Nacional de Cuba." Rich's gesture took in the hotel and surrounding gardens. "Toblinsky operated the hotel's bar and casino in the 50's. She looks pretty good for a lady of nearly ninety, doesn't she?"

She did indeed. An eight-story structure of cream stone rose up before them, a blend of 1930's angular practicality topped by Spanish Colonial architectural elements complete with twin red-tile roofed bell towers. Online pictures viewed before they left Miami had revealed that luxury had not completely disappeared under the Castro regime. The hotel had been remodeled and updated in 1992. Tourists remained an important part of the economy, after all.

Checking into the hotel brought an unexpected surprise. Rich took the lead, speaking in Spanish to the desk clerk. With room key in hand, he opened his mouth to speak on behalf of Liz and Hugh, but the clerk anticipated him. He looked at Hugh. "Welcome sir. Would you prefer a double room or a suite?"

Hugh glanced at Liz, then smiled at the young man behind the desk. "A suite with an ocean view would be great. Do you have one available?"

The clerk consulted his computer screen. "At the moment, I'm afraid the only room of that kind is on the top floor. It's our honeymoon suite. Will that be suitable?"

Liz's involuntary intake of breath not only surprised her, but it brought a flood of heat to her face. She saw a brief smile skitter across the clerk's face before he regained his professional composure, while a frown flickered across

Rich's features. She didn't dare look at Hugh. She snatched her gaze toward the view of the pool and surrounding gardens through the front windows. Why she should care what the clerk thought was a mystery. His appearance in her life would surely be limited to this one moment. That she gasped at the mention of the honeymoon suite made her just plain stupid. She exhaled slowly and squared her shoulders. Feeling flummoxed was not the right mindset to begin her quest. It would need her full concentration. If all went as anticipated, tomorrow morning they would drive to the agreed upon location, set out a recording device, ask a few questions, and be on a return flight to Miami tomorrow evening—a straightforward, simple plan.

Chapter 41

The following morning after a late brunch, the trio made their way to the main entrance where their transportation waited.

Liz took one look at the vehicle and laughed. "A limo? Really Rich?"

He shrugged and grinned. "It was the only car available on short notice. Don't you love it though? Just look at those tail fins. Sweet ride, huh?"

Hugh smiled and patted a fin. "Well, it's certainly a classic. Shall we?"

Instead of Rich riding beside the driver as he had in cabs, all three passengers were able to sit in back since there were two seats. After a brief argument with the driver, Rich said they were ready to roll. Their early, afternoon appointment took them into the countryside. Once they left the city proper, the roads became less well maintained, eventually becoming dirt. About an hour and a half from Havana, their driver turned onto a rutted lane that ran between tobacco fields spreading out as far as they could see. Another twenty minutes brought them to a village with what appeared to be one general store and a gas station. Their driver guided the car down a lane behind the store and slowed in front of a modest house, no better than most of its neighbors, but not as disheveled as some.

Rich spoke to the driver in Spanish and shrugged. Turning to Liz, he said, "He doesn't want to wait here in the car, so I told him to go have a coffee and come back in an hour. Do you think that will be enough time?"

"Probably. All we were promised is the identity of the man in the picture."

While they stood on the porch waiting for their host to answer their knock, Liz watched the car speed away from the yard. The driver seemed to be looking at them in his rearview mirror. He had acted grumpy and uncommunicative throughout the trip from the city. Now he watched them as though he suspected them of something. Liz shrugged mentally. Perhaps living in a dictatorship did that to people. They never knew who they could trust.

The front door opened and a brown, deeply wrinkled face gazed up at them. The little women could not have been more than 4' 11". She squinted at them and asked something in Spanish. Rich answered and they were waved inside, down a long central hall, and out the backdoor into a garden area. Beneath the shade of an ancient banyan tree, an old man sat in a wooden lawn chair puffing on a cigar, a glass of amber colored liquid on the table at his elbow. The old woman shuffled to the table and cleared away the remains of a meal, muttering to herself and flashing unhappy glances at Liz, Hugh, and Rich as she gathered the soiled dishes. A roar from the old man sent her scuttling back into the house.

Their host indicated that they should be seated in the other chairs beneath the tree. After introductions through translation and awkward handshakes, he looked at Rich and asked a question. Rich translated. "Sr. Mendoza said, 'So, you are wanting information from the time of the Revolution?' He asks what would you like to know?"

Liz withdrew the pictures from her bag and spread them out on the table. She pointed to the man with the scars on his face in each photo. Looking at the Cuban, she said, "We were told you might know who this man is. Do you know him, sir?"

She looked to Rich to translate, but the old man waved a hand and answered her in English. "Of course I recognize him. He came several times to the office where I once worked." Liz's brows rose nearly to her hairline. The old man chuckled. "Which surprises you more? That I speak good English or that I know this man?"

"I'm not sure. Maybe both. Sr. Mendoza, perhaps you could tell us why this man came to your office."

The old man nodded. "Before I speak of him, it is important that you know what I did before the Revolution. At that point, I was just Juan. No señor or sir." He paused for effect, meeting the gaze each of his guests before continuing with a smug smile. "I was a clerk in the Havana Merrill Lynch office. I reported directly to the branch manager. We were both in the office the day Havana fell."

Chapter 42

Sam guided the truck through Havana's quiet streets with the headlights off. Only the moon and the occasional street lamp lit his way. Having been to Cuba many times at the behest of Moshe Toblinsky, Sam knew the streets and the address to which he was to report. With this trip, Toblinsky had ordered Sam to undertake two tasks. The first was to retrieve documents that would prove damaging if they fell into the wrong hands. The second was far more dangerous.

Sam applied the brakes, down shifted at a small intersection, and squinted through the darkness at what looked to be a street sign. The lettering was impossible to make out in the darkness that blanketed the city. There was nothing for it but to flash the headlights for a moment. Yep, this was the place. The crack of gunfire broke the stillness, echoing from a nearby block. Sam jumped and slammed the lights off with one hand while the other jerked on the gear shift. He drew a shaky breath and leaned his forehead against the steering wheel. With luck he would be back in Miami in less than forty-eight hours. There would be other problems to deal with at that time, but at least he wouldn't be trying to get stuff done in the middle of a goddamned revolution.

He turned left into an alley behind an apartment building. No lights shone through the multiple windows of the four-story structure. The political upheaval presently tearing Cuba apart must have ordinary citizens, like the occupants of this building, cowering in closets and huddled under beds.

When Toblinsky's business partner, the dictator Fulgencio Batista, fled the country at the turning of 1959, the gangster knew the end had come to their lucrative partnership. All that remained was the repayment of personal debts, one owed by Toblinsky to Batista, the other owed by Sam to Toblinsky. Sam's arrival in Cuba for this one last time took care of both, at least he hoped it did. With men like Toblinsky, you never knew what they might expect.

Despite the cooler temperatures of early winter, sweat trickled down Sam's back and from his armpits. Snatching his handkerchief from his pocket, he swiped at the moisture on his forehead and upper lip. These days, stress elicited a liquid response and drove his blood pressure through the roof. A twinge of pain stirred in his chest. Getting old was a real pain in the ass. Sam dug in his pocket again and withdrew his vial of nitro tablets. He placed one under his tongue. This job required him to be at the top of his game.

Once his chest eased, Sam went to the building's back entrance and up a flight of stairs to the top floor. Going to the door of the apartment that overlooked the alley, he knocked twice, waited for a count of seven seconds, and knocked three more times. The scuffling of shoes on bare floorboards and hushed whispers sounded through the closed door. After a considerable time, the door creaked open just a crack and a pair of dark eyes peered at Sam from the other side. Sam glanced down at the muzzle of a revolver that appeared in the opening, as well.

Great. Getting shot would be a perfect beginning, or more likely end, to this little venture. Hell, might as well get on with it. "Put the gun away and open the door. Toblinsky sent me." The man behind the door didn't seem to understand a word of English. Shit. Sam mustered up what little Spanish he knew and pointed to himself. "*Un amigo. Amigo de* Toblinsky." He made a wavy motion with one hand. "*Un barco.*" The man stared blankly and edged the gun closer to Sam's midsection. Sam's temper flared. He leaned in close to the crack and hissed, "I'm here to help you, you stupid son-of-a-bitch. Now open the fucking door."

The eyes suddenly disappeared and a different pair took their place. They traveled over Sam from top to bottom, finally settling into direct eye contact. "How do we know what you say is true?" A heavy Spanish accent colored the man's words. "These are perilous times."

Sam reached into his pocket and withdrew several photographs. He held them up one-by-one so that the man behind the door could get a good look at each.

The man's eyes narrowed. "So, you have been with General Batista and Sr. Toblinsky on several occasions. What does that really prove?"

"That I am here because Toblinsky sent me to save your sorry ass. Right now, I'm wondering why I shouldn't just leave you here. The Castro boys will catch up with you sooner or later." Sam half turned, but stopped long enough to say over his shoulder, "Have fun rotting in Fidel's prison. I bet he's picking out your cell right now. From the sound of the gunfire I heard, the rebels are taking the city block by block."

Sam took a couple of steps toward the staircase when a hand gripped his arm. "Wait. Come back. We will let you in. We have no choice but to trust you."

Sam's mouth lifted in a lopsided grin. "No, you really don't. Lucky for you, I'm on your side."

Once inside the apartment, Sam let out a small whistle. "Are all of these people coming?"

The man who seemed to be the leader nodded. "Yes, all or none."

"I was told five, but there must be twelve of you." Sam massaged his left arm. "Hell, it's no matter. We probably won't make it to the city limits anyway."

Fear clouded the eyes of every man in the room except the leader's. His grew hard, but his tone remained calm.

"Perhaps, but we will all stand a better chance if we are well rested." His gaze swept the room. "Go to bed. All of you. This gentleman and I have business to discuss."

When the room was clear, Sam spoke to his host. "We, that's you and me, only have one piece of business. And it's that you and your men do exactly as you are told. Right now, I need a bed. I've got business in the morning that has nothing to do with you. All of you will be ready when I get back here tomorrow. Got it?"

"Si, señor. Do we really have a choice?" When Sam's only response was a hard stare, the man sighed and gestured toward the room's far wall. "You will prefer sleeping on the sofa. All of the beds have three or four people in them already. Sheets are in that closet. I will bid you goodnight."

Chapter 43

Sun slanting through the Venetian blinds woke Sam from a restless dream populated by people long dead. Faces filled with terror faded as the waking world took hold. Goddamn that son-of-a-bitch Bateman. He and the 1926 hurricane's innocent victims got all jumbled together in his dreams. They played hide and seek through his nights like alligators lurking in the Glades. Always just below the surface ready to attack when you weren't paying attention. Sam rubbed his eyes groggily and started to rise, but his joints and muscles screamed and raged. He lay back, trying to get a handle on his surroundings. For a moment, he couldn't understand why his neck had such a crick in it or why he was on a sofa, but the reasons came flooding back, and his heart lurched at the memory of where he was and what he had to do.

The apartment was dead silent. The sounds of gunfire no longer drifted through the blinds from the streets four stories below. Maybe even ardent revolutionaries had to sleep. He squinted at his watch. 7:00. Too early to get started. Stretching his back to work out the stiffness, he rolled over and closed his eyes. If he couldn't sleep, at least he could rest.

~ ~ ~

The fragrance of strong coffee was the next thing Sam was aware of. He must have gone back to sleep after all. Sitting up, he stretched and glanced toward the kitchen door. A shadow moved across the opening followed by the person himself. It was the guy who took the leadership role last night. Sam rotated his wrist. 9:30. He had just enough time to swallow a cup and get to his appointment, if you could call it that.

The figure emerged from the kitchen, steam curling from an ironstone mug that he offered to Sam. "I am glad you have awoken. I would not have let you sleep much longer. The others are getting restless cooped up in the bedrooms."

Sam's brows rose in surprise. "Why didn't they just come on out here? I was awake at seven."

"We wanted you to be well rested. You appeared tired when you arrived last night. Lack of sleep leads to mistakes. We cannot afford mistakes."

Sam sipped the bitter, black brew and nodded. "True on both counts. Thanks for letting me sleep and for the coffee." Sam placed the half-drained mug on the side table and stood. "I have to go into downtown this morning. I don't know how long I'll be. You guys need to be ready when I get back."

"As you said last night. We will be ready, just as I said as well."

~ ~ ~

Sam shuffled down the four flights to the farm truck waiting where he had left it and eased his way out of the alley. He expected to have to dodge gunfights and roadblocks on his way to the business section, but the city lay eerily quiet as though the eye of a hurricane had settled over it. Doors were closed and barred. No faces appeared in the drapery-covered windows. No children played in the courtyards. No shoppers came and went from the neighborhood markets. No pedestrians roamed the sidewalks and alleyways. Havana held its collective breath waiting for the other side of the storm to slam ashore.

After entering the business district, Sam passed deuce and a half trucks coming and going. Bearded young men in olive-drab fatigues, rifles bristling at their shoulders, rocked along in the beds as the trucks rumbled toward their assigned posts. By the rumpled appearances of the uniforms and their lack of insignia, these were Fidel's boys. Havana was falling to the revolutionaries at that very moment. Sweat popped out on Sam's face and rolled from his forehead despite the cool breeze coming through the open windows. He scrubbed his handkerchief across his face and tried to look as much like a Cuban farmer come to town as he could.

The place he was headed sat on one of the best streets in Havana, a fancy dress shop on one side and the city's richest bank on the other. In other times, men in tropical business wear and women in the latest fashions would have strolled on its wide sidewalks. Today, the street looked deserted. If nobody had opened the office, Toblinsky was shit out of luck. Sam couldn't waste time waiting for someone who might never show. He parked in front of the Merrill Lynch office and stepped on the brake. Peering through the brokerage office front window, he searched for signs of life within. A flicker of movement toward the back of the building gave hope that he might be able to complete this part of his mission.

Sam drew a long breath and let it out slowly. This was a dangerous game he played for Toblinsky, and he didn't have as much time as he thought he would. Getting out of the truck, he strode to the office door and grasped the handle, half praying it wouldn't open and that no one would come to let him in. The knob turned easily, and the door opened wide at his slight push. He walked in and stopped to look around.

The shadow he had seen emerged from a back office in the form of a dark-haired man of about twenty-five. Dark eyes swept over Sam. "How may I help you, *senor*?" The words were English, but the voice was definitely Cuban. Sam glanced down at his wrinkled, white polo shirt and soiled seersucker slacks. A sheepish smile lifted the corners of his mouth. So much for impersonating a Cuban farmer.

Sam eyed the young man before asking, "Is your manager in?"

"*Si*. This way, *por favor*." He led Sam to an office where a slender, handsome man sat with his shirtsleeves rolled up to mid forearms casually reading the *New York Times*. The whole country was falling to revolutionaries, but the goddamned Gray Lady still got through.

The young man cleared his throat. "This gentleman wishes to speak with you, sir."

The manager, who looked to be in his late-thirties, dropped the newspaper on his desk and graced Sam with a somewhat puzzled smile. "If you are wanting to speak with the New York office, I'm afraid we can't help you. I'm sorry, but our communications have been cut. The phones lines went dead two days ago."

Sam licked his dry lips. His throat burned from a lack of saliva. "No, I don't need New York. I'm here to pick up some documents that you are holding for one of your customers."

"That's doubtful. Who's the customer?"

Sam reached into his front pants pocket and withdrew a wrinkled, smudged envelope. He handed it over to the manager. The man read the contents and commented, "I see. We do have the documents mentioned in the letter."

The younger man stepped forward. "Sir, forgive me, but are you sure the letter is authentic?" He seemed to know exactly what Sam was here for. Maybe the kid also knew who had sent him.

The manager tossed the letter on his desk. "I've seen that signature enough to know it. General Batista may have fled the country, but he still has business here. Give the man what he came for."

The young man's eyes grew larger when he glanced at the letter. He turned to Sam. "Follow me please." When they drew abreast of a large safe room, he stopped. "I'll only be a moment." Keys clanked in locks and metal scraped against metal. The boy emerged holding a lockbox. "We will go back to the manager's office to remove the contents."

The manger cleared space on his desk for the box, and the boy unlocked it. Sam did not know what could be so important to Toblinsky, but it better be good for all of this trouble. The clerk handed a small stack of documents to Sam. He thumbed through them and let out a low whistle. No wonder Toblinsky wanted this stuff. These were the deeds to the properties he and Batista held in partnership and a couple belonging to Batista alone—hotels, casinos, a sugar plantation. They must be worth a fortune.

The manager leaned back in his chair with his hands behind his head as though he was in the most relaxed of states, but his eyes were riveted to the building's front plate-glass windows. "Juan, take the box back to the safe room, and lock the door." He paused to glance at the letter before taking a box of matches from his desk drawer. Within seconds, the letter lay in the bottom of a metal trashcan, nothing but a pile of ash. "Mr. Ackerman, hide those documents. Put them in your underwear or down your shirt. We're about to have company. Just go along with whatever I say."

At that moment, the front door banged open followed by the sound of tramping boots. Sam stepped away from the desk and turned to see who approached. His heart leapt into his throat. He swallowed hard to keep from choking. He recognized two of the five men from newsreel and newspaper reports. The beard and cigar clamped between the teeth of the lead man made him unmistakable.

The manager rose from his chair and came around to stand in front of his desk. His mouth split into a cool smile. "Good morning, gentlemen. Welcome to Merrill Lynch. May we be of service in helping you establish accounts?"

The newcomers looked at one another and laughed. The lead man turned back to the manager. "No, no open accounts. We here to close them."

The manager's smile faded from cool to puzzled. "I'm not sure what you mean."

"We here for stocks, bonds, cash, things . . ." Fidel looked to Raul who supplied, "Of value."

"I see." The manager beckoned toward the back of the group. "Juan, show Mr. Castro and Mr. Castro to the safe room. Show them whatever they ask to see." He paused and looked over the group of revolutionaries. "I'm afraid the rest of you gentlemen must wait here. The safe room is rather small."

When most of the group made to follow, Juan spoke to them in Spanish. From the office, Sam heard the safe room door open and snatches of Spanish, at first relatively polite, then increasingly angry. Metal scraped and banged for about fifteen minutes, after which, the Castro brothers returned to the office with a white-faced Juan in tow.

Fidel walked to within inches of the manager and leaned in. "Nothing. Where is gone?"

The manager stepped back until the backs of his thighs rested against the edge of his desk. "Our customers . . . how shall I say it?" The manager tilted his head in an apparent display of searching for the right words. "They anticipated your success. Assets held here were transferred out of Cuba some months ago."

"Where?"

"Primarily to the Miami and New York offices. In any event, the bulk of their holdings were already spread over international portfolios. We held only the simplest of their assets in this branch."

Fidel's already sun-ruddied complexion grew redder as he placed his fists on his hips. His gaze traveled over the room until it fell on Sam. "Who are you?" Sam felt the blood drain from his face.

The manager stepped beside Sam. "This is Mr. Jacob Goldstein from the home office in New York. He is here to audit the books in preparation for our Havana branch's closing." Suspicious expressions crawled across Fidel's and Raul's faces, their eyes fixed on Sam. The manager placed a hand on Sam's shoulder and continued, "Mr. Goldstein is an American citizen traveling on a US passport. He reports directly to the president of Merrill Lynch. Our company president is on a first name basis with President Eisenhower." He paused to let his meaning register. "A diplomatic incident is in no one's interest."

Fidel's mouth and eyes hardened. His expression rolled from anger to defiance, finally settling into acceptance. He sighed heavily. "No. We no need more enemies." Turning to his men, he spoke to them in Spanish.

When the front door slammed shut, Sam blew out a long breath, bent over, and placed his hands on his knees.

The manager spoke to Juan. "Get Mr. Ackerman a chair and a glass of water." To Sam he said, "The feeling will pass, and you can now leave Cuba without delay."

But that was exactly the problem. Sam looked up at the manager from beneath his lashes. He couldn't leave. He still had an unfinished task more dangerous than the last.

Chapter 44

Liz had to press her arms across her stomach and squeeze to keep herself from flinging them around Mr. Mendoza's neck. Samuel Ackerman. Finally she had a name. All it had taken was a flight into a country that had been under a travel ban for nearly sixty years.

She bit her lower lip lightly to force down her excitement and leaned in toward the old man. "You have no idea how much this means to my research. I cannot thank you enough for being willing to talk to us. I hope there is something I can do for you to return the kindness you have shown me."

Mendoza's brow wrinkled in thought. His gaze drifted down toward his feet. He seemed to study his shoes for a moment before his head snapped up, and he met Liz's eyes. "Do not tell anyone where you came by this information. If you write an article, do not mention the incident in the Merrill Lynch office. There is still danger for people like me who were once seen as staunch participants in imperial capitalism. I have no desire to be recognized for who I really am."

Liz's heart sank a little. The Merrill Lynch story would have made for interesting reading and was *prima facia* evidence from an important day in Cuba's history. If she must bear this disappointment, perhaps Sr. Mendoza might be willing to satisfy her curiosity on a small matter. She mustered her most winning smile.

"I hope you will forgive my curiosity."

"It depends on what you wish to know."

"I believe you know a Sr. Cruz who now resides in Miami." The old man's eyes grew wary as he nodded. "Did he communicate with you directly?"

"No."

Rich coughed to cover the choking sound he had just made. Liz glanced at him. His face drew up on one side in an expression of ambiguity. It was as though he said it was up to her, and that he would take no responsibility in her little drama.

"May I ask how the communication was made?"

"Communication with those in the United States is difficult, but it can be accomplished. The US is not the only country in the Western Hemisphere, you know. More than that I will not say."

Chastised by both his words and tone, Liz shifted her gaze away from Sr. Mendoza, pretending studied fascination in work taking place in a nearby tobacco field. When the tension in the atmosphere around the little group eased, she took up her quest once again.

"I understand, of course. Will you permit a final question?" The old man nodded, but an expression of irritation flashed in his eyes. "Did you know Sr. Cruz before he left Cuba?"

Instead of the anger Liz feared her question might elicit, Mendoza snorted and chuckled. "Joaquin Cruz is my cousin."

"So how did . . .?" Liz stopped herself from blurting out what she was thinking.

Sr. Mendoza finished her question for her. "How did he get out of Cuba while I did not?"

Mortified by her lack of subtlety, Liz could only nod. Mendoza continued, "He was serving as an extra waiter for the New Year's Eve party thrown by General Batista the night he fled Cuba. Joaquin overhead the general discussing his escape plan. My cousin took his life savings and bought a ticket on the last plane to leave Havana on New Year's Day 1959. He landed in Miami with nothing but a change of clothes stuffed into a paper bag." He fell silent for a moment. In the stillness, the sound of a phone ringing somewhere deep in the house drifted out to the quartet beneath the tree. A little puff of air escaped Sr. Mendoza's lips as a look of regret crawled over his face. "And to think my mother said Joaquin would never amount to anything because my father's sister married beneath herself. She had Joaquin a few months after the wedding. After the birth, the father deserted her and the child. It was a scandal. My mother said it was the shame that killed my grandfather before his time." He sighed deeply. He picked up his glass from the table and began swirling its liquid.

Liz couldn't help it. She reached out and touched the old man's hand. Looking earnestly into his eyes, she said, "So you know he has become wealthy." It was a statement, not a question.

An ironic smile lifted the corners of Mendoza's mouth. "Beyond anyone's wildest imaginings from what I have been told."

"A person might understand if you felt some animosity toward your cousin."

"No. He did what he had to do. He informed the rest of the family of what he had heard, but no one wanted to believe him, least of all my parents and grandmother, so we stayed."

The backdoor of the dwelling slammed and Sra. Mendoza marched toward them. When she stopped, it was mere inches from her husband's feet. She planted her fists firmly on her hips and began speaking rapidly. Liz didn't need to be bilingual to catch the theme of her remonstrance.

Sra. Mendoza's gestures swept over Liz and the guys while her scowl settled upon Rich. When she turned back to her husband and began shaking her finger in the old man's face, Rich rose from his chair. "Time to go, folks. The taxi's returned and Señora is none too pleased that we have kept her husband from his afternoon rest."

Something in Rich's manner signaled there was more to what the old woman had said than he chose to share. Barely allowing Liz time to thank Sr. Mendoza, Rich practically yanked them to the front door and out to the taxi. When the doors were closed, he gave directions in rapid Spanish. The driver stepped on the accelerator. The sudden speed jerked Liz back.

She leaned forward over the front seat. "Is something wrong, Rich?"

Rich jumped slightly and turned to look at her. "I'm not sure. The old woman was angry about a phone call. She wouldn't say exactly why, but she wanted us gone."

Liz glanced at Hugh, who shrugged and asked, "Do you think someone has figured out who you are, Rich? It seems highly unlikely, but she certainly gave you the evil eye before we left."

Rich's mouth thinned and his eyes narrowed in thought. "I don't see how. My name is as American as they come."

Hugh nodded. "True, but what about your Spanish? I suspect you speak like a native Cuban."

Rich's face went blank as though he couldn't face the prospect that Consuelo had been right, that coming to Cuba presented a danger to anyone with Batista connections. After several beats, he laughed, but it sounded a little forced to Liz. "Can't be. Aunt Connie says I sound like an American trying to sound like a Cuban, so I end up talking like a cartoon version of Ricky Ricardo."

Liz patted his shoulder. "I doubt you speak like that. All the same, I'm glad we are leaving tonight."

Chapter 45

The trip from the brokerage office back to the apartment where the men waited took twice as long as it had going. Three times Sam had to squeeze the truck down alleyways to avoid roadblocks. When he found the alley behind the apartment building deserted, he breathed a sigh of relief. He strode up the stairs and knocked at the door.

The door creaked back on its hinges and again a gun muzzle greeted him. "It's me. Ackerman. Open the door. We need to get going."

Once admitted, the leader of the group stopped Sam with a hand on his arm. "Shouldn't we wait until darkness covers our departure?"

"Have you seen the roads we have to drive?"

"No, but surely it will be less dangerous at night."

"Hardly. The road turns into a muddy track long before we get to the farm where the boat is docked. You got a man that Fidel's guys won't recognize?"

"Actually, something better. We have a man who can pass as a farmer. He will drive and do the talking if we are stopped. He even has bales of hay to stack in the back to conceal our presence."

"Is he going to Miami with us?"

"No."

"So why do you trust him?"

"He is the son of my valet. He is doing this in return for his father going with us and a certain consideration."

"And what does the son want?"

The Cuban stopped speaking and snapped his fingers as though he searched for words. Finally he sighed and responded, "*El truckl.*"

The guy's excellent English had failed him. Sam looked closely at the Cuban. His eyes had dark circles beneath them, and the lines in his face spoke of exhaustion. No telling when the guy last had a decent night's sleep. Sam made a guess. "He wants the truck?"

"*Si.*"

Sam chuckled. "I don't know who it belongs to, but I don't imagine anyone's gonna come looking for it or complain to the cops. Sounds like a fair trade. Get your people ready to move."

The man started to walk away, but hesitated and turned back to Sam. "You have never asked our names, and I have not heard yours."

Sam held up a hand. "Stop right there. I ain't giving you my name, and I don't want to know yours. It's safer for everybody that way."

The leader looked thoughtful, but did not respond. After several beats, he nodded. "Perhaps you are right, but for the sake of communication, please call me Paco. This is not my real name, of course."

"Okay, Paco. I guess you can call me Fred. Not my real name either."

In the alley, Sam swung himself up onto the truck bed last after all the other men except their new friend Jesus, who got into the cab behind the wheel. Sam settled himself against the stack of hay bales that lined the truck bed's side walls. Shafts of sunlight crept in between the bales, allowing at least a little fresh air onto the space. Paco signaled to one of his men and together they stacked the last of the bales at the back end of the bed until they almost touched the truck's canvas top. After patting the stack to check its balance, Paco lowered the truck's back flap and drew a tarp over the three-sided fortress of hay. The engine roared to life and the truck rumbled through the lesser used streets and alleys of Havana. The back of the truck, packed with men and their rucksacks, soon filled with the odor of sweating bodies and the dusty fragrance of hay. The men sneezed and coughed from the particles that drifted from the bales with every bump in the road. Sam's whole body ached with every jerk, jolt, and sway.

Please Adonai let this end with everybody alive. A small smile lifted the corners of his mouth. Praying. Something he hadn't done since he was a kid trying to survive a hurricane.

Squealing brakes sent Sam banging into the men behind him and hay toppling onto him. Scrambling to shove the bales aside, Sam sat up coughing and wheezing. The guy next to him pushed the bales back into place. He motioned to Sam and together they braced their backs against the reconstructed wall to keep it from toppling over again. Someone pounded on the truck's hood. Voices began shouting in Spanish. A pistol shot rang out and all fell silent. The driver's door creaked open and Jesus's footsteps sounded on the running board. Sam squinted into the swirling dust filled dimness. All of the Cubans were frozen in place, the irises of their eyes completely surround by white. Paco lifted a finger and placed it over his lips. Sam nodded. The sudden silence was more frightening than the shouts and banging had been. Pain reverberated through Sam's chest, but he dared not dig in his pocket for his nitro tablets. He massaged the muscles over his breastbone with his fist. Just have to wait it out.

Footsteps crunched on gravel. They moved from the front to the rear of the truck. Canvas rustled. Sunlight wedged itself between the tarp and the bales beneath, creating strange patterns in the stifling air. The men within the hay fortress held their collective breath.

Spanish words spoken by quiet voices drifted with the dust. Jesus spoke in jocular tones. He must be trying to convince their human impediment to travel that he was hauling a simple load of hay. The voice belonging to the stranger sounded angry, authoritative, full of self-importance. Sam shot an inquiring look at Paco, who hunched his shoulders in uncertainty. Sam closed his eyes and concentrated on forcing calm thoughts, quiet breathing, and a slower heart rate.

Without warning, a top bale closest to the tailgate rocked a little. Sam and the guy beside him moved into a crouch and slid their hands up the stack. The blade of a bayonet swished between the men. It withdrew, followed by sawing sounds announcing the location of its next port of entry. The metallic scrape of blade against straw came to within an inch of Sam's head, stopped, and slid away.

More quiet talk followed by feet crunching on gravel again, this time moving toward the front of the truck. Sweat streamed down Sam's face, back, and from his armpits. His heart pounded, but funny thing. The pain had stopped. The sound of the engine turning over was the sweetest sound Sam had heard since beginning this Godforsaken journey.

The truck rolled along on the city streets and highway pavement without further incident. When they began bumping over a washboard, Jesus pulled over and came around to the back. He lifted the back cover and shoved a bale off the top of the pile. His grinning face appeared over the top of the hay wall. He spoke to Paco, who nodded and stood up.

"Jesus says we have reached farm roads. He believes it is safe to remove the back bales so we may have more air."

Sam tried to stand, but his knees gave way. He slumped down and leaned against the bales. Worry flashed in Paco's eyes. "Are you unwell? We cannot afford for you to become unable to travel."

Sam leaned his head back against the wall and looked up at the Cuban. "Your concern touches me deeply." Sam couldn't tell if his sarcasm had hit the mark or not. This Paco was one cool customer. Sam sat up and continued, "Give me a minute and some water. I'll be good to go soon enough."

"We all need to get out and stretch. You rest while my men remove the bales."

With the job of the end bales completed, Sam scooted to the edge of the bed and squinted into a late afternoon sun. Dropping to the road, he shuffled over to a tree and slumped down at its base. One of the Cubans handed him a canteen. He took a long swig and surveyed their surroundings. Since it had been dark when he drove into Havana, he couldn't really gage how far away the farm was. He searched his memory trying to get a feel for how long it had taken him to reach the paved highway from the farm's sugar warehouse. His tired brain refused to make the calculation.

What did it really matter? They would have to wait until after midnight before they set out anyway. With luck, a panel truck waited for them at Dinner Key Marina in Miami as promised. Toblinsky's connections came through with favors or they paid the price. Sam chuckled to himself. He was living proof of that.

~ ~ ~

A ribbon of gold showed at the Atlantic's eastern edge when Sam steered the sport fisherman into the mouth of Biscayne Bay. By the time they docked at Dinner Key, the dawn glowed full strength, painting the sky in shades of yellow and pink. When the boat bumped against the dock, Sam could finally breathe a sigh of relief. They had made the trip across the Florida Straights without a single problem. No Coast Guard, no engine trouble, no one even puking over the sides. Sam searched the near empty parking lot. There it was. A white-panel truck waited near the marina clubhouse. Now all that remained was to figure out what to do with his passengers once they were in the truck. He bent down and knocked on the cabin hatch. It slid open immediately. Paco's fear-filled eyes looked up at him.

Sam leaned down. "You can relax now. We're in Miami and nobody's come asking any questions. Get your men ready to roll."

They settled all of the Cubans except Paco in the back of the truck. Sam lowered the canvas back flaps before climbing behind the wheel. He turned to Paco in the passenger seat. "Where should I take you guys?"

All color drained from the Cuban's face. "What were you told? Surely Sr. Toblinsky told you something."

"Not a frigging thing."

"You did not ask?"

"It ain't healthy to ask too many questions." Tino's long ago admonition echoed through Sam's mind. "Boss don't like them." Sam shifted his gaze to the driver's side window and bit down on his lower lip to keep from shouting in frustration. When he had control of himself, he turned back to his passenger. "So, I'm guessing I'm stuck with your asses until we figure something out."

"I regret that it is so." The Cuban at least had the good grace to look sorry for all the trouble he was creating.

Sam drummed his fingers on the wheel. What the hell was he supposed to do with this bunch?

"I tell you what. Why don't I take you to a hotel? There's plenty of good ones in Miami."

"No!" Paco's shout filled the truck cab. He drew a deep breath and let it out slowly. "What I mean to say is even here we are in danger. We do not know who we can trust beyond you and Sr. Toblinsky. There are those who would gladly kill us because of our association with General Batista."

"And you think they went to all the trouble of following you to Miami?" Sam couldn't tell if Paco caught his sarcasm or not.

Paco's eyes became hard as his lips thinned. "Can you ensure they have not?"

"I guess you got a point." Sam massaged the muscles at the base of his skull. It had been a damned long thirty-six hours. "Okay. I only got one place where nobody would come snooping."

Sam turned the ignition key and put the truck in gear. They reached the alley behind the store while the streets were still fairly empty. The business day would not start for another couple of hours. Sam unlocked his rear entrance and ushered his unwelcome guests into the windowless storeroom. The Cubans looked around in dismay as though they couldn't quite figure out where they were or why they had been brought there. Paco explained to his men in quiet Spanish and he turned to Sam.

"My men have not eaten in many hours. Would it be possible to get something? We can pay." Paco stuck his hand into his pocket and withdrew a large roll of US dollars.

Before the Cuban could peel off any bills, Sam held up his hand. "Wouldn't hear of it. Keep your cash. You're gonna need it." He pointed toward the front of the storeroom. "Restroom's in there. You guys do what you can to get cleaned up while I go get us some breakfast. There's a good deli around the corner. Won't be long."

The trip to the deli took longer than Sam planned. For some reason no one could explain, there was a line waiting for bagels. When he finally got back to the store, he found the showroom lights on. He had not turned them on himself. He patted the pocket where his pistol lay loaded and waiting, then unlocked the front door as quietly as he could. Shouts came from the back of the building. Sam drew out his gun and broke into a run.

He gasped for breath as he threw the storeroom door open. In the center of the room stood a terrified Jimmy in the grasp of two of the Cubans, one of whom held a gun to the boy's temple.

Sam waved his pistol toward the bigger Cuban. "Let him go, you ungrateful, spick bastards." While they didn't speak English, the two men understood Sam's intent and released their grip on Jimmy's arms. The boy slumped to the floor and put his head between his knees.

Sam knelt down beside him. "What the hell are you doing here so early?" Sam did not try to keep the anger out of his voice.

Jimmy drew a shaky breath. "I didn't finish restocking the shelves like you asked. I had to study for a big test, so I thought I'd get the restocking finished before the store opened."

The kid looked like he might puke. Sam put his hand on Jimmy's head and gave him a little nudge. "You're a good kid. Did you get the restock finished?"

"No, sir. I didn't even get started."

"Don't worry about it now. I got a bigger problem." Sam's gaze swept the Cubans. "Let's eat while I try to figure out what to do with these guys."

Sam had no choice but to tell Jimmy who their guests were and why they were in the storeroom. Paco finished the tale while Sam chewed on a bite of bagel. "As you can see, we cannot allow ourselves to be seen. We have many enemies and some of them may be in Miami."

Jimmy nodded. He may be just a hick kid from the swamps of north Florida, but he was smart. Sam was about to suggest taking the Cubans to the airport when Jimmy snapped his fingers and grinned.

"I think I know what we can do."

Chapter 46

The trip back to Havana took them over the same bumpy, rutted country lanes as before, but it seemed to Liz that it took twice as long. Dusk bathed the outskirts of the city in purple shadows and painted the western horizon in pink and orange streaks that diminished by the second. As the limo approached the *Malacòn*, Rich looked at Liz and Hugh. "I'm going to ask the driver to drop me here. A walk along the seawall might clear my head. This trip has been harder than I ever dreamed."

Liz cut her eyes at Hugh, sending him a nonverbal plea. He ran his teeth over his lower lip and replied, "I can understand how that might be, but I don't think it's a good idea for you to stroll around on your own. I've had a bad feeling about your situation since we arrived. Too many odd stares. Too many sidewise glances. And there was the old lady and the phone call this afternoon."

Rich's gaze shifted to the waves breaking against the seawall. "Yeah. But I don't think anything will happen out in the open in sight of every car that passes."

Something in Rich's manner set off warning bells. Liz searched his face and her concern grew. She grabbed his shoulder. "Don't do it. It would be a stupid move."

Rich's face flamed. "So, you've turned mind reader and mother superior all in one?"

"Do what?" Hugh's voice held a note of alarm.

Liz looked from Rich to Hugh and back. "He's going to try to get into his family's home, aren't you?"

Rich laughed, but there was little humor in his tone. "I guess you are a mind reader. I've come all this way. I've got to try."

"Why? What could be so important that you would go against all common sense?"

Rich glanced at the limo driver and ran his tongue over his lips. He didn't answer for several beats. Perhaps he never would. Families like his must have secrets that they don't want known to all and sundry. Finally, he spoke to the driver in Spanish. The Cuban switched on the radio while Rich slid the communicating glass shut.

Liz heard Hugh draw breath to speak when Rich finally answered her question. "$10,000,000, at least that's what it was when last seen."

"Good lord, just hidden in the house?" Disbelief coursed through Liz. "It can't still be there after all this time."

"It's not. It never has been. It's in Switzerland in a numbered account, and that's the problem."

"So why do you have to go to the house?"

"When it became clear the Revolutionaries would win, grandfather hid his account numbers and pass codes. He inconsiderately died without telling anyone where they are, but I think I know where to find them. Grandfather kept a journal, and the clues are there if you know how to interpret his cryptic thoughts."

Hugh chuckled. "You're certainly a dark horse, Rich. But from what Liz tells me, money is not a problem for your family."

"Yeah, I guess you could say that, but nothing like we should have. Think about it. 2% interest accrued over 60 years. It should be about $40,000,000. Would *you* leave $40,000,000 untouched if you could get your hands on it?"

"When you put it like that, perhaps not, but I'm not sure even that much money is worth my life. I might let it go if it meant living into old age."

"Well, that's you, not me. I have plans for that money, and I'm the only legitimate heir. My grandfather has no other direct descendants."

An image of Rich injured or worse flashed through Liz's mind. "Hugh, if he is determined to do this, I think we need to go with him. He's gone to a lot of trouble for me. I feel like I owe him."

Hugh stiffened beside her and threw her a disgruntled look. "You have a disturbingly exaggerated sense of indebtedness to everyone who does anything at all for you. You do know that, don't you?"

Liz ignored Hugh's question. "Okay. Stay at the hotel, but I'm not letting him go alone." She hated the petulant tone in her voice, something that sometimes surfaced when she didn't want to admit she was in the wrong.

Hugh rolled his eyes. "You really are going to do this harebrained thing, aren't you? In that case, I don't really have a choice."

"Of course you do, but I would much rather you went with us," Liz snapped.

Rich held up a hand. "Hey, you two, don't get mad at each other because of me. I've done you some favors, Liz, but do you think I could have come to Cuba without your academic visas? By listing me as a research associate, you got me into the country. I could never have come on my own. You owe me nothing, especially if I get what I came for."

Liz put her hand on Hugh's arm and squeezed. His lips tightened for a moment before he spoke. "All right. We'll go with him." Hugh looked at Rich. "Tell him where to drop us."

The driver retraced the route they had taken coming in from the airport at the beginning of their visit. At the end of the block where Rich had pointed out his grandparents' former home, the trio stepped onto a crumbling, deserted sidewalk. Rich bent through the passenger side window and said something to the driver.

Liz watched in dismay as the vehicle moved away from the curb. "Why did you send him away? We'll need a ride back to the hotel."

Rich grinned. "He hasn't been paid. He'll be back in thirty minutes. He wanted to get dinner rather than wait by the curb." With that, he turned and started down the sidewalk toward their objective.

The low hum of conversations could be heard coming from the interiors and courtyards of the houses that lined their route. In the middle of the block, Rich stopped and pointed. "This is it. It's got to be. It fits the descriptions and old photographs."

Liz looked over its pockmarked facade. The walls needed touching up where the stucco had crumbled away and the architectural ornaments wanted a good scrubbing. The front door stood open, as though the mansion awaited the return of its rightful owner.

Rich stepped into the foyer and glanced around rather furtively, then motioned for Liz and Hugh to follow him. Hugh slipped a protective hand under Liz's elbow as they entered. In other circumstances, she would probably have resented the show of protectiveness, but a tingle of trepidation settled in her midsection as she surveyed the once opulent space.

The marble floor tiles were now cracked and several were missing. The richly carved crown moldings and ceiling medallion remained in place but were in need of serious refurbishment. No sounds greeted them, yet Liz felt sure that on the trip into the city from the airport, people had been sitting on the front steps and lingering in the double-door entry. As the trio approached the ornate staircase, no one cracked open an interior door or offered to challenge their right to be there. Odd that strangers should be allowed to roam freely through a house where they had no business being. A prickle of fear slithered down Liz's spine. She stared at each door, willing someone to come out and put a stop to this insane quest, but no one did.

With Rich in the lead, the trio began ascending the steps, treading as quietly as possible. When they reached the third floor, a thud floated up from the foyer. Liz froze. Being closest to the bannister, she peered over it. No one stood in the foyer or on the stairs below. No interior door clicked shut. No step sounded. Still, she couldn't shake the feeling that someone followed them.

She tapped Rich's shoulder. He turned to her with his finger over his lips and nodded toward the upper floors before continuing on. Liz and Hugh had no choice but to follow. At the top of the house, the ornate staircase and broad landings ended abruptly, replaced by utilitarian, unfinished floorboards in a cramped space. Rich turned right, walked softly to the end of the hall and opened a door. He revealed another set of stairs, but this one was narrow, steep, and covered in dust and cobwebs. No one had been up to the attic in a very long time.

Rich, followed by Liz and Hugh, crept through the low-ceilinged space with the aid of a small pocket flashlight. Dust tickled Liz's nose. She put a finger up to stifle a sneeze. Cobwebs hung suspended between the rafters and the ceiling joists, creating gossamer curtains backlit by a single window in the roof's gable end. Liz swiped at the filaments that covered her hair and clung to her face. When they reached the attic's center, Rich stepped to a low wall created by the meeting of roof valleys. He began tapping along the crude baseboard. After a couple of minutes, a hollow sound drifted up. Rich took a small file from his pocket and applied it to the seam between two boards. The one on the right popped away, revealing a small vacant space. Using his flashlight, he swept the beam over the hole and stopped when it illuminated a dust covered brown envelope. He extracted it from the place where it had lain hidden for the last sixty years.

Rich looked up at Liz and grinned as he slapped the envelope across his palm. "This is it. It's got to be." Placing the flashlight in his mouth, he tore open the flap, but his face filled with bewilderment. "I don't understand. This can't be." He turned the paper over several times as though the words on the page would somehow change. In the end, he balled the paper up and threw it across the attic. In frustration, he pounded the wall with his fist.

At the third blow, Hugh grabbed Rich's arm. "Stop. We don't need the attention your noise may already have drawn."

Rich slumped to the floor and buried his face in his upturned palms. Liz knelt beside him. "What was in the envelope?"

Rich's angry eyes met hers. "The transaction numbers and routing codes from when Grandfather transferred funds from the Merrill Lynch office here in Havana to the home office in New York. We've had all of his money the whole time. There's not anything else. This was all for nothing." Desolation clouded his handsome features and turned down the corners of his mouth.

"Is there anything else in the hole?"

"*Nada. Niet. Nein.* No. Not a damned thing."

Liz looked to Hugh for support. To Rich she said, "I think we should go. It's dark now, and the car will be waiting for us."

The trio retraced their steps without a soul calling out, approaching, or even peeking at them through the crack of a door. It was as though the house was deserted yet light shone at every threshold. When they reached the front door, Rich stopped and hung back.

"I'll be out in a minute. I want to spend a few moments alone in the house. If there had been no revolution, it would be mine now. I'll probably never see it again. My mom and grandmother described it to me so often it feels like I've been here all my life."

Despite feeling uneasy at leaving Rich, Liz stepped out to the sidewalk ahead of Hugh. Her head swiveled left and right. "Maybe we should walk down to the corner. The car could be waiting where the driver dropped us off. We can ask him to come around to the door."

Halfway to the corner, an angry shout followed by an agonized yelp emanated from Rich's former family home.

Liz grabbed Hugh's arm. "That's Rich's voice."

The thud of running steps echoed through the empty street. Liz and Hugh skidded to a halt in front of the house. The door stood ajar as before, but instead of the foyer being empty, three figures struggled. The glint of a knife blade held by one of the assailants flashed in the meager light. Liz gasped and grabbed Hugh's arm. Suddenly two of the figures melded into one ghastly creature. The third stood before it, panting, knife raised, preparing to strike. Liz screamed involuntarily as Hugh jerked out of her grasp.

He rushed the man with the knife, yanked him off his feet, and slammed him against the closest wall. The clatter of metal striking stone rang in the space. Liz's heart rate hit full gallop while she edged toward the knife. Dizziness clouded her brain. Scooping up the weapon, she placed a hand on the near wall before throwing the knife out onto the sidewalk and turning frantically back toward the men battling in the foyer.

Hugh seemed to be holding his own, thank God. It helped that he was almost twice the size of his opponent. One blow sent the assailant's head lolling to one side. Hugh dropped his quarry, who slumped in a heap on the floor. Turning toward Rich and his captor, Hugh grabbed Rich's shirtfront and wrested him from the assailant's embrace. Once Rich stood aside, Hugh lunged at the remaining attacker and landed a blow on his shoulder as the man raced for the safety of the sidewalk. His retreating footsteps rang on the concrete. Breathing heavily, Hugh leaned over and placed his hands on his knees. Rich looked dazed, as though he could not process what had just happened to him.

Liz rushed to Hugh and knelt so that she could see his face. "Are you okay? You scared the life out of me. What were you thinking?"

Still panting, Hugh looked up at her and grinned. "I haven't had that kind of workout since my Golden Gloves days."

She drew back and her eyes narrowed. "You've never told me you boxed. Exactly when was that?"

"High school and college. I thought I was going to be the next heavyweight champion, or at least make the Olympic team. Neither worked out, so I decided to become an academic instead." Hugh's self-deprecating chuckle echoed in the quiet hall.

Apparently Hugh's joke hit Rich as hilarious because one minute he stood leaning against a wall for support and the next he bent double with laughter. He sniggered; he chortled; he guffawed until his eyes streamed. His hysteria became contagious. First Liz chuckled followed by Hugh's laughing. Within moments, the trio's howls rang through the building. Still, no resident ventured out into the foyer or hung over the upper floor bannisters.

When Rich's assailant began to stir, Hugh grabbed Liz's hand and yanked her through the door out onto the sidewalk. Rich stumbled after them, wiping his eyes with his forearm. By the time they reached the corner, the limo stood idling at the curb, the Cuban driver tapping out a nervous tattoo on the wheel.

When Rich opened the passenger door, the man behind the wheel looked at him with wide, startled eyes. He nodded to Liz and Hugh before fumbling with the ignition. He pumped the accelerator until the engine flooded. Cursing under his breath, the driver let it rest for several moments and tried again.

This time, the engine caught. Jerking the wheel, he stamped on the accelerator with such force that the car leapt away from the curb, sending Liz and Hugh crashing against the door. The driver sped from the neighborhood and back through the city like bank robbers on the run from the law. The car dashed through yellow lights and jumped reds. Every few blocks, the guy glanced in the rearview mirror. Clearly, he expected to be followed.

Liz turned sideways in the seat so that she could watch their rear as well as approaching traffic. Hugh raised an eyebrow in question. She jerked her head toward the front seat, pursed her lips, and shook her head. Hugh nodded.

Headlights picked up the limo somewhere in the old quarter and stayed on its tail for blocks until they reached the seawall and a red light. This time, the cab driver was forced to stop as traffic had become heavier. Havana nightlife had awoken and business must be good. The buildings along the seawall glowed.

Headlights loomed up behind them. The crunch of metal bumper against bumper filled the cab and propelled it into the intersection. Their driver swerved and dodged amid the blaring horns and shouted curses of other drivers. Liz glanced back. Their assailant followed them into the onrushing traffic. This was no casual accident. Someone intended them harm or worse. Liz's heart leapt into her throat. She felt physically ill as she swayed in her seat while the car maneuvered in and out of traffic. Surely whoever followed them wouldn't try to kill them in the presence of so many witnesses, but of course, Cuba was a dictatorship with its own set of laws and rules for police. Perhaps it was the authorities that pursued them. At this point anything seemed possible.

Liz sought Rich's face to gage his reaction. He was deathly pale beneath his normal tan and terror glowed in his eyes. He clearly believed someone wanted him dead. Liz closed her eyes and bit down on the interior flesh of her cheek to maintain control. The three of them were young with many years to live unless it all ended here. *Please, Lord, not here.*

Their driver jammed on the brakes, and they slid sideways toward the seawall. Horns blared and tires screeched as their driver jerked the wheel back toward their correct lane and took advantage of a space opening before them. The cab leapt forward just before other cars closed the gap. Liz stared through the back window. Their pursuer was stalled in the chaos they left behind.

Giddy with relief, she looked at Rich. "Are you going to tell Consuelo she was right?" Her voice trembled despite her effort to maintain control.

Rich shook his head. "Are you nuts? She would have a coronary. And don't you tell her either."

Liz felt Hugh stir beside her. He slid his arm around her shoulders. "We certainly have no desire to upset your aunt. Liz really has no reason to visit her again. This trip has been a little more exciting than either of us bargained for. You can rest assured your secret is safe."

A little flicker of irritation tingled within Liz. Hugh had said what she herself felt, but she resented his taking charge. She cut her eyes at him so that he could see her displeasure. He raised an eyebrow while his mouth remained firm. Their gazes remained locked until Hugh's mouth curved up in an apologetic, questioning smile. He understood her so well. Her anger melted away.

To Rich she said, "I assure you I will never do or say anything to distress Consuelo. I owe her and you too much." She would have said more, but the cab made a jarring turn onto hotel's driveway.

At the entrance to the hotel, Hugh took out his wallet, but Rich held up his hand. "Nothing doing, man. You saved my life. There's no way you're going to pay for the ride."

Liz and Hugh got out, but Rich stayed in place and rolled up his window. Liz couldn't hear their exact words, but she suspected from the gestures and the angry tone occasionally drifting through the glass that the topic under discussion was less than cordial. After a particularly loud exchange, Rich grabbed the driver's shirtfront and raised his fist.

Liz nudged Hugh. "Do you think we should do something about that? Rich looks like he might actually hurt that man."

Hugh tilted his head and watched for a moment. "Nope. Rich looks like he has things under control. Besides, based on this guy's behavior, I'd say he had something to do with the attack or at least knew about it." Inside the car, the Cuban flew back against the door, his hands held up in submission. Hugh grinned. "I'd say Rich has convinced the bum to tell what he knows."

The Cuban's lips moved rapidly while his eyes looked pleadingly at Hugh and Liz. After five or so minutes of monologue, Rich let the man go and got out.

Watching the disappearing taillights, Liz asked, "So what did you say to him, and what did he tell you?"

Rich clasped his hands, stretched, and cracked his knuckles. "That felt good. Ready for dinner?"

Liz batted his hands down. "Good grief. Don't keep us in suspense."

"Okay. I told him you two were CIA and that you would put a hit out on him if he didn't tell me what he knew."

Liz and Hugh looked at each other. With their laughter bouncing off the hotel's glass front, Hugh slipped his arm around Liz's shoulders. "We're about as unlikely a pair of spies as you'll find."

Rich shrugged. "Whatever. He bought it."

"And?" Liz's volume attracted the glances of passing hotel guests.

"And he said there are people here who know I'm related to General Batista. People with long memories and healthy grudges."

"Did he know how you were identified?"

"He said not. My guess is someone in the States sent a message. How else could anyone have known?"

"But who?"

Rich shrugged. "No idea, but I intend to find out."

Chapter 47

"Wait, Mr. A., just hear me out. It's not as harebrained as you say." Jimmy had clearly recovered from the experience of having a pistol pressed against his temple.

The expression in the boy's eyes did nothing to reassure Sam. The kid seemed to think this was some kind of adventure, that they were playing a child's game instead of hiding hunted men from dedicated revolutionaries with a sizable grudge. Unfortunately, Sam didn't have a better idea.

"Ok. Tell me again about how you would get these guys out of Miami."

Jimmy grinned and waggled his eyebrows. "Well, first I'd take the back roads up the coast. At Daytona, I'd swing inland to Ocala where we'd catch 41 North. If we take turns driving, we won't have to stop until we reach Lake City." Jimmy's words tumbled over one another as he warmed to his subject. "We put the guys up at the Blanche Hotel for the night. We can put them on the train to New York the next morning. Simple. Doable. Nobody will suspect a thing."

"So we just show up in your hick hometown with a bunch of Cubans who don't have no luggage and can't speak English and nobody's gonna suspect nothing? Yeah, right."

Frustration flickered in the boy's eyes. "I worked in the men's shop on the first floor of the Blanche when I was in high school. The hotel manager is my first cousin once removed. If I tell him we're coming and to keep it a secret, he will. We get all kinds of celebrities coming through town staying at the hotel. Most of them don't want to create a stir, so my cousin is used to keeping things quiet."

"Uh-huh. What kinds of celebrities?"

"Johnny Cash. He's that country and western singer who performs in prisons. They say he's going to be a star."

"Never heard of him."

"Not a C&W fan, I take it. Well, how about Al Capone. Know who he is?"

Sam had only been half listening to the boy's chatter, but the mention of the gangster riveted his attention. "Of course I know who he is. What was he doing in that part of Florida?"

"It was back in the '30's. He was traveling from Chicago to Miami. Lake City is the natural place to stop when you're coming from up north. It's a day's drive from Chattanooga, so you don't have to stay overnight in South Georgia where there isn't much in the way of hotels."

Sam sucked on his lower lip. He glanced at Paco to get a read on his reaction. The Cuban nodded. "It sounds like a good plan. We must remain anonymous until we reach our friends in New York. Airplane passengers attract attention. Travelers by train are not so noticed I would think."

Sam wasn't sure about this, but he kept his concerns to himself. "Okay. If you're happy that's what we'll do." He turned to his employee. "We mess this up, kid, and none of us may live to tell the story. You sure about everything you've told us?"

The reality of the situation finally seemed to sink in, for Jimmy's features settled into an expression reflecting equal parts trepidation, concentration, and caution. He was quiet for several beats before answering, "I'm sure. We should wait until dark to leave. We'll be in Lake City by breakfast tomorrow."

"And you know the way even at night?"

"Sure. I've gone home for every holiday since I started school down here. I know the route we're taking. Florida's not that big, after all, and I've driven most of it between Miami and home."

~ ~ ~

As Jimmy had promised, the trip north was uneventful. Approaching the little town from the south, the forests, fields, and pastures gave way to farmhouses and craftsman bungalows bunched ever closer together until they were replaced by Queen Anne Victorians with little space between them. Sam's stomach growled loudly as the truck sat idling at a red light on the edge of what passed for downtown Lake City. Glancing at the road signs, he saw that they would cross over US 90, the major east-west route running from Jacksonville to Los Angles. How bad would it be to simply get out of the truck, put Paco behind the wheel, and tell him to turn left and not stop until they reached the Pacific?

A snort interrupted the light snoring coming from the other side of the seat. Jimmy stirred and settled with his cheek against the window. He had insisted on driving until dawn to give Sam a chance to rest. Well, let the boy sleep for another few moments. That's all they had remaining of this godforsaken journey. Up ahead, Sam saw an open town square. A bank and a couple of drug stores stood on three corners on the other side of the square and just beyond them, the hotel's green awning with white lettering shaded the sidewalk.

The light changed. Sam shifted gears and pressed down on the accelerator. He guided the truck between the town square and the storefronts. At the end of the block, he turned left between the two drug stores and crept along until the entrance to an alley came into view. Jimmy had said they could park the truck behind the hotel and unload their cargo with minimal chance of observation. With a right turn, the truck's tires crunched on gravel covering the alley and a small parking area. The brakes' squealing roused Jimmy, who yawned, stretched, and grinned at Sam.

"You made it. Have any trouble?"

"No. It's not like this is New York or Miami. Better see to our passengers." They got out of the truck and went to the back.

When Sam rapped on the truck's side panel, the muzzle of Paco's thirty-eight poked through the canvas first, followed by his face.

Sam's patience deserted him. "Oh, for God's sake. Put the piece away and get out of the fucking truck."

They must have made an interesting sight for the Blanche's staff as they trouped through the kitchens to the front desk, scruffy and foreign-looking all except Jimmy, who the cooks and waiters knew by name. Jimmy's cousin once removed greeted them and checked the Cubans into the hotel without requiring them to sign in under their real names. So it was that a series of Mr. Smiths, Joneses, and Browns were assigned the suit on the top floor once occupied by the gangster, Al Capone.

Sam looked at Paco. "Well, I guess that's it until the train leaves tomorrow. You guys can go get some rest."

The Cuban shook his head and turned to Jimmy. "Is there a place where we may purchase clothing? We will stand out in our Guayaberas."

Jimmy glanced at the reception area clock. "Give it another ten minutes, and you can go right next door."

By noon, the Cubans had bought clothes and luggage, and were waiting for room service to bring them lunch. When a knock sounded, Paco drew his pistol and crept to the door. He edged it open an inch and slid the muzzle into the crack. Letting out a deep sigh, he opened the door completely and motioned to someone standing in the hall. A white-faced waiter rushed into the room, deposited clattering dishes and cutlery onto the closest table, and fled without waiting for his tip.

Sam yawned, stretched, and rolled his stiff neck and shoulders. "Me and Jimmy are going to stay with his parents." Sam withdrew a scrap of paper from his pocket and handed it to Paco. "Here's the phone number, if you need to talk to me. Otherwise, we'll see you guys bright and early in the morning."

By 6:30 a.m. the following day, Paco and his band of fugitive Cubans were settled in a passenger car on a train headed north for New York and Sam and Jimmy were in the truck headed south for Miami.

As the pine forests and Spanish moss draped live oaks flashed by the truck windows, Sam rubbed the area over his breastbone. The nitro tablet he had slipped under his tongue a few seconds ago would take effect any moment now. With the easing of his angina, an unexpected feeling settled over Sam. The last few days had been a rush toward danger and frenzied flight from it, each day more exhausting than the last. The only thing he had left to do was deliver the package of documents to Toblinsky. After that, he was finished with this business. They were headed back to their ordinary lives—something he should be glad of—yet somehow he felt . . . Disappointed? Let down? Anticlimactic. That was it. But why? Maybe his younger self, the boy who had once dreamed of adventure, fame, and fortune still lurked within him, so deeply hidden that Sam had forgotten he existed until Toblinsky called in his debt of "friendship." A rueful smile flickered across his lips.

Sam ran a hand over his face and leaned his head against the seat back, staring at the fabric lining of the cab's ceiling. Debts. Some people thought of them only in terms of money to be repaid, but those were the easy ones. Money could be gotten in a variety of ways, if you knew where to look and worked hard enough. The type of debt he owed Tolbinsky was much more difficult. There was no physical evidence that it ever existed, unless you counted the fact that he had lived a full life all these years instead of ending up a corpse floating in the East River back in 1926. The worst part was that Sam had no idea whether Toblinsky considered the debt paid in full because a man like Moshe Toblinsky could pretty much do whatever he wanted. Sam rubbed his temples. That was the thing that worried him the most.

Sam glanced sidewise at Jimmy, who whistled under his breath as he drove. There was something Sam wanted to discuss with Jimmy, but he was unsure how to start the conversation. It was a lie he had told Rebecca that had reshaped itself into a possible solution to several problems.

Chapter 48

The plane touched down and bumped along the tarmac at Miami International on schedule. Liz, never a completely secure passenger, eased her grip on the seat arms and opened her eyes. The last forty-eight hours had been like an out-of-body experience. First the high of learning her quarry's name and business, followed by the terrifying attacks.

Liz glanced at Hugh, whose head nodded in rhythm to the plane's progress toward the terminal. He was so handsome and smart. She had always known that. Over the course of their relationship, she had also found him to be a truly good man. But a warrior against crime and a protector of the vulnerable? She would never have guessed. He had always seemed so mild mannered. In fact, a lack of that touch of danger she had always thought she needed in her romantic attachments had nearly doomed them, but his persistence and patience had finally opened her eyes. Of course, he had gotten serious help from that cheating jerk, Jonathan, her previous boyfriend.

Even so, she, herself, had changed during her research into Al Capone while uncovering the horrors that a black child of the 1930's had experienced. She liked to think she had finally matured, that she was no longer the totally work absorbed geek she had once been, that she no longer rebelled against type and her mother's expectations by seeking out the worst possible romantic entanglements. She liked to think that she had achieved balance in her life and a big part of that balance was this beautiful man beside her. She leaned over and kissed his temple. His eyes fluttered open.

He reached up and drew her lips to his. The crackle of the PA system and the captain's voice welcoming them to Miami broke the moment.

In the row ahead, Rich removed his gear from beneath a seat and turned to face Liz. She looked straight into his eyes. His expression held touches of longing, regret, and resolve. After a moment of intense eye contact, he shifted his gaze away and back again. "So I guess you and I each have a quest. Do you think we'll ever see each other again?"

The unexpected question caught Liz off guard. She searched for just the right way to answer the man who had made possible a successful end to her search. "Of course we will. You're our friend. We expect you to visit us in Gainesville and Hugh hasn't been to your amazing restaurant. We must get together in the new year."

A crooked smile lifted one corner of Rich's mouth. "Yeah. We should, but I may be tied up. I am going to find the guy who ratted me out to the Cubans."

"Oh, Rich. Do you think you should? You may spend a lot of time and energy without result. It could even be dangerous. Why not go home to Tampa and enjoy your success? You've certainly earned it."

"Oh, I'm going home as soon as I get my car out of the garage, but I have contacts and I intend to use them. Anyway, my sous chef has been left to his own devices longer than is healthy. I'll probably get home to a full-blown coup." A rueful chuckle died on Rich's lips as he searched Liz's face in anticipation of something she was unable to give. The momentary pause edged into awkward silence.

Liz mustered a sincere smile. "I doubt that."

Rich's gaze dropped. "Doubt what?"

"That your staff has defected. They adore you."

"Oh, they do, do they? They adore the man who yells at them if they make a mistake or the one who has been known to throw the occasional kitchen utensil?"

"Both. They also admire you for your talent and drive. I have observed their affection first hand, you know."

He looked at her once again, but this time resignation colored his expression. "Okay. I'll accept your analysis since you witnessed it."

Hugh tapped her shoulder. "I hate to break up this fond farewell, but they want us to go to the jetway. Everybody has deplaned but us, and we need to get to our hotel before they give our room away."

When they reached the garage, Liz gave Rich a quick hug and Hugh shook his hand. Silently, they turned in opposite directions toward their vehicles. Liz fought the urge to look over her shoulder. She had made her choice long before she ever met Rich, but she could not deny that she owed him a lot. A little trickle of guilt curled its way through her. She had disrupted his life for her own purposes. She could be fiercely self-centered when it came to her work, but he had been willing enough to let her. In fact, he had insisted upon it, by gosh. She gave herself a mental shake. Enough. Guilt was a wasted emotion in situations like this.

She took Hugh's arm and snuggled against his shoulder. He bent and kissed her hair. He felt good, safe, dependable, which was what she had grown to realize she needed in a partner. A small smile drifted across her face. A partner. Why had she never thought of her previous relationships that way? What a foolish girl she had been, but if she had figured it out earlier, she wouldn't be with Hugh now. To everything there is a season, and a time to every purpose under heaven. Yes. That was it.

Rich was right. They probably would not meet again. Their brief season was now passed, for in reality, all that needed to be said or should be said had already been spoken.

~ ~ ~

A search of the Dade County Records and Miami Herald Archives revealed that Samuel Ackerman, native of Brooklyn, New York, owner of Miami Party Rentals and Restaurant Supply, husband of Rebecca, and father of Jacob from Cleveland and Rachel from Dallas, passed away in July 1963 surrounded by his family. Cause of death was listed as heart failure. The business had run for another fifteen years until Mrs. Ackerman's death, when the doors were closed for good, according to a J. M. Peterson, Esq., who posted a legal notice in the newspaper alerting anyone to whom the business owed money.

Liz closed the files and pushed her chair away from the table. The Ackerman kids were a long shot after all these years. They must be well into their seventies, maybe older. Anyway, they lived too far away to approach for information before she and Hugh left to spend what remained of the holidays with her mother in Seattle. Would Peterson still be practicing law? A quick internet search revealed not, but a White Pages search of southern Florida listed a man by the same name residing in the Gold Coast Senior Community in Hobe Sound. She glanced at the big clock on the wall. Hugh would be nearly home by now. He had not been able to stay longer in Miami because of work he had left undone to go to Cuba with her. One more day and she would have to return to Gainesville as well. She tapped the phone number given for J. M. Peterson into her cell and prayed. After several rings, an elderly male voice answered.

Chapter 49

Liz guided the rental car between the rows of palms lining the Gold Coast Senior Community's front drive. A low whistle escaped her lips. J.M. Peterson must have done well as a lawyer to be able to retire in this kind of style. The four-story building sat on the narrow strip of land between the Indian River and the Atlantic, its white Italian Renaissance facade styled as a miniature version of the Palm Beach playground of the rich and famous, The Breakers. The meticulously manicured grounds and beds must keep a small army of gardeners busy. If there was a dead flower among the roses, bougainvillea, hibiscus, and other flowers she couldn't name, Liz certainly couldn't see it. Turning into the residents' parking lot, she pulled in between a huge Mercedes and a Bentley—serious money dwelt within the halls of this place.

She switched off the ignition and gazed up at the luxury apartment building. A wrinkle creased her brow. Years of chasing history's criminals had left her with a suspicious bent of mind. The connection between the development of the Gold Coast and the mob was well documented. How much mafia money had found its way into this place? Given Samuel Ackerman's links to Moshe Toblinsky, did attorney Peterson enjoy the same resources and protection? Liz shook her head. Just stop it. Judging someone before even laying eyes on them was not appropriate research methodology.

She found him where the girl at reception directed, seated on the back veranda, gazing out over the breakers rolling in from the Atlantic. She cleared her throat so as not to startle him. He glanced over his shoulder and smiled.

"You must be the professor who requested an interview."

"I am. Thank you so much for agreeing to see me." Liz hesitated beside the chair opposite Mr. Peterson.

"Sit. Please. No need to hover or stand on ceremony." When Liz had done his bidding, he continued, "Now what was it you wanted to know about Sam?"

Liz spread the photographs from Richard Whitehead, Sr.'s 1989 article on the table between them. She tapped each image of the man with the scared face. "Can you confirm this is Samuel Ackerman?"

Peterson adjusted his readers and picked each one up in turn. An affectionate smile lifted the corners of his mouth. "Yes, that's Sam, the old reprobate. In his younger years, of course, before I worked for him in the store, but it's Sam all right. I'd recognize those scars anywhere. How he got them is quite a story."

Liz wasn't sure which interested her more—that Mr. Peterson had apparently worked for Samuel in a capacity beyond family lawyer or that he knew something of Sam's early life. "Anything you are able to tell me would mean a great deal to my research." Liz went on to explain her purpose as a historian and her hopes for her latest project.

Peterson rubbed his chin in thought. "So, you teach history by telling the stories of ordinary people. I would guess today's students find it more interesting that way."

"I certainly hope they do. I always worry until class registration is finished."

"And are your classes popular?"

"So far, they have a pretty good track record. My students seem to relate to the little guy caught up in the events of history. And that's why I think Mr. Ackerman's story would be such a wonderful addition to the new course I have planned."

"Which is?"

"*Florida's Underbelly, 1920-Present: the Mob in the Sunshine State* or Gangsters on the Gold Coast for short."

"Catchy title." Peterson frowned and looked out over the Atlantic. He seemed deep in thought. Finally, his gaze snapped back to Liz. "I don't suppose telling you Sam's story can do any harm at this point. Both of Sam's kids are dead. Sadly, neither of them had children. There's no one to be shocked or hurt by Sam's past. To understand Sam, it is important to know how he came to be in Miami. It all began when he was seventeen in 1926. Did you know he worked in Tops Monza's speakeasy in New York?" Liz shook her head. "Well, you really don't very much about Sam, do you?"

For the better part of two and one half hours, James M. Peterson filled in the blanks of Samuel Ackerman's life with considerable emphasis on his relationship with Moshe Toblinsky and the debt of friendship Sam owed, ending with the trip to Cuba and the ferrying of Batista's men to the Blanche Hotel in the little town of Lake City. At the mention of the hotel and town, a little gasp of surprise escaped Liz.

Jimmy, as he insisted she call him, smiled. "Do you know Lake City?" Liz nodded. "Oh, I suppose that's not surprising considering you teach at the University of Florida in Gainesville. Lake City's just 45 miles north of you." Liz shared her research findings with regard to Al Capone, the hotel, and the town. Jimmy laughed and slapped his thigh. "I thought I knew your name when you called. So you're the young lady who created such a stir in my hometown. Well done. It was a story that needed telling. But that's old news for you, isn't it? Is there anything else about Sam you want to know?"

Liz considered his question for a moment before asking, "Do you think Toblinsky considered Sam's debt paid in full?"

"You know, I've never been sure. My guess is not based on what Sam always said about his mob connections."

Should she ask it? Might as well. "May I ask how you avoided entanglements with the mob since you became so deeply involved in the Batista affair?"

The old man's eyes twinkled. "How do you know I didn't become involved with them?"

Heat rose from Liz's cheeks to her hairline. She cast about for the right reply. "When you put it like that, I guess I don't, except that you are an attorney, and you seem like a nice man who cared about his friend."

A distant expression clouded Jimmy's face. "You know, I did care about Sam and his family. He gave me the best advice I've ever received and made sure that I was in a position to take it. He told me to never talk to certain people who came into the store, that their bosses were always on the lookout for smart, educated young men, but that once I took their job and money, I would never be free of them no matter what I tried."

"Were they Mafia?"

"Oh, yes. Definitely."

A thrill of anticipation tingled in every inch of Liz. "Did he do anything to help you beyond giving advice?"

Jimmy became thoughtful. His gaze drifted into a past only he could see. "When I graduated college, jobs were not exactly falling off trees. Sam knew I wanted to go to law school but couldn't afford it. He offered to pay my tuition in exchange for my taking care of his wife and business after he died. You see, he knew he was dying. His cardiologist had told him as much. It's a wonder he survived the trip to Cuba. It was a major miracle he lived for another four years afterward. He stayed around long enough to see me graduate and sign on with a big Miami firm. It was like he waited until I was established to make sure that I was in a position to keep my end of the bargain. And I did. I took care of Rebecca.

"By the time I graduated, their children had been gone from Miami for several years and didn't come home too often. I think they realized Sam was and always had been, as they say in the movies, *connected*. The kids wanted nothing to do with that life and Rebecca refused to leave Miami. She was lonely after Sam died and was clueless about the business. I saw to it that the business ran smoothly and profitably until she passed away. I looked after her, but she looked after me, too. I was pretty much on my own after high school. Sam and Rebecca did more for me than my own parents ever thought about doing. I loved them."

"If you essentially ran the business for her after Sam died, how did you keep from becoming involved with the Mafia yourself?"

"First, understand that I did not run the business on a daily basis. I hired good managers. Next, I made sure the favors that had always come Sam's way were no longer accepted. The bottom line suffered, but the store still made enough to take care of her needs, make payroll, and pay the bills. It was an honest profit."

"I don't understand how you could just stop the favors. The Mafia has always been tenacious when it wanted something."

"That's just it. Without Sam, there really wasn't anything anyone wanted anymore. Sam died and his debt to Toblinsky died with him."

As Liz mulled over Jimmy's revelations, the irony of one detail struck her. "I wonder what became of the property deeds Sam retrieved from the Havana brokerage office. I don't suppose even Toblinsky anticipated that Castro would nationalize every business in Cuba."

A smile tinged with sadness drifted over Jimmy's features. "If Toblinsky kept them, they would be part of his estate. Their only value would be historical. Sam risked his life for pieces of paper that ultimately proved worthless."

Liz sat silently for several minutes while she let Jimmy's last statement sink in. All for nothing. Unless saving Batista's men counted. It would have been nice to know how Sam felt, but Jimmy said Sam slammed the door on all discussion of Toblinsky and Batista once they returned Miami. They never spoke of that time again.

After a few pleasantries, Liz left Jimmy where she had found him, gazing out over the Atlantic. With his help, she now had enough information to ensure that her course met her own expectations and to publish at least an article, maybe two, with new revelations on the mob's Gold Coast involvement. With time and work, she might stretch her course into a monograph featuring Sam's story as an illustration of the mafia's long reach and influence in South Florida.

Sam had repaid his debt to Toblinsky several times over. Did the gangster at last consider the debt repaid in full or did Sam continue to live in fear of another undeniable request from his former boss? Liz could only guess. She let go a long, slow sigh. Non-monetary debts. Debts of friendship, family, personal obligation. Something she had in common with Sam. But unlike the unfortunate gangster's pawn, Liz knew that her debt had been repaid. In fact, some people, like Hugh, would say the debt had never existed at all, that it had only lived in her overly developed sense of obligation and the deep emotional bond between mother and daughter. Perhaps Hugh was right, but the work she had done to exorcise her personal demon of debt had been necessary. She had needed to expel it from her heart, not just her mind. It is one thing to know something intellectually and quite another to know it emotionally.

She could now move forward fully into the future, which included more frequent trips to Seattle. She would spend whatever time remained with her mother and father, giving them all of the comfort and strength within her power. Hugh would join her there on New Year's Eve after Christmas week spent at his Cross Creek farm with his sister and her family. While they were apart, she would have time to adjust to her new definition of having it all.

Originally, she believed that having it all meant living life solely on her own terms, terms that were dominated by her drive to succeed and dictated by the demands of her career above all else.

But over the last months, she had come to understand that having it all was really about compromise, about taking happiness where she found it and holding onto it for dear life. This new understanding was the foundation of a momentous decision.

It meant she would never be able to move too far away from the North Florida area, no matter how great another university's offer might be, for Hugh would never live so far away from his farm as to not be able to reach it on a Friday night. North Florida was his home, and like so many small-town southerners, home for him was more important than professional advancement through relocation.

What she had come to understand about having it all was that loving and being truly loved in return were the greatest accomplishments of one's life. All else was, and should be, secondary. She wanted more from her life than the successes or failures of other people's children, dusty tomes with her name on the binding, and prying into the lives of the dead.

She wanted a life with Hugh.

She wanted children.

She wanted permanence and Hugh's love.

These things and a teaching career she enjoyed meant she had it all.

Indeed, it meant she had found a lifetime of happiness.

Turn the page for a preview of, *Al Capone at the Blanche Hotel*, available now!

Chapter 1

Saturday
June 14, 1930
O'Leno, Florida

Jack jammed a finger into each ear and swallowed hard. Any other time, he wouldn't even notice the stupid sound. The river always sorta slurped just before it pulled stuff underground.

His stomach heaved again. Maybe he shouldn't look either, but he couldn't tear his eyes away from the circling current. When the head slipped under the water, the toe end lifted up. Slowly the tarpaulin wrapped body, at least that's what it sure looked like, went completely vertical. It bobbed around a few times and finally gurgled its way down the sinkhole. Then everything went quiet . . . peaceful . . . crazily normal. Crickets sawed away again. An ole granddaddy bullfrog croaked his lonesomeness into the sultry midnight air.

Crouched in the shelter of a large palmetto clump, Jack's muscles quivered and sweat rolled into his eyes, but he remained stock-still. His heart hammered like he had just finished the fifty yard dash, but that was nothing to what Zeke was probably feeling. He was still just a little kid in lots of ways.

When creeping damp warmed the soles of Jack's bare feet, he grimaced and glanced sideways. Zeke looked back with eyes the size of saucers and mouthed the words *I'm sorry*. Jack shook his head then wrinkled his nose as the odor of ammonia and damp earth drifted up. He'd always heard that fear produced its own peculiar odor, but nobody ever said how close you had to be to actually smell it. He prayed you had to be real close; otherwise, he and Zeke were in big trouble.

The stranger standing on the riverbank stared out over the water for so long Jack wondered if the man thought the body might suddenly come flying up out of the sinkhole and float back upriver against the current. Funny, the things that popped into your head when you were scared witless.

The man removed a rag from his pocket and mopped his face. He paused, looked upstream, then turned and stared into the surrounding forest. As his gaze swept over their hiding place, Jack held his breath and prayed, but he could feel Zeke's chest rising and falling in ragged jerks so he slipped his hand onto Zeke's arm. Under the gentle pressure of Jack's fingers, Zeke's muscles trembled and jumped beneath his soft ebony skin. When Zeke licked his lips and parted them like he was about to yell out, Jack clapped a hand over the open mouth and wrapped his other arm around Zeke's upper body, pulling him close and holding him tight. Zeke's heart pounded against the bib of his overalls like it might jump clean out of his chest.

With one final look 'round at the river and forest, the stranger strode to the hand crank of a Model T. The engine caught momentarily, then spluttered and died. A stream of profanity split the quiet night. The crank handle jerked from its shaft and slammed back into place. More grinding and more swearing followed until the thing finally coughed to life for good and a car door slammed. Only then did Jack relax his hold on Zeke.

"I want outta here. I wanna go home," Zeke whispered hoarsely.

Lucky Zeke. Before Meg left home to move into town, Jack would have felt the same way. Now he didn't care if he ever went home.

Jack cocked an ear in the Ford's direction. "Hush so I can listen. I think he's gone, but we're gonna belly crawl in the opposite direction just to be sure we ain't seen."

"Through that briar patch? I ain't got on no shoes or shirt."

"Me neither. Come on. Don't be such a baby."

"I ain't no baby," Zeke hissed as he scrambled after Jack.

When the pine forest thinned out, Jack raised up on his knees for a look around. Without a word, Zeke jumped to his feet and started toward the road. Jack grabbed a strap on Zeke's overalls and snatched him back onto his bottom.

"You taken complete leave of your senses?" Wiping sweat out of his eyes, Jack pushed his shaggy blonde hair to one side. "Check it out before you go bustin' into the open."

"Why you so bossy all the time? I ain't stupid, ya know. Just cause you turned twelve don't make you all growed up."

Zeke's lower lip stuck out, trembling a little. Whether it was from fear or anger, Jack wasn't sure. Probably both. Peering into the night, he strained for the flash of headlights. Nothing but bright moonlight illuminated the road's deep, white sand. Finally confident that no vehicles were abroad, he grabbed Zeke's hand and pulled him to his feet. With one final glance left, then right, they leapt onto the single lane track and ran like the devil was on their tails.

Chapter 2

August 15, 2011
Gainesville, Florida

Liz Reams glanced at the caller ID and grimaced. She didn't have time for this, but guilt wouldn't let her put the conversation off any longer. Sighing, she pressed the talk button and prepared to listen with forbearance and humility.

"Hello, Roberta. I'm so glad to hear your voice. I was beginning to think we were going to play phone tag forever." Internally, Liz squirmed. Her conscience yelled, *liar, you returned calls when you figured you'd get her voicemail.*

Roberta's reply made Liz cringe. While she endured the diatribe pouring through her cell phone, Liz eyed her purse, book bag, and laptop case huddled together on the sofa. She couldn't afford to be late today of all days. Her eyes narrowed as her gaze paused on her laptop. She had paid more than a month's rent for the thing, but as much as she loved its power and speed, it was also a constant reminder of her dereliction. It only compounded her guilt that everything Roberta said was true.

Also from **Linda Bennett Pennell**
and **Soul Mate Publishing**:

AL CAPONE AND THE BLANCHE HOTEL

Lake City, Florida, June, 1930: Al Capone checks in for an unusually long stay at the Blanche Hotel, a nice enough joint for an insignificant little whistle stop. The following night, young Jack Blevins witnesses a body being dumped heralding the summer of violence to come. One-by-one, people controlling county vice activities swing from KKK ropes. No moonshine distributor, gaming operator, or brothel madam, black or white, is safe from the Klan's self-righteous vigilantism. Jack's older sister Meg, a waitress at the Blanche, and her fiancé, a sheriff's deputy, discover reasons to believe the lynchings are cover for a much larger ambition than simply ridding the county of vice. Someone, possibly backed by Capone, has secret plans for filling the voids created by the killings. But as the body count grows and crosses burn, they come to realize this knowledge may get all of them killed.

Gainesville, Florida, August, 2011: Liz Reams, an up and coming young academic specializing in the history of American crime, impulsively moves across the continent to follow a man who convinces her of his devotion yet refuses to say the three simple words "I love you." Despite the entreaties of friends and family, she is attracted to edginess and a certain type of glamour in her men, both living and historical. Her personal life is an emotional roller coaster, but her career options suddenly blossom beyond all expectation, creating a very different type of stress. To deal with it all, Liz loses herself in her professional passion, original research into the life and times of her favorite bad boy, Al Capone. What she discovers about 1930's summer of violence, and herself in the process, leaves her reeling at first and then changed forever.

Available on Amazon: <u>AL CAPONE AND THE BLANCHE HOTEL</u>

CONFEDERADO DO NORTE

October, 1866

Mary Catherine is devastated when her family emigrates from Georgia to Brazil because her father and maternal uncle refuse to accept the terms of Reconstruction following the Confederacy's defeat. Shortly after arrival in their new country, she is orphaned, leaving her in Uncle Nathan's care. He hates Mary Catherine, blaming her for his sister's death. She despises him because she believes Nathan murdered her father. When Mary Catherine discovers Nathan's plan to be rid of her as well, she flees into the mountain wilderness filled with jaguars and equally dangerous men.

Finding refuge among kind peasants, she grows into a beauty, ultimately marrying the scion of a wealthy Portuguese family. Happiness and security seem assured until civil unrest brings armed marauders who have an inexplicable connection to Mary Catherine. Recreating herself has protected Mary Catherine in the past, but this new crisis will demand all of the courage, intelligence, and creativity she possesses simply to survive.

Available on Amazon: <u>CONFEDERADO DO NORTE</u>

Linda Bennett Pennell

I have been in love with the past for as long as I can remember. Anything with a history, whether shabby or majestic, recent or ancient, instantly draws me in. I suppose it comes from being part of a large extended family that spanned several generations. Long summer afternoons on my grandmother's porch or winter evenings gathered around her fireplace were filled with stories both entertaining and poignant. Of course being set in the South, those stories were also peopled by some very interesting characters, some of whom have found their way into my work.

As for my venture in writing, it has allowed me to reinvent myself. We humans are truly multifaceted creatures, but unfortunately we tend to sort and categorize each other into neat, easily understood packages that rarely reveal the whole person. Perhaps you, too, want to step out of the box in which you find yourself. I encourage you to look at the possibilities and imagine. Be filled with childlike wonder in your mental wanderings. Envision what might be, not simply what is. Let us never forget, all good fiction begins when someone says to herself or himself, "Let's pretend."

Favorite quote regarding my professional passion: "History is filled with the sound of silken slippers going downstairs and wooden shoes coming up." Voltaire